M
Rendell

Rendell, Ruth,
1930-

Harm done.

DATE			

Mynderse Library

Seneca Falls, New York

BAKER & TAYLOR

HARM DONE

ALSO BY RUTH RENDELL

A Sight for Sore Eyes
The Keys to the Street
Blood Lines
The Crocodile Bird
Going Wrong
The Bridesmaid
Talking to Strange Men
Live Flesh
The Tree of Hands
The Killing Doll
Master of the Moor
The Lake of Darkness
Make Death Love Me
A Judgement in Stone
A Demon in My View
The Face of Trespass
One Across, Two Down
Vanity Dies Hard
To Fear a Painted Devil

CHIEF INSPECTOR WEXFORD NOVELS

Road Rage
Simisola
Kissing the Gunner's Daughter
The Veiled One
An Unkindness of Ravens
Speaker of Mandarin
Death Notes
A Sleeping Life
Shake Hands Forever
Some Lie and Some Die
Murder Being Once Done
No More Dying Then
A Guilty Thing Surprised
The Best Man to Die
Wolf to the Slaughter
Sins of the Fathers
A New Lease of Death
From Doon with Death

BY RUTH RENDELL WRITING AS BARBARA VINE

The Chimney Sweeper's Boy
The Brimstone Wedding
No Night Is Too Long
Anna's Book
King Solomon's Carpet
Gallowglass
The House of Stairs
A Fatal Inversion
A Dark-Adapted Eye

Harm Done

AN
INSPECTOR WEXFORD
MYSTERY

RUTH
RENDELL

CROWN PUBLISHERS
New York

The quotation on p. 109 is from "The South Country" by Hilaire Belloc, from *Complete Verse*, published by Random House UK Ltd. With permission from The Peters Fraser & Dunlop Group Ltd. © 1970 The Estate of Hilaire Belloc.

Copyright © 1999 by Kingsmarkham Enterprises, Ltd.

All rights reserved. No part of this book may be reproduced or transmitted in any form or by any means, electronic or mechanical, including photocopying, recording, or by any information storage and retrieval system, without permission in writing from the publisher.

Published by Crown Publishers, 201 East 50th Street, New York, New York 10022. Member of the Crown Publishing Group.

First published in the United Kingdom in 1999 by Hutchinson.

Random House, Inc. New York, Toronto, London, Sydney, Auckland
www.randomhouse.com

Crown is a trademark and the Crown colophon is a registered trademark of Random House, Inc.

Printed in the United States of America

DESIGN BY KAREN MINSTER

Library of Congress Cataloging-in-Publication Data
Rendell, Ruth
Harm done / Ruth Rendell.—1st ed.
I. Title.
PR6068.E63H37 1999
823'.914—dc21 99-20432
CIP

ISBN 0-609-60547-X

10 9 8 7 6 5 4 3 2 1

First American Edition

MYNDERSE LIBRARY
31 FALL STREET
SENECA FALLS, NEW YORK 13148

HARM DONE

THE CHILDREN'S CRUSADE, HE CALLED IT AFTER IT WAS ALL over, because children played such a big part in it. Yet it wasn't really about children at all. Not one of them was physically injured, not one of them suffered bodily pain or was even made to cry beyond the common lot of people of their age. The mental pain they endured, the emotional traumas and psychological damage—well, those were another thing. Who knows what impression certain sights leave on children? And who can tell what actions those impressions will precipitate? If any. Perhaps, as people once believed, they are character-forming. They make us strong. After all, the world is a hard place and we may as well learn it young. All childhoods are unhappy, said Freud. But then, thought Wexford, some childhoods are unhappier than others.

These children, the crusaders, were witnesses. There are many who believe children should never be permitted to be witnesses. As it is, laws are in place to protect them from exploitation by the law. But who will stop them from seeing what they witnessed in the first place? His daughter Sylvia, the social worker, said that she sometimes thought, after what she had seen, that all children should be taken from their parents at birth. On the other hand, if any busybody of a social worker tried to take her children away from her, she'd fight him tooth and nail.

The children in question, in Wexford's questions and questioning, came from all over Kingsmarkham and the other small towns and villages, from an estate the newspapers, in their current favorite word, called "infamous," from the millionaires' row they called "leafy," and from the middle class in between. They were given, or occasionally baptized with, the names that had become popular in the eighties and nineties: Kaylee and Scott, Gary and Lee, Sasha and Sanchia.

In one class in Kingsmarkham's St. Peter's Primary School it was tactless to ask after someone's father because most of the children were unsure who their father was. Raised on crisps and chips and chocolate and take-away, they were nevertheless the healthiest generation of children the country has ever known. If one of them had been smacked, he or she would have taken the perpetrator to the European Court of Human Rights. Mental torture was another story, and no one knew what that story was, though many tried to write it every day.

The eldest of the children Wexford was interested in was on the upper limits of childhood. She was sixteen, old enough to marry, though not to vote, old enough to leave school if she so chose and leave home too if she wanted to.

Her name was Lizzie Cromwell.

CHAPTER 1

On the day Lizzie came back from the dead the police and her family and neighbors had already begun the search for her body. They worked on the open countryside between Kingsmarkham and Myringham, combing the hillsides and beating through the woods. It was April but cold and wet, and a sharp northeast wind was blowing. Their task was not a pleasant one; no one laughed or joked and there was little talking.

Lizzie's stepfather was among the searchers, but her mother was too upset to leave the house. The evening before, the two of them had appeared on television to appeal for Lizzie to come home, for her abductor or attacker, whatever he might be, to release her. Her mother said she was only sixteen, which was already known, and that she had learning difficulties, which was not. Her stepfather was a lot younger than her mother, perhaps ten years, and looked very young. He had long hair and a beard and wore several earrings, all in the same ear. After the television appearance several people phoned Kingsmarkham Police Station and opined that Colin Crowne had murdered his stepdaughter. One said Colin had buried her on the building site down York Street, a quarter of a mile down the road from where the Crownes and Lizzie lived on the Muriel Campden Estate. Another told Detective Sergeant Vine that she had heard Colin Crowne threaten to kill Lizzie "because she was as thick as two planks."

"Those folks as go on telly to talk about their missing kids," said a caller who refused to give her name, "they're always the guilty ones. It's always the dad. I've seen it time and time again. If you don't know that, you've no business being in the police."

Chief Inspector Wexford thought she was dead. Not because of what the anonymous caller said, but because all the evidence pointed that way. Lizzie had no boyfriend, she was not at all precocious, she had a low IQ and was rather slow and timid. Three evenings before, she had gone with some friends on the bus to the cinema in Myringham, but at the end of the film the other two girls had left her to come home alone. They had asked her to come clubbing with them but Lizzie had said her mother would be worried—the friends thought Lizzie herself was worried at the idea—and they left her at the bus stop. It was just before eight-thirty and getting dark. She should have been home in Kingsmarkham by nine-fifteen, but she didn't come home at all. At midnight her mother had phoned the police.

If she had been, well, a different sort of girl, Wexford wouldn't have paid so much attention. If she had been more like her friends. He hesitated about the phrase he used even in his own mind, for he liked to keep to his personal brand of political correctness in his thoughts as well as his speech. Not to be absurd about it, not to use ridiculous expressions like *intellectually challenged*, but not to be insensitive either and call a girl such as Lizzie Cromwell mentally handicapped or retarded. Besides, she wasn't either of those things, she could read and write, more or less, she had a certain measure of independence and went about on her own. In daylight, at any rate. But she wasn't fit just the same to be left alone after dark on a lonely road. Come to that, what girl was?

So he thought she was dead. Murdered by someone. What he had seen of Colin Crowne he hadn't much liked, but he had no reason to suspect him of killing his stepdaughter. True, some years before he married Debbie Cromwell, Crowne had been convicted of assault on a man outside a pub, and he had another conviction for taking and driving away—in other words, stealing—a car. But what did all that amount to? Not much. It was more likely that someone had stopped and offered Lizzie a lift.

"Would she accept a lift from a stranger?" Vine had asked Debbie Crowne.

"Sometimes it's hard to make her like understand things," Lizzie's mother had said. "She'll sort of say yes and no and smile—she smiles a lot, she's a happy kid—but you don't know if it's like sunk in. Do you, Col?"

"I've told her never talk to strangers," said Colin Crowne. "I've told her till I'm blue in the face, but what do I get? A smile and a nod and another smile, then she'll just say something else, something loony, like the sun's shining or what's for tea."

"Not loony, Col," said the mother, obviously hurt.

"You know what I mean."

So when she had been gone three nights and it was the morning of the third day, Colin Crowne and the neighbors on either side of the Crownes on the Muriel Campden Estate started searching for Lizzie. Wexford had already talked to her friends and the driver of the bus she should have been on but hadn't been on, and Inspector Burden and Sergeant Vine had talked to dozens of motorists who used that road daily around about that time. When the rain became torrential, which happened at about four in the afternoon, they called off the search for that day, but they were set to begin again at first light. Taking DC Lynn Fancourt with him, Wexford went over to Puck Road for another talk with Colin and Debbie Crowne.

When it was built in the sixties, on an open space that would now be called a "green field area," between the top of York Street and the western side of Glebe Road, the three streets and block of flats on a green in the midst of them, it had been called the York Estate. The then chairman of the housing committee, who had done *A Midsummer Night's Dream* for his school certificate and was proud of the knowledge thus gained, named the streets after characters in that comedy, Oberon, Titania, and Puck. This last had always been a problem to tenants, the police, and the local authority because of the opportunity it gave the local youth of transforming, with a can of spray paint and the minimum effort, an innocent name into an obscenity.

Muriel Campden had been the chair (as she must now be designated) of Kingsmarkham Borough Council longer than anyone else, and when she died, the York Estate was renamed after her. A move was afoot to erect a statue of her on the green opposite the council offices, a building newly named the Municipal Centre. Half the population was in favor and half was vehemently opposed.

"I'd have thought this place was memorial enough," said Wexford, eyeing the triangle of squat sixties houses in the midst of which reared up a truncated tower, six stories high. Titania, Oberon, and Puck Roads looked as if built out of absorbent breeze blocks that had soaked up the rain of two dozen wet winters and had rendered them the darkest shade of charcoal. "Very appropriate for Muriel Campden. She was a dark, gray, gloomy sort of woman." He pointed to the street sign at the beginning of Puck Road, once more defaced. "Look at that. You'd think they'd get bored with doing it."

"Little things please little minds, sir," said Lynn just as the door was opened and they were admitted to No. 45 by the occupier of No. 47. This was a neighbor called Sue Ridley, who conducted them into the presence of Debbie and Colin Crowne, sitting side by side on a sofa. They were both smoking cigarettes and both watching, or at any rate looking at, a television quiz show.

Debbie jumped up and screamed when they came in, "They've found her! She's dead!"

"No, no, Mrs. Crowne, we've no news for you. Nothing has happened. May I sit down?"

"Do what you want," said Colin Crowne in customary surly tones.

He lit a cigarette and gave his wife one without asking her. The atmosphere in the small room was already thick with smoke. Rain beat relentlessly on the windows. On the screen a quiz contender, asked if Oasis was a town in Saudi, a pop group, or a West End cinema, was unable to answer. Debbie Crowne called fretfully to her neighbor to make another cup of tea, "Would you, Sue, love?"

Wexford and his team had already asked all the relevant questions, and he was there more to convince Mrs. Crowne that everything was being done that could be done than to elicit more information. But he did press once more for the names of any relatives or even friends living in distant parts of the country to whom Lizzie might conceivably have gone. Such a man or woman would have to have been marooned on a newspaper-less, radio-less and TV-less island in perhaps the Outer Hebrides not to have known that Lizzie Cromwell had vanished and that the police were hunting for her, but he still asked. For something to say, for the sake of something to distract Debbie Crowne's mind from the horror of her fears.

The doorbell rang at the very moment Sue Ridley brought in their tea, four mugs of it with the teabags still in as well as the milk and no spoons. She deposited the mugs in a bunch on the table and went to answer the door, saying it would be her partner, come back from going out with the search party.

Her loud shout made Wexford jump. "You naughty girl, wherever have you been!"

Everybody stood up, the door opened, and a girl came in, water running from her hair and clothes as if she had just stepped out of a bathful of it. Debbie Crowne screamed and, screaming, threw her arms around her daughter, oblivious of her soaking clothes.

"I'm cold, Mum," said Lizzie, smiling waterily through chattering teeth. "I'm ever so cold."

She was back and safe, and apparently unharmed, and that, at first, was all that mattered. Wexford left, deputing Mike Burden and Lynn Fancourt to talk to Lizzie after she had had a hot bath. He was to question her himself on the following day and several times on subsequent days because her response was far from satisfactory. In other words, she refused—or was unable—to say where she had been.

He said nothing, he knew nothing, of this when he walked into his own house at six, early for him, but he did tell his wife Lizzie Cromwell was found. "Rather, she seems to have come back of her own accord. It'll be on the news at nine."

"Where had she been?" said Dora.

"I don't know. Off with some boy, I dare say. That's usually what it is. The fact that their parents don't know there *is* a boy means nothing."

"I suppose it was the same with us. I suppose Sylvia and Sheila had boyfriends we never knew about, as well as the ones we did. Which reminds me, Sylvia is bringing Robin and Ben to us for the night. Neil's away somewhere and she's got this new job."

"Ah, The Hide helpline. I didn't know she had to work nights."

"I wish she didn't have to. It's far too much for her, with her day job as well. I don't suppose The Hide pays much."

"If I know anything about it," said Wexford, "The Hide pays nothing at all."

He was on the phone to Burden when his elder daughter arrived with his grandsons. Burden had made the call, incensed at Lizzie Cromwell's refusal to talk.

"You mean she won't say where she's been?"

"I thought she *couldn't* talk. I honestly thought she was dumb. Well, she's not entirely normal, is she?"

"She can talk," said Wexford repressively. "I've heard her."

"Oh, so have I—now."

"And she's as normal as you are or as normal as half the people in this place. It's just that she's not a genius." Wexford cleared his throat. "Like you and your ilk," he added nastily, for Burden had just gained membership of Mensa on an IQ rumored to be 152. "Why won't she say where she's been?"

"I don't know. Scared. Obstinate. Doesn't want her mum and Earrings to know, I'd guess."

"Okay, we'll have another go tomorrow."

Wexford's daughter Sylvia was a social worker. She had been a mature student when she studied for her sociology degree, for she had married at eighteen. The two boys who came running out of the kitchen when their grandfather put down the phone were the offspring of that marriage. Wexford said hello to them, admired a new Nintendo and a Game Boy, and asked if their mother was still in the house.

"She's talking to Gran," said Ben in the tone of disgust someone might use when castigating deeply antisocial behavior.

All parents have a favorite among their children, though they may, like Wexford, strive always to conceal that preference. He had failed to hide his bias in favor of his younger daughter and he knew it, so he kept on trying. With Sylvia he was more effusive, he never missed giving her a kiss each time they met, listened attentively when she spoke to him, and pretended not to be ruffled when she rubbed him the wrong way. For Sylvia lacked her sister's charm and, although pleasant enough to look at, was without Sheila's beauty. Sylvia was an opinionated, didactic, often aggressive feminist, with a talent for saying the wrong thing, a fault-finder, bad at marriage but expert at rearing children. She was also—and Wexford knew it—good as gold, with an oversize social conscience.

He found her sitting at the kitchen table with a mug of tea in front of her, lecturing her mother on domestic violence. Dora had apparently asked the classic question, the one that, according to Sylvia, betrays ignorance of the whole subject: "But if their husbands beat them, why don't they leave?"

"That question is just so typical," Sylvia was saying, "of the sort of woman who is completely out of touch with the world around her. Leave, you say. Where is she—we'll say she, not they—where is she to go? She's dependent on him, she has nothing of her own. She has children—is she to take her children? Sure, he beats her, he breaks her nose and knocks out her teeth, but afterwards, every time, he says he's sorry, he won't do it again. She wants to keep things normal, she wants to keep the family together—Oh, hi, Dad, how are things?"

Wexford kissed her, said things were fine and how was work on the crisis line.

"The helpline, we call it. I was telling Mother about it. Mind you, it breaks your heart, all of it. And some of the worst is the attitude of the public. It's extraordinary, but a lot of people still think there's something *funny* about a man beating up a woman. It's a joke, it's a seaside-postcard kind of thing. They ought to see some of the injuries we see, some of the *scars.* And as for the police..."

"Now, Sylvia, wait a minute." Wexford's resolutions flew out of the window. "We have a program here in Mid-Sussex for dealing with domestic violence, we emphatically do not treat assaults on women in the home as a routine part of married life." His voice rose. "We're even putting in place a scheme to encourage friends and neighbors to report evidence of domestic violence. It's called Hurt-Watch, and if you haven't heard about it, you should have."

"All right, all right. But you have to admit all that's very new. It's very recent."

"It sounds like the Stasi or the KGB to me," said Dora. "The nanny state gone mad."

"Mother, suppose it is a nanny state, what's wrong with having a nanny to look after you? I've often wished I could afford one. Some of these women are utterly helpless, no one *cared* about them until the refuges started. And if that isn't evidence enough of the need, there aren't refuge places enough, there aren't *half* enough to meet the need..."

Wexford left the room quietly and went to find his grandsons.

The boys' school was on the outskirts of Myfleet, and next morning Wexford drove them there before going on to work. His route took him through the Brede Valley, under Savesbury Hill and along the edge of Framhurst Great Wood, and he never went that way without thankfulness that the bypass, started the previous year, had been shelved on a change of government. Newbury was completed but Salisbury would never be built, nor would Kingsmarkham (insofar as you could ever say "never" in connection with such things). It was unusual to feel glad about frugality, relieved that something couldn't be afforded, but this was a rare instance of that happening. The yellow caddis would be saved and the map butterfly. You could even say that some kinds of wildlife benefited from the bypass plans, since the badgers retained their old setts and gained man-made new ones, while the butterfly had two nettle plantations to feed on instead of just one.

At the point where the bypass had been due to start and where work on it had begun, earth had been shifted by diggers and excavators. No one, it appeared, had any intention of restoring the terrain to its former level, and grass and wild plants had grown over the new landscape of mounds and declivities, so that in the years to come these hills and valleys would seem a natural phenomenon. Or so Wexford said, commenting on the strange scenery.

"And in hundreds of years, Granddad," said Robin, "archaeologists may think those hills were the burial ground of an ancient tribe."

"Very likely," said Wexford, "good point."

"Tumuli," Robin said, savoring the word, "that's what they'll call them."

"Are you pleased?" Ben asked.

"What, that they didn't build the bypass? Yes, I am, very pleased. I didn't like them cutting down the trees and tearing up the hedges. I didn't like the road building."

"I did," said Ben. "I liked the diggers. I'm going to drive a JCB when I'm grown up and then I'll dig up the whole world."

It was the loveliest time of the year, unless early May, still a month off, might be more lush and floral, but now in April the trees were misted over with green and pale amber, and the Great Wood, which in May would be carpeted with bluebells, showed celandines and aconites, both bright gold, studding the forest floor. After he had dropped the boys at the school gate and waited a moment or two to see them shepherded into the building, he drove back, musing on children's taste, and on the beauties of nature and when children were first affected by them. Girls sooner than boys, he thought, girls as young as seven, while boys seemed not to notice scenery—rivers and hills, woodland, the distant landscape of downs, and the high skyscape of clouds—until well into their teens. And yet all the great nature poets had been men. Of course, Sylvia might be right and there had been great women poets too, born to be unrecognized and waste their sweetness on the desert air.

Meanwhile, he had a girl to talk to, one who might or might not care about pastoral beauty and badgers and butterflies, but who seemed amiable enough and who smiled timorously when her stepfather scolded her and when she was soaked to the skin. Not a wild teenager, not a rebel.

She was sitting on the sofa in the front room of 45 Puck Road, watching a dinosaur cartoon video, designed for children half her age, called *Jurassic Larks.* Or staring unseeing at it, Wexford thought. Anything rather than have to look at him and Lynn Fancourt.

At a nod from Wexford, Lynn picked up the remote off the table. "I think we'll have this off, Lizzie. It's time to talk."

As the pink brontosaurus faded and the pterodactyl with baby ichthyosaur in its mouth vanished in a flicker, Lizzie made a deprecating sound, a kind of snort of protest. She went on staring at the blank screen.

"You won't get anything out of her," Debbie Crowne said. "She's that obstinate, you might as well talk to a brick wall."

"How old are you, Lizzie?" Wexford asked.

"She's sixteen." Debbie didn't give her daughter a chance to answer. "She was sixteen in January."

"In that case, Mrs. Crowne, perhaps it would be best for us to talk to Lizzie on her own."

"What, not have me here?"

"The law requires a parent or responsible adult to be present only when a child is under sixteen."

Lizzie spoke, though she didn't turn her head. "I'm not a child."

"If you would, please, Mrs. Crowne."

"Oh, all right, if you say so. But she won't say anything." Debbie Crowne put her hand up to her mouth as if she had just recollected something. "If she *does* say something, you'll tell me, won't you? I mean, she could have been anywhere, with anyone. There's no knowing, is there? I mean, she could be *pregnant.*"

Lizzie made the same sound she had when her video was turned off. Saying, "It's all very well grunting like that, but I reckon she ought to be examined," Debbie Crowne left the room, shutting the door rather too smartly behind her. The girl didn't move.

"You were away from your home for three days, Lizzie," Wexford said. "You'd never done anything like that before, had you?"

Silence. Lizzie bent her head still farther so that her face was entirely concealed by hanging hair. It was pretty hair, red-gold, long, and wavy. The hands in her lap had bitten nails. "You didn't go alone, did you? Did someone take you away, Lizzie?"

When it was clear she wasn't going to answer that either, Lynn said, "Whatever you did or wherever you went, no one is going to punish you. Are you afraid of getting into trouble? You won't."

"No one is going to harm you, Lizzie," said Wexford. "We only want to know where you went. If you went away because you wanted to be with someone you like, you've a right to do that. No one can stop you doing that. But, you see, everyone was looking for you, the police and your parents and your friends were all looking for you. So now we have a right too. We've a right to know where you were."

The grunt came again, a straining sound like that made by someone in pain. "I can understand you might not want to tell me," Wexford said. "I can go away. You could be alone with Lynn. You could talk to Lynn. Would you like that?"

She looked up then. Her face, a rather pretty, pudgy face, freckled about the nose and forehead, was blank, her pale blue eyes vacant. She moistened her thin, pink lips. Frown lines appeared as if she was concentrating hard but as if the intellectual effort of whatever it was, was too much for her. Then she nodded. Not as people usually nod, repeating several times the up-and-down motion of the head, but just once and jerkily, almost curtly.

"That's good." Wexford went out of the room into the hall, a narrow passage that contained a bicycle and a crate full of empty bottles. He tapped on a door at the end and was admitted into a kitchen-diner. Colin Crowne was nowhere to be seen. His wife was sitting in the dining area on a high stool up at a counter, drinking coffee and smoking a cigarette. "There's a chance your daughter may feel more able to talk to DC Fancourt on her own."

"If you say so, but if she won't talk to her own mother..."

"What would your attitude be if it turns out she's been with a boyfriend?"

"She hasn't," said Debbie Crowne, stubbing out her cigarette in a saucer, "so I couldn't have an *attitude*."

"Let me put it another way. Could she be afraid of what would happen if you found out she had been with a boyfriend?"

"Look, she hasn't got a boyfriend. I'd know. I know where she is every minute of the day, I have to, she's not—well, you know what she is. She's a bit—she's got to be looked after."

"Nevertheless, she was out on her own with friends on Saturday evening, and though she went to Myringham with them, they left her to come home on her own."

"Well, they shouldn't have. I've told them over and over not to leave Lizzie to do things on her own. I've *told* them and her."

"They're sixteen, Mrs. Crowne, and they don't always do as they're told."

She shifted off the subject to one obviously nearer to her heart. "But what about like I said if she's pregnant, she ought to have a medical, she ought to be looked at. Suppose he did something to her, we don't know what he did."

"Are you suggesting she was raped?"

"No, I'm not, of course I'm not, I'd know that all right."

Then if she hasn't a boyfriend and she wasn't raped, how could she possibly be pregnant? He didn't say it aloud but went back to the living room, first knocking on the door. Lynn was there but the girl was gone.

"I couldn't exactly stop her, sir. She wanted to go upstairs to her bedroom and I couldn't stop her."

"No. We'll leave it for now." In the car he asked Lynn what had been the result of the interview, if there had in fact been an interview. "Did she say anything?"

"She told me a lot of lies, sir. I know they were lies. It was as if—well, she'd realized she had to say something to get us to leave her alone. Unfortunately for her, she has rather a limited imagination, but she tried."

"So what tall stories did this limited imagination come up with?"

"She was waiting at the bus stop and it was raining. A lady—that's how she put it—a lady came along in a car and offered her a lift but she refused because Colin had told her never to accept lifts from strangers. The bus didn't come and it was pouring with rain so she went into an empty house with boarded-up windows—the house with the apple tree, she calls it—and sat on the floor waiting for the rain to stop..."

"I don't believe it!"

"I said you wouldn't. I didn't."

"How did she get in?"

"The door wasn't locked. She pushed it open. Then when the rain had stopped and she thought she'd go back to the bus stop, she couldn't get out because someone had come along and locked her in. She stayed in there for three nights and three days with nothing to eat, though she could get water from a tap, and she found blankets to wrap herself in and keep herself warm. Then the door was unlocked, she escaped and caught the bus home."

No one believed Lizzie's story, but it was worth going to Myringham and taking a look.

"No need for you to do that, sir." Lynn meant it was beneath someone of his rank. "I can do it."

"It's either that or back to the paperwork," said Wexford.

Vine had talked to the two friends, Hayley Lawrie and Kate Burton, and both said they had walked with Lizzie to the bus stop. They had promised not to leave her alone and they hadn't, not really, only for five minutes, the bus was due in five minutes. Hayley said she wished now she had stayed with Lizzie till the bus came, but Kate said it didn't matter anyway because no harm had come to Lizzie.

The bus stop was the nearest one to the cinema where they had been, but still it was on the outskirts of Myringham, on the old Kingsmarkham Road. The first thing Wexford noticed was the derelict house. The bus stop was directly in front of it. All its windows boarded up, half the slates off its roof, its front gate hanging from a single hinge, the house stood in an overgrown patch of garden in which the one beautiful thing about the whole place was the cherry tree in rose-pink blossom. Not an apple, as Lizzie had said, but a Japanese kanzan. The front door of the house had been painted an aggressive dark green some twenty years before, and now the paint was peeling. Wexford turned the blackened brass knob and pushed it, wondering how he would feel about Lizzie if the door yielded. But it was locked.

They went around to the back. Here the boards were hanging off one of the windows, or someone had been at work attempting to remove them. Wexford made a quick decision. "We'll get in that way. And afterwards we'll have the window properly boarded up. Do the owner a service, whoever he or she may be."

Perhaps Lizzie had got in that way or out that way or both. The aperture was big enough for small or slight people to squeeze through, but Donaldson had to enlarge it for Wexford with the aid of tools from the car boot. Wexford stepped in over the ledge and Lynn and Donaldson followed. Inside it was cold, damp, and smelled of fungus. Floorboards had been taken up to disclose black pits, in some of which oily water lay. Most of the furniture had been taken out long ago, though a black horsehair settee remained in the room where they were and the iron basket in the fireplace was full of empty crisp packets and cigarette ends. Paper hung from the walls in long, curling swaths.

In the only other downstairs room, apart from the kitchen, two oil paintings still hung on mildewed walls, one of a stag drinking from a pool, the other of a girl of vaguely Pre-Raphaelite appearance picking up shells on a beach. No blankets anywhere. Upstairs still remained to explore. Wexford was inspired to investigate the filthy hole of a kitchen. He tried both taps. One was dry while the other emitted a trickle of rusty water, red as blood. Lizzie hadn't drunk from that. The back door had no key in its lock and no bolts. Wooden battens had been nailed across its architrave. Lizzie hadn't come in through the front door either. It was bolted on the inside. The bolts were rusty and couldn't have been drawn back without the use of tools.

"Can we get up the stairs, Lynn?" Wexford asked. "They look as if someone's been at them with a pickax."

"Just about, sir." Lynn eyed him, not the staircase, as if she doubted his athleticism rather than the stability of treads and risers.

An attempt had apparently been made to replace the treads or remove them or to widen the whole structure and had been abandoned, but not until the staircase was partially demolished. Wexford let Lynn go first, not so much out of politeness as from knowing that this way, if he fell over backward, he wouldn't fall on top of a small, slim woman who probably weighed less than eight stone. He trod gingerly, holding on, perhaps unwisely, to the rickety banister and got safely to the top. His efforts were rewarded by the sight of a large gray blanket covering some sort of tank or at any rate large cuboid object. Nothing else at all was in the two small attic bedrooms.

"I suppose she could have wrapped herself in this," said Lynn, extending to Wexford the hand she had brought away damp from contact with the blanket. "Though it smells a bit musty." Above them, through a hole in the stained plaster, the edge of a tile could be seen, and beyond, a segment of blue and white sky.

"She might have drunk from a bathroom tap," said Wexford, "if there were a bathroom." He shook his head. "She may have been here, but not for three days."

"Does it matter, sir?" Lynn asked as they made their way back down the perilous staircase. "I mean, she's back and she's not hurt. Is it any of our concern where she was?"

"Maybe not. Maybe you're right. I suppose it's just because I'd like to *know*."

He said much the same thing to Burden next day when the inspector protested about his interest in something so trivial. They were not at the police station but in the Olive and Dove, for a beer at the end of the day's work.

"Only I don't seem to have done any work," said Wexford, "just filled in those damned forms."

"Perhaps we're beating crime at last."

"You jest. I don't suppose a crime was committed against Lizzie Cromwell or that she committed one, but I'd like to know. *Three days* she was away, Mike, three days and three nights. She wasn't in that house—oh, we could only establish that for sure by taking her fingerprints and going over the place—but I know she wasn't. She couldn't have got in, or if she had, she couldn't have got out again and restored that window to the way it was when we found it. She lied about drinking water from a tap, she lied about wrapping herself in a blanket, and she lied about being locked in and then let out. So she wasn't there at all. I'm wondering if it would be worth putting out a call for that woman, the one who offered her a lift."

"That may be a lie too."

"True. It may be." Wexford downed the last of his best bitter. "So where was she?"

"With a man. They're always with a man, you know that. The fact that her mother says there's no boyfriend means nothing, and saying she never had the chance to meet a boyfriend means nothing either. It doesn't matter what a girl looks like or how simple she is—all right, don't look like that, you know what I mean—or how shy or whatever, the instinct in young human beings to reproduce is so powerful that the most unlikely ones get together like—like magnets."

"I hope there'll be no reproduction in this case, though I agree the most likely thing is that she was with a man, a boy. It still doesn't tell us where."

"At his place, of course."

"Ah, but there's the difficulty. If he's her age, the most likely thing is that he lives with parents or one parent and maybe siblings. If he's older, he's likely to be married or, as they put it these days, 'in a relationship.' The other people involved would know of her disappearance. Somebody would have come to us."

"He could have taken her to a hotel."

"For *three days and three nights*, Mike? Is he that well-off? No, the only possibility that I can see is that he lives alone in a room or flat of his own and that he took her there. He kept her indoors for the whole of the three days and three nights, and no one in the house or block of flats saw her. I don't like it, I don't really believe it, but we know what Sherlock Holmes said."

Burden had heard it too often from Wexford's lips to be in any doubt about it. "If all else is impossible, that which remains must be so, or something like that." Burden went to renew their drinks. Although he wasn't going to say so, or not yet, he was sick of Lizzie Cromwell and bored with the whole thing. Wexford, in his opinion, was beginning to get obsessive again, only in the past when he had had a bee in his bonnet, it was over events rather more earthshaking than this. But if, when he returned to their table with the two halves of Adnams, he hoped that Wexford would choose a new subject of conversation, he was disappointed.

"So when her friends left her at the bus stop, she was waiting for this guy to come along in a car, was she? Why a bus stop then? Why not somewhere warm and dry like a café?"

"Because she had to make her friends believe she was waiting for a bus." Burden said it repressively. He hoped he might have had the last word.

"You're fed up with this, aren't you? I know you are, I can tell. I won't bore you much longer. I think you're right about her reason for waiting at the bus stop, but I'd like to dig a little deeper into that. Why did she want to make her friends believe she was waiting for a bus?"

"So they wouldn't know about the boyfriend."

"But why wouldn't she want them to know? Wouldn't she be proud of having a boyfriend? Especially one with a car and a place to take her? She could have trusted them. They'd be the last to tell her mother."

"Maybe he's married."

"Then he wouldn't have a place to take her," said Wexford, and though Burden waited for the next phase of this reasoning, he said no more about it. "Hurt-Watch meeting in the morning," he said instead. "Remember? Ten sharp. Southby will be there, in case I haven't told you."

At the prospect of an encounter with the new assistant chief constable designate, Burden groaned softly. Operation Safeguard, which the program had originally been called, held little interest for him. His personal belief was that what happened in the home belonged in the home and should come as little as possible within the province of the law. But he knew where Wexford's sympathies lay, so he held his tongue.

Next morning, half an hour before the meeting was due to begin, a woman came into the police station on her way to work to say that she had seen Lizzie Cromwell at the bus stop the previous Saturday evening. It was a matter of chance that Wexford spoke to her at all. He and Barry Vine happened to be passing the desk in the foyer of the building where she was talking to the duty sergeant. Even so, Barry came out with the usual formula, that he would see to it, that it was hardly necessary for Wexford to...

Bother my pretty little head about it, Wexford thought but he didn't say aloud. "We'll go up to my office," he said.

CHAPTER 2

It was Friday now and Lizzie had come home on Tuesday afternoon. Wexford imparted this information to Mrs. Pauline Ward, surprised that she seemed not to know it already. "May I ask why you didn't come before?" he asked her.

"I never saw her picture till last night. It was in a paper wrapping up a crab."

"It was what?"

"Look, I don't take a paper. I mean, a daily paper. And I don't watch television news. I watch television but not the news. It upsets me. I mean, if it's not atrocities in Albania or kids burnt to death in a fire, it's baby seals getting clubbed to death. So I don't look at it anymore."

"The crab, please, Mrs. Ward."

She was in her midfifties, smartly dressed, her skirt too short and her eyelids too blue, but a handsome, well-kept woman who had arrived—and parked it on the parking place reserved for the assistant chief constable designate—in a dark blue Audi, polished to a gleam. When she smiled, as she now did, she showed a fine set of bright white teeth.

"Oh, the crab," she said. "Yes, I stopped off at that good fishmonger in York Street on my way home from work last evening. I had a friend coming to supper and I'd nothing for a starter, so I thought a crab would be nice and the fishmonger wrapped it up in this newspaper. *The Times*, I think it was. Anyway, when I unwrapped my crab, I saw her picture and I remembered seeing her on Monday night."

"I see. And when your friend came, did you say anything to her about it?"

"Him," said Mrs. Ward. "It's a him, my friend." Her tone was that of a woman who would hardly bother to buy a crab for a female guest. "Well, no, I didn't. Should I have?"

"He might have told you Lizzie Cromwell was found. That is, unless he too shies away from the news."

Pauline Ward gave him a suspicious sideways look. "I don't know whether he does or not. We don't talk about that sort of thing." She very nearly but not quite tossed her head. "Don't you want to know about Saturday night?"

Wexford nodded.

"All right, then. I work in Myringham. I'm the manager of the Crescent Minimarket on the Heaven Spent mall and we stay open till eight-thirty on Saturdays. It was twenty to nine when I left. I had to lock up and go to my car so, what with one thing and another, it was ten to when I drove past that bus stop."

Wexford interrupted her. "How can you be so sure of the time?"

"I always am, to the minute. I'm a clock-watcher. Well, I suppose I'm a watch-watcher. I noted the time when I left, and I saw that digital clock on the Midland Bank just when I started driving off, and it said eight fifty-four. I thought, 'That can't be right, not as late as that,' and I checked it with my watch and the clock on the car—I knew they were both right to the nearest second—and they both said eight forty-nine. Well, I thought, I'll go into the Midland and tell them—and I did, I went in on the Tuesday. And by the time I'd thought that, about the bank I mean, I was passing that bus stop and the girl was there, and I thought, 'Poor thing, having to wait for a bus in the rain. Shall I offer her a lift.' I thought, and then I thought, 'No, better not,' because you never know, do you?"

So this wasn't the woman who had offered Lizzie a lift and had her offer rejected. But ten to nine...Had the girl really waited at the bus stop for twenty minutes?

"Are you quite sure it was ten to nine?"

"I've told you, haven't I? I always know the time. What d'you want to know all this for, anyway, if she's come back?"

"I can't tell you that, Mrs. Ward."

She got up. "Aren't you going to thank me? I didn't have to come in here, you know. I wouldn't have if I hadn't happened to buy that crab."

He took her downstairs and at the exit doors she looked back over her shoulder and said, "You have an attitude problem, you know. You want to get it sorted."

Wexford restrained his laughter until she had gone. He certainly had a problem, but it wasn't one of attitude. Rather, he was allowing himself to be ridiculously involved in this Lizzie Cromwell business. She was back, as everyone kept telling him, she had been away with a boyfriend, but she was back and no harm was done. Had the boyfriend kept her waiting at that bus stop for twenty minutes? In the rain? Perhaps. It was possible. It struck him—and the idea was very unwelcome—that Lizzie, sweet, childishly pretty, not very bright, and probably highly gullible, was the kind of person of whom the unscrupulous would take advantage.

Did she go to a special school? And if not, why not? Even if she did, would that school be the kind of place to nurture her self-confidence and her street wisdom? He doubted it. But he resolved to turn his back on Lizzie and her problems and her family. It wasn't a police matter. Police time and the taxpayers' money had been wasted on it, but that happened all the time. You had to be thankful there was no crime, there was no fatality or even injury, and some would say the money and time had been well spent when the outcome was such a happy one. So goodbye, Lizzie Cromwell, and let's hope you're not pregnant.

The Hurt-Watch meeting passed off uneventfully, even satisfactorily. For once, Wexford and Malcolm Southby were in agreement. Both wanted to prioritize (Southby's word, Wexford wasn't in agreement with that) domestic violence as serious crime, and both thought providing women who were its victims with mobile phones and pagers a good move. Simply knowing the police were on their side was to take a step in the right direction.

"What about the ones who are victims but who have never called us?" Karen Malahyde asked. "There's a lot of secrecy in this area. Many of these women will do almost anything not to admit to being victims."

"I hardly see what we can do about that, DS Malahyde," said Southby, who was parsimonious with the taxpayers' money, "short of supplying every lady in Greater Kingsmarkham with expensive electronic equipment." Even when he approved a cause, the assistant chief constable designate could scarcely resist sarcasm. He elaborated. "Oh, excuse me, only those in a meaningful relationship, of course," and he cackled with laughter at his own wit.

Karen, who didn't think it amusing, kept a straight and glowering face while deploring the sycophantic smiles of certain of her fellow officers. "That's all very well, sir." She didn't quite dare say that was all very funny, and she knew the "sir" didn't justify everything. "But don't we have to do more to find out where the victims are? I mean, the ones who'll conceal what happens to them at any price?"

"We have Hurt-Watch, Karen," said Wexford, and got a look from Southby for using her Christian name. "We're alerting everyone through advertising in the *Courier* and leafleting every household. A police representative—and that'll be one of us—will go on *Newsroom South-East* and talk about it. I don't see at the moment what more we can do."

"Okay. Thank you, sir. It's just that the whole business is on the increase—but, thanks."

He had concentrated on the meeting for the hour that it lasted, and he also had resisted smiling, without much difficulty, at the ACCD's wit. The moment it was over, the thought came winging back into his head: Talking of secrecy, what was there about this boyfriend that he had to be concealed from Lizzie's friends as well as her parents, and why wouldn't she admit to him now?

The Hide was probably not the dullest and least interesting looking structure in the whole of Kingsmarkham. The Muriel Campden tower was uglier and some office blocks starker, but among sizable houses standing in their own grounds The Hide had no rivals in the category of boring buildings not worth a second glance. That few people would have given it that second glance or even noticed it at all had been a factor in its purchase by Griselda Cooper and Lucy Angeletti as a center and temporary home for the victims of domestic violence.

It was necessary for the house to be inconspicuous yet appear to have nothing to hide, dreary without being sinister, and dull with a dullness that excited no comment. Once it had been numbered 12 Kingsbrook Valley Drive, but the number plate had been removed and no nameplate lettered THE HIDE had replaced it. Its telephone number was unlisted. Only its helpline number was known. Every call box in Kingsmarkham, Stowerton, Pomfret, and the villages had posted in its interior The Hide's helpline number. But nothing on the cards said where the house was or its purpose, or who sought and found sanctuary there.

Almost the first question Sylvia Fairfax had asked when she first went to work for the helpline was, "Why the secrecy?"

"In nine cases out of ten," Griselda Cooper said, "husbands or partners or boyfriends, whoever's responsible for the abuse, come looking for them. This way it makes it harder to find them. Not impossible but harder."

"But they do get here?"

"Some do. We had one got over the wall. It's ten feet high with barbed wire on the top, but he got over. After that we changed the barbed wire for razor wire."

The garden was large. Trellis raised the height of the walls between The Hide and Nos. 10 and 14 Kingsbrook Valley Drive. The lawn was mown and the shrubs occasionally pruned, but otherwise the garden was untended. There was a swing and a climbing frame for the children, and Lucy Angeletti, who was The Hide's fund-raiser, was trying to get enough money together to create a proper play area.

The neighbors at Nos. 10 and 14, and at Nos. 8 and 16 too, had got wind of this intention and were mounting a rival campaign to put a stop to it. The Hide and its occupants were not popular in Kingsbrook Valley Drive. People thought it constituted a danger to the peace of the area and an encouragement to crime. The house itself was a big square box without wings or gables or porch, built in 1886 by a man with a large family who wanted to save expense. Even the roof, though not entirely flat, was scarcely discernible from the street, being concealed by a bald brick wall that ran around the top of the house above the fourth-floor windows. The only decorations on the dull reddish-brown brick house were the buff-colored stone facings around the flat sash windows. All this was half-hidden by the laurel bushes that dominated the front garden and by the two ilexes, cemetery trees whose leaves never fell but merely grew darker and dustier with time.

Inside, it was quite different, pale colors and pretty curtains, and pictures on the walls. Well, posters rather than pictures. Lucy had had the bright idea of buying sheets of wrapping paper, the kind that has flower paintings on it or maps of the world or *La Dame à la Licorne*, and getting them framed. The furniture was from secondhand shops or contributed by supporters, and the floor covering came from the carpet warehouse on the Stowerton Road where all the stock was cheap because it had been damaged by fire. There was never sufficient money. Lucy's hair had gone gray through worrying about getting enough funds to keep The Hide going, though perhaps it would have changed color anyway as premature grayness ran in her family.

Lack of money was the reason Sylvia and Jill Lewis and Davina Crewe got no pay for answering the phone to the women who appealed for help and sometimes for refuge. Ideally, the helpline should have operated from elsewhere. But there was no elsewhere. Griselda Cooper lived on the premises and Lucy Angeletti in a one-bedroom flat in Stowerton. The Hide had no offices apart from two poky rooms in the basement at 12 Kingsbrook Valley Drive. The two phone lines manned by Jill and Davina, sometimes by Griselda and Lucy, and now by Sylvia, were in a room on the top floor alongside Griselda's tiny flat. Space was so precious that the other two rooms on that floor had been converted into bedsits for fugitive women, two single beds in one and three plus a cot in the other. It wasn't ideal but it was the best they could do.

There was no lift. Sylvia had to toil up three flights of stairs, from the ground floor where the living rooms were—the lounge and the television room and the children's playroom and the kitchen and the laundry room—through the first and second stories, given over entirely to bedsits and bathrooms—more bathrooms were another priority when Lucy could get the funds—and up to the top where the phones were. Children were usually playing on the stairs. They weren't supposed to, or to slide down the banisters, but when the playroom was crowded and it was raining, they hadn't much choice.

Sylvia worked at The Hide two evenings a week, not always the same evenings, up till midnight. Her husband was usually at home to look after the boys, and if he couldn't be there, she knew they could go to her parents. She had taken on the job partly from the pressures of her social conscience and her commitment to women's causes, and partly to get herself out of the house. When she was at home, she and Neil either sat in silence or addressed each other through the medium of their children or quarreled. Although she never talked about the state of her marriage to her mother or her father, she did to friends and she was fast making a friend of Griselda Cooper.

Griselda's shift ended when Sylvia took over, but sometimes she stayed on for half an hour or even longer to talk. She was a dozen years or more older than Sylvia, a single woman who had a lover who took her out and about, and away when she had a weekend off, an enviable lot. Sylvia couldn't help being envious, though Griselda had no children and would now never have. One evening Sylvia told Griselda about her marriage, that she and Neil had married young and discovered too late they were less than well-suited.

"Too late?" said Griselda, who had been divorced.

"I couldn't break up the family. If we split up, it would devastate my kids."

"That sounds like the sort of thing some of our callers say. He's half killed her and he will again, and she knows he will, but she can't break up the family."

The phone rang and Griselda picked up the receiver. "The Hide helpline. How can I help you?" She spoke in the calmest, warmest, and most comforting tone she could achieve, and that was very calm and warm and comforting.

Sylvia could tell there was silence at the other end. There often was. Women lost their nerve or didn't know what to say or, worst of all, the man of the house had come into the room where the phone was.

Griselda waited, repeating her words, "How can I help you," then, "We're here to help you," and "Won't you tell me what your problem is? Anything you say will be in confidence."

After ten minutes' perseverance she put the phone down regretfully. "I could hear her breathing," Griselda said. "I heard her sigh. God knows, I hope she'll call back. Maybe she will and you'll take it."

"What you were saying just now," Sylvia said, "before the call came, about a man half killing a woman but still she won't break up the family, Neil has never laid a finger on me. And, d'you know, working here and listening to all this, hearing from these women and what they go through, has done me good. I mean, it's actually done my *marriage* good."

"You're joking."

"The other night I went home from here and it was the middle of the night, of course, and I went home and got into bed—oh, yes, we share a bed—crazy, eh?—and I got into bed beside him—he was asleep, sleeping so peacefully, like a child, and I—I thought, you've always been kind to me and gentle and patient, and I've never appreciated that. And I—I put my arm around him and lay beside him and hugged him. That's something I haven't done for years..."

"Come on," said Griselda, "don't cry. Well, *do* cry if it makes you feel better."

She put her arm around Sylvia, but only for a moment, because the phone was ringing again.

A designer in textiles who lived and worked in Pomfret had had her entire stock stolen. The collection, quilted coats and waistcoats, bed-covers and throws, as well as batik wall hangings, dresses, tablecloths, and napkins, had been housed in the basement, which had been converted two years before into a workshop. The basement window was barred and the door into the area double-locked and bolted, but the window of the cloakroom, a cupboard-sized place containing lavatory and diminutive washbasin, was open. Whoever had got through that window must have been thin and lithe, and he or she had evidently removed the entire haul through the same aperture.

"Or unbolted and unlocked that door from the inside," said Inspector Burden, "taken the stuff out, gone back, bolted and locked the door again, and escaped through that broken window."

"I couldn't do it," said Wexford sadly. "If it were half the size, I couldn't." He looked critically at Burden, whose new taupe-colored suit enhanced his slimness. "And I'm bound to say you couldn't either, Mike. Did they put a kid in there? A kind of Oliver Twist?"

"God knows. We've found no prints apart from her own and the guy she lives with. She values the stuff that's gone at fifty thousand pounds."

"Does she now? I thought these craftspeople were supposed to be on the breadline. You know what they say, that they'd make more dosh going out cleaning than they do from their exquisite needlework, pots, batik, et cetera."

"That's what she *values* it at. It's got nothing to do with whether she can sell it or not. By the way, before I forget, we've had another mum phoned up to say her daughter's missing."

Wexford banged the desktop with both fists. "Why didn't you say so before?"

Burden didn't answer. Always particular about his appearance, he fingered his tie, also a shade of taupe but patterned discreetly in dark red and pale blue, and looked about him for a mirror. A small one had always hung on Wexford's yellow wall between the door and the filing cabinet.

"It's gone," Wexford said impatiently. "I don't like mirrors or 'looking glasses,' as my old dad used to call them. I look in one to shave in the morning, I have to, and that's enough for the day. I'm not a male model."

"Evidently," said Burden, by now studying the best image of his face and neck he could get, their reflection in the glass that covered Wexford's Chagall print. "I don't know what's wrong with this tie, it goes crooked whatever I do."

"For God's sake, take it off then. Or do as I do and have two ties to wear on alternate days, the blue one on Mondays, Wednesdays, and Fridays and the red one on Tuesdays and Thursdays, and vice versa the next week. Now perhaps you'll tell me about this missing girl."

Burden sat down on the other side of Wexford's desk. "It's almost certainly nothing, Reg. Do you know that there are more than forty thousand teenagers missing in this country? Of course you do. Anyway, this one won't be missing, she's not a child, she's eighteen and she's probably done a Lizzie Cromwell."

"And what might that be?"

"I mean she's gone off with a boy or gone to visit friends, or dropped out or something."

"What do you mean, 'dropped out'?"

"She's at university somewhere. She came home here for the weekend, went out on Saturday night, and hasn't been seen since."

"Time was," said Wexford, "when universities used to stop undergraduates leaving the place to go home or anywhere else at weekends. Pity the custom's changed. I suppose the mother knows she hasn't just gone back to her college—had they had a family row, for instance?"

"She says not. And the girl hasn't gone back. Barry's checked with her hall of residence and her supervisor."

"What's she called and where's her home?"

"She's called Rachel Holmes, Oval Road, Stowerton. The mother's Mrs. Rosemary Holmes, divorced, lives alone when the girl's not there. She's a medical secretary in Dr. Akande's practice."

Turning away from his reflection, a ghostly face dimly mirrored behind Chagall's flying lovers, Burden began to explain. Rachel had gone out at eight or thereabouts on Saturday night with the intention of meeting a group of friends in a pub. Her mother didn't know which pub nor yet where Rachel was going afterward, but it would have been some club or a friend's house. It was unlikely that she would be home before two or three the next morning.

"When she was younger," Mrs. Holmes had said to Detective Sergeant Barry Vine, "I made her carry a mobile with her and she'd ring me to tell me where she was. But you can't do that when they're over eighteen, can you? She's at university, after all. I don't know what she's doing when she's there, do I? I don't know what time she comes in at night when she's there. So what's the point of worrying if she's late when she's at home? I do worry, though, of course I do. I didn't sleep a wink on Saturday night."

"So she phoned us today, did she?" Wexford asked.

"Phoned and came in to report a missing person."

"Why did she wait so long?"

"Don't know. Vine got the impression the girl's one of these bolshie teenagers, the kind who might give her mother a hard time if she reported her missing when she's just off somewhere up to her own devices."

Wexford sat silent for a moment. He was anxious not to become obsessive, not to let a single not very important case take over and dominate his mind. But he was also aware that it is hard to alter one's nature, especially at his age. This was the way he was, and to attempt a change would be a violation of his character and not necessarily otherwise advantageous.

"You surely aren't thinking of going to see Mrs. Holmes?" said Burden almost derisively. "Barry's got it in hand."

"I'm thinking of going back to see the Crownes and Lizzie Cromwell." Wexford got up. "If they know the Holmeses or the two girls know each other, it would be very interesting indeed."

CHAPTER 3

"No, we don't know her," Debbie Crowne said, spitting out the words. "She's not our class, is she? The likes of her wouldn't want to know the likes of us."

Since Rachel Holmes and her mother lived in a back-street terrace, in a poor little house rather smaller than the one he was now in, Wexford wondered at the fine distinction Mrs. Crowne made. But at the same time he knew he was being disingenuous. There *was* a difference. Rosemary Holmes owned her house, she had a white-collar job—if that description could be applied to a woman—and Rachel was at university. Somehow, if she had begun in the working class, Mrs. Holmes had elevated herself a grade or two, while the Crownes had remained where they started. In some ways he didn't like these gradations, but he knew they were a fact of life, not a culture specific or, as some said, confined to this country.

"Were she and Rachel at the same school?"

As soon as he said it, he knew he had made things worse. Lizzie herself gave him one of her lowering looks, head drooping but nervous rabbit's eyes peering upward. It was an expression more usually seen in children half her age.

Her mother said, "There's two years between them, you said. That's like centuries when you're her age."

"But Lizzie does go to Kingsmarkham Comprehensive," he persisted, "where Rachel went?"

"Along with a couple of thousand others. Anyway, she's in the Learning Difficulties stream." Debbie Crowne eyed him with the same expression as her daughter's. "That's like the bottom of the pile."

Nevertheless, they must have been at the same school at the same time over a period of years, perhaps as many as four. Was that the link? Was there a link? Colin Crowne came into the room before any more was said. Wexford studied him while Mrs. Crowne talked about Lizzie, repeating her fears as to what might have happened to her during her absence from home and adverting in querulous tones to the possibility of her being pregnant. She kept glancing at her husband while she talked.

Most people would have called Colin Crowne handsome. He was tall and slim, dark-haired and dark-eyed with firm, clear-cut features. But the length of his hair and the beard that might have been just a week-long failure to shave, as well as the triple earring arrangement, gave him a sinister look. His wife's faded appearance, her pinched face and dry, shaggy hair, contrasted almost ludicrously with the impression he gave of youth and sensuality. Wexford remembered them on television when Crowne had made an eloquent appeal for Lizzie's return, staring into the camera and enunciating his words clearly and with what seemed like real emotion, while his wife had sat by, biting her lip and only just restraining her tears. If it wasn't true, what that caller had said, that those who appeared on television to appeal for the return of a missing child were often themselves responsible for that child's death, there was a grain of truth in it.

There had been cases of a parent, later found guilty of child murder, whose outpourings of grief over that child's disappearance moved viewers to tears. And such behavior wasn't necessarily hypocritical; these people felt genuine grief, real emotion, and sometimes bitter regret. What, after all, is likely to pain you more and stimulate more remorse than committing murder? But Lizzie wasn't dead, Lizzie had come back. He had no reason at all to suppose Crowne responsible for her three-day absence or guilty of anything in connection with her.

After a moment's soul-searching, he decided to mention the derelict house in Myringham to Lizzie. Even supposing she had spoken to Lynn Fancourt in confidence, no discretion had been asked for. Besides, the truth must be that she had never been in the place. Perhaps a girl such as she couldn't be blamed for lying, but she had lied.

He spoke to her gently. "Lizzie, you were never in that house by the bus stop, were you? You told"—he sought for words she would understand—"the woman police officer, you told her you had been three days in that house and wrapped yourself in blankets? You told her you took water from a tap, but that wasn't really true, was it?"

He saw at once from their reaction, or because there was no reaction, that Colin and Debbie Crowne had been told the same story. The likelihood was that Lizzie, rather than being afraid to tell this fantasy to her mother and stepfather, had only thought it up in the moments before she'd revealed it to Lynn. Probably she had gone through the whole tale again to Debbie Crowne once he and Lynn had left.

Now she said, with the liar's too vehement indignation, "Yes, it was! I did go there!"

"There was no water in the taps, Lizzie. It was very cold. There was a blanket, but it was damp."

"I did go there!"

Crowne said roughly, "There you are, you've got your answer. What more d'you want?"

A great deal. But it would be useless, and perhaps pointless, to persist. And yet Wexford was suddenly sure that she *had* been in that house, not for three days and nights certainly, but she had been inside it, she knew it. She had seen that blanket and had at least attempted to get water from the taps. Had Rachel been there too?

Burden had implied that it would be quite unnecessary for Wexford to go to Oval Road, Stowerton; that this was an altogether different missing-person case from that of Lizzie Cromwell, for Rachel was older, for the most part living away from home, and an intelligent young woman very much in charge of her own life. But since then all inquiries had had negative results. None of her relatives had heard from her, and it seemed that none of her friends was harboring her.

A second call to the University of Essex revealed only that she had not turned up to the lecture she was due to attend at ten that morning. But a different picture was emerging. Rachel, apparently, had never intended to go straight to the pub but first to her friend's home in Framhurst. Because the Framhurst-to-Stowerton bus route had been discontinued when work on the bypass began, Caroline Strang's mother, who would be passing that way on her way home from work, would pick Rachel up at eight on the Kingsmarkham Road, five minutes from Oval Road, take her to Framhurst to pick up Caroline, then drive the two girls to the Rat and Carrot. Vine had talked to Mrs. Strang and been told that she had reached the pickup point some minutes after eight owing to a traffic holdup and had parked and waited.

"They're always late for everything, these girls. I know, I've got two and I thought I'd got there long before Rachel, even though I was late." She had waited for ten minutes, then driven off. "I'd have gone to her house only I don't know where she lives. I'd got the phone number but not the address."

Caroline Strang thought Rachel must have been confused about the arrangement and gone straight to the Rat and Carrot. Nevertheless, she had phoned Rachel's home before she herself left but got no reply. She naturally supposed no one had answered the phone because Rachel was on her way to the pub and her mother was out.

Vine had talked to the remaining three young people Caroline and Rachel were to meet that night. All said she hadn't come. None had been worried. They supposed she had changed her mind. Vine concluded they were very casual indeed about such matters as forgetfulness, indecisiveness, phoning to explain, or apologizing when a better prospect for the evening turned up.

There was a chance Rachel had gone to Kingsmarkham by bus, and Vine had talked to bus drivers. The buses on the Stowerton–Kingsmarkham–Pomfret run had no conductors, and the driver took the money and issued tickets. Vine showed Rachel's photograph to the drivers of the 8:10 bus and the 8:32 bus. Neither remembered her, but one said he was sure he wouldn't remember her and the other said that he had no memory for faces.

That convinced Wexford Rachel hadn't been on the bus, for to any man she would be unforgettable, an exceptionally good-looking girl with luxuriant dark hair, large dark eyes, and voluptuous features: full mouth, rounded chin, and high, smooth forehead. These seemed an inheritance from her handsome mother. If Rosemary Holmes was forty, she was not much more. Wexford could imagine her being flattered by people taking her and her daughter for sisters. Her own dark hair was plaited and coiled at the nape of her neck, an old-fashioned style that suited her oval face. She was slim, with long, shapely legs. Dr. Akande must keep his secretary well hidden, Wexford thought, for he would have remembered her if he had ever seen her in the medical center.

In his own mind he had compared the Crownes' home with this one, but theirs, though clean enough, betrayed that none of them took much interest in their surroundings, while Rosemary Holmes's house was furnished with taste if not much expense. Well-tended houseplants grew green and lush in troughs on both windowsills in the living room, a big bowl of orange tulips was on the table, and one wall was fitted from floor to ceiling with bookshelves. British country people might be class-conscious still, but a warped reasoning was behind their elitism and their sense of inferiority.

Though he knew he was wrong to do it, Wexford couldn't help linking the two cases in his mind, and now he had somehow convinced himself that because Lizzie had come back after three days and three nights, Rachel would come back too and after the same period of time. That would be tomorrow afternoon, Tuesday afternoon. So he was unable entirely to share Mrs. Holmes's fear. When she said, as she now did, "I keep thinking I'll never see her again," he felt strangely, as if he were in possession of some superior knowledge, some secret information, that it would be cruel not to reveal to her. And yet, of course, he wasn't, he knew nothing; he had no reason to align one girl's disappearance with another's. To tell her that everything would be all right, that she had no need to worry, would be the unkindest thing, for which of us can say that we guess right more often than we guess wrong?

"Are you," she asked him, "going to... well, search for her? I mean, the way you see people on television searching—in a line—with sticks? Beating the... well, you know, the ground?" She began to wring her hands. Wexford understood very well what she meant: that they would only do that if they had good reason to believe her daughter was dead.

"It's early days for that, Mrs. Holmes." Karen Malahyde saved him the trouble of answering. "Let's wait awhile. Rachel has only been missing since Saturday evening, that's less than forty-eight hours."

They had already inquired about boyfriends. Vine had asked her and now Karen did so again. "You say there's no boyfriend now, but what about in the past, when she was living here and going to school?"

Rosemary Holmes gave two names. She had done so before, to other police officers, but if she felt impatient with these repetitions, she gave no sign of it. She was anxious to help, she would have done anything to assist in finding her daughter and done it without complaint.

"And yourself, Mrs. Holmes?" Karen asked it delicately. "Are you perhaps in a relationship?"

"I've got someone, yes. But you're not thinking…?"

"We're really not thinking anything at the moment," Wexford said, reflecting that nothing could have been further from the truth. "We're asking questions and sizing up the information we get, that's all. It's useful for us at this stage to have the names and addresses of all your friends and your daughter's, Mrs. Holmes."

She named a doctor with a practice in Flagford. They had been going out for about a year and sometimes they spent weekends together. Rachel, she said in a burst of frankness, didn't like him, but she hadn't liked any friend of her mother's. So high is the profile of a doctor of medicine in society that Wexford immediately placed Dr. Michael Devonshire beyond suspicion, then, with quick self-admonition, put him back inside it again. A medical man was also a man, and you could never tell.

"You went out yourself on Saturday evening, Mrs. Holmes?"

She flushed faintly. "Well, yes. May I ask how you know that?"

"Caroline Strang phoned here at about twenty-five past eight. You weren't here."

"Michael took me out to dinner. It's ridiculous, I know, but I feel guilty about being out when—when whatever was happening to Rachel was happening."

"Did you know about this arrangement with Mrs. Strang?"

Rosemary Holmes said uneasily, "I knew someone was picking her up on the Kingsmarkham Road. She said. I thought it was a…well, one of the boys she was meeting." Suddenly she burst out, "You can't stop them doing things, you know. You can't keep tabs on them all the time." Again she dropped her guard. "I don't suppose it's important, I just want to say that we have our problems, Rachel and I. She's a lovely girl, a really marvelous person and I get on with her fine, but she doesn't exactly get on with me. I expect that's quite usual with people her age, isn't it?"

"Quite usual, Mrs. Holmes," said Karen.

Back in the car Wexford suggested Karen speak to Michael Devonshire, perhaps catch him before his evening surgery. "Though he obviously has an alibi with Rachel's mother. Do you think it worth taking a second look at that house in Myringham?"

"But Rachel never went near Myringham, sir." Karen sounded surprised.

"So far as we know."

"Surely it's just coincidence that Lizzie Cromwell went missing the Saturday before last and Rachel Holmes disappeared last Saturday."

"But we don't like coincidence, do we? We know that when events happen in sequence or according to a pattern, those events are most likely linked."

Karen looked dubious. As well she might, Wexford thought, as well she might. He must rid his mind of tying in one girl's disappearance with the other's. There was no point in returning to the derelict house, just as there was no real link between the girls—except for their having attended the same school. Except for their both being young and pretty and unattached and female. Except for their disappearing on successive Saturday nights...Stop it, he said to himself, but when he encountered Burden at the end of the day's work, it was to the Rat and Carrot instead of the Olive and Dove that he suggested they go for their evening drink, a twice weekly event when they could make it.

Burden gave him a sidelong look. "She never got there, you know. Rachel Holmes, I mean. Whatever happened to her happened in Stowerton. Waiting for a bus."

"Like Lizzie Cromwell," said Wexford.

"You've no reason to connect the two, none at all. Rachel shouldn't have been waiting for a bus, we know that, she should have been waiting for a lift. But they're so dozy, these young girls, they're as forgetful as old people. Now if Lizzie Cromwell had been found dead and *then* Rachel Holmes had disappeared, I'd have said, now you're talking. No, it's just that you've got another one of your obsessions. I thought you'd given all that stuff up, but you haven't, you're as bad as ever."

"Can the leopard change his spots?" asked Wexford rhetorically. "Or the Ethiopian his skin?"

"If I'd said that, you'd have called me a racist."

The nearest bus stop to Kingsbrook Valley Drive was at the eastern end of the High Street. From there it was ten minutes' walk to the Rat and Carrot, an ornate Victorian building on the corner of Kingsbrook Valley Drive and Savesbury Road. The area was mainly residential, but two shops were next to the pub, one of them a small supermarket and the other a jeweler, and opposite it was a pharmacist. All were closed by now and the jeweler had taken the valuable stock out of his window and pulled down a metal grille to cover it.

It was a district of hodgepodge housing, thirties bungalows neighboring on near-mansions and seventies blocks of flats alternating with gloomy houses dating from the late nineteenth century. The Rat and Carrot was the residents' local. Not long ago the pub had been called the Duke of Albany, but that was considered by whoever rules in these matters to be outdated and meaningless to most people, so it had been given this new, and to those who rechristened it amusing, name. Unfortunately, within six months local people were dubbing it the Rotten Carrot, and this sobriquet stuck.

It evidently put itself out to supply everything patrons could want from a pub, as well as a good many things that probably wouldn't have occurred to them. "Good" meals were served in the restaurant as well as the bar; snacks and sandwiches were available all day long; the pub ran its own lottery and gave away scratch cards as prizes in contests to guess the number of pints consumed there each day or how much money had been raised in the bar for charity since Christmas; and the Rats' Hard Rock Club met every Tuesday and Thursday evening. Children were welcome in the King Rat Kids' Room, where orange juice and Coke were on sale, or on fine days outside in the play area, furnished as it was by a large purple dinosaur, a giant Yogi Bear, two climbing frames, and a huge Looney Tunes character with a table and chairs in a cavity where its stomach should have been. As Wexford remarked, you could have been forgiven for entirely missing the point that the primary purpose of a public house was to sell alcoholic drinks to customers.

He and Burden went in through the main entrance, under a sign informing patrons that the licensee was one Andy Honeyman, edging their way between boards advertising bumper breakfasts, line dancing, and a talent contest (Be the Next Posh Spice).

"I wouldn't much care to live down here," said Burden gloomily. "Summer evenings must be a nightmare."

"Ah, well," said Wexford, carrying their drinks to a table, "in the midst of life we are in karaoke. It could happen to you, you know. That pub down your road, it's a free house. Get a change of licensee and you too could have a view of cartoon characters from your living-room windows and aspiring Spice Girls warbling away half the night."

Pretending not to hear, Burden surveyed the place, glass in hand. The bar was brightly decorated. Red and gold flock wallpaper shared the walls with mock linenfold paneling, there were a number of pictures of doe-eyed girls, gamboling kittens, wistful dogs, and mountainous panoramas, and all the chairs were black and gold with pale primrose upholstery. The girl who walked about wiping the already spotless tables wore skintight scarlet leggings and earrings that hung to her collarbones.

Apart from her and them, the only other person in the bar was a bearded man of about forty, whom she addressed as Andy and who was sitting on a high stool behind the counter reading *Sporting Life*.

Burden shook his head ponderously in the manner of one asking what the world was coming to. "Rachel Holmes, you can't understand what a girl like her would be doing in a place like this."

"I dare say a good many men ask her that question," said Wexford gravely.

"You what? Oh, yes, I see. Right. But seriously, a good-looking girl from a nice background who's got into a university—what would she find here?"

"Her friends, presumably. Anyway, she didn't find anything, she didn't come. Ah, more customers. I can't say I'm sorry. I don't much care for being the only people in a pub, do you?"

Two men had come in, closely followed by a man and a woman. "As a matter of fact, I prefer it," said Burden. "I like a bit of hush."

Wexford grinned because that was the response he had expected. "I've just thought of something. Mrs. Strang was late, she didn't get to the pickup point—outside the Flag, was it?—until some minutes after eight, let's say at least five past eight. Just suppose, though, that Rachel *wasn't* late, that Rachel got there on the dot of eight or even a couple of minutes to. And someone else came along and offered her a lift and she took it."

"Why would she? She was waiting for Mrs. Strang."

"True. But I've got an idea about that..."

Wexford broke off and edged his chair back to allow for the passage of a group of women who had just come into the Rat and Carrot by the swing doors. There were four of them, two young and two in early middle age, and Wexford was immediately struck by the air of wariness and timidity most of them had. But the one who led the way up to the bar, a thin and rather beautiful young woman in jeans and shabby sweater whose long black hair was tied back with a chiffon scarf, had a resolute manner as if before coming in here she had gritted her teeth and sworn to stick to her purpose. Screwed her courage to the sticking place, he thought.

The others followed her and stood in a line along the counter. The black-haired woman cleared her throat, but this had no effect on Honeyman, who kept his eyes on his *Sporting Life*.

There was a brief silence, then—and Wexford heard her draw in her breath—she said in a voice probably higher pitched than her normal tone, "We'd like a drink, please. Two glasses of white wine and two of lager and lime."

The licensee slammed the paper shut and looked up. "You come from that place up the road, don't you?"

She took a step nearer the bar. "*What?*"

"That house that's full of women who've walked out on their menfolk. You come from there."

An older woman, taking courage, said, "That's a funny way of putting it, but what if we do?"

"I'll tell you what. I'm not serving you, that's what."

The black-haired woman had gone very pale. Wexford thought he saw the hand that rested on the counter begin to tremble. "You can't do that," she said. "What reason have you got for doing that?"

"Don't have to have a reason. You ask anyone if I'm not within my rights to refuse to serve anyone I don't want to serve."

"He is too," Burden said softly.

Wexford nodded. He doubted if the women would put up a fight and they didn't. They said no more but turned away and made for the door.

The licensee called after them, "You'd best go down the High Street where they don't know where you're from. They'll serve you there till they find out who you are."

The black-haired woman turned around and said in ringing tones, "You bastard!"

"Charming," said Honeyman when the door swung to behind them. "I wonder if you gentlemen heard that? Ladylike, wouldn't you say?"

Wexford got up, went to the counter, and having ordered two more halves of Adnams, said that he was a police officer and showed his warrant card.

Honeyman said rather too hastily, "I was right, wasn't I? I don't need a reason for not serving people."

"You were within your rights, but you must have had a reason and I've been wondering what it is."

The licensee filled the two tankards. "It's on the house."

"No, it's not, thanks all the same." Wexford produced a fiver and put it down with precision. "We came in here to ask you about the missing girl, Rachel Holmes, but just tell me about those women first, will you?"

"They live in a house in Kingsbrook Valley Drive, up the road here." Honeyman's whole manner had changed, becoming obsequious and conciliatory. Even his voice was different, the South-of-England burr replaced by a refined drawl. "They're what they call battered women, if you know what I mean. Or they say they are. Husbands gave them a little tap when they cut up rough, if the truth were known."

"All right, I get the picture. But what have they done to get up your nose?"

"Let me tell you. There was two of them in here a couple of weeks back, and some poor devil comes in and gets hold of one of them, asks her to come home, she's left him with the kids, if you please. Well, of course, she's not going to do as he asks, is she? Don't suppose she ever has. So she struggles and gives him a push and he starts slapping her around, which he was driven to, and then the other one joins in, banging on his back with her fists, and then I had to intervene. Naturally, as I'm sure you'll agree, out you go, I said, the lot of you, and don't come back. Actually, I regret having to put him out, he seemed a decent fellow. You know something? Well, of course you do. When folks got married in the old days, the woman used to have to say she'd obey him. Pity that was ever changed, if you ask me."

"I don't know that I do ask you, Mr. Honeyman," Wexford said blandly. "I'm rather inclined to think I wouldn't want your advice on anything much." He watched Honeyman blink his eyes and slightly recoil. "But you could take some. You'd be well advised to call us next time a decent fellow slaps a woman around on your premises. And now perhaps you'd like to tell me if to your knowledge this girl has ever been in here."

A deep red flush had suffused Honeyman's face. It was probably a relief to him to have something to look at and be distracted by. He stared at the photograph Wexford showed him, then muttered, "I don't know, I don't recall."

Burden, who had come up to the counter, said, "Does that mean you never saw her meet her friends in here on a Saturday night? She's very good-looking, isn't she? Not the sort of face you'd forget."

"I may have seen her." The burr was back and the sulkiness. "I reckon I did, maybe two or three months back. She was in here with some other kids—well, I don't mean kids," he said quickly, remembering what the law said about selling alcohol to those underage, "they was all over eighteen—and they had a bar meal."

"But you didn't see her on Saturday night?"

"Absolutely not," said Honeyman, shaking his head to give a kind of earnest vehemence to his denial.

"Sylvia's working there," Wexford said when he and Burden were outside and approaching The Hide. "I can't remember if I told you. Answering calls on the helpline among other things. Have you ever hit a woman?"

"Of course I haven't," Burden said, shocked. "What a question."

"Oh, I don't know. I haven't either. D'you know what Barry said to me the other day? 'All men hit their wives sometime or other,' that's what he said. I was a bit taken aback."

"My God." Burden sounded horrified. "I hope and trust we haven't got a wife-beater on the team. That would be a fine thing, just when Hurt-Watch has got going. And by the way, just how are we to go about distributing those pagers and mobiles? We may know that domestic violence is very prevalent in all societies, but how many prosecutions for assaults on wives and girlfriends have there been in our area? Precious few. Presumably that doesn't mean male-female relationships are more idyllic here or men more easygoing. It's just because in the past women haven't called us and haven't wanted our intervention."

"So how are we going to find the ones that are in danger? Is that what you mean? Maybe by consulting the people who run this place."

Wexford stopped outside The Hide and looked up at the windows. Those on the ground floor were almost entirely hidden by the tall evergreens that filled the front garden. From a top-floor window a white face framed in black hair looked back at him and he recognized its owner as the woman who had shouted at Andy Honeyman.

"There'll have to be some such method. We can't very well put an ad in the *Courier* offering free communication systems to anyone who applies. As Southby says, the entire female population would want one."

Burden obviously wasn't much interested. "Talking of the female population, what was this idea of yours?"

"Idea?"

"You said you'd an idea about Rachel waiting for Mrs. Strang. Presumably you meant you'd found some sort of answer."

"Oh, right. Yes. But I wouldn't go as far as that. I only wondered if Rachel and Mrs. Strang had ever met. I mean, would they recognize each other?"

Burden seemed mystified. He gave Wexford a dark look and said he had better be getting home, his mother- and father-in-law were visiting and he was inexcusably late already. And Wexford went home too, with Burden's remarks to nag at him while he ate his dinner and afterward, when a television documentary on a European single currency failed to hold his attention. Operation Safeguard, and its subsidiary scheme Hurt-Watch, would only work if he and his team probed the whole domestic-violence situation.

A ludicrous picture presented itself to him of five hundred mobile phones and pagers landing in his office, perhaps even on his desk, and he without a clue as to which women were eligible to receive them and which would be affronted to be offered what amounted to a defense against the men who shared their lives. Once that hurdle had been got ever, how were they to react when a call on one of these mobiles was received? Go to the caller's home and arrest the perpetrator. Simple. Only most of the time it wouldn't be as clear-cut as that. She'd say she didn't want him charged, she didn't want him taken from the house, he was the breadwinner, he'd promised not to do it again, he was sorry, he was ashamed, she shouldn't have called the police, only she was frightened and hurt and at her wits' end, but she didn't want the family broken up…He must talk to Sylvia. Meanwhile, there was this missing girl, Rachel Holmes.

Dora seemed quite keen on the boring television program, which meant he couldn't turn it off. The evening would stay light till past eight, so he went out into the garden and walked about, finally sitting down in the little paved area, which was the centerpiece of Dora's rose garden. His seat was one of a pair of French café chairs that Sheila had given them for Christmas, an elegant affair of pale gray metal scrolls and twists and curlicues, but not the most comfortable to sit on. Above him the sky was a deepening blue, and heading this way, probably by now passing over Pomfret, was a red and yellow balloon whose passengers he could see waving to him. Or waving to someone. Wexford waved back and in doing so nearly fell off his delicate and perilous seat.

Tomorrow would be Tuesday and in the afternoon Rachel Holmes would come back. Both girls had been to the same school, both were still in their teens, both were attractive, if in very different ways, each was the child of a divorced mother, both had been waiting for a lift, one returning from an evening out with friends, the other anticipating such an evening. Both had gone missing on a Saturday, and on successive Saturdays. In spite of all that, Burden would say it was a ridiculous assumption to make. Wexford was making it every time the girl entered his thoughts. It kept him from worrying about Rachel as he should have been worrying. Did it also prevent him from taking all possible steps and measures to find her?

Should he, for instance, have put Rosemary Holmes on television? Should he have instituted a search of the countryside between Stowerton and Kingsmarkham? Perhaps the question he should have been asking himself was, would he have done so if Lizzie Cromwell hadn't gone missing exactly a week before and come home three nights and three days later?

The balloon sailed overhead and a little breeze sprang up to ruffle the new leaves and send a shower of petals scattering off the pear tree. The pretty chair was so uncomfortable it might have been designed as an instrument of torture. Sit on it for twelve hours under bright lights and answer the interrogator's questions...My God, he thought. He got up and went into the house, resolving to talk to Caroline Strang's mother first thing in the morning.

CHAPTER

4

THE SEARCH BEGAN AT TWO ON TUESDAY AFTERNOON. THERE were ten uniformed officers, some of them reinforcements from the Regional Crime Squad, and sixteen members of the public, all volunteers from among neighbors and friends of the Holmeses'. Rosemary Holmes wanted to join them but Wexford advised against it. He still believed, against the odds, that Rachel would turn up later in the afternoon, and what he had discovered in Framhurst that morning only reinforced his belief. Olga Strang had never met Rachel, had never even seen a photograph of her. The two girls had met at university, not through living only five miles apart or having been to the same school. Rachel was a stranger to Olga and she to Rachel.

"How were you to know her?" Wexford had asked. "You were to give her a lift, but how were you to recognize her?"

"You mean, she wore a yellow ribbon and I wore a big red rose? There was nothing like that. I never thought about it, I was just *there* and she was supposed to be *there* but she wasn't."

A scatty woman who seemed unable to collect her thoughts for two minutes at a time, Mrs. Strang gave the impression of being harassed by everything in her surroundings and perhaps by life itself. The cottage she lived in with her husband and three children was frighteningly disordered, with papers mixed with clothes, chairs laden with newspapers and magazines, used cups and glasses set or left beside vases of dead flowers, an iron switched on, its red light glistening, standing upended between a naked loaf of bread and an open packet of kettle descaler.

She herself, perhaps about to use the iron, wore a diaphanous dressing gown over blouse and slip and clutched in her left hand something made of crumpled red material that might have been a skirt or a pair of trousers. Without relinquishing her hold on it, she sat on the edge of the table, crumpling the red stuff to a worse state of creasedness while running her right hand through her wispy, reddish gold hair.

"I won't keep you long," Wexford said. "I can see you're getting ready to go to work." He couldn't keep his eyes off that iron, which seemed to come closer and closer to her muslin frills as she swayed nervously back and forth. "But did Rachel know the make of your car? Its color?"

"Oh, I don't know, I can't answer."

"Had Caroline described you to her?"

"You'll have to ask her. I can't remember." She brightened and suddenly smiled. "I knew she had dark hair. I was looking for a dark-haired girl. And Caroline said she was very good-looking."

"Mrs. Strang, you're about to singe your, er, dressing gown."

"Am I? Oh, God. Thank you. Caroline's not here, she's back at college, you could phone her and ask her. Or I could. I must get this skirt ironed, you must excuse me, I'm late..."

He knew enough. Rachel had no more idea as to the woman due to give her a lift than that she was middle-aged and driving a car. Someone else had come along at eight and picked her up, and when Rachel said, "Mrs. Strang?" or some such thing, this woman had agreed, had fallen in with the misapprehension, and used it to her advantage.

Was she the same woman who had offered a lift to Lizzie Cromwell? And had Lizzie, in spite of what she'd said, accepted it? To risk acting on this wild intuition would be criminal. There must be a search, and next day, if she hadn't come home, he would have Rosemary Holmes up before the television cameras. But she'd come home. She'd walk into the house on Oval Road. She wouldn't be distraught or soaked to the skin, she would simply stroll in and, after her mother had had hysterics, ask what all the fuss was about. Or else, instead, she'd turn up at her university, with a considerable amount of explaining to do. He turned his attention to his post, first to the document that lay uppermost on his desk.

If someone addresses you, in a letter, by your given name and signs himself "yours always," you may confidently expect your correspondent to be a close friend. This printout of an E-mail began "Dear Reg" and ended "Yours always, Brian," but Wexford would not have placed Brian St. George, editor of the *Kingsmarkham Courier*, in that intimate category. The very sight of it filled him with apprehension. No communication he had ever received from St. George had been supportive or even cooperative with police strategy. He had looked at this one without putting on his reading glasses, and he stared at a glazed muzziness of dancing print for a moment. But he knew that was no good, and after only a brief hesitation, he put on his glasses and read St. George's letter.

Dear Reg,

It has come to my attention that the infamous pedophile, Henry Thomas Orbe, is due to be released from detention at the end of this week. His home was and still is on the Muriel Campden Estate in Kingsmarkham and I have been reliably informed that he intends to return to the house, currently occupied by his daughter and her partner, when he leaves prison, where he has been for the past nine years, on 17 April.

Now, a large number of parents with young children, to whom Orbe must pose a threat, live on the Muriel Campden Estate and my intention is to run a lead story in this week's edition of the *Courier*, informing interested parties of Orbe's return. I am sure you will agree that Orbe is a dangerous man and that no child can be safe while he remains at large.

I will be interested to receive your comments. If the Mid-Sussex Constabulary would care to supply me with a statement of Orbe's current situation and perhaps their general opinion on the arrangements made for released pedophiles, I will be delighted to print it.

With my very good wishes,
Yours always, Brian

Wexford sighed. It wasn't only a wonder what induced St. George to call him by his first name and end in that affectionate way, but a mystery why the man should want to. At their last meeting, which had been in connection with the hostage-taking over the proposed bypass, he, Wexford, had been atrociously (but justifiably) rude to the editor and had received a good deal of abuse in return. The answer, no doubt, was that St. George wanted something. Wexford's approval?

He decided—quite quickly—not to reply. After all, much as he would have liked to, he couldn't stop St. George and the *Courier* in their mission. Barring an injunction to restrain them, they would go ahead whatever happened. Wexford tried to remember Orbe but could recall only a newspaper photograph from long ago of a fat-faced man with bleated chin and forehead. That didn't mean much. Anyone would look dreadful in one of those blown-up snaps. Orbe, the man, had entirely faded from his memory. Of course the crime, whatever it was, hadn't happened in the Kingsmarkham area and he hadn't arrested him.

He was wondering whether he was capable of summoning up Orbe's CV or dossier on his computer, of filling with information the pretty blue screen over which clouds swam and birds flew, when Barry Vine came in. "How's the Rachel Holmes search going?" Wexford asked.

"Nothing new, sir. But I came to tell you something else. You know we had a second clothes robbery?"

"Oh, yes. The First Gear boutique."

"Well, we've got someone for both, the First Gear and the craftswoman, the designer. You were right when you said they used a child to get in. 'A sort of Oliver Twist' were your words if I remember rightly. I don't know how old Oliver Twist was—I can't say I've ever read the book or seen the film—but this kid's four."

For a moment Wexford said nothing. Orbe's face, the remembered face, reappeared in some picture frame of his mind, and he asked himself which was worse, to use a small child sexually or to teach that child to break and enter and steal. The former, no question about it, but still...

"You mean this villain—what's his name, by the way?"

"Flay. Patrick Flay. He lives in Glebe Road."

"This Patrick Flay put a child of four through that fanlight and instructed him how to open the door?"

"Not quite, sir," said Vine. "It was a girl, his own daughter, and while it was a fanlight the first time, my belief is that this second time she went in through the cat flap."

"The *cat flap?*"

"Yes, sir. It's a sort of trapdoor that hangs on hinges that the cat pushes open with its head and—"

"I know what it *is*." Wexford shook his head, more in sorrow than in anger. "Before the things were invented they used to cut a hole in the door, and the story is that Isaac Newton cut a hole for his cat, and when she had kittens, he cut six more holes."

Vine stared at him. "He must have been bonkers."

"Well, no. They didn't have Mensa in those days, but he was just as bright as Mr. Burden. He was a great physicist, he discovered gravity, among other things. But that's the point, that very clever people can be daft in some ways. Anyway, I don't believe it. I told you just to make it plain that I know what a cat flap is. Where's this Flay? Downstairs?"

"He's called his solicitor and the guy's on his way."

"I hope and trust you haven't brought the little girl along as well?"

Vine looked a little affronted. "I left her with her mum, sir. I've talked to her…"

"In the presence of her mother, I hope?"

"Of course. Mother claims to know nothing about it, but the child—she's called Kaylee, K-A-Y-L-double-E—told me her dad got her to wear gloves. He said it was cold and she must keep them on, and they went out together and round the back of this house where her dad showed her the little door that belonged to 'the pussy cat,' I quote, and he said never to tell what she did, so she wasn't going to tell me. But afterwards her dad gave her a Dracula."

"Gave her a *what?*"

"It's a kind of ice cream," said Vine.

They went downstairs together. On the way Wexford asked if the missing textiles had been discovered and Vine had to admit that they had not. Flay, a man of twenty-five who wore his reddish hair in dreadlocks, though he was white and that hair was sparse, sat at the table in the interview room, smoking while he awaited his solicitor. PC Martin Dempsey sat on a chair inside the door, his back to the wall, his eyes fixed impassively on the table legs.

Vine switched on the recorder. "Detective Chief Inspector Wexford and Detective Sergeant Vine have entered the room at four fifty-two. Present also are Police Constable Dempsey and Patrick John Flay."

"I'm not saying a word till my lawyer gets here," said Flay.

Wexford didn't answer. He had been sitting down for no more than a minute when Lynn Fancourt brought the solicitor in. This was a young man Wexford had never seen before but whom he knew to be James Beamish of Proctor, Beamish, Green. Vine noted his arrival and began questioning Flay, whose sullen expression had changed to one of pleasurable anticipation once his solicitor was beside him. His smiles turned to laughter when Vine asked him about his daughter. "You've got that wrong for a start. She's not my kid, she's the wife's. I'm like her stepdad. The wife had her before we like moved in together."

"You seem to have a good relationship with her," said Wexford.

"What, with Kaylee? Of course I do. I love kids."

"You love her so much that you teach her to go into someone else's house and steal someone else's property."

"I don't know what you're talking about," said Flay, grinning widely. "If you believe what a four-year-old kid, practically a toddler, tells you, you're barking. She's got an imagination, has Kaylee. She tells stories, right? Well, some would call them lies. I mean, I wouldn't, not me, I'm a tolerant sort of guy, but there's some as'd give a kid a clip round the ear for telling the sort of porkies Kaylee tells."

"So you didn't make her wear gloves and put her through a fanlight into the householder's cloakroom and then through a cat flap into the householder's basement?"

Wexford was aware of how ridiculous it all sounded. Any outsider would almost have thought Flay's mirth justified. He was looking at Beamish now, grinning and shaking his head.

"You didn't teach her how to open the window and put the property out from the inside."

"Zilch. Are you kidding?"

"Kaylee wasn't taught to enter that house and steal the property?"

Beamish raised his eyes languidly. "My client has already told you no, Mr. Wexford."

Wexford was thinking how to rephrase his questions when a note was brought to him by Lynn Fancourt. He didn't even glance at it he was so sure it was to tell him Rachel Holmes had come back, but he spoke into the recorder to announce he was leaving the room and that Lynn had taken his place. Outside, he unfolded the paper. Not a word about Rachel but a message from the assistant chief constable designate asking him to call him as a matter of urgency. Of course, it was a bit early for Rachel's return. If she came back at the same time as Lizzie Cromwell had returned, she wouldn't be in Stowerton before six. The moment he was back in his office he phoned Southby.

"Orbe," said the voice that always barked out its clipped sentences. "Henry Thomas Orbe. Mean anything to you?"

Would he have known if he hadn't had St. George's letter? Wexford would never have thought he had reason to be grateful to the editor of the *Kingsmarkham Courier*. "Pedophile, sir," he said promptly. "He's been inside for nine years, coming out and home here next Friday."

"Right." Southby sounded faintly disappointed. "I just thought you should know that the local rag's going to run an in-the-public-interest story about it on Friday. I dare say it will pass off without incident."

So Southby too had had a letter from St. George. I wonder if that one began *Dear Malcolm*, thought Wexford. He started up the computer and after several false moves resulting in rather frightening admonitions on the screen, managed to access—hateful computer language but nevertheless a source of pride when you got it right—Henry Thomas Orbe.

"Born South Woodford, London E18," he read, "20 February 1928, the third son of George and Annie Orbe, of Churchfields, South Woodford. Educated Buckhurst Hill County High School until age sixteen. Convicted of gross indecency 1949 and again in 1952, sent to prison on the first offense for two months and on the second for eighteen months. Convicted of gross indecency with a minor in 1958 and sent to prison for eight years."

Sickened by the dreary repetition almost as much as by the squalid nature of the offenses, Wexford pressed the page-down key and was gratified to find that it worked. It actually did the job it claimed to do, which was far from being the case, in his opinion, with most computer moves. Up onto the screen came the last page of Orbe's sorry catalog. Wexford drew in his breath. The man had gone to prison for manslaughter nine years before, having been sentenced originally to fifteen years for his part in the rape and death of a twelve-year-old boy.

Two other men had been involved, of whom one had received the same sentence as Orbe and the other eight years. There was no mention in the dossier of Orbe's marriage or marriages and nothing about a daughter. Wexford noted that Orbe must be an old man now, more than seventy. Would he still be a danger to children? You would have to know the man and know a lot more about pedophilia than Wexford did to answer that. But of one thing he was sure: something was wrong with a society that set free such a monster, even a worn-out, aged, broken monster, into a community with a bigger population of small children than anywhere else in the neighborhood.

By nine he knew he had been wrong and the Rachel Holmes disappearance wasn't going to follow Lizzie Cromwell's pattern. A kind of guilt overwhelmed him, as if it were his fault she hadn't come back. He was thankful he had said nothing of that hope and certainty of his except to Burden. What he had said to Burden would remain between them. He had tried to compensate by suggesting that the search go on after dark, but even he had to admit this was impossible, for it was a black, moonless night of heavy rain.

Vine, whom he phoned before he went to bed, told him he had had to let Patrick Flay go. Without enough evidence to charge him Vine was obliged to release the man, still laughing, in the company of his solicitor. For a while Wexford stood at the landing window, looking out at the night. It was a habit of his, to stare out, when all was still and silent, and it amused him to see that Sylvia did it too. Maybe you could inherit a gene of meditative sky-watching. Rain fell steadily, insistently, long silver needles of it puncturing the dark. He thought then of Lear's words when he reproaches himself for having paid too little attention to the plight of the homeless and dispossessed—*poor naked wretches... that hide the pelting of this pitiless storm*—the women who cried to Sylvia for help, such victimized children as Kaylee Flay and the missing girl. But she, probably, was dead by now, lying in a waterlogged ditch.

In Detective Sergeant Vine's opinion people like the Flays—and he made no such reservations as Sylvia Fairfax did—shouldn't be allowed to have children and, if by some contravention of the law they did have them, should not be allowed to bring them up. What was the care system for if not to protect children against the likes of Patrick Flay? Why was there fostering and adoption if these processes weren't put to better use?

He arrived at the ground-floor flat in Glebe Road, the half of a shabby, run-down house, to find both Patrick Flay and Kaylee's mother at home, and the little girl, when he began to talk to her, firmly set on the stained and battered sofa between them, squeezed between them, with no possibility of escape. She was a child of mixed race, born of a white mother, a woman as fair, freckled, and ginger-haired as Patrick.

But Kaylee had dark brown hair in tight ringlets all over her head, dark brown eyes, and a light olive skin. Under the left one of those eyes was a darker mark, a bruise that hadn't been there before, and Vine knew, as surely as if he had seen the blow struck, that one of those two had hit her in the face. Jackie Flay, perhaps, but more probably Patrick, and Vine also knew why that blow had been inflicted.

A choking feeling of impotence and frustration almost inhibited him from speaking, and as he afterward told Wexford, the worst part was knowing there was little he could do about it.

"You can notify the Social Services," said Wexford. "There's a good case here for threatening the Flays with putting the child into care. So what happened?"

"Kaylee told me it *hadn't* happened. She's an intelligent kid, you know. I mean, she's really very bright. She just said none of it was true, she had made it up. In other words, just what Flay said. And he had the nerve to say to her, 'You know what happens to you when you tell lies, don't you, Kaylee?' And he was grinning in that revolting way of his."

"And the mother?"

"She just sat there, silly-scared, if you know what I mean, looking as if she'd say anything and do anything to stay on the right side of Flay. She probably held the kid while Flay hit her. I can just hear him saying it, 'You say you never did it, you never went there—right? You want my fist in your face again?' "

Wexford shook his head. "Jackie Flay may be just as much a victim. And the worst thing is that Flay'll get the child to do it again, he'll get her into the habit of it and soon she won't even consider telling the truth—poor little Olivia Twist."

Vine, who had been frowning gloomily, brightened a little and said, "What happened to him, sir? This Oliver Twist?"

"He got saved by an old gentleman who turned out, by an amazing coincidence, to be his own great-uncle."

"That won't happen to Kaylee."

"Probably not, though I dare say she has no more idea who her grandfathers are than Oliver had."

Vine considered this, pursing his lips. "Why would a woman want to marry Flay? If they're married. Why would any woman shack up with him? Does she want to be a victim and make her kid a victim?"

"You're getting into deep waters, Barry, when you start asking why anyone would marry anyone else. It's a mystery. But I doubt if many people choose to be victims unless they're masochists, and masochists are few. The thing is people want to be part of a couple, what they call these days 'being in a relationship.' And most of them would rather have a bad one than none at all. It's nature. By the way, you didn't really mean you hit your wife, did you?"

"Me? Oh, right. It was just the once. She hit me and I hit her back. That's all I mean."

Wexford had spent the best part of the morning in Oval Road, where Rosemary Holmes, who knew Lizzie Cromwell's story, had perhaps also believed her daughter would return on the previous evening. But Rachel hadn't come home and Rosemary was distraught, pacing the room and at one point throwing herself into an armchair where she collapsed in a storm of tears. Wexford asked himself why on earth he had thought this disappearance would have a happy outcome just because Lizzie's had. Thank God he hadn't let his ridiculous hunch impede the search or prevent any serious investigation.

The searchers had begun again soon after first light, combing the rain-drenched fields, glad of shelter inside the quiet dimness of woodlands, but while the rain remained no more than a drizzle, pressing on. Karen Malahyde and Lynn Fancourt had widened the inquiry beyond Rachel's immediate circle of friends, had talked to people she had been at school with. They were now in Brighton with the girl's father, Rosemary's divorced husband, hearing how he hadn't seen his daughter for the past seven years. Michael Devonshire, the Flagford GP, had not only taken Rosemary out to dinner but admitted frankly that he had spent most of the night with her, leaving the house in Oval Road at five the next morning.

Rachel had now been missing for four nights and almost four days. Uneasily, Wexford set up a press conference for five that afternoon—his reluctance stemming from the certainty that Brian St. George would be there—and at that conference, as part of it, Rosemary Holmes would make her appeal for Rachel's return. She shrank from it, at first flatly refusing. She was too little in command of herself, she told Wexford, she would make a mess of it.

"That doesn't much matter," he said to her gently. "I don't want to sound cynical, but the more emotion you show and the more...well, frankly, upset, you appear to be, the more likely the appeal is to succeed."

"But they don't care, those viewers. They're just going to gloat."

"I wouldn't be so sure of that, Mrs. Holmes. There are a lot of people out there who have real sympathy for you."

And your attractions may have some effect, he thought, not saying it aloud, your pretty, youthful face and nice voice, not to mention that figure and those legs. We live in a world where good looks get you everything, where the preservation of youth is at a premium. Those journalists would write better stories and longer ones because this woman was beautiful and had a voice like a Shakespearean actress. The photographers would take more trouble and the television cameramen be more enthusiastic.

And would all that bring Rachel back? No one could tell him.

A car was sent for Rosemary Holmes at four-thirty. Wexford saw with approval that in spite of her terrible anxiety, she had dressed herself with care for this confrontation in a black suit and pink-and-white blouse. She had made up her face for the cameras. Her hair was newly washed and her nails painted pink pearl. St. George's reporter stared as if he had never seen a presentable woman before. The cameras closed in before she had taken her seat at the table between Wexford and Burden.

"Look this way, Rosemary!"

"Just turn your head a fraction, Rosemary!"

"Thank you, that's great. Just one more, Rosemary, and I'm done."

Wexford clenched his teeth. Why couldn't they call her Mrs. Holmes? Did they think that using her first name would allay her anxiety, put her at her ease, make her *happier?* It was such crass impertinence.

He listened while she made her appeal in that rich, modulated voice, her eyes downcast. "If you are holding my—my beloved daughter, please let her go, let her come back to me. Please have mercy on us, she's all I've got and I—I'm all she's got. *Please.* She's a lovely, good, clever girl, she's never done harm to anyone in the whole of her short life. Please send her back to me..."

And here Rosemary Holmes could sustain the steadiness of her voice no longer. She broke into sobs, her throat heaving, her pretty hands flying to her face, her weeping eyes. Wexford helped her to her feet and took her out. He sent for tea and left her in his office with Lynn Fancourt. Burden would conduct the rest of the press conference, they didn't really need him, but he made his way back downstairs all the same and was just in time to hear someone, not the *Courier* reporter, ask in strident tones if it was true that Thomas Orbe would be coming out next day and returning to his home in Oberon Road.

"No questions will be answered not relevant to the Rachel Holmes disappearance," Burden snapped.

The reporter took no notice. "Will he be coming out tomorrow?"

"No," said Burden with perfect truth. Orbe's release date was not Thursday but Friday. "That ends the conference. Thank you very much, ladies and gentlemen."

Wexford went back upstairs. What must it be like to be a pedophile? To want to have sex with small children? Something told him that if you could imagine it, just as if you could imagine being a sadist or a necrophile, really live it yourself in imagination, then you would understand. *To understand all is to forgive all* ought to be changed to *to imagine is to understand* and leave off the forgiving bit. In the Lord's Prayer, which he hadn't said in church or anywhere else for forty years, there was a bit about forgiving us our trespasses as we forgive those that trespass against us.

Against *us*, not against other people. He couldn't forgive those offenses against others, and God, if there was a God, ought not to either. Maybe religious people would call that blasphemy.

In his office he thought about going home, putting some of these papers in his expensive hide briefcase—another gift from Sheila. Did she ever let him and Dora buy things like that?—paperwork to do at home, worse luck. The phone rang but he didn't dare think of not answering it.

A voice he didn't recognize—they were always changing—said, "I have a Mrs. Holmes on the line for you, sir."

And then the beautiful tones he had heard no more than half an hour ago, appealing for her daughter's return: "Rachel's home. She was here at home when I got back. I'm so happy, I still can't believe it, but it's true, she's home."

CHAPTER 5

SHE WAS TWENTY-FOUR HOURS LATE BUT SHE HAD COME BACK. He felt curiously gratified because he had been right, especially as she was so obviously unharmed, a beautiful girl, tall and slim, with a flawless skin and dark, shining hair. It was plain, though, that she was far from pleased to see him and Karen Malahyde. She didn't want them there. If it had been left to her, Wexford thought, the police would never have been notified of her return.

He could almost see inside her head, imagine her thinking, "I'll just quietly go back to Essex and then Mum can tell them after I've gone. It's nothing to do with them, it's my business." She had greeted them by saying in a loud and surly tone that she had a bad headache.

"You should see a doctor," Wexford said. "You must do that anyway."

Rachel had flushed brilliantly. "I don't need a doctor. I've just got a headache. No one's done anything to me."

What she meant was clear. But she explained, her eyes on Karen Malahyde. "It's because I'm a woman. People just assume a woman must have been raped. Well, I haven't been. I'd know."

A very strange remark, Wexford thought it. How could she not know? How could anyone not know? "Have you been assaulted in any way?"

"No. Not in *any* way."

He wasn't imagining the scorn in her voice. She was one of those clever girls, brought up to have a high opinion of themselves, who when as young as this show their self-confidence in contempt for others they estimate as lower down the intelligence scale. Police officers would come into that category, he thought with concealed amusement.

"Have you been given any substances? I was thinking of a blood test."

"I don't know," she said sharply. "I don't know what I've been given,

I can't remember. But I'm not having any blood test. If you've got AIDS in mind, I've told you, I've not been raped."

He hadn't had it in mind. "I would like a doctor to see you."

"I wouldn't and I won't." She said savagely, "I won't see a doctor and I won't have a doctor see me. I hate doctors. I never go near them. If I need anything like that, I go to an alternative practitioner. Chinese medicine or an herbalist."

"I hardly think an herbalist would be much use in the present situation," Wexford said dryly. He thought of Rosemary Holmes's friendship with her doctor. Was that the cause of Rachel's dislike of orthodox medicine? Perhaps. "If you're so set against a doctor, I can't compel you. Now perhaps you'll tell us where you've been."

They were wonderful banisters to slide down, dark red mahogany polished over a century by a hundred hands, many of them gloved, and in the staircase's early life, by half a dozen housemaids. The banisters flowed, an unbroken river of wood, from the top floor to the basement, unbroken but not consistent in their gradient, for while on the main areas of the flights they declined at an angle of forty-five degrees, above the bends they became briefly almost vertical and at the landings they relaxed into the horizontal. It was at the second landing that Sylvia, toiling up, stepped back to avoid contact with a protruding foot as a child of about six came flying down, hanging on with both hands and shrieking at the top of his lungs. Shrieking, Sylvia had often thought, seemed a natural concomitant of pleasure in the undersevens. His momentum was just insufficient to carry him on across the landing horizontal to the next downward slope, and waving to Sylvia, he cried, "Give us a push, miss!"

This was the way the children at The Hide tended to address her and Lucy and Griselda, as if they were teachers at school. Deciding not to admonish him, but dreading an accident, she put out her hand and gave him a feeble shove in the middle of his back.

"Harder," he said. "Go *on*."

Sylvia pushed a very little harder; the little boy slid along the straight and tipped over onto the next slope with another shriek. Before climbing up the last flight, she watched him reach the bend and, more riskily, negotiate the vertical banister at the bend in safety. Lucy was in the helpline room and the two phones were quiet.

"I'm not on my own, am I?"

"Afraid so," Lucy said. "Jill's got flu and Davina's giving up. She says she can't afford an unpaid job, and that I understand."

"What do I do," Sylvia asked, "if both phones ring at the same time?"

"It seldom happens, thank God, it's not as if we're in the center of a big city. But if it does, you'll just have to put one on hold. Use your own judgment which one."

"When they get their mobiles, we'll have a lot more, won't we? Though I suppose that's not something we should complain about."

Lucy laughed. "No, we shouldn't, but I know what you mean. I'm going to leave you to hold the fort now."

After she had gone, Sylvia stood by the window, looking down into this garden and the next one, and those behind, all the big, shrubby, well-treed gardens, divided from each other by walls of stone or brick, or creeper-hung fences or cypress or yew hedges. Apart from this one, all the leafy gardens were empty of people but for one man mowing a distant lawn, the hum of the mower faintly audible as its owner took advantage of a rainless day. In The Hide's garden two toddlers supervised by their mothers clambered up the climbing frame while bigger children occupied the swing. The banister slider came out into the garden while she watched, holding a red, white, and blue football, which he dropped onto the grass and kicked hard at the trunk of a flowering cherry, dislodging from its blossoms a cascade of petals. The pink shower he achieved evidently pleased him, for he aimed another, harder kick at the tree and, when it had the effect he wanted, gave one of his famous shrieks.

She turned back into the room. Two of its walls were papered with press cuttings of domestic-violence cases. Big black letters, big stark photographs, a haggard woman with a black eye, another with a split lip, a well-known black boxer whose smile showed his dazzling teeth, an equally famous white footballer wearing his notorious scowl. The former had put his girlfriend into a wheelchair for life, the latter had killed his wife by accident while punching her head. On the wall above the table where the phones were, hung a calendar and a large sheet of card that showed details of the four refuges in the area and what space, if any, was available in each of them. Currently there was no room at the Kingsmarkham Hide and none in Myringham, but the smaller house in

Sewingbury had one room free, and the most distant of all, a onetime B & B outside Lewes, had two. Sylvia had read all the cases on the walls several times over, and now, for the intervals of quiet, she brought a book with her.

The phone's ringing, after a quarter of an hour of silence, made her jump. She picked up the receiver. "The Hide. How can I help you?"

A woman's voice, cultured, gentle, diffident, said, "I'm not one of those battered women, you know."

"Right," said Sylvia cheerfully. "Would you like to tell me what your problem is? Take your time. I've plenty. Everything you say will be in absolute confidence."

She heard the rough intake of breath and its expulsion before the woman spoke again. "I would like to know if you could recommend a psychiatrist."

Sylvia was a little taken aback. "This is The Hide helpline. Are you sure you have the right number?"

"Oh, yes. I know who you are and I'd like you to recommend a psychiatrist. My husband says he'll stop hitting me if I put myself in the hands of a good psychiatrist."

"There are lots of bits I can't remember," Rachel Holmes said. "You just have to accept that. I've got a sort of amnesia. It's the shock, I expect."

"Let's have the bits you do remember," said Karen Malahyde dryly. If this girl was going to be uppity, was going to try to put her down, she too could be crushing. "Begin at the beginning, will you? At eight on Saturday evening. You were to be picked up by Mrs. Strang at eight?"

"You know all that," the girl said. "You don't want me to repeat it, I suppose? I was early. My mother's boyfriend was calling for her and I thought I'd get out of their way." This last remark was accompanied by a resentful glance in her mother's direction. "I don't come home all that often and I'd have thought the least she could do was give up a night out with *him* just for once..."

"But, Rachel," Rosemary protested faintly, "you were going out yourself, you'd told me you were going out."

"Oh, what's the use?"

Rachel seemed about to expand on her resentment, but Karen

Malahyde cut in with a swift and rather curt, "Let's get back to your movements on Saturday night, can we?"

"I left here at a few minutes to eight." Rachel was sullen now. "I got to the bus stop opposite the Flag when it was just on eight. There's a seat there and I sat down to wait. I'd have thought all that was pretty obvious."

Wexford couldn't help recalling how Mrs. Holmes had said, no more than an hour or so before, that her daughter was a "lovely, good, clever girl." Clever she might well be. "Did you know Mrs. Strang's car, its color and make?" he asked.

The girl gave an impatient sigh, but at last she spoke more reasonably. "I know I ought to have found that out. I ought to have found out what the woman looked like, but I didn't and I've been punished for that, haven't I?"

"You tell us," said Wexford equably.

"I am telling you. A car came along and stopped. A woman was driving it—oh, she was about fifty, I suppose. Maybe more, I don't know," said Rachel with the indifference of an eighteen-year-old for the age of anyone over thirty-five. "She wound down the passenger window and I went over and said hi or something and 'I'm Rachel,' and she said, 'Get in, Rachel,' and I did. I just thought she was Mrs. Strang, I took it for granted. When I was sitting down, she said, 'I'm Vicky,' but I didn't know what Mrs. Strang was called, did I?"

"Mrs. Strang's name is Olga."

"Pity no one told me that earlier. Still," said Rachel with unusual graciousness, "they weren't to know, were they? Anyway, I did call her Vicky and we talked, and I suppose I didn't take much notice of where we were going. If I had, it wouldn't have helped. I don't know those villages, I've never been to Framhurst, so I wouldn't know where we went. It was country, I know that, fields and woods and whatever. I was talking to her, she wanted to know all about me..."

"What, she asked you to talk about yourself?"

"Yes, and you could say I fell for it. I told her my parents were divorced and I lived with my mother, and that I'd be nineteen in June and I was at university—oh, and all sorts of things about my friends and what I liked doing, and my interests and everything." She laughed suddenly, an angry, self-mocking sound. "Vicky was a good listener," she said bitterly.

"Where did she take you?"

"I don't know. I didn't take any of it in. You see, I simply trusted her to take me to her house and pick up Caroline. She talked about Caroline. Of course I see now that she could talk about Caroline because I'd talked about her first, said we'd met in our first term at Essex and then found out we lived near each other, and how Caroline was doing Latin American studies and I was doing anthropology. She talked about Caroline's Spanish being so good because they'd lived in Spain for a year when she was a child, and I said I'd never known that, and of course it wasn't true, it was all made up—but you can see why I trusted her, can't you?"

"What happened when you got to where you were going?"

Rachel sighed. "I wish I could tell you where it was and describe the house, but I can't. I have a vague impression of shingles on the front of the house and a fir tree—well, a sort of Christmas tree—but that's all. I didn't look, I didn't know then that I'd have to remember. Vicky unlocked the front door and we went inside, and she called out 'Caroline!' as if Caroline was somewhere getting ready or something. My God, she was such a good actress I'd have sworn I heard Caroline answer." Rachel looked at her mother. "Can I have a drink of water?"

Rosemary Holmes shot out of her chair, happy to obey any commands now she had her daughter back. Karen watched with carefully disguised disapproval as Rosemary came running back with a tall glass that had ice in it and a bottle of Perrier.

Taking it without a word of thanks, Rachel tipped the ice into an ashtray and filled the glass with water. "I'll go on now, shall I?"

"If you please," said Wexford.

"Vicky asked me to sit down and I did, and she offered me a drink and I said yes, which was a big mistake, but I didn't know that."

"How a big mistake?" Karen asked.

"She put something in it. She must have..."

"Oh, Rachel!" It was a wail from Rosemary Holmes, a cry of anguish.

"I've told you they didn't do anything to me!" Rachel was almost shouting. "Not what you mean, anyway. There's no need to make a fuss." She seemed to notice the effect her rage was having on the two police officers, their quiet awareness that might cover disapproval, and she lowered her voice. "I asked for vodka with tonic or lemonade or whatever, and she brought it. She wouldn't have anything herself because she'd be driving Caroline and me to the Rotten Carrot. Oh, yes, I'd told her where we were going, she wasn't a thought reader. My drink tasted like a normal vodka and tonic, and it didn't have any weird effects, not at first.

"I did start wondering why Caroline was taking so long, as I must have been there ten minutes. We were supposed to be at the Rotten Carrot by eight-thirty and it was past that. Vicky offered me another drink—'Freshen your glass?' was what she said—but I wouldn't, I was starting to feel a bit woozy. And then this man came into the room. At first I thought he must be Caroline's brother, though he'd have been old for that. He was maybe thirty, a small, thin guy with weird eyes."

"What does *weird* mean?"

For a moment Karen thought Rachel was going to shout at her to consult a dictionary, so contemptuous was her glance, but she only gave one of her impatient sighs. "Strange," she said, "piercing but sort of dull. Like stones. He had rather a high voice and he didn't look at you while he was talking." She drank some of her sparkling water and set the glass down. "And after that I don't remember, I don't remember what happened till the middle of the next day, the middle of Sunday."

"Oh, Rachel!" exclaimed Rosemary Holmes once more.

"Oh, Rachel," her daughter mocked. "I've told you, I know I wasn't... touched. What Granny would call 'interfered with.'" She looked at Wexford as if she would include him in the Granny category. "I was lying on a bed and Vicky—I'm sure it was Vicky and not him—had taken off my jeans and my sweater. I was in my top and bra and pants, *and nobody'd done anything else to me.* Right? Is that clear? Vicky brought me a cup of tea and said to get up and have a bath and dress." Rachel hesitated. "So I did. I mean, I argued, I said where was I and to take me home, but when I saw there was no way of getting out—she'd locked me in and wouldn't let me out till I'd had a bath—I just did it. I suppose I thought I'd be better able to get away from there if I was clean and dressed and everything.

"Vicky had taken away my jeans and given me a skirt, a longish sort of A-line skirt it was, awful, but I wasn't going to go out there in just my knickers, so I put it on and went out and *he* was there—she called him Jerry—and she told me to cook the lunch."

"She told you to cook the lunch?" Wexford said in a neutral tone. The incredulity was in his face.

"I was to cook the lunch and clear it away and wash up. I said, 'Don't be ridiculous,' and that I was going home, she was to take me home *now*. I knew it was a crime to take someone away and shut them up against their will, and I said that to them and Vicky said, 'Too bad,' or something like that. I tried to run to the front door—well, I did run to the front door but it was locked on three locks, so I tried a window but all the windows were locked and I think they were double-glazed too. I didn't tell you I felt awfully ill, like an outsize hangover it was, a tremendous headache and sort of trembling and shivering. So in the end I just did what she said. I said could I have some paracetamol first and she gave me two capsules. I saw her take them out of the paracetamol pack, so I knew they were okay."

Rachel laughed that same bitter laugh. "Then I peeled some potatoes and washed a cauliflower—I'm not much of a cook, I've never had to cook." Rachel eyed her mother reproachfully just as she must have looked at her when, in the past, any tentative suggestions had been made that she might care to learn how to boil an egg or grill a chop. "They watched me all the time, Vicky and Jerry. Anyway, we ate the lunch and then I washed up and Vicky said to get the vacuum cleaner and clean the bedrooms, but not *her* bedroom, the door to that was locked. I said, 'Can I go home if I do?' and Vicky said, 'We'll see,' so I cleaned the bedrooms and when I came back, she gave me a great pile of Jerry's socks and said to mend them. 'Darn' them was what she said and I didn't know what that meant—"

"Rachel," said Wexford, interrupting her, for he could stand it no longer, "have you ever read a novel called *The Franchise Affair* by Josephine Tey?"

She looked at him with raised eyebrows. "What?"

"It's about a young girl who accuses two women of kidnapping her and forcing her to do their housework. The accusation is false. She has, in fact, been away with a man she picked up in a hotel. The novel is sometimes set as a GCSE text."

The flush that spread across Rachel's face was one of the most intense and glowing he had ever seen. But he knew that it is not only guilt and shame that make us blush. Being suspected of lying may be just as effective in causing a rush of blood to the face.

"Have you read it?" he asked, gently this time.

"Yes, I have."

"Well?"

Rachel spoke in a high voice, near to hysteria. "You came here and—and wanted me to talk to you and I said yes—I said I'd tell you everything—and now I—I have—you—you don't believe me! You accuse me of getting it out of a book!"

"Did you darn his socks?" asked Karen, barely concealing her amusement.

"No, because I can't! I don't know how! I got supper instead and put my jeans and shirt in the washing machine and washed up, and all the time this Jerry never said a word, he just watched me. Why won't you believe me?"

"Go on," said Wexford.

"Not if that woman's going to laugh at me."

"I'm not laughing," said Karen. "Even you must have felt it was pretty ludicrous trying to get you to mend his socks. Did you try to escape?"

"They hadn't a phone, or if they had, I couldn't find it. I tried all the windows. I tried to attract someone's attention but there wasn't anyone, it was just a country lane. Cars went past but the drivers couldn't see me. I got up in the night but Vicky'd locked my bedroom door. I could have broken the window if I'd really tried, but there were bars outside."

"This was a bungalow?"

"No—yes, just two stories, yes. But big, a lot of rooms. On the Monday I felt better, the headache had worn off. Vicky got me up early and told me to defrost the fridge and clean the oven. Then I was to take Jerry his breakfast in bed. That was the only time Vicky touched me. She shook me to wake me up and slapped my face. I'd—no one had ever slapped me before. I didn't know what to do, I don't know how to fight people. It was a shock, being hit like that. I took Jerry's breakfast in on a tray, it was cereal and toast and honey and an orange. He was sitting up in bed in striped pajamas, and he took the tray and said, 'Thanks.' That was the only time he spoke to me, though he spoke to Vicky."

Rachel seemed to have forgotten her restraint. Now she was voluble, pouring it all out. "I did housework all day and cooked. I suppose I thought that if I did it, they'd let me go. I had plenty to eat and Vicky offered me drinks, but I wouldn't have them in case she'd doctored them with whatever that was. But I did a silly thing. On Tuesday I started feeling ill, it was my period coming, and I asked Vicky for a paracetamol and again the pack came out. But she'd done something to it, put capsules with this drug in through the plastic so the foil seal wasn't broken. And that deceived me, so I took two and they had the same effect as the first one, only worse, and I don't know what I did for the rest of the day, I can't remember anything, I may have done housework, had some food, I don't know, but when I woke up it was midday today and I was lying there"—she looked dubiously in Wexford's direction—"well, in a bit of a mess, and there was a packet of Tampax beside me and my jeans and sweater.

"I felt dreadful but Vicky made me wash my sheets. She hung them on the line herself, she wouldn't let me outside. And then, at about six, she said I could go home. I had such a hangover I could hardly see. Jerry wasn't around. Vicky unlocked the front door and took me out to the car, the same one we'd come in. I could have run away then, but I felt so ill and besides I didn't see the point. I let her bring me back here and she dropped me off where she'd picked me up."

It was not Wexford or Karen Malahyde who eventually persuaded Rachel to be seen by a doctor, but Lynn Fancourt, who seemed to strike some chord with her or ignite some spark of affinity. Perhaps it was only that Lynn was nearer her own age. Not that Devonshire, though, Rachel said, pulling a face as if she could smell something nasty. So it was Dr. Akande whom she saw and, after more grumbling and truculence, allowed to take a blood sample and peer into her eyes and down her throat.

"I think she was given Rohypnol," Wexford said. "Akande found no trace of it but it's virtually undetectable anyway, and by now it would have passed out of her system."

Burden raised his eyebrows. "Is that the stuff they call the rape drug? No smell, no taste, put in drink it sedates, and next day the subject has a massive hangover but can't remember what's happened to her?"

"More or less."

"Then we find out who in the area's been prescribed Rohypnol and Bob's your uncle."

"Not quite," said Wexford. "Rohypnol's only obtainable on prescription now and only, in fact, on private prescription, but until recently you could buy it over the counter, anyone could buy it."

Burden, who had been walking up and down, not so much pacing as strolling while he considered, sat down on the edge of Wexford's desk. "How much of this tale of hers do we believe? I mean, is it any less of a farrago of lies than Lizzie Cromwell's story?"

Wexford was silent, thinking. He had begun by not believing it. The parallels with *The Franchise Affair,* a favorite book of his, had been responsible in part for his incredulity, but gradually, as Rachel went on, he had doubted his own disbelief. Now he half believed. That a middle-aged woman had taken Rachel to a house somewhere in the countryside he could give credence to. And that she had been drugged and locked up, all that was possible. But the silent, stony-eyed Jerry and the demands that Rachel cook and do housework, most of all that she darn the man's socks, these must be figments or fantasies. "What's a farrago, anyway?" he said irrelevantly.

"God knows. It's just a phrase, a figure of speech, a 'farrago of lies' is. You're such a pedant, you are. You ought to have been a professor among the dreaming spires."

"Maybe I should at that," said Wexford wistfully.

"You talk about a tissue of lies—well, you don't but I might—so I suppose a farrago is something like that, like sort of embroidered material or something."

Wexford watched him resume his walking, take up a station at the window, against which a sudden shower was dashing hailstones. "She's described those two people quite circumspectly," Wexford said. "The woman in her fifties, gray-haired, blue-eyed, wearing a wedding ring, overweight—but any normal person's overweight to these girls." Wexford tightened his belly, as people always do when talking of fatness or thinness in others. "The man about thirty, small, she says around five foot four, dark, receding hair, and the stony eyes. She sticks to these descriptions, she's repeated them twice to me and given the same details to Lynn. I believe in them."

Apparently fascinated by the hailstones that stung the glass, Burden didn't turn his head. "Does it matter? No harm's been done. She wasn't hurt. It probably did her good, cooking and cleaning and all that, spoilt little madam."

"You know better than that, Mike. I don't have to tell you that taking someone away and detaining her against her will is a very serious offense. Not to mention drugging her. And now it's happened to two young women. It's false imprisonment. Of course it matters."

"All right. Point taken. You mean you think this Vicky woman took Lizzie away too?"

"You remember she mentioned a woman offering her a lift, which she didn't accept? Well, I think she did accept it and she too was taken to this house for the same purpose, whatever that was."

"The woman and the man were mother and son, were they?"

"Don't know. It's possible." Wexford thought of the strange relationships he came across in his work, the bizarre combinations of disparate types and the unlikely conjunctions of ages. He wasn't going to draw any facile conclusions about this one. "What on earth are you gawping at?" he asked. "You've seen hailstones before, haven't you?"

"Come and look at this."

Wexford got up. Through the streaming window he could see two people sheltering from the hail in a shop doorway. Both wore sandwich boards, the woman's cut out in the shape of a girl child, the man's in the shape of a boy, faces and hair and clothes painted in quite realistically, one bearing the words SAVE OUR CHILDREN and the other PEDOPHILE OUT. The storm ceased as abruptly as it had started, and both of them stepped out onto the pavement and crossed the road, holding up hands to halt the traffic. Taking no notice of the honking of horns and yells of motorists, they reached the police station side and stood looking up at the windows.

Wexford rubbed at the steam on the glass left by his breath. "The man's Colin Crowne," he said. "I don't know the woman's name, but she's from the Muriel Campden Estate too, Oberon Road, I think."

"Where Orbe returns tomorrow," said Burden in fatalistic tones. "Shall we get on over there and kill two birds with one stone?"

"And have a word with those two first."

But by the time they reached the forecourt the two people and their child-shaped sandwich boards had gone.

For no apparent reason, the Muriel Campden Estate was designed so that no house faced another, but all, looking inward from the three sides of the triangle, fronted on the squat tower in its center. Around this building, from all the windows on the second floor, at bedroom-window height in the houses, a banner had been hung, bearing the same legends in red and black paint as those on the sandwich boards. It girdled the tower like a belt, running almost all the way around and announcing to anyone looking out of windows or passing by: PEDOPHILE OUT. KEEP AWAY FROM OUR CHILDREN. Of the sandwich-board bearers there was no sign.

In the raised flower beds at the foot of the tower, hail had beaten the tulips to death. Orange-and-green-striped, feather-edged, they lay broken and crushed against the pale chalky soil. And the pink-blossoming street trees, cherries and prunus, had dropped all their petals in one mighty shedding under the hail's onslaught. The pavements were slippery with them, bright mother-of-pearl under the blazing sun, which had suddenly come out. In the distance, beyond these charcoal-colored houses, these anthracite walls and roofs, the green meadows shone brilliantly enough to hurt the eyes.

Wexford rang the bell at 16 Oberon Road. Standing on the doorstep, he had only to turn his head to receive the full force of that banner, some twenty yards away. But it would be the same wherever you lived on the triangle. The protesters had seen to that. Here, though, at this point, by careful design and strategic positioning, the single word PEDOPHILE stood out most assertively.

The woman who opened the door looked sixty but was probably forty. She appeared to have never taken the least care of herself, to have never heard that it is possible to file and clean one's nails, keep one's hair clean, go to a dentist, iron one's clothes, and smell sweet. Her face was greasy and her hair, fastened back with an elastic band, was the same dull charcoal as the fabric of the house she lived in. She wore a dress that should have had a belt but was unbelted and was probably, by the shape and style of it, a hand-down from her grandmother, wrinkled brown stockings, and bedroom slippers. The smell of her, as Burden remarked later, was very like that emanating from the hamburger stall set up in Queen Street on market day. Her teeth—but Burden said he didn't want to remember her teeth, he wanted to put them right out of his mind.

"Ms. Orbe?" said Wexford. "Ms. Suzanne Orbe?"

"That's me. What d'you want?"

"Chief Inspector Wexford and Inspector Burden, Kingsmarkham CID. May we come in a minute?"

She stepped back and, when they were inside, slammed the door hard. "Haven't I got enough to put up with," she asked of no one in particular, "with that scum out there?" In the living room a man sat staring at the television screen. He took no notice whatever of the newcomers; Suzanne Orbe might have come into the room alone, or as far as he was concerned, no one at all had come in.

"You expect your father to come home here on Friday—tomorrow, that is?" Wexford asked.

"I reckon. He's nowhere else to go, the old bugger."

This remark stirred the man at the other end of the room. He took his eyes from the screen, turned his head, and stared in their direction. Suzanne Orbe made a kind of introduction: "That's my fiancé."

Neither policeman acknowledged him. "We're not anticipating trouble," Burden said with a confidence he didn't feel, "but I'll leave you this number." He wrote it down and handed it to her. "And if need be, you can speak to me, Inspector Burden. B-U-R-D-E-N—have you got that?"

She nodded. Loyalty to her father forgotten—or perhaps Wexford had misinterpreted her tone—she made a sound of exasperation, a "huh" noise, and cast up her eyes.

The man at the other end of the room spoke. "That's right, girl," he said, and added in a voice so deeply vindictive and vicious that Wexford found himself flinching, "Put the likes of him in the gas chamber'd be best. Or the chair."

Outside, in the relatively wholesome air, Burden remarked that Suzanne Orbe's "fiancé" probably had no idea capital punishment had ceased in this country over thirty years before. His whole notion of life came from television; so much transatlantic culture had he absorbed from that source that he believed death by gas chamber or electrocution were United Kingdom options.

"So long as he and she don't give the wretched Orbe up to the mob," said Wexford.

"You're joking, I hope," Burden said severely.

"So do I hope. There is no mob, there's only a banner. We must look on the bright side."

Wexford looked about him. The sun had gone in but the day was still bright and the sky blue, with scurrying clouds rushing across its face. The belt-banner flapped in the breeze. In two of the gardens men who looked civilized and law-abiding mowed their lawns. "This isn't a very pretty place," he said, "but it's quite nice, isn't it? It's comfortable, rustic, the air's pure, and if it's not like wine, it's like the best mineral water. There's no vandalism or very little. If the local authority plants trees, they don't get pulled up. Hail spoils the tulips, not human hands. A far cry from those inner-city estates one reads about, wouldn't you say? Those places where the old go in terror of their lives or daren't go out at all, where gangs roam the walkways and the residents deal in controlled substances."

"Sure. So what are you getting at?"

"Just that—let's hope it stays that way. And now we'll pay a call on the Crowne family, shall we?"

Inevitably, the banner was visible from this front room too. Lizzie Cromwell was sitting in the window, gazing at it, as if she expected it to change shape, fall off, or be joined at any moment by even more inflammatory material. Wexford, deterred neither by the smoky atmosphere nor Debbie Crowne's grim expression and headful of heated rollers, pulled up a chair beside Lizzie and proceeded to tell her what had happened to her on Saturday two weeks before.

"After you'd waited twenty minutes for the bus you accepted a lift from a lady in a white car and she drove you to a house in the country. There was a man there. Her name was Vicky and his was Jerry. They gave you something to drink which made you sleepy and made you forget a lot of what happened to you. I'm right, aren't I, Lizzie?"

She turned to face him. He thought how healthy she looked and blooming, her face flushed and her eyes bright and knowing. "I'm not supposed to say."

"Who told you not to say? The woman who took you away? The man, Jerry?" Lizzie didn't get a chance to answer. Debbie Crowne interposed herself between Wexford and her daughter. There was a strong smell, suddenly, of overheated hair. He saw that she was trembling.

"What is it, Mrs. Crowne?"

"I'll tell you what it is. She's pregnant, that's what it is. He's made my daughter pregnant."

CHAPTER 6

WEXFORD'S FIRST REACTION WAS TO SAY, "IT'S NOT POSSIBLE to tell so soon. It's less than a fortnight."

"Where have you been living?" Debbie Crowne asked rudely. "On the moon? I done a test, haven't I? A home pregnancy kit's what they call them in case you didn't know. And I done it and she's fallen pregnant. If I'd done it last week, it'd have shown the same. And what I'd like to know is, what are you going to do about it?"

"It would help us to do something," said Burden, "if Lizzie would tell us the truth about what happened to her."

"She's scared, isn't she? He raped her and now she's scared what he might do."

At the word *raped*, Lizzie's eyelids flickered. It was as if something hot or a bright light had suddenly been brought close up to her face. Her head jerked back.

"Did you sleep a lot while you were there, Lizzie?" Wexford asked. "Did they give you drinks to make you sleep?"

"I don't know. I'm not to say. I'll be punished if I say."

Burden looked at Colin Crowne, who had just come into the room. "You won't be punished, Lizzie. No one will punish you. If you tell us about them and about the house you went to and where it was, they will be caught and punished. I'm sure you understand that, don't you?"

Debbie Crowne shouted suddenly, "You leave her alone! It's not right, bullying her in her condition. She could have a miscarriage!"

Surely the best thing imaginable, Wexford thought, then castigated himself for callousness. "No one is bullying Lizzie," he began, but the rest of his sentence dwindled away as Lizzie broke in, and he forgot that he had once thought her meek and not inclined to rebellion.

"No, I won't, I won't have a miscarriage. I'm going to have my baby, I want my baby. Then I can go away from here and get a flat and live with my baby. I can get away from you and *him* and have my own place and be—be *happy!*" Her face crumpled and she burst into a storm of tears.

"Now see what you've done," said Debbie Crowne. "That's rubbish, that is. Wants her baby! She ought to have had the morning-after pill. If she'd had the morning-after pill the day she come back..."

"She wouldn't be in the shit now," said Colin Crowne.

"*Farrago,*" said Wexford next morning. "I looked it up in the dictionary. It doesn't mean anything like tissue, it means 'mixed fodder for cattle,' and it comes from the Latin. Interesting, don't you think?"

Burden threw the *Kingsmarkham Courier* down on Wexford's desk. "It only confirms what I said about you being a pedant. Have you seen the paper?"

With a hint of that feeling that is usually described as a sinking of the heart, Wexford said, "Why? Should I have?" He knew what he was likely to see but not how bad it would be. "Oh, God," he said, "what's the point of doing this, I wonder. What does St. George get out of it?"

"A boost to his circulation, I suppose. God knows it needs it."

The headline was ORBE FREED, and under that, KINGSMARKHAM PEDOPHILE COMES HOME. Wexford read:

> All parents with small children will live in terror from this weekend onward, knowing that Thomas Orbe, convicted pedophile and child-killer, is back in their midst. Released after serving nine years of a fifteen-year prison sentence, Orbe, seventy-one, is expected to return today to the home he left nearly a decade ago in Oberon Road on Kingsmarkham's Muriel Campden Estate.

"He could only have spelt it out more thoroughly if he'd given the house number," Wexford said gloomily. "I wonder why he didn't."

> An elderly man by now, Orbe is nevertheless understood to have admitted he may still be a danger to children. His home in

> Oberon Road, currently occupied by his daughter, Ms. Suzanne Orbe, and her partner, Mr. Garry Wills, backs onto Kingsmarkham's only public park with its children's play area. Until an order is in place restraining Orbe from places frequented by children, such as York Park, this popular venue for youngsters will most likely stand empty, and that at the most favorable season of the year for outdoor play...

"I can't stand his English or his reporter's English, never mind the content," said Wexford. "That word *pedophile*, no one knew what it meant five years ago—well, no one but psychiatrists and Greek scholars. Now it's on everyone's lips. Even a moron like that Colin Crowne knows what it means."

"There's a leading article as well," said Burden. "Would you like me to give you a synopsis? It won't do you any good to read it yourself. Your blood pressure's showing all over your face as it is."

Wexford sighed. "Okay. What does it say?"

"That pedophiles should be kept under restraint for the whole of their natural lives, given the option of castration, never allowed within any area where even one child may live, given more severe sentences in the first place—all that, if not necessarily in that order. Oh, and he—it's St. George himself this time, by the way—he says the government isn't acting fast enough and how about these steps they are supposed to be taking to monitor released pedophiles? It couldn't be worse."

"I don't know about that. He could have advocated compulsory castration." Wexford dropped the paper on the floor where he couldn't see it. "I've been thinking about that banner thing, Mike. We don't have any powers to make them take it down, do we?"

"I doubt it. We could if it led to trouble. Then it'd be an offense against public order. But it hasn't led to trouble."

"Not yet. Orbe's not home yet, but he will be today. I dreamt about the Muriel Campden Estate last night and I woke up yelling there was a bomb planted under the tower. Dora thought I'd gone mad. What are we going to do about Lizzie Cromwell?"

"It's a job for Lynn now, don't you reckon? Get Lynn around there and see if she can ferret out what really happened. Rachel Holmes got on fine with her, so why not Lizzie?"

"They're a very different type of girl, Mike. But it's a good idea. Lynn should persuade Mrs. Crowne to take Lizzie to her GP, that's a priority. When he or she confirms it, I'll believe she's two weeks pregnant."

The hunt for the house with the shingles on its front and the big Christmas tree hadn't yet begun, but Wexford, whose knowledge of the surrounding area was considerable, had given it thought. He had pictured villages in his mind's eye, seeing their churches and clustering cottages, bigger houses, village greens with war memorials, and had been presented with several possible bungalows, but none of these stood alone in open countryside. Seeing stretches of roads and lanes, dipping valleys and swelling hills, was harder. So, on the previous evening he had driven back and forth across the area where the bypass was to have been built.

To himself he confessed that he enjoyed going there to gloat. There was a sweet, almost physical pleasure in seeing, bursting into fresh leaf, trees scheduled last year to be felled, in hearing the song of birds going to roost, and driving along the one narrow road through Framhurst Great Wood, eyeing through the long, still glades the tiny blossoms of celandine and wood anemones on the forest floor. He had even lingered on the edge of it, parking the car for a moment or two, while he reflected that here, on this very spot, he and everyone else in Kingsmarkham had expected to see by this time a huge trunk road ripping through the wasted valley. It did him good, he sometimes thought, to sit and look and rejoice, it brought him a calm satisfaction. And he felt revived and keen again when he started the car and set off for Framhurst and Savesbury and Myfleet.

All the way along the roads, some of them narrow lanes with high banks studded with primroses and cowslips, he looked for a house that would conform to Rachel Holmes's description. But although a shingled front is a feature of many Sussex dwellings, there were few of these in the area and even fewer that were bungalows. After driving around for an hour, going as far as Myringham in one direction and Stringfield in the other, he had come across only two, and of these one was in the center of a hamlet and in any case was a house on two floors. The other, on the edge of downland, had no trees near it apart from its own Leyland cypress hedge.

That had been last evening. This morning he resolved to take Rachel reconnoitering with him and Karen Malahyde, and to go south of the town, always supposing Rachel had kept her promise and not yet returned to the University of Essex.

Sylvia had been at The Hide for no more than ten minutes when the doorbell rang. It wasn't one of her days for being there and it wasn't one of her times. In fact, it was the day she was owed to take off from her regular job and she had been at home, planning a morning in the garden and an afternoon at the cinema, when Lucy Angeletti had phoned and said that Jill Lewis still had flu and she had a morning meeting set up with Myringham Housing Department, and could Sylvia possibly be an angel and come in? Just for a few hours till Griselda took over at three. So of course Sylvia had said yes and had phoned her mother to ask her to pick up the boys from school, just in case she was late, and had come down here by eleven.

When she was herself a child, when she was ten, no one would have thought twice about letting her come home from school alone. No one would have considered it unsafe for her to bring her little sister home with her. But these days people were terrified of letting their kids out of their sight for five minutes. And they would be even more frightened after reading the *Courier*, as she had done that morning, taking it and her cup of tea back to bed with her. Presumably, there had been pedophiles when she was a child, there must have been, and just as many—human nature didn't change—but you seldom heard about them, while today there seemed to be one behind every bush and around every corner.

She was hanging up her raincoat in the hall and no one else was about apart from two three-year-olds sitting on the stairs, so it seemed obvious that she should answer the door. But even as she put up her hand to the latch, she remembered instructions she had received during her brief training for this job. Be careful when you answer the door, look through the spyhole first, put the chain on. It could be a violent spouse or partner looking for the woman he had assaulted and who had escaped from him. So Sylvia drew back her hand, put on the chain, lifted up the little circular flap over the spyhole, and squinted through it.

An old, anxious-looking woman was what she saw. She slipped off the chain and opened the door. The woman held out a sheaf of papers fastened to a clipboard. She spoke as if she had learned her words by heart and painstakingly. "I wonder if you would care to put your name to the Kingsbrook Residents' Association's petition? It is a protest against the residential home where they plan to make a children's playground."

"Do you mean The Hide?" said Sylvia.

"That is what they call it, yes. You may care to read some literature I have here first. It fully explains the situation and why the Kingsbrook Residents are so strongly opposed to it."

Sylvia had difficulty suppressing her laughter. She put one hand up to her mouth, took a deep breath, and said in a polite tone, "This *is* The Hide."

"This is? This house?" The woman couldn't have sounded more aghast. She rallied, as people do, by taking refuge in unreasoning attack. This hadn't been learned in advance. "How on earth is one supposed to know? There's no name up, there's no number. It ought to be against the law for a house not to have a number."

"Right. I'll tell the police," said Sylvia, and closing the door, burst into laughter. She would tell the police, she'd tell her father if she saw him that evening. It would amuse him. She climbed the stairs. As she crossed the first landing, a black woman with two small children in tow came out of one of the bedrooms. Black people were thin on the ground in Kingsmarkham and its environs, though there were more now than a year ago, and Sylvia wondered where she had come from and what her particular story was. She was tall and majestic, her braided hair wound and woven into a crown on top of her head. Sylvia said hello and that it was raining again and passed on to the top floor.

Lucy Angeletti was there on the phone. It didn't sound as if she was answering a distress call. Sylvia heard Lucy say, "Yes, well, thanks. If someone will call this morning, I'll show him or her the letter I've had. Good-bye."

Sylvia raised an eyebrow.

"A death threat," Lucy said. "Anonymous, of course. *You have got my wife. If she don't come back, I will kill you, bitch.*"

"Was that the police you were phoning? Are they sending someone round?"

"It won't be your dad," said Lucy, laughing. "He's too high-ranking. But just so that they know. I'll leave you to it, then, shall I? We've got a new woman coming in any minute. She's been at the Pomfret police house all night with a baby and a two-year-old. She'll have our last available room, and after that I don't know what we'll do. And now I must get over to Myringham."

From the window, Sylvia watched the woman arrive. She came in a taxi, for the payment of which Sylvia knew the Social Services Department would have provided her with a voucher. The baby was tiny, snuggled up like a nestling bird in the harness the woman wore across her thin chest. The toddler was crying, pushing fists into his eyes. Lucy came out of the front door and down the steps and took the case the woman had brought out of the back of the cab. The driver did nothing to assist her. The voucher, Sylvia thought, probably didn't allow for a tip. She watched the taxi reverse down the drive between the green banks of shrubs and was back to her desk when the phone started ringing.

"The Hide. How can I help you?"

Silence. There usually was silence or else a hurried rush of speech. Most women were embarrassed about phoning. Guiltless, they were ashamed. After all, they were complaining to outsiders about the man they had chosen for their life partner. They often began with excuses for themselves or for the man who had beaten them. While the silence endured, she thought of the woman she had spoken to the other night, the one whose husband abused her because he said she was mad and would only stop when she found a cure for her madness. From her, once she had unburdened herself, they had heard no more, and Sylvia had no way of knowing if her advice to go to the police had been taken.

She said again, "This is The Hide. How may I help you?"

A voice said abruptly, "Is that the Women's Aid Federation of England?"

"No, this is The Hide helpline. We offer you the same kind of service as the Women's Aid Federation. Can I help you?"

"What will you—what will you do for me?"

Sylvia spoke gently. "Won't you tell me what the problem is? Has someone hurt you? Have you been hurt?"

"It was last night. Before he left for work. He's at work now, he'll be back around eleven, maybe sooner. I thought he'd broken my arm, but he hasn't. It's not broken if I can move it, is it? I'm all over bruises and my face is a real sight."

Sylvia looked at the clock. It was nearly ten-thirty. She didn't ask why the woman hadn't phoned before, why she had waited so long. She guessed what it must have cost her to have phoned at all, the sacrifice of pride and privacy, the revealing to a stranger what her marriage had come to.

"The best thing for you to do is go straight to your nearest police station. Are you in Kingsmarkham?" The woman wouldn't want to give her address, Sylvia sensed, but she got a grudging murmur of assent. "Would you tell me your name?"

"I'd rather not."

"That's fine. That's quite all right. It doesn't matter. Go to Kingsmarkham Police Station. Do you know where it is? It's in the High Street at the beginning of the Pomfret Road, opposite Tabard Road. I'll phone them and alert them to expect you. Will you do that?"

"Oh, I don't know..."

"I'll phone them as soon as I've said good-bye to you. I'll tell them to expect you in half an hour."

"Good-bye," the voice said abruptly. "Thank you. Good-bye."

The phone went dead and a dial tone began. Sylvia had no means of knowing if her caller would take her advice, but she phoned Kingsmarkham Police, spoke to Sergeant Camb, whom she had known since she was in her teens, and told him to expect the arrival of a woman with a badly bruised face, name unknown. The phone rang immediately when she put the receiver down. A man this time.

"Fucking bitch," said the voice. "Frigid lesbian cow. Do you know what I'm going to do to you? I'm going to..."

Sylvia held the receiver at arm's length. She noted that the hand holding it was shaking, her whole arm was trembling. Lucy had laughed when Sylvia told her the last time it had occurred and said she knew all about that shaking and trembling, it had happened to her, but it wouldn't always. Sylvia would get used to these calls and eventually take them in her stride.

Obscenities gobbled and chattered out of the receiver. Sylvia put it down and drew a deep breath. Was it the husband of the woman who wouldn't give her name? Had he come home while she was still talking? Sylvia desperately hoped not. That was the worst of this job. Half the time, more than half, you didn't know what the outcome had been, you couldn't guess the next phase in a caller's perilous life.

No more calls came for half an hour, three-quarters of an hour. Then the phone rang. Perhaps because there had been silence for so long, the bell seemed more than usually loud and insistent. A shrill phone bell, a soft, cultured voice.

"My name is Anne. I don't want to give you my surname."

"That's fine," said Sylvia. "Will you tell me what your problem is?"

A hesitation, then in a slightly bewildered tone, "But surely it's always the same problem, isn't it?"

"Basically, perhaps it is. The details vary. Usually it's a woman who's been hurt, but not always. It may not be physical, it may be psychological abuse."

The laugh Anne gave was unearthly, cold and echoing, the least humorous laughter Sylvia had ever heard. "Oh, there's nothing psychological about my hurt, I can tell you."

"I'd like to help you." Sylvia hazarded the Christian name she didn't entirely believe in. "I'd really like to help you, Anne. Won't you tell me what's wrong?"

"I'd have to see you, I'd have to be face-to-face with someone, it's a long story, it would take days, weeks."

Anne stopped and a silence followed. Sylvia listened to the silence, discerning faint breathing sounds.

Then, piteously, desperately, a cry for help if Sylvia had ever heard one came on a thin, keening note out of the receiver: "What shall I do?"

"Are you in Kingsmarkham?"

"Yes."

"Is there anyone else in the house with you?"

"He's in the garden. The baby's with him. I can see them from the window. Oh, God, he's coming in, I can't talk, I shouldn't have rung you, he'll want to know who I was speaking to—what shall I say?"

"Phone again when you're alone," Sylvia said in the calmest tone she could muster. "I'll say good-bye now."

There was no answer. The phone went dead. Sylvia sat hunched over the desk, her head in her hands. It had shaken her, that call. So far it was the worst she had had. There was something particularly horrible in the fact that this was a middle-class woman—yes, Sylvia had to admit this—a woman perhaps gently brought up and living in this country, in this town, who could speak in the tones of a victim of imprisonment and torture. She imagined the man coming into the room, taking the phone from her, hitting her with his free hand, and she shuddered.

On this job you needed a drink, she sometimes thought, but that was impossible, she knew where that would lead, drinking at midday. She told herself there were others to think about besides "Anne" and made herself phone Kingsmarkham Police Station again, but no woman with a bruised face had come in.

"Describe the house to me again," Wexford said. They were in Karen Malahyde's car. Karen was driving, with Rachel Holmes in the passenger seat and Wexford in the back.

"I've *told* you." One thing you could say for Rachel, she wasn't scared of the police. "It stood all on its own with fields and woods around, there weren't any other houses, it had shingle tiles all over its front—well, not all over, just over the top part, the rest was red brick—and a big tree in the front garden. I think it was a pine tree, maybe a Scotch pine."

"You said a Christmas tree before."

"That's a pine, isn't it? I don't know but I know what I saw. I've been thinking about it, shutting my eyes and trying to make a picture form, and what I see is a Christmas-tree sort of tree."

What she meant was that the tree was coniferous, but Wexford didn't correct her. He knew how easy it would be to put her off and drive her into a sullen silence. If only he knew equally how to put her into a cheerful and responsive mood! "Now, Rachel," he said, "while you were being kept a prisoner, you must have known that on your release the police would be involved. Did you think of that?"

"Sometimes I thought I'd never be released."

"All right, but you've made it plain you weren't particularly frightened by your ordeal. While you were with Vicky and...er, Jerry, you no doubt thought that when the time came, the police would want you to recall as much as you could of your surroundings. Did you, for instance, take note of what you could see from the windows?"

Rachel sniffed. She had an unattractive habit of sniffing where others might have shrugged. "They gave me that stuff, you know they did. You said what it was. It messed up my memory. Anyway, all you could see was fields. That's all there was, just fields for miles and miles."

They drove south from Stowerton toward Flagford. A few stretches of this road were bare of houses, but all were widely separated, each from its nearest neighbors, which might be a quarter of a mile away. And the architecture was varied, ranging from farmhouses and what had perhaps been dower houses to cottages, converted barns, modern villas, and even, on the outskirts of Flagford, a couple of blocks of flats, thinly disguised as mansions, but few bungalows. Rachel made a sullen face and Wexford guessed this was because they were passing either Dr. Devonshire's home or the medical center where he practiced.

The village itself was not worth lingering in, for Rachel was adamant that the place to which she had been taken was surrounded by open meadows. Karen took byways and narrow lanes, through woodland and on to the downs. The great sweep of gentle hills and higher peaks was inhabited only by sheep. Not a house was in sight. Rachel, moreover, insisted that she had been nowhere near here, nowhere like this terrain at all: "I said *fields*, fields and woods; it wasn't hilly."

"You'll be hard put," Karen said crisply, "to find anywhere round here that isn't hilly."

She didn't like Rachel, Wexford had noticed, and she let her dislike show. A not altogether helpful attitude in this situation. "Drive on," he said. "Keep north of the downs."

Southwest of Pomfret they came upon a house that perfectly answered Rachel's description, or so Wexford thought. It was what is known as a chalet bungalow, its upper floor consisting of only one room and that up in the roof, and it stood alone in an isolated place at a crossroads, though the roads in question were no more than narrow lanes. On its upper story were scallop-shaped shingles, while its lower floor was of pale reddish brick. The windows were latticed panes and its front door a lead-and-glass anachronism. In the front garden, which was otherwise lawn and gravel drive, stood a tall and beautiful tree, its shape roughly that of a Lombardy poplar, and evidently deciduous, for it was just coming into leaf, its elegant skeleton misted over with a delicate tracery of pale bright green. Wexford thought it might be a swamp cypress, native to the bayous of Louisiana, and said so.

"I said a pine tree," said Rachel.

"A pine or a fir. Let's settle for a coniferous tree, shall we?"

"Then why hasn't that one got—what d'you call it? Needles, right—why hasn't it got needles?"

Wexford wasn't going to get into that one. "Could this be the house?"

"No, it's not a bit like it."

"It answers your description," said Karen.

"The front door's wrong. I know I haven't said anything about the front door, but I remember now and that one's wrong. The tree's wrong and the door and the tiles are the wrong color. And," said Rachel triumphantly, "it wasn't on a crossroads."

They took her home. She was evidently relieved. On Sunday she would return to Colchester and the University of Essex and put her experience with Vicky and Jerry in the house with the pine tree behind her. If the house she described ever existed, as Karen said on the way back to Kingsmarkham. If there was a house. She was cleverer at invention than Lizzie Cromwell, but not much cleverer.

"Then what happened to those two girls that they're so anxious to hide from us?" Wexford asked.

"Rape, apparently, in Lizzie's case."

"I don't believe that."

Karen's look had something of disappointment in it, as if she had hitherto categorized him as a man who took rape seriously but now had cause to change her mind. "She *is* pregnant, sir."

"So far as we know. And if she is, there are other ways of getting there." Wexford looked hard at her. "Another time, Sergeant Malahyde, make your dislike of the girl a bit less obvious, will you? What you'd no doubt call emotional involvement has no place in police practice."

No general practitioner in the area had prescribed Rohypnol to a patient in the past two years. If any had, it would have been next to impossible to get a name out of him or her. Pharmacists in Kingsmarkham, Stowerton, and Pomfret all said they had stocked it but did so no longer. None had any records of purchases, but four of them kept no records of this kind of sale.

While Rachel Holmes was being driven about the countryside, helping (or obstructing) the police in their inquiries, the GP who attended the Crowne family confirmed Lizzie's pregnancy. That is, Debbie Crowne and her daughter said she had confirmed it. To Wexford the doctor declined to give any information about her patient.

Lizzie had had several long conversations with Lynn Fancourt, on whom she was developing a "crush." "I'd like to be a policeman when I grow up," she said, a statement that Lynn saw as so pathetic it nearly brought tears to that tough young woman's eyes.

"A police *officer*, Lizzie," she said gently.

"A police *officer*, that's what I meant."

"And I think you're grown up now, aren't you? People can't have babies till they're grown up." If only that were true!

"If I get a flat to live in, Mum could come and look after my baby while I did my training to be a policeman—I mean, a police *officer*. I wouldn't want *him* near my baby, but Mum'd be okay."

Lynn told Wexford that Lizzie appeared to dislike Colin Crowne intensely. Lynn suspected sexual abuse. Lizzie's pregnancy was beginning to show, which was absurd if conception had only taken place two weeks previously. But when Lynn asked about Colin Crowne and, emboldened by the girl's evident desire to list all Colin's faults, all the "nasty things" he said and did, hinted that sexual relations might have taken place between her and him, Lizzie laughed so incredulously and was so obviously amazed at the idea that Lynn almost gave up. But perhaps her hints had been too oblique. She spelled things out more freely.

"I'd give him a punch he wouldn't forget if he ever come near me," Lizzie said, more aggressive than Lynn had ever known her.

Her renewed laughter did more to convince Lynn than her stalwart denials. She wasn't in the least upset. On the other hand, relaying Rachel's story to her seemed to cause distress. She didn't want to hear. She had abandoned her tale of spending three days and nights in the derelict house, saying instead that she had never been there, that it was a "dream."

No one had taken her to any other sort of house either, no one had taken her anywhere, she had roamed the countryside, sleeping in barns and under hedges. It had been to get away from *him*. It had been to get away from Colin, who said she was mental. He was always getting at her because she wasn't brainy.

"Did you like Jerry, Lizzie?" Lynn asked.

She gave a small sigh of relief when Lizzie, distracted by her dislike of Colin, said, "Don't know any Jerry. I liked Vicky all right."

It was the only breakthrough, but it wasn't much of one.

CHAPTER 7

It was dark when Thomas Orbe, always called Tommy, came home to Oberon Road. He came on foot from the station, and because those who interested themselves in his return were certain it would be by cab or in a police car or even a prison van, his arrival went unnoticed. The last train brought him to Kingsmarkham, and just after eleven-thirty he rang the bell of the house of which he was the tenant. No doubt he had possessed a key, but during the nine years he had been in prison that key had been mislaid. The house was in darkness, as if no one lived there.

His daughter Suzanne opened the door. He entered without a word and she closed the door after him.

"You've aged," he said when she switched on the light.

"I suppose you think you haven't."

Six years had passed since she had last visited him. She didn't like the looks she got in there. Everyone knew what he was in for and took it out on him. But why take it out on her? It wasn't her fault. She watched him walk into the living room and look out of the window. He knew something was hanging out of the windows in the tower, but he hadn't lingered to look at it by the light of the solitary streetlamp and the few lights on in the flats. The streetlamp was still on, though it would go out in twenty minutes. He read the legend on the banner impassively. He had little feeling left and reacted to nothing, cared about nothing except staying alive, though why he desired life he couldn't have said. A chaplain in the prison had once told him he was in danger of losing his soul and Tommy had shrugged his shoulders.

Now he said to his daughter, "What's that thing?"

She didn't answer. He made out the word *pedophile*, and if he flinched, ow. He turned away from the window, said, "That chap of still here?"

y fiancé."

y laughed. His laughter sounded as if it came from an instrument and by a mechanism long disused. It was as if he were speaking a language learned at his mother's knee but for years superseded by a different and harsher idiom. In the quiet, dark house it echoed a little.

"I got your bed ready," she said, "in the back."

"Taken my room, have you? You and your fiancé?" Into that last word he put infinite scorn. "I don't want anything to eat or drink," he said, as if she had asked.

He picked up the suitcase he had left in the hall and went upstairs without turning on more lights to guide him. His daughter waited at the foot until he had disappeared. She opened the front door and looked out into the silent, empty street, the rows of houses, the tower and the banner, which swayed a little in the wind. When, on the stroke of midnight, the streetlamps went out, she closed the front door, bolted it, and put on the chain. Then she too went to bed.

In the large, inconvenient, rather beautiful, and incompletely modernized former rectory where she lived with her husband and sons, Sylvia lay awake, worrying about The Hide. The woman who had come in that morning (yesterday morning by now) had taken the last room for herself and her children. What would they do when the next caller appealed for sanctuary? Only a couple of hours after that woman's arrival another had rung and asked, with such hope and innocence, "Can I come and stay with you? Can I bring my baby?" And then, when Sylvia had asked for details of her problem, "Would I get a flat for myself and my baby?"

Some had such optimistic expectations, others almost none. Some wanted no more than a listening ear, another human being to confide in, while there was always one who thought that once she had taken that initial small step—that vast, enormous, almost impossible step—all else would follow: substantial accommodation found for her, the law invoked on her behalf, the man who was the author of her troubles chastised, warned, and brought to behave as she had believed he would when first she threw in her lot with his.

What became of the ones who phoned in but never went to the police or the Social Services? The one with the battered face, for instance? And what about the woman called Anne who had laughed that dreadful bitter laugh when Sylvia mentioned psychological abuse and who had sounded so terrified when she saw her husband coming in from the garden?

What had been her fate when he confronted her and perhaps understood whom she had been phoning? Had he hit her again? Injured her again? And what of the baby she had mentioned? Where did that baby come into all this? It worried Sylvia, it kept her awake at night, lying beside the nice, kind, dull man she had ceased to love long ago. He was as likely to raise his hand to her, she thought, as he was to change into the interesting, exciting, and charming lover she had expected him to be when she married him. A lot of those abusive spouses and partners, "fiancés" and boyfriends, were charming men—courteous, considerate, and altogether delightful to all but the woman they lived with. Sylvia wondered why this was. She had asked her father what he thought when she called round last evening to collect Robin and Ben.

"To throw a blanket of deceit over their true activities maybe," he had replied. "Only you'll think that so psychologically unsound I hesitate to say it."

"Yes, it can't be that," she had said in her dismissive way, "that's ridiculous," then wished she'd been nicer to him as she often did wish.

He made considerable efforts to behave as if he loved her as much as he loved her sister. She noticed the efforts, but her awareness didn't make her feel tenderly toward him. She thought he ought not to prefer Sheila. Why did he? She loved her two sons equally, she made no difference between them, for she genuinely had no favorite.

He'd gone on talking to her as if she hadn't snapped at him. "We've got a meeting set up for next Thursday. The ACCD and I, and a couple of people from the Regional Crime Squad and a woman called Griselda Cooper from The Hide. It's to discuss methods of supplying those mobiles to women in need."

Confiding in her, she thought, making a conscious effort to talk about things he calculated she'd be interested in.

"Do you know Ms. Cooper?"

She observed the *Ms.*, uncharacteristically used. A placating tactic, no doubt. "Well, of course I do," she said sharply. "We haven't got a staff of hundreds, more's the pity."

Now, lying wakeful beside Neil, she remembered her sharpness. She was too old for this behavior. What was wrong with her, anyway, that she couldn't get on with her own husband and her own father? Her own mother, come to that. She was great with children. She was marvelous with the disadvantaged, the poor, the socially excluded. Everyone said so. Why not with her kind, forbearing father? And then a thought so daring and bold came to her that she sat bolt upright in bed. Hadn't she always maintained, hadn't she been taught this in therapy, that the proper thing to do in such circumstances was to "talk it through"? Why, then, not talk it through with her father?

She said it aloud, half waking Neil, so that he muttered at her, "What's the matter? What's wrong?"

Talking to Neil of their differences had only ever resulted in his retorting that there was nothing to talk about, they were incompatible, that was all, but must remain together for their sons' sake. She looked at him in the half-light of dawn, at his closed eyes, the frown lines on his forehead that never relaxed, then she bent over and gently kissed his cheek. He smiled in his sleep. That smile brought tears to her eyes and she thought, when he's asleep, I still love him. She lay down again, close up beside him.

A beautiful day, the first really fine day for a month. The sky was blue, the sun shining, and every blade of grass, every new leaf, every spring flower, bright and fresh, fed by weeks of rain. Wexford and Dora were going to London by train to shop, to visit the Bonnard exhibition at the Tate and in the evening see Sheila in the revival of Somerset Maugham's *Home and Beauty* at the Theatre Royal, Haymarket. Because it was such nice weather, they walked to the station, discussing on the way whether they would have to leave immediately after the curtain fell in order to catch the last train or if the play would end early enough for them to have a glass of champagne with Sheila in her dressing room.

Burden was in his garden. His wife had planted boxwood all around a formal flower bed and now he had to decide how to trim it. To cut it square or up to a point? To turn each small bush into a ball? He doubted if he was capable of this last. Wasn't it, anyway, too early in the year to cut it at all? Perhaps he should just trim off the bits that stuck out. He decided to leave it for now and mow the lawn instead.

On the Muriel Campden Estate the street sign had been repainted and the loop in the *P* of *Puck* restored entire. It wouldn't last, as Hayley Lawrie remarked to Kate Burton on their way to the Crownes' house to ask Lizzie Cromwell to accompany them to the new shopping arcade in Myringham. Kate had just had her sixteenth birthday and wanted to spend the fifty pounds her father and stepmother and two half brothers had sent her for a birthday present.

Lizzie, who hadn't been to school since her abduction and didn't intend to go back, said she couldn't come out because she was pregnant and had to rest. The two girls were astounded at her news, astounded, delighted, and somewhat overawed. Details were demanded. Who, why, and when? Lizzie had scarcely begun to answer when Colin Crowne came in, lighting a cigarette from the stub of the last one. He had overheard Lizzie say she couldn't come out and, anxious to get rid of her, said what was she, simple or something? Of course she must go, it would do her good, they weren't living in "olden times." Kate, who fancied Colin, cast him languishing looks, of which he took no notice, having other fish to fry.

When the girls had gone, he and his wife went down the road to call on Brenda Bosworth, the mother of three small children. The young Bosworths were out playing, unsupervised, in York Park with a number of other children from the estate. Colin and Debbie and Brenda Bosworth walked to the end of Puck Road and into Oberon Road where they rang the doorbell of Tommy Orbe's house. Suzanne withdrew the bolts and opened the door but kept the chain on. This allowed it to stand about six inches ajar.

"Where is he?" asked Colin Crowne.

"What's that to you?" said Suzanne.

"Is he inside?"

"Maybe he is and maybe he isn't."

"We want a straight answer to a straight question." Brenda Bosworth elbowed Colin aside and tried to get sight of the hallway behind Suzanne. "And that question is," she cried theatrically, "where is the infamous pedophile, Thomas Orbe?"

"Fuck off, the lot of you," said Suzanne, and slammed the door in Brenda's face.

Undaunted, they went around the back, Colin first, with the two women following. The house was semidetached, with a gate of wire netting on a wooden frame between the side wall and the fence dividing this garden from next door's. Colin kicked the gate open and they walked through into the back garden. It presented a startling contrast to those on either side of it, both of which were trim, with neat lawns and flower beds. The Orbes grew nettles, thistles, and docks as luxuriantly as the next-door gardens grew tulips and wallflowers. In among the weeds, where the neighbors on one side had a birdbath, lay a rusty iron bedstead.

Colin, Debbie, and Brenda took no notice of any of this. Having peered at the front window as they passed and seen that the curtains were drawn, they now made for the French windows. Through these they saw Garry Wills, the man they knew as Suzanne's fiancé, watching television, and a yard from him, in an armchair, a much older man who was doing nothing at all, just staring at the opposite wall. He was short and stocky, with a bloated, puffy face and iron gray hair, surprisingly long and luxuriant. The hands that lay slack in his lap were large and thickly veined, his nails as thick and yellow as hooves. He was dressed in gray flannel trousers far too big for him and a blue-and-white-striped T-shirt far too young for him.

Debbie Crowne banged on the window. Garry Wills turned his head and scowled at her. The other man moved not at all but continued to stare straight ahead of him, even his hands remaining perfectly still on his bony knees. "We've seen you, Tommy Orbe," Debbie shrieked. "We know it's you."

"We know you're in there," said Colin, as if Orbe were hiding in a cupboard. "Don't think you can get away with this."

Suzanne Orbe's fiancé turned his eyes back to the screen. Orbe stayed immobile. He might have been a waxwork of himself. At a loss how to act, Colin and Debbie Crowne and Brenda Bosworth walked away back to the front of the house where, in the street, they encountered two women carrying sheets of cardboard mounted on broom handles. One said PEDOPHILE GO AWAY and the other PROTECT OUR CHILDREN. The banner still rested, like a belt, around the waist of the tower. Colin persuaded the women to join forces with him, Debbie, and Brenda, whereupon the lot of them made their way into York Park where they collected all the children playing on the swings, seesaws, and climbing frames and brought them back, protesting, to Oberon Road.

With the exception of Brenda Bosworth they assembled outside the Orbe house, chanting "Ban the pedo" and "Save our children," to the tune of "Men of Harlech." Soon heads appeared out of the windows of the tower and the neighbors came out of their houses to swell their numbers. Brenda Bosworth went back to her own house where she phoned the *Kingsmarkham Courier.* No one was in the offices except the woman who took the small ads, but she gave Brenda Brian St. George's home number. Brenda phoned him and, showing some contempt for a newspaper that appeared only once a week, asked how she could get hold of *Independent Television News.* He would do that, St. George said, gladly abandoning his earlier plans to spend the day at a point-to-point.

A train crash, owing to a signal failure on the line between Bath and Bristol, occupied the media that Saturday to the exclusion of almost all other news. Almost all, because at approximately the same time as the engine of the local train plowed into the last carriage of the Paddington-to-Bristol Intercity, a bomb exploded in a Belfast pub, killing no one but injuring four people. Therefore television and radio showed little interest in the Kingsmarkham fracas, and although both the *Sunday Mirror* and the *Mail on Sunday* responded favorably to Brian St. George's frenzied efforts to get his story recognized as major, nothing of what he had written appeared in their pages on the following day.

There having been a soccer match of international significance on the Saturday afternoon, occupying a television channel from three till five, most of the residents of Puck, Titania, and Oberon Roads, occupied in watching it, had no inclination to follow Colin and Debbie Crowne and Brenda Bosworth into battle.

"A bit of a damp squib" was the comment of a peace-loving neighbor of the Orbes', who had watched the Crowne-Bosworth activities and listened to the chanting for as long as he could bear it. But at five to three, just before the soccer was due to start, he walked around to York Street where he encountered two police officers on the beat, PC Martin Dempsey and WPC Lydia Wingate.

They went back with him to Oberon Road and advised the chanters and banner carriers to go home. Colin Crowne argued with them, but not for long. The children who had been removed from York Park were whining about missing their lunch and noisily demanding food, so by three-fifteen everyone had departed or "dispersed to their homes," as PC Dempsey put it.

He and Lydia Wingate went into the tower and up in the lift to the second floor where they banged on the door of a flat tenanted by John and Rochelle Keenan. Martin Dempsey asked them to take the banner down. Expecting a refusal, he got meek acquiescence—John Keenan would have agreed to anything so long as he could watch the soccer—and by the time Dempsey and Wingate were on their way back to York Street, Keenan had sent Rochelle around to the neighbors and together they had removed the strip of cloth with its inflammatory lettering. On the corner, Dempsey looked back and saw to his surprise and gratification that it had gone.

Not in all this time had Tommy Orbe shown his face at any window or door of 16 Oberon Road. Suzanne Orbe ventured out at four and came back three-quarters of an hour later with two carrier bags of shopping. The place was dead, not a soul about, for everyone was watching the match, including her father and her fiancé. Garry Wills left the house alone at seven to go to the pub, as was his habit, but instead of the Crown and Anchor in York Street, his usual venue, he thought it wiser to go farther afield to the Rat and Carrot, where no one knew him.

The Sunday papers were full of the bomb and the rail crash. With her morning tea Wexford took them upstairs to his wife, who was having a lie-in after her late night, but first he checked that there was nothing in them about Orbe. A mile away, in the triangle of streets with the central tower, all was as yet calm. The banner had disappeared. The curtains in the front window of 16 Oberon Road remained drawn. At ten Colin Crowne was still in bed, sleeping off a hangover, the result of drinking round at Brenda Bosworth's until the small hours with Brenda and her live-in lover, Miroslav Zlatic. Brenda and Miroslav were also still asleep, so the two small boys and the small girl had got up on their own, got their breakfast unaided, and taken themselves off to York Park with two little Keenans and three children called Hebden from Titania Road.

Saturday had been one of the most enjoyable days of Lizzie Cromwell's life. For once she had been feted and admired. Hayley had bought her ice cream, and Kate, having treated them all to lunch out of her birthday money, persuaded Lizzie to have a vodka and black currant to "build her up." She had to look after herself now she was pregnant, they said. After several illegal drinks in a pub that boasted it never closed, they went back to Kate's mother's flat on the Stowerton Road, had fish and chips and mushy peas fetched in by Kate's brother Darryl, and watched a video of *L.A. Confidential.*

Lizzie hadn't got home till nearly midnight. She expected trouble but none came, for, as Debbie said, "It's too late for that, isn't it?"

And Colin said, "No point in shutting the stable door after the bloody horse has bolted."

Next day looked like being nearly as good, for soon after ten Kate and Hayley called for her with another girl whose name was Charlotte. This Charlotte, as well as being over six feet tall and stunningly beautiful, with red hair that reached to her waist, knew hundreds of boys, including four who all had motorbikes and were coming over from Pomfret to meet up by the bandstand at eleven. The four girls all went down to the High Street and bought Twix bars and crisps from the only shop in the town center open on a Sunday, then they made their way into the park.

The day's promise was destined not to be fulfilled, for the boys failed to turn up. Lizzie and Kate and Hayley and Charlotte hung about the bandstand for a long time, eating their crisps and chocolate, and eventually lying down on the grass to listen to Lizzie's account of the origin of her pregnancy. Each time she told this story she gave a different account of events, and by this time she had invented three possible fathers for the child. Hayley noticed this and pointed it out, but Lizzie said not to argue with her, she mustn't be upset in her condition.

When it was obvious the boys weren't coming, they all got up and trailed back. Not the way they had come, for that would have brought them out into the High Street, but via the children's playground, which was in that part of the park closest to the Muriel Campden Estate. A young Keenan and a young Bosworth were on the swings, another Bosworth and two Hebdens were on the climbing frame, and the rest of them were kicking a ball about. The four girls lingered and Hayley said she was going down the slide, she'd never dared to when she was little.

Most of the houses in Oberon Road backed onto the park, but only those numbered between 14 and 19 actually overlooked the playground. Hayley, descending the slide for the second time, looked up and saw a man standing at an upstairs window, apparently staring at the children in the playground. It wasn't No. 16 and it wasn't Tommy Orbe, but the man next door but one at No. 18, the one who had fetched the police on the previous afternoon. Tony Mitchell was six inches taller than Orbe and twenty years younger, but Hayley didn't let these minor matters bother her. Descending with a whoosh, arms and legs in the air, she screamed out, "The pedo! The pedo's up there, watching us!" The other girls took up the cry and so did the children, bored by now with what the playground had on offer. With Hayley in the lead, they started back for the Muriel Campden Estate, running now, and all yelling, "The pedo, the pedo!"

They pounded down the passage that led into Oberon Road, Lizzie running with the best of them, her condition forgotten. Nine children and four teenagers all shouting at the tops of their voices make a considerable noise. Heads appeared at windows in Oberon Road and Puck Road, doors flew open, and people came out into their front gardens to see what was going on.

"That old pedo's up at his window watching the kids," Charlotte gasped, and Lizzie cried equally breathlessly, "He's watching them and he's going to come down and get them!"

Brenda Bosworth, who had come out in her nightdress with a coat over it, let out a loud scream and seized hold of her Sean, her Dean, and her Kelly, clutching all three of them to her in a protective embrace, but let them go again when Colin Crowne began ushering all the children into his own house, declaring that they would be safe there until "something has been done about it." He slammed the front door on them, and he and Debbie marched up the road to No. 16.

By this time John and Rochelle Keenan had appeared on the lawn that surrounded the tower, where they were joined by a dozen other people, two of whom, young men, had armed themselves, one with a length of lead piping and the other with a brick. The banners with PEDOPHILE GO AWAY and PROTECT OUR CHILDREN now reappeared, carried by Joe Hebden and a pal of his who had dropped in to talk about a twenty-five-year-old Triumph Herald he was trying to sell for two hundred pounds. The Triumph Herald man was only the first of many strangers to the estate who came to join in the fray. How they knew about it, how news of it had reached and fired them, remained a mystery. But by the time the majority of Muriel Campden parents had gathered on the lawn where Brenda Bosworth was haranguing them on "this menace in our midst," people were streaming into Titania Road from all parts of Kingsmarkham, most on foot but some in cars or on motorbikes, as well as a party in a minibus.

The peacemaker, Tony Mitchell, whom Hayley had mistaken for Tommy Orbe, saw it all but this time did nothing. Last evening, while he was out watering his front garden, an old woman had gone by, spat at him, and called him a quisling, an epithet he was far too young to understand. He hadn't liked it, though, and he hadn't liked his neighbor at 19 turning her back when he said good evening, so he resolved to stick his neck out no further. He told his wife not to get involved and she said she wouldn't. She just quietly popped across the road to the tower, borrowed her sister Rochelle Keenan's camcorder, and from an upstairs window, began recording the whole thing on videotape.

The three streets were now packed with cars. Drivers, trying to get in through the approach road from York Street, left their hands on horns and shouted out of their windows. One of them was Brian St. George, who abandoned his car to block the roadway and went off into Oberon Road on foot. The crowd on the lawn cheered and clapped Brenda Bosworth, and two men had the idea of carrying her on their shoulders to take up a position outside No. 16.

There they stood, flanked by the banner carriers, while something like a hundred people assembled behind them. Things were still quite orderly, with the crowd merely chanting once more, this time to "Abide With Me," the tune a suggestion of a Manchester United supporter and not because it was Sunday. Who threw the first brick was never established. The stack of bricks stood in the front garden of 21 Oberon Road, whose occupants were out for the day, ready for use in the building of a wall to separate their lawn from the pavement and replace the wire fence. The bricklayer had left them there on Friday, covered up with a plastic sheet.

John Keenan pulled off this sheet, but whether he actually picked up a brick, no one knew. But somebody did and hurled it at No. 16. This first brick, flying past Brenda Bosworth's ear, caused her bearers to duck and the banner carriers to retreat, but it missed its mark and crashed against the front wall of the Orbes' house instead of through the window. The noise it made slightly daunted everyone and the crowd hesitated.

At this point a man called Carl Meeks realized that fewer children were about than there should have been. Notably, his own son. He shouted out, "Where's my Scott?" and John Keenan took up the cry with "What's happened to my Gary?"

Brenda Bosworth jumped down from her bearers' shoulders, assured herself with a glance around that her children were missing, and screamed out, "He's got them! The pedo's got them in there!"

All the little Bosworths, Keenans, Hebdens, and Scott Meeks were inside the Crowne house where, although any of them could have opened the front door and escaped, they preferred to remain and enjoy themselves eating the crisps they had found in the kitchen and watching one of Colin Crowne's porn videos. Colin had shut them in there, but no one knew that, and somehow Colin had forgotten all about it. So he too began shouting that Orbe had got the children and he too threw a brick. This time it didn't miss but went through the front window of No. 16. A hail of bricks followed it, and when the bricks ran out, the crowd threw stones they picked out of the tower flower beds. Someone could be heard shrieking inside the Orbe house. It was Suzanne herself, but Linda Meeks claimed to recognize the voice of her son Scott, whereupon the crowd surged forward up to the gate of No. 16, to kick that gate down, to trample down the flimsy wire fence, and form a human battering ram against the front door.

The police arrived just as the door went down. Suzanne had rung them when the first brick was thrown. She would have phoned before but for her fiancé saying that if anyone had told him someone belonging to him would call the police, he'd never have believed them. What Orbe thought no one knew. He sat silently in his upright chair, doing nothing except for getting up sometimes to make himself another cup of tea. Between nine in the morning and three in the afternoon he had drunk fifteen cups.

The police dispersed the crowd and arrested John Keenan, Brenda Bosworth, and Miroslav Zlatic, all of whom would be charged with making an affray and causing criminal damage. They sent a carpenter around to rehang the front door of No. 16 Oberon Road and board up the broken windows. Sergeant Joel Fitch had a long talk with its occupants about the situation and their future, or rather he talked in Orbe's presence, but whether Orbe listened or cared was another matter. Should he remain where he was or be moved? And if moved, taken where? Possibly a police station would be the best, though temporary, sanctuary for him. But not Kingsmarkham, where the only accommodation was two cells, both currently occupied by John Keenan and Miroslav Zlatic, Brenda having been released because there was no one to look after her children.

Those children, along with the small Keenans and Hebdens, were not discovered for some hours. By the time Debbie and Colin and Lizzie got home, they had left, having consumed everything edible in the house, helped themselves to the five hundred duty-free cigarettes Colin had brought back from a day trip to France, and gone down to Kingsbrook weir for a swim.

When things had quieted down, Shirley Mitchell came out of her house and onto the green, where she picked up all the litter dropped during the afternoon and put it into a plastic bin liner: crisp packets and chocolate wrappers and a couple of Coke cans. No one was around to hear her angry mutterings on the theme of those too ignorant to value their environment.

Later in the evening a man came out of 16 Oberon Road, carrying a suitcase. Suzanne Orbe's fiancé was heading for the station to catch the last train for London. He had a pal in Balham he could stay with. When it had "all blown over" he might come back, he told Suzanne, but the way things were, the stress was too much for him.

Wexford watched it all on television, on the Sunday-night news at ten to nine. Most of the footage came from an amateur video and this was acknowledged, though no names were mentioned. He thought it unhelpful that included in the news item was a still of Thomas Orbe, one of those rogues' gallery photographs that make the subject look like a hideous and debased thug. Of course, it was quite likely that Orbe was just that, he thought with a sigh, and he hoped he wouldn't have to meet him but feared he soon would.

The sight of the Orbes' house, even after the boarding-up had taken place, shocked Dora deeply. Such a thing would have been unthinkable when she first came to live in Kingsmarkham and the place was a quiet, law-abiding, peaceful country town.

"Not all that law-abiding," said Wexford.

"Nothing like it is now, Reg, you know that."

"Yes, of course I do. What are we going to do with this chap, this Orbe? Lock him up forever?"

"Wouldn't that be best? It makes me shudder to think of him."

"It makes us all shudder," said Wexford.

Rumor ran wild around the Muriel Campden Estate. Shirley Mitchell had received £5,000 for her video, she had received £10,000, she had received no more than £500, she had got nothing. It wasn't even her video that had been used but another made by a professional cameraman secreted into the Keenans' flat. Tony Mitchell had personally smashed his sister-in-law's movie camera, and as a result he and Shirley were splitting up.

The children had been snatched by Orbe but Colin Crowne had rescued them. Or only the Bosworth children had been snatched and Miroslav Zlatic had done the rescuing. Orbe had committed suicide or had told Suzanne he intended to commit suicide. Far from being charged with anything, Brenda Bosworth was to be recommended for a bravery medal.

All these stories proliferated. More important and more dangerous was one that began to do the rounds on Monday morning. The man who had been seen leaving 16 Oberon Road at nine-thirty the previous night wasn't Suzanne's fiancé but Orbe himself. One of the Keenans' neighbors knew that for a fact because he had seen Garry Wills at his bedroom window at ten. Another older man, one of the original residents on the Muriel Campden Estate, recognized Orbe; he would have known his walk anywhere and the way he carried his suitcase in his left hand.

Where had he gone? No one knew, but that didn't stop them from guessing.

CHAPTER
8

"THERE'S NO HOUSE WITHIN TWENTY MINUTES' DRIVE OF Kingsmarkham that answers Rachel's description," Wexford said. "She made it up. For some reason, she doesn't want us to find Vicky and Jerry."

"If Vicky and Jerry exist," said Burden.

"Vicky does. Both girls admit to Vicky. So what is true and what is false? Certainly it's false that Lizzie is only two weeks pregnant, she's more like three months. And certainly it's true that Rachel wanted to keep her engagement at the Rotten Carrot but was prevented by someone or something. Both of them were taken somewhere but perhaps not to the same place. Whoever took Lizzie away managed to frighten her. If she told, they would find her and punish her, something like that. But that wouldn't succeed with Rachel, so I'm wondering if while she was with this person or these people she did something she regards as shameful and she doesn't want it to come out."

"We stand a chance of finding out if they take another girl."

"God forbid."

"You're always telling me where things come from," said Burden. "I mean expressions, quotes, that sort of thing. I bet you don't know where what you've just said comes from."

"Where what comes from?"

"God forbid."

"*What?* Oh, I see. Well, where does it come from?"

"Paul. The apostle Paul. He says it all the time in his letters."

"How do *you* know?"

"I don't know. I just know."

Wexford had expected another girl to be abducted on Saturday evening. While he was in London and next day during the Muriel Campden crisis, his thoughts had reverted from time to time to Rachel and Lizzie, to Vicky and Jerry, and the mystery house, and he wouldn't have been at all surprised this morning to hear of another missing girl. But there had been nothing. And what was to be done about Orbe overrode all other considerations.

On the Muriel Campden Estate things were quiet. Miroslav Zlatic and John Keenan with Brenda Bosworth were currently appearing in Kingsmarkham Magistrates Court, but Wexford knew they would all be put on probation or bound over to keep the peace and released by lunchtime. What would be the result of Orbe's showing his face outside 16 Oberon Road? He couldn't remain shut up in there forever. And there was no knowing when some other Muriel Campden firebrand would decide that his children were in danger and make a renewed assault on the house. Wexford was beginning to revise his opinion of the estate as being different from its inner-city counterparts and its occupants law-abiding. On the other hand, wouldn't most parents of small and subteenage children rise in wrath and fear when an Orbe came among them?

Superintendent Rogers of the uniformed branch had told him that Orbe, on leaving prison, had made a private appeal for protection. He wouldn't guarantee, he said, that he was no longer a danger. He couldn't say what would happen if he had access to children. At any rate, if nothing worse than that, he liked looking at them. It gave him great pleasure to watch them, and he couldn't rightly see why he should relinquish that pleasure. It did no harm. Apart from the boy who died—and that, he averred, was a tragic accident—Thomas Orbe maintained that he had never done any harm. He was one of those pedophiles—"*Pedos*," said Wexford scathingly. "A new word enters the English language"—who insisted that children, even very small ones, desire, enjoy, and need sexual relations. "He asked for it, pestered me for it" was his principal defense.

And if Wexford had been inclined to pity Orbe, it was this attitude more than anything that made him harden his heart. *Evil* was a word freely bandied about these days and he looked on it with suspicion, but Orbe and what he did were evil, that he knew. And when he heard how Orbe justified his actions, even at this late stage, when he heard that the old man still made excuses for himself on such grounds, Wexford felt much the same kind of fury as that displayed by the Muriel Campden residents. If his own grandsons lived anywhere near Orbe's home, wouldn't he at any rate want to react as they reacted?

Still, if in no more than the interests of public order and civilized behavior, the pedophile must be protected from his neighbors, just as little boys must be protected from him. Superintendent Rogers was in favor of removing him to Myringham, either to the police station or to the Mid-Sussex Constabulary Headquarters. Both had accommodations that could temporarily be adapted to house him. For, as Rogers said, obnoxious as the whole idea of the man and his activities might be, he had (in the superintendent's own words) "paid his debt to society" and was technically an innocent person, who could not legitimately be lodged in a police cell without some adaptations being made to it.

The assistant chief constable designate wanted him left where he was, at home, in his own house. For the present. His theory was that once the ringleaders, in this case John Keenan, Miroslav Zlatic, and Brenda Bosworth, had appeared in court, been dealt with, and severely warned, there would be no more problems. This was a community of country folk whose recent forebears had lived in cottages in villages and hamlets, who had kept their sheep and looked after the landowner's game. Such people were naturally law-abiding, peace-loving, and tolerant. "Besides," he said, "they'll get used to it. They will accept. They'll see no harm comes to their children and everything will simmer down."

Detective Constable Lynn Fancourt had established a pleasant relationship with Lizzie Cromwell, albeit one that was sympathetic on her part and sycophantic on Lizzie's. Lizzie called her by her first name and felt herself privileged, even daring, to do so. On Monday afternoon Lynn had managed, in a friendly talk, to extract from Lizzie an admission that she had in fact accepted a lift from the woman called Vicky and been told that Vicky drove a white car, registration number and make unknown. It was a triumph for Lynn and she decided to leave it there and revert to the subject of Lizzie's pregnancy, of which she deeply disapproved. A termination was what she advocated and as soon as possible.

Debbie said it was a funny thing but Lynn had just missed the social worker who had been around to see Lizzie and asked her to take part in their new project. Lizzie was proud to have been one of the girls selected. No, Debbie said, she hadn't said anything about Lizzie's pregnancy and Lizzie hadn't, it didn't seem necessary, and anyway, it wasn't the social worker's business.

By now Lynn had guessed that the project was Kingsmarkham Social Services' initiative to discourage teenage pregnancies, a campaign called Project Infant Simulator, and when she went into the living room where Lizzie was, she found her with a life-size baby doll on her lap. The doll wore a Babygro over a disposable napkin and little white socks.

"I'm to keep him for the week," said Lizzie. "His name's Jodi."

She seemed bemused. As well she might be, thought Lynn. She asked, "Is he a sort of robot?" And then she realized Lizzie wouldn't know what that was, so she said, "Does he cry and pee and need feeding and all that?"

"He's done some crying. I changed him. I'm learning how to look after him."

Lynn saw that Lizzie, and perhaps Debbie too, had missed the point. The provision of Jodi to selected candidates or volunteers was to demonstrate to adolescent girls the hard work, lack of sleep, and overall responsibility caring for a baby entailed. Thus, they might think twice before engaging in unprotected sexual activity. Lizzie, on the other hand, saw it as training for her future.

"Well, I'm afraid you're in for some sleepless nights," said Lynn. "How many weeks pregnant do you think you are?" She asked it conversationally, in a friendly instead of hectoring tone, and Lizzie, preoccupied with staring into Jodi's fathomless blue eyes, answered her just as casually, "I reckon fourteen weeks, that's what Mum says. I haven't seen since January."

Interpreting this last statement with some difficulty but pretty sure she had got it right, Lynn said, "Jerry had nothing to do with it, did he?"

Lizzie's muttered answer was lost in a sudden sob from Jodi, who began to cry without prior warning, as indeed real babies do. Saying she had to get his bottle, she handed the robot to Lynn and went outside. DC Fancourt was left in the ridiculous situation of being landed with a weeping baby doll, down whose plastic cheeks water trickled and who mouthed piteous whimpers.

She got up and walked it up and down, the way she remembered her

MYNDERSE LIBRARY

mother doing with her infant brother. Jodi continued to sob and weep and thrash his arms about. His crying had reached a crescendo by the time Lizzie came back. She took him tenderly into her arms, murmured to him, and slid the nipple into his mouth. A sweet smile came to her lips as the robot sucked, and she turned to Lynn with such a naked look of love and pride that DC Fancourt almost flinched. To question her now seemed like interrupting with practicalities the celebration of some holy rite. Lizzie, with a lump of plastic on her lap, was earth mother, priestess, and the essence of sacred maternity all at once.

So Lynn waited, rather uneasily, until the bottle had been emptied, deciding to speak when Lizzie began removing Jodi's napkin and fastening on another. After all, no one, however moved by the girl's devotion—curiously it brought to Lynn's mind those orphaned ducklings who, imprinted early, attach themselves to a mother dog as surrogate—could become sentimental over these hygienic measures. "You were going to tell me about Jerry, Lizzie," she said.

"He never touched me. Never touched me and never said a word." Lizzie realized she had betrayed herself and put one hand over her mouth.

Lynn said casually, "Was it a nice house?"

Jodi replaced in his carrying cot, Lizzie turned on Lynn a resentful look. "I'm not to say, you know that. They'll get to me and punish me. They'll drill holes in my knees, they said, they'll break my fingers. If they hurt me, I could lose my baby, Mum says."

"So you've told your mum?"

"No, I haven't," Lizzie shouted. "I just said, I'd like a nice bungalow like that, modern like and out in the real country, and not joined on to next door."

"And Jerry never spoke to you, is that right?"

Lizzie said with bitterness, "Never spoke a word, but they never do. *He* never did. Just 'Leezee, Leezee.' "

About to ask her to explain, Lynn was interrupted by the entry of Debbie, fetched in by the sound of Lizzie's raised voice. "What's the matter? What have you been saying to her now?"

"I'm just leaving, Mrs. Crowne. Lizzie has been very helpful."

"Oh, has she? Well, wonders will never cease. To change the subject, I thought you lot might like to know that old pedo's gone. There you are, you didn't know, did you?" Debbie smiled complacently. "It's funny how the police never know what the rest of the world does. He's gone, left last night. There's dozens of people saw him. He had a suitcase, one of them on wheels, and he was running like all the devils in hell was after him and pulling that case behind him. It's not likely any folks here'd stop him going, is it? Good riddance to bad rubbish is what I say. It's no good asking me," she went on, as if Lynn had asked, "where he went, because I haven't a clue. Chucked himself under a train, hopefully, only if he'd done that, there'd be a body. What amazes me is he's the criminal, he's the one ought to be hung, but it's poor John and Brenda and that Miro-what's-he-called that's up in court."

When this conversation was relayed to him, Wexford said, "If they believe he's gone, so much the better. That way we'll have a bit of hush. Sooner or later they're going to find out he's still there, but unless he goes out, and I doubt if he will, there'll be no trouble."

"I thought you subscribed to Southby's view," Burden said.

"I do in a way. But I know that crowds are the same the world over, in city centers and rustic paradises alike, and all subject to mob psychology. Shall we go out and have another look for a bungalow?"

They knew it was a bungalow now. Both girls wouldn't be lying, not in that particular way. Lizzie had called this one "modern," which meant forgetting about the shingles. To Orbe, as Lynn said, *modern* might mean anything put up in his lifetime, but to Lizzie it would be no more than ten years old. And this one stood alone, without neighbors. They had asked her to come with them and try to point it out, but Lizzie refused. She felt ill, she said, and she was frightened, she might have that much dreaded miscarriage. Her mum had once "brought it on" by going for a ride in a truck on a bumpy road.

They drove to the villages along the abandoned bypass route, as far north as Myfleet, then south to Flagford, Pickvale, and Sayle. Three bungalows were possibilities, and one of these was soon dismissed. No one, not even Lizzie Cromwell, would call a converted train carriage, even though the conversion was recent and the house stood alone at the end of a lane, "modern" or "lovely." But the bungalow on the outskirts of Pickvale was another matter. Planning restrictions forbade new building there except on a site where a previous house had been. This one probably had the vestiges of the original cottage incorporated somewhere inside it, but its outside was pristine ivory rendering, white paint and black weatherboard. No other house was in sight. Its garden was young, bleak, and laborsaving, more paving than lawn, and the trees and bushes of a kind that would never grow big.

Burden rang the doorbell and they waited. A young woman answered it, a young man standing behind her. Somehow, as soon as he saw them, Wexford knew this wasn't the place. They showed their warrant cards and the young couple studied them earnestly. Unless they were consummate actors, they weren't lying when they said they knew no one called Vicky, had never heard of Jerry, and owned a black BMW, presently in their garage, but which Wexford and Burden were welcome to look at.

On the way through Pickvale, taking the lane for Sayle, Burden said he thought the whole thing was a waste of time. No one had been harmed, both Rachel and Lizzie were home safely, and the girls themselves were obviously anxious that no further steps should be taken.

"And that makes it all right, does it?" Wexford had been looking out of the window across the meadows to the start of the downs, but now he turned around. "The law has been broken, and broken twice, in a very serious way. Two young women have been forcibly taken from their homes and families and falsely imprisoned for three days. Two police investigations have been mounted at enormous cost to the taxpayer, and you say no harm has been done."

Burden would have liked to tell him not to go on so and would have done but for the presence of Donaldson, the driver, whose tongue might be discreet but whose ears were not. Instead he said, "Prolonging that investigation is just costing the taxpayer more. And for what? What kind of—"

Wexford interrupted him. "Look at that! That's it!"

Donaldson pulled onto the shoulder. They had stopped outside a house previously seen but dismissed because it had no shingles on its front. The bungalow, called Sunnybank, stood indeed upon a bank, planted with alpines and small junipers, which would have been sunny if the sky were not heavily overcast. In the middle of its front lawn grew, not a conifer as Rachel had said, but a deciduous tree with foliage the like of which Wexford had never seen before, pale yellow-green leaves shaped like a square joined to a triangle. Those leaves would, of course, have been only in bud when she was there. If she had been there, if this was the house.

"We've seen it before," said Burden. "We didn't give it a second glance."

"Because the tree was wrong and there were no shingles. But we know Rachel has lied and Lizzie didn't mention shingles or a tree. This place is just what would appeal to a girl like Lizzie."

It was dazzling white with a pink front door, unsuitable Georgian pillared portico, and roof of jade-green pantiles. The separate garage was a little house in itself, also with pantiled roof and two small diamond-paned windows. In describing the house where she had been as two-storied, shingled, and with a gravel drive, Rachel could hardly have diverged more from the truth. Had that been her purpose? To outline its opposite?

But again they were disappointed, though this time they went in, sat down, and talked to Mrs. Pauline Chorley for half an hour. She was in her fifties, a tall, thin woman with dyed ash-blond hair, married to a businessman who commuted daily to London. He was there now and wouldn't be home till seven-thirty. Mrs. Chorley was a keen gardener, gardening occupied most of her time, that and the maintenance of her home in exquisite condition. She had painted the exterior herself last year and really thought it already needed doing again. White wasn't suitable for this country, the rain discolored it so, but she did love white, she was crazy about it, couldn't have enough of it. And this preference showed in her furnishings of the large open-plan living-dining room, the bright white net curtains, white carpets and cushions and fluffy rugs, and in her own clothes, the frosty white lace-trimmed blouse and glossy white pumps.

Her taste for white had its full scope in the kitchen, visible through double glass doors and as sparkling white as icebergs in an icy sea. Not in the garden, though. There she must have color. And the view from the French windows confirmed this, the blaze of pink and orange azaleas, with the strident yellow of doronicum and Crown Imperials. Mrs. Chorley supplied the names, unasked.

"What's that tree in the front?"

"*Liriodendron tulipifera*," she said with perfect articulation.

Wexford said he hoped he would remember but rather doubted it. Didn't it have a common name?

"The tulip-flowering lyre tree, I suppose." Mrs. Chorley said it distastefully, as if she wondered at anyone wanting to sink so low as to call vegetation by English names. She had already told them she had never heard of Vicky or Jerry and had had no visitors to the house for months. "I don't have time to entertain. The garden and the house take all my time. Drive? A car, d'you mean? My husband does that. I never learnt."

And yet there was something, Wexford said when they were returning to Kingsmarkham, something he had missed or should have asked.

"That woman wouldn't have those two girls in her house," said Burden. "Not in any circumstances, she wouldn't. They might make the carpets dirty. I'm sorry for that poor devil, Chorley."

"Really? I've always thought you a bit of a fusspot about the house yourself."

"I'm not a crazy fanatic," said Burden huffily, "thank you very much."

"What is it we've failed to ask?" Wexford speculated, but Burden couldn't tell him.

Three years in the police force, ambitious and hoping for promotion, Lynn Fancourt still looked much younger than her twenty-five years. Her face was round and rosy, her eyes willow-pattern china blue, and her thick brown hair, short and with a fringe, cut like an old-fashioned child's under a pudding basin. People took her for eighteen, and a drunk she'd arrested, for an offense against public order, asked her if her parents knew where she was at that time of night. Her home—some two hundred miles away from those parents—was the top half of a house in Framhurst with a carport at the end of the garden where she kept her Ford overnight.

Lynn usually went to work by car, but lately, ever since the return of Rachel Holmes, the Fiesta had stayed in the carport. Lynn had caught the bus halfway and walked the rest. Going home was more carefully planned. One evening she walked half a mile or so to a lonely stretch of Pomfret Road and waited at the bus stop, not exactly thumbing for a lift but looking hopeful. On another she chose Flagford Road where the traffic was light and the roadway darkened by overhanging trees.

The driver of the van that was the only vehicle that stopped for her gave her such a lecherous look and was so repulsive that even if she had genuinely wanted a ride, she would have turned him down. Generally, she ended up catching the bus, but on the day she had visited Lizzie and seen her with Jodi the virtual baby, she accepted her first lift. It seemed entirely natural only to allow herself to get into a car driven by a woman. This one was middle-aged, gray-haired, and friendly, her car a cream-colored Honda. Not wanting to lead the woman to her own door, Lynn had said to drop her off in Savesbury.

Her excitement mounted when the driver took the first wrong turn and seemed to be heading in the direction of the old bypass. But she had only lost her way—"I've no sense of direction whatsoever, my dear!"—and within ten minutes Lynn found herself set down in the middle of a Savesbury village street, waving cheerfully to the departing Honda.

Then she had to walk the two miles home.

Some two hours later, Wexford was thinking about going to bed. The phone rang but it was a wrong number and he was replacing the receiver when the question he had forgotten to ask Mrs. Chorley came back to him. Not so much a question, perhaps, as an *omission* in that house, which he had subconsciously noticed but had not commented on. There had been no telephone.

Or he hadn't seen one. He was trained to observe absences of things as well as their presence, and he had seen no phone. These days that was so rare as to be an eccentricity. Rachel Holmes had said that the house to which she had been taken had no phone or she had been unable to find one…

His own phone rang while he was standing there pondering. At this hour! And undoubtedly the wrong-number woman again.

He picked up the receiver and heard a voice he hadn't heard for years, the frightened child's voice of his mature, competent, controlled daughter Sylvia: "Oh, Dad, something so horrible's happened. I know I'm a fool but—would you come, Dad? Would you?"

CHAPTER 9

He pulled on a sweater instead of his tweed jacket and got to The Hide a quarter of an hour later. There he had difficulty in getting inside, due to the woman who opened the door mistaking him for another angry husband in search of his wife. After profuse apologies and some relieved laughter, he found Sergeant Fitch and PC Dempsey arresting the man Sylvia had seen cutting the wire on top of the wall. Quincy Miller had led them on a dance from one end of the house to the other, yelling, "Tracy, where are you? I'm going to get you," kicking down two doors and punching a woman he had never seen before and could not possibly have taken for his wife. Tracy slept peacefully through it all and so did her two daughters in the beds beside her.

Wexford found Sylvia in the helpline room at the top of the house, drinking tea and recovering from her two confrontations with Miller, the first when he'd looked up and met her eyes as he crossed the garden, the second when he'd burst into this room, shook her till her teeth chattered, and bawled obscenities at her. Wexford took her in his arms and held her in a long, comforting embrace.

After a minute or two, during which she clung to him, she said, on a sob, "Oh, Dad, and I thought I was tough. All those years with the Social Services..."

"No one," he said, "is that tough. Believe me."

She thought of her resolution to "talk it through" with him and how that no longer seemed necessary. Misery and terror were succeeded by a great calm, a warmth that spread through her like drinking something hot and strong. She caught his hand and held it.

"Show me the place," he said. "What's that list up there? Where are all these cuttings from?" And when she had taken him on a little tour of the room, "What do you say when you answer the phone? What do you do?"

She told him about "Anne" who had phoned some days before in great fear, the man who had apparently entered the room and how the phone had crashed down, and about the woman whose husband offered to stop hitting her if she went to a psychiatrist. Among her failures, those had been, so she told him about her successes too and her victories. When it got to midnight and Jill came to relieve her, Wexford said to leave her car and let him drive her home, he'd much rather she didn't drive, she could get Neil to bring her next time she was on duty. So he had driven her home, all the way out into the country, ten miles from Kingsmarkham, and seen her into the house and driven home himself, getting into bed beside Dora a few minutes before two.

Because he was weary and a bit light-headed, he had decided to walk to work in the morning. For the fresh air and the exercise, healthy options Dr. Akande was always telling him he needed. It was a beautiful day too, warm and still, the sun pleasantly hazy. He thought how pleasant it was when the litter on the pavements was fallen blossoms and green-pollen-dusted flowers instead of packaging and cigarette ends. In spite of sleeplessness—for he hadn't slept much after getting home—it had been a most satisfactory night, rewarding him with the affection of that difficult elder daughter, whom, with luck, he might soon find he loved as much as her younger sister. At the police station he went so far as to walk upstairs, all four flights, instead of using the lift.

A brief on his desk attracted his eye and it was the first thing he read:

Action on Sex Offenders

An enhanced system for identifying and dealing with any high-profile sex offenders released into the community was announced this week by the Home Secretary.

A new national steering group will be established, including representatives of the Home Office, the Association of Chief Police Officers and the Association of Chief Officers of Probation, and sex offender treatment specialists.

The new group will:

Identify high-profile, difficult-to-place sex offenders while

> they are still in prison and also assess the plans for their release;
>
> Oversee their handling after they have been released; and
>
> Consider any funding necessary to meet the likely additional accommodation costs. There has been obvious public concern about the way some high-profile sex offenders are released back into the community…

You can say that again, Wexford said to himself, also reflecting that all this would be too late for Orbe. But perhaps there had been a settling down on the Muriel Campden Estate. He was a great believer in people's ability to accept a situation through getting used to it. If Orbe did nothing, and of course he would do nothing, if he became a high-profile offender keeping a low profile, his neighbors would do no more than ostracize him and his and hold themselves aloof.

His reverie was interrupted by the entry into the room of Karen Malahyde. "Another girl's gone missing, sir."

Afterward he regretted his facetiousness. "Spirited away to a lovely bungalow with a tree in the front, I suppose?"

Karen didn't smile. "I don't think so, sir. This is serious, it's a child and she's not quite three years old."

Ploughman's Lane is Kingsmarkham's millionaires' row. Yet to the visitor it might appear not to be a street at all but rather a country road passing through woodland. And the woods of Sussex are the most beautiful in England, for the trees are taller, of more diverse kinds, their foliage more luxuriant, and among them grow the viburnum and the wayfaring tree. Loveliest of all are the beeches with their branches like feathers, like spread green wings, and their trunks the smooth silvery gray of sealskin, neatest the round-crowned hornbeam, whose natural shape looks as if the topiarist has been at work on it.

The great hills of the South Country,
They stand along the sea;
And it's there walking in the high woods
That I could wish to be,
And the men that were boys when I was a boy
Walking along with me.

That was how Wexford felt when he came up here, though there was no sea, of course, the sea was twenty miles away. And the woods were full of houses now and had been since he was a boy. More had been added, that was all. But you still failed to see most of them until you looked, until you peered through a grove or copse, supposing some dwelling must be hiding itself behind the trees because there was a gate that told you so and a letter-box and perhaps even a name such as Woodland Lodge or The Beeches. Sylvia had once lived up here, when Neil's business was at its most prosperous, but even then her house had been among the more modest examples. The one Wexford had come to call at now was among the more grandiose, with the tallest trees in its grounds, the longest drive, and the highest degree of invisibility from the road.

No greater contrast within a mile's radius could be found than that between this place and Glebe Road or the Muriel Campden Estate. Even those without radical leanings could hardly fail to notice it and be made, in spite of themselves, uneasy. Wexford thought of that contrast each time he came up here, and as they drove along the approach to Woodland Lodge, a route to the house that was more like a country lane than a garage drive, he looked from side to side, with that same sense of the inequity of life.

The house that they reached was almost a mansion, an Arts and Crafts house dating from the first decade of the century, red brick with solid white facings, casement windows, a studded oak front door. The big double garage was evidently a conversion from the original coach-house. Before he got out of the car he realized that from here it was quite impossible to see any neighboring houses or for any neighbors to overlook it. This feature of Woodland Lodge, Ploughman's Lane, so advantageous to estate agents and desirable to house buyers, would be a hindrance to the police in their investigation.

He had known even before he was admitted and stood in the presence of the distraught mother and father that this was a very different matter from the abductions of Lizzie Cromwell and Rachel Holmes. The Devenishes' daughter had not been offered a lift or lured away but snatched by night from her own bed in her own bedroom in her parents' house. But that was not to say that the Cromwell and Holmes episodes were not forerunners of or rehearsals for this one.

Stephen Devenish had opened the door to Wexford and Karen Malahyde. He was very protective of his wife, intent at first on keeping her out of the investigation. She could tell them nothing he said, she was far too upset, he didn't want her troubled, made to suffer more than she need. There was nothing she could tell them that he couldn't.

"I'm afraid I must talk to Mrs. Devenish, sir," Wexford said. "We shan't upset her. I think she would want to help us."

Devenish had a gracious manner, not apparently aggressive or assertive, and he gave a rueful smile as he nodded acceptance of what Wexford said. He took them into a lavishly furnished drawing room, at one end of which French windows were open onto a terrace and a lawn. Beyond, the trees began, mature, even ancient trees that had been here since long before the house was built, but even they were not tall enough to hide the distant blue sweep of the downs.

In the middle of a three-seater sofa upholstered in cream satin sat a small, thin woman with the pinched face and huge eyes of a flying fox. This marriage was an instance, Wexford could see at once, of that not uncommon phenomenon in which a tall, strikingly handsome man has married and established a successful marriage with a plain and insignificant woman. Stephen and Fay Devenish, he already knew, were both thirty-six, but while he looked in his early thirties she could have been taken for forty-five.

She got up when they entered the room and held out her hand, gestures of a well-brought-up woman who needs more than the horror of that morning's discovery to make her forget her manners. She said in a low, sweet voice, "Thank you for coming, it's good of you to come."

"Sit down, darling," Devenish said. "You must take it easy, you have to conserve your strength."

For what? Wexford wondered, but aloud he said, "Your daughter, she's three years old, I believe?"

"Thirty-three months, to be precise," said Devenish.

"And her name is—let me see—Sanchia?"

"That's right."

"Have you any other children, Mr. Devenish?"

"We have two sons. They're at school. I sent them off to school this morning, I thought it the best thing. They're called Edward and Robert, and they're twelve and ten."

Karen said, "Would you like to tell us what happened here last evening and this morning, Mrs. Devenish?"

Although it was his wife who had been asked, Devenish said quickly, "Last evening was just normal, an absolutely normal weekday evening. It was what happened in the night that was so—so horrendous, so terrible." He sat down beside his wife and took her hand, drawing it onto his own knees. Next to her, he looked twice her size, a burly, though not fat, man, dark almost to swarthiness, with a Byronic head and the poet's striking features. "Sanchia went to bed at seven as she always does and my wife read her a story, as she always does, everything was entirely normal."

"I left the bedroom window open," Fay Devenish said in a despairing voice, as one confessing to a dreadful solecism. "It was a beautiful night and I left the window open. It didn't seem a dangerous thing to do, not in this place, not in England, in the spring."

"Well, darling," Devenish said, "you know you do silly things sometimes."

He spoke in a loving, almost bantering tone, but Wexford was surprised. Not "*we* all do silly things sometimes" but "*you* do silly things," you're the fool and to blame. "We'll go up and see Sanchia's room in a minute," he said. "Did you hear anything untoward during the night?"

"I never do hear a thing, I take a sleeping pill before I go to bed." It was a surprising admission from such a strong, healthy-looking man. "It makes me sleep like a log. I need my rest, I've a demanding job."

"Doing what, Mr. Devenish?"

"I'm the chief executive of Seaward Air," said Devenish, naming one of the principal trans-European airlines using Gatwick Airport. "I should be there now, but obviously..." He lifted up his hands in a gesture of inevitability.

"And you heard nothing in the night, Mrs. Devenish? Do you also take sleeping pills?"

She shook her head, then looked at Wexford with such naked pleading that he had to turn away his eyes. But he had to go on asking. "What time would you expect Sanchia to wake up in the morning?"

Again it was Sanchia's father who spoke. "Six. Very occasionally six-thirty." He smiled, as one paterfamilias to another. "They all wake early at that age."

"So you thought she was sleeping late, as she had done before?"

Karen said. "What time did you go into her room?" Devenish was evidently about to supply the answer to that, but Karen said firmly, "Mrs. Devenish?"

"I—we—we overslept a bit." She looked at her husband as if seeking permission to continue. He nodded reassuringly. "It was seven when I woke up. I got up and rushed in to Sanchia. I thought she must have been awake for an hour and I hadn't heard her. Of course, if she'd been there, she'd have got up and come in to us, she could have done that, but I didn't think of it, not then. I rushed into her room and the bed was empty and—oh, God—I thought—I thought..."

"Don't upset yourself, darling," said Devenish. "Try to keep calm. You know it's not wise for you to get excited. I'll tell the rest." Once more he took his wife's hand and pulled it close against his own body. "We thought Sanchia must have got up and gone downstairs. She'd never done that but they change so much at that age, there's always something new.... Anyway, she hadn't. We searched for her, we even searched the garden, though all the doors had been locked and still were locked. That door"—he pointed to the French windows—"that was locked and the key was taken out as it always is." He nodded. "By me," he said as if no one else in the household would be capable of taking a key out of a lock.

Wexford got up. "We'll see Sanchia's room now, if you please."

The house was beautiful, immaculately kept, its woodwork typical of its period, dark, carved, and highly polished, the spacious hallway and wide staircase carpeted in an ivory close-pile. Strange choice, Wexford thought. It was one thing for the childless, middle-aged Mrs. Chorley to enjoy and maintain pristine whiteness everywhere, but for a couple with three children, the eldest of whom was not yet in his teens? Yet it was spotless. Presumably Mrs. Devenish had daily help or even a live-in maid. As they climbed the stairs, he asked.

"My wife sees to all that," said Devenish with pride. "She's a splendid housewife. Not that I would stand for anything else," and he smiled to show he was joking.

Upstairs was all ivory too, and standing about on the landing were those articles of furniture that only the wealthy have: a couple of small white-and-gilt chairs, a jardiniere with a huge flower arrangement, a pink chaise longue. A door on the right had an enameled medallion inset and on it the words SANCHIA'S ROOM. Devenish opened the door and they went inside, the missing child's mother covering her face with her hands. She gave a low sob.

"Now sit down, darling," said Devenish. "It would have been better if you hadn't come up. All this is too much for you." He lifted his eyes to give Wexford a significant look, though significant of what it was impossible to say. "My wife isn't very strong."

By this, Devenish seemed to mean much more than the common, though old-fashioned, usage implied. Was she recovering from some illness? Had she heart disease? Wexford couldn't guess. He surveyed the room. It was at the back of the house and its windows overlooked the garden. The carpet here was pink, the bed canopied with pink curtains. It was evidently as it had been when the child left it, was taken from it, its pink-and-white floral duvet folded back and the menagerie of furry animals—several bears, a dog, two cats, and giraffe—piled at the foot. One of the windows was still open, wide enough for an adult to pass through. The other was more in the nature of a glass door, and when Wexford unlocked and opened it, he found that it gave onto a balcony with a wrought-iron railing. He went outside. The drop to the ground was only about fifteen feet, still too high for anyone to jump with a child in his arms.

"The bed would normally be made by this time, of course," Devenish said, apparently apologizing. "But, in the circumstances, I thought..."

Wexford made no answer to that, if answer was required. "Have you a ladder on the premises?" he asked Devenish, who had come out onto the balcony with him.

"I'm afraid we have. An extending one. It's in the garage and—again, I'm afraid, I blame myself—the garage wasn't locked. In a place like this, I mean, a country town, a very select neighborhood, you don't expect to have to lock up the garage every night."

"And I'm afraid the select neighborhood is the reason you may have to," said Wexford dryly.

Devenish shrugged. "May we shut the window now? Your people have been over everything, fingerprinting and whatever, and I showed an officer the garage and the ladder."

Wexford sat down next to Fay Devenish. Her head was still in her hands, but now she took them away and looked at him, presenting a ravaged face, marked with tears. "Mrs. Devenish," he said, "what kind of a child is Sanchia? She's thirty-three months old, so presumably she is talking quite well and has a strong, clear voice?" He was thinking of children accompanying their mothers to supermarkets. The voice of the three-year-old is the most earsplitting of all. "And she has been walking for a year and a half?"

Fay Devenish hesitated, then said, "She was a late walker, she was eighteen months before she walked." Her voice was monotonous, all on one level, as if she had been drugged. "And she doesn't talk much, not as much as she should."

"Darling, please don't make my child out to be retarded." Devenish's genial and indulgent manner softened the harshness of the reproof. "Chief Inspector, Sanchia is simply one of those children who come rather late to talking. My sons both walked at a year and were fluent by two. Sanchia's a girl and maybe it's that which makes the difference."

Karen's intake of breath was only what Wexford would have expected from her, but he gave her a quelling look just the same. "Would she let a stranger lift her from her bed and take her out of her bedroom down a ladder? Would she protest? Surely she'd cry out?"

The father said he didn't know, he couldn't answer that, and Wexford wondered how much time Devenish had actually spent with his children. Had Seaward Air kept him so busy that, though he might have seen them briefly in the mornings, he usually failed to get home until after they had all gone to bed?

On a choking sob Fay Devenish said, "She's a nice little girl, a friendly little girl, she might—she might go with someone who was—who was nice to her." And with that she broke into a storm of tears, sobbing and swaying from side to side. Her husband took Wexford's place and put his arms around her.

It wasn't necessary to spell it out. Montague Ryder, the chief constable, hadn't been explicit on the phone, but he had said all that needed to be said, and Wexford hadn't named names or given details to Karen and Burden and Vine, but they understood what Wexford meant just as he had understood Ryder. It would be wiser at this stage to keep the snatching of Sanchia Devenish out of the press, off the media, to keep it for the time being a secret.

This meant no television appearance for Stephen and Fay Devenish to appeal for the return of their child, something of a relief to Wexford, who was beginning to feel that after the Crownes' appeal and Rosemary Holmes's, another would be an embarrassment. Besides, he pinned his faith on Vicky and Jerry. Whatever lies Lizzie and Rachel had told, Vicky and Jerry came into both accounts; they existed.

"Someone'll have to go to the University of Essex, I suppose," said Burden, "see Rachel and get the truth out of her. I imagine she may stop lying when she's told it's a three-year-old that's been taken."

Wexford shook his head. "No, Mike, that won't do. I want her back here. Karen is going to Colchester to bring her back here. She can get permission from her tutor or supervisor or director of studies, whatever he or she is called. One day here will be enough. I'll drive her round myself till she finds that house and identifies these people."

"She may refuse to come."

"In that case," said Wexford, "I'll have her charged with perverting the course of justice. She's over eighteen, she's a grown woman."

Vicky was evidently very persuasive, a woman of charm perhaps. If she hadn't been, would she have been able to entice Lizzie into her car and convince the far more intelligent Rachel that she was a friend's mother? Was she also what is called "good" with children? Was she the kind of woman a little child will immediately take to, go with, feel at ease with? Such say, "Suffer the little children to come unto me," and they come willingly, happily, with trust. Because if it wasn't such a Pied Piper, Wexford decided, it must be someone Sanchia knew, a relative or family friend, a frequent visitor to the house in Ploughman's Lane. How unlikely that seemed, how difficult to imagine such a person taking a ladder out of a garage at dead of night, climbing it, getting in through the window, and waking that sleeping infant, taking that infant away without her uttering a single cry.

Later that day he went back to Woodland Lodge and extracted from Stephen Devenish a list—a very short list—of relatives and friends Sanchia knew and saw often. *Extracted* was the word, for Devenish was most unwilling to give it. None of these people was remotely capable, he insisted, of kidnapping a child, let alone *his* child. He gave a strange impression, as of one of whom his few friends were in awe, or deeply respected or even feared. But then he smiled and it struck Wexford, not for the first time, that Devenish didn't seem as upset as he should be. Wexford imagined how it would have been for him if Sylvia or Sheila had been taken from their beds when they were less than three years old. Rage and incredulity would have beset him, and panic and grief. But this man smiled, albeit ruefully. Well, people were different, you had to face it. And some were good at concealing their feelings.

Devenish gave him a list and Fay Devenish another. The husband looked at what the wife had offered and shook his head. "Look here, darling, you've put down Gerard Morgan and Sarah Pilgrim and—let's see—Carmel Finn, whoever she may be. None of these people has been in this house for *years*—well, certainly not since Sanchia was born." He smiled to soften his words as he had in a similar situation that morning. "I wouldn't have allowed it." His wife's hand received a comforting squeeze. "Sanchia didn't know any of them, she certainly wouldn't have gone with them. Their ugly faces would have frightened her to death."

At that final word Fay Devenish burst once more into tears.

Wexford took the lists, doubting whether they would help him much. "I expect you have a recent photograph of Sanchia," he said.

They hadn't. Perhaps in a family group, Devenish said doubtfully, a snapshot that would be not anything like a portrait. Wexford looked from one to the other of them, recalling his own young parenthood when photography was not the almost weekly routine it was today, but still he and Dora had pictures faithfully and regularly taken of their daughters. And they had scarcely been well-off...

Alone with Devenish, who took him into a room he called the study, Wexford asked if the man had any enemies.

"Enemies?" Stephen Devenish made it sound a ludicrous suggestion.

"Have you ever received any threats?"

"Yes, of course. Any man in my position receives threats."

Wexford found this an astonishing response. "Really?"

"I mean, threatening letters, I've had a few of those, the kind that are full of obscenities and the writer says he wants to kill me."

"You take it very casually, Mr. Devenish. Did you inform us? Have you kept these letters?"

"No to both. Look, I know there are people at work with me, subordinates, you know, or people who *have* been at work, who don't like me, but that's a far cry from stealing my child, isn't it?"

Wexford didn't answer. When it came to people's behavior, he knew, nothing was a far cry. He looked around the room. It was an abode of maleness but almost a parody of a study, an office where men's things were done, men's work and men's business, but where a man could luxuriate too among things alien to women. A stage designer might create something like it as set for a play about a tycoon or a politician. The furniture was all big and heavy, the woodwork mahogany with brass fittings, and the upholstery tan-colored hide. No photographs, no flowers, no calendar. Crossed swords in leather scabbards hung on one wall with an unsheathed dagger beneath them. An ancient flintlock gun reposed in a glass case and next to it, in another, a large, dead, possibly stuffed fish. The window had a blind, not curtains, and on the hearth of the black marble fireplace stood an array of polished brass fire-irons.

"What did you mean by people who 'have' been at work with you, Mr. Devenish?"

"Oh, only that I had to sack a chap for incompetence and drinking. The general manager he was. He resented it. Naturally, I dare say. And there've been others. But all this is reaching too far out."

"I'll have the general manager's name just the same, sir."

Once more out in Ploughman's Lane, Wexford peered down the drives of the houses on each side of Woodland Lodge, both of them separated from the Devenishes by a good forty feet. Vine had already called on their occupants, none of whom had heard or seen anything in the night. He and Lynn were still carrying out house-to-house inquiries.

The chief constable came on the phone again as soon as Wexford got back. "When does that local paper of yours come out, Reg?"

"Kingsmarkham's, sir, not mine. The *Courier*'s on the streets on Friday morning."

"I see. That girl, the second one to be taken, Lizzie Crowne is she called?"

"Lizzie Cromwell."

"Lizzie Cromwell. I dare say you weren't thinking of questioning her about the little girl?"

What a lot you could say, Wexford thought, and make your meaning very clear, without calling a spade a spade. "No, sir."

"Right. Good man."

Lizzie Cromwell wasn't exactly backward, certainly not retarded, far from being the kind who were candidates for an institution. But she was slow, innocent, with rather a low IQ. Devenish had denied that his daughter was behind others of her age, but that was something he would deny. Everyone associated with him, his wife, his children, his home, had to be perfect, you could quickly see that. Still, eighteen months old was extraordinarily late to walk, especially these days when babies seemed to do things earlier and earlier, and if one of his daughters had been unable to talk at nearly three, Wexford thought, he would have been seriously worried.

Was there a link? Did whoever had abducted Lizzie also abduct Sanchia because they liked or needed or were attracted by something in the unintelligent? It was an unpleasant thought. And in that case why had the same people, if they were the same people, chosen to abduct the highly intelligent Rachel Holmes? He wished he knew what the child looked like, but in the absence of a photograph—he had refused the family group—he had no idea.

Karen brought Rachel home that evening. She hadn't wanted to come, she had refused to come, so Karen had stopped trying to persuade her, told her what she could be charged with, and spoken first to her supervisor, next to the head of her department, and finally to the vice-chancellor himself. Sulkily, Rachel gave in. The journey took a long time because although it was possible to drive from Colchester to Kingsmarkham without going into London, there was a traffic jam on the M25 all the way from Brentwood to the Queen Elizabeth II Bridge over the Thames and another one on the M2. It was nearly nine before they reached Stowerton, where Karen left Rachel to spend the night in her mother's house.

Wexford said he would see Rachel first thing in the morning. He had personally phoned all the people on the Devenishes' lists, even those three Devenish said Sanchia had never known. All sounded innocent, shocked, sympathetic. He asked them to tell no one of their conversations with him, and they undertook not to do this, but you couldn't really trust men and women to be discreet in a situation like this one.

Most people on the Muriel Campden Estate believed that Orbe no longer lived there. The man seen departing from 16 Oberon Road was certainly Orbe himself—who else could it be? The question was, where had he gone? Various answers, all speculative, were supplied. Colin Crowne said he had been moved to the Mid-Sussex Constabulary Headquarters outside Myringham. It was big enough, for one thing, and it had suites in it, he knew that for a fact. Orbe ought to be locked up in a cell, but they wouldn't do that, they were too soft. They would put him in a suite with luxury bathroom and fitted kitchen. Brenda Bosworth said he had been sent to a former health farm, one of those that, as everyone knew, had been converted into detention units for high-profile sex offenders who had served their time.

In the opinion of Tony Mitchell, the peacemaker, Orbe had been given a flat in some distant place, probably in the North, as part of a Government Witness Protection Scheme, but John Keenan said witness of what and that was only in America anyway. His wife, Rochelle, adhered to the suicide theory. That was where he had been going on Sunday night, to kill himself. They would probably find his body in the river or hanging from a tree in Cheriton Forest and good riddance to bad rubbish. Miroslav Zlatic said nothing, being incapable, even after twelve months in this country, of speaking a word of English, but he waved his arms about and shouted imprecations in Serbo-Croat. Live and let live, said Sue Ridley, he won't do any harm, he's too old and worn-out.

All, however, were unanimous in the belief that Orbe was no longer among them. Of Suzanne and her fiancé they had seen nothing. Too ashamed to show their faces, said Debbie Crowne. Then, passing along Oberon Road on his way home from work, Joe Hebden spotted a man coming out of No. 16 and putting two milk bottles out on the step. A little old man, it was, with the face of an ancient baby and a mop of gray hair, wearing a T-shirt and trousers far too big for him. He scurried back and slammed the door as if menaced by a gunman, but not before Hebden had seen who it was. Tommy Orbe, beyond a doubt.

In his own words, Hebden went back to his and got straight on the blower.

CHAPTER 10

HER MOTHER HAD STAYED AT HOME, TAKING THE MORNING OFF work, to be with her. As if she were a child, Wexford thought with some disgust, as if she couldn't look after herself. And it wasn't even as if the girl were moderately nice to her. Their home life must be hell. Rachel's going off to university would have been a relief.

"It's time you told us the truth, Rachel," he said. "You know that, don't you? You know that the latest girl to go missing is a child of not yet three years old?"

"They wouldn't have taken her."

"Rachel, darling, how can you be sure of that?" Rosemary said it in the kindest possible way.

Perhaps it sounded like someone humoring the simpleminded, for Rachel snapped at her, "Because she wouldn't serve their purpose. Because I was there and I know these people. You weren't and you don't."

Karen Malahyde looked as if about to say the girl could know nothing about it, but with a glance at Wexford she restrained herself. "Still, I think you do know where this house is that they took you to."

"You are aware of what it looks like," said Wexford, "and, frankly, the description you gave us matches nothing in the neighborhood. There is no such house. There is no house or bungalow with shingles on its front and a coniferous tree in the front garden." Then he said, watching her mutinous, petulant face, "However, there is a house in Sayle that has a big *deciduous* tree in its front garden, a white house called Sunnybank of just one story, with a rose-pink door and a green pantiled roof."

Rachel Holmes was much given to blushing, no doubt to her own mortification. She put her hands up to her face but couldn't hide the deep flush, as pink as Mrs. Chorley's door, making her denial, "I don't know what you're talking about," particularly ineffective.

She sniffed, eyed her mother, then turned away. Not knowing where to look, she stared at the door as if longing for carpet and floorboards to part and welcome her into a concealing world below.

"Mrs. Pauline Chorley," Wexford went on, determined to be relentless. "What can you tell us about her?"

"I've never heard of her!"

People would lie less—or learn to deceive more skillfully—if they understood how easy it is for a trained investigator to detect lying. For a while after she first told her story, when she came voluntarily into the police station, he had believed her but largely because she was a victim, because there seemed no motive for not telling the truth. Now, as she expostulated, he knew she had never heard of Pauline Chorley just as she clearly knew Pauline Chorley's house.

"I think Detective Sergeant Malahyde told you that we'd like to take you on another drive, this time to Sayle, to see if you recognize the house."

"Okay. I don't mind," Rachel mumbled. She sat up straight and some of her old assertiveness came back. "But I've got to get back to the university tonight. So long as you know that."

"Would you like me to come with you to Sayle, darling?" Rosemary Holmes asked.

Wexford wondered if he had ever talked so humbly and ingratiatingly to Sylvia. He hoped not, he thought not, it obviously didn't work anyway, as Rachel showed, rounding on her mother.

"No, I would not. I'm not a child!"

It was difficult to say who was the more embarrassed by the confrontation, Pauline Chorley or Rachel Holmes. Unless this was some bizarre conspiracy, some deep-laid plot—and Wexford knew it wasn't—they had never seen each other before. Like all people in this situation who have led sheltered lives, Mrs. Chorley was fearful that she was going to be accused of something she hadn't done, wouldn't have dreamt of doing, but might still find herself for years ahead suspected of. Rachel stood there with hanging head. She barely reacted except to stare, quite suddenly and compulsively, at an area of the white carpet approximately in the middle of the living room. It was as if she were looking for something that should have been there but wasn't. Wexford concluded that this was simply a technique for holding herself aloof from the situation, and he insisted they go over the rest of the house.

But back in the car, she admitted that if Mrs. Chorley wasn't Vicky, her house was *the* house. She had been taken there by Vicky on that Saturday evening two weeks before. In those rooms she had been drugged, told to cook and mend socks, and in one of those bedrooms she had been put to bed and given "suitable" clothes to wear. Apart from their both being women and much the same age, she said, Vicky and Pauline Chorley had nothing in common. They were completely different physical types. Vicky could drive and Mrs. Chorley couldn't. Mrs. Chorley was plainly nervous, while Vicky wouldn't have been afraid of anything.

"You cleaned that house?" Wexford asked, remembering how he had doubted that explanation when it was first given. "Those white carpets?"

"Yes, those carpets. And I dusted all that junk and all that naff furniture. And I cooked and everything. I *told* you. And I tried to mend the guy's socks."

Wexford went back to the house. Pauline Chorley opened the door tentatively and was aghast to see him again. She went white, he thought she was going to faint, and he stepped quickly into the hall.

"Sit down, Mrs. Chorley.... That's right. Believe me, I don't suspect you of anything. I believe you too are a victim of some very unscrupulous people, but you are guilty of nothing."

The color returning to her thin, pinched face, she gave a little nervous laugh. "The way I go on," she said, "flapping around and nearly passing out, I'm amazed you don't think me guilty."

"That's only on TV. Now, will you help me? Will you answer a few more questions?"

She nodded.

"Have you and your husband been away on holiday lately?"

"How could you possibly know?"

"Say I guessed."

"We went to Cyprus for a fortnight and came back at the end of last week."

"And you had a house-sitter, didn't you? You didn't want to leave your beautiful house"—God forgive me, he thought—"empty and perhaps a prey to burglars, so you answered an advertisement from someone offering to house-sit. Her name was Vicky something and she had impeccable references."

Mrs. Chorley stared at him in wonderment. "Her name was Victoria Smith and she did have good references, but I'm afraid I didn't follow them up. She was so—well, so practical and down-to-earth and nice, and obviously a really good housewife, that I...well, I suppose I've been a fool."

Not to check out references, you have, he thought, but he didn't say so. "How about Jerry? Was he her husband, her son?"

"I never saw or heard of any Jerry. She came on her own, she was here a day and a night before we left, so that I could show her everything, if you know what I mean, and she never mentioned any Jerry." Mrs. Chorley asked her question tentatively and as if expecting no answer. "What...what has she done?"

"I'm afraid I'm not at liberty to tell you that."

"I see."

He could tell she was relieved, she didn't really want to know, it might be too unpleasant. But she had to ask, her husband would expect her to ask. He could almost hear her thoughts.

"Will you let me have her address, please, Mrs. Chorley?"

"Yes, of course, I'll be glad to."

He was positive it was false. Not that it didn't look all right, just a normal Myringham address, a poor street of terraced houses between the bus station and, ironically, the police station. But it would be a place this Victoria Smith—"Smith" indeed, was it likely?—would have lighted on by consulting a street plan or a driver's road map. He thanked Mrs. Chorley, promised to let her know what came of it, and on the doorstep asked her a final question.

"A phone? Yes, of course we have one. It's in my bedroom. But I mostly use a mobile and have it with me when I'm out in the garden."

If anything more was needed to confirm Rachel's account, this was it. The phone was in the principal bedroom, and Vicky had kept that bedroom door locked. He went back to the car. Mrs. Chorley would have something to tell her husband when he returned home from his long commuting that evening. Was he the kind of man who would be interested and laugh and long to know the outcome? Or the other kind, one only too happy to have an excuse for admonishing and berating his wife for her carelessness?

Rachel was sitting in the back, mouth set, brows drawn together. "Can I go back to Essex now?"

"Sorry, Rachel," said Karen, "we've got a few more questions we'd like answers to." She was driving. "Back to the police station, sir?"

Wexford nodded. He said nothing.

They went back through Pomfret. After about ten minutes Rachel said, "I haven't done anything wrong, you know. You haven't any right to keep on at me like this." When neither Wexford nor Karen replied, Rachel repeated what she had said, but more querulously.

"You've done your best to obstruct police business," Wexford said quietly, "and you're lucky not to be charged with that."

Tasneem Fowler was a woman of Pakistani parentage, born in west London, who had been married at seventeen to an Englishman and had two children before she was twenty. At the group therapy sessions sometimes conducted by Griselda Cooper, Tasneem had told the others that for years she had endured her husband's brutality, and when he beat her, as he did most frequently on a Saturday night, she had never called the police. She was afraid that if she did so, Terry Fowler, the breadwinner, would be taken away and the family broken up. But when he broke her jaw and knocked out three of her teeth—previously he had never knocked out more than one at a time—after a weeklong stay in hospital, she had been afraid to go home and had come to The Hide.

Things should have been better for her after that, and in many respects they were. Some satisfactory dental work had been done on her damaged mouth, she had the promise of a flat from Kingsmarkham Borough Council, and she had signed up with Myringham University as a mature student to take a BA degree. But when she came to The Hide, she had had to leave her sons behind. They were only six and four and got on well with their father, who had never raised his hand to them. Tasneem had a legal separation from her husband and awaited a divorce, but she had no chance of getting custody of Kim and Lee while she had no home.

What she hadn't aired at the group therapy was that every day she spoke to her friend and former next-door neighbor in Titania Road,

Maria Michaels, to ask about the boys, how they were and sometimes if they had forgotten her. She phoned from the pay phone in the hall at The Hide or Maria phoned her. Tasneem was afraid to go home to see them, and their father wouldn't allow them to come and see her.

"I'll go and see them if you like," Sylvia said to her. "I'll say I'm a social worker. Well, I *am* a social worker."

"You're very kind."

"I know how I'd feel if I were separated from my boys."

Sylvia felt like crying but she controlled herself, and next day she went around to the Muriel Campden Estate and gained admittance to 27 Titania Road by saying she was from the council's Family Department. Terry Fowler was a weedy little man and as fragile-looking as his wife. Sylvia, who was a big woman, tall and well-built, thought that if he tried anything with her, she'd give him as good as she got, she wouldn't stand for it. But she knew how fallacious was this argument. Men *are* stronger than women, and abused women are often too demoralized even to try to fight back.

He might be little, but he was as aggressive as a small game bird. A frustrated sergeant major, Sylvia thought, one who wouldn't have had a hope in hell of finding himself in that position but who nourished secret dreams of power and bullying. Realized through domination of his little boys? She didn't think so. Although he spoke curtly to her, barking out "yes" and "no" and "right," with them he was gentle and patient. People were odd.

Out in the hall, as she was leaving, the older boy, Kim, said, "Our mummy's gone away and she's never coming back."

A heartstrings wrencher if ever there was one, Sylvia thought as she walked back along Oberon Road. That was something she wouldn't be telling. She had hoped to have a moment alone with those boys, to tell them their mother sent her love, but there had been no opportunity. When she got home, she phoned The Hide and spoke to Tasneem, telling her that she had been to Titania Road and that all was well, the children were happy and healthy. Tempted to tell a lie, to say they missed their mother and sent her messages, she restrained herself. It wouldn't do.

After Sylvia had rung off, Tasneem remained where she was, in the big hallway of The Hide, holding the receiver. She had felt a real physical pain in the area where her heart was when Sylvia had said the boys were happy. Healthy was one thing, was good, but that they were happy, which meant happy without her, was one of the greatest hurts she had ever known, worse than when Terry smashed up her face. Perhaps Sylvia had made it up, perhaps she thought hearing Kim and Lee were happy would *please* her. Maria Michaels never said anything like that. She only said the children were okay. Just that, just okay. But Tasneem had understood. She knew okay meant they weren't ill or in danger and that was all she really wanted. Once more unhooking the phone from the wall, she put twenty pee in and dialed Maria's number. Best to do it now before there was a queue for the phone as there often was in the evening.

Maria answered. She was Tasneem's friend and a nice woman, but she had this funny habit of calling you "my darling" almost every sentence she spoke.

"Happy, my darling? Who told you that? . . . A social worker? You want to steer clear of the social, my darling. Need I say more?"

"You mean they're not happy?" Now thinking of them being miserable was just as bad.

"Now I didn't say that, my darling. But you know what kids are. They miss their mummy, naturally they do, so you couldn't call them exactly over the moon. Now I've got some news for you. That old pedo's come home, that Orbe. You never knew him, did you? Before he went to prison, I mean. You weren't here then, my darling, you're too young, but he's come back as large as life."

"What's a pedo?"

"A ped-o-phile, one of them that messes about with children, only this one murdered them as well."

Tasneem began to cry. She wailed and sobbed and banged her head against the wall until Lucy Angeletti came down the stairs to see what was going on.

When she had given a precise description of Vicky and Jerry, filling in all sorts of details like eye color and the clothes he and Vicky had worn, and coming as near to estimating their ages as she could, Rachel returned to her insistence that while at Sunnybank she had been made to do housework, cook, and mend clothes. "And it's got nothing to do with *The Franchise Affair*," she said sulkily. "It really happened." She shrugged her shoulders as if exasperated by the whole exercise. "Jerry never said a word, he just sat there and stared at me. I'll tell you something, though, something I've just remembered, as a matter of fact. Vicky wasn't very well. I mean she'd something wrong with her. She coughed a lot and she got tired. It was that which made me..."

"Made you what, Rachel?"

"Nothing. It doesn't matter."

Wexford looked hard at her, thinking that it probably meant a lot. But she had been helpful, she had told them more than anyone else had. He asked her to describe the car. Of course she didn't know the registration number, but she was able to tell him it was "average size" and what she rather surprisingly called "middle of the market"; a white, or rather cream, car and an automatic.

"Now I'd like to know why they let you go and how they did."

"They just did," she said in her sullen mode. "I'd vacuumed the place and dusted, and I said I was going. 'I'm going now,' I said, and she just said I could and she'd drive me back."

"Just like that? They'd abducted you and virtually imprisoned you and drugged you, they'd forced you to work and do menial tasks, yet when you said you were going they didn't argue, they just agreed."

"Not Jerry. Jerry never spoke."

"Right. Vicky, then. Vicky just agreed?"

"I've *told* you."

"I'm wondering what else happened in that house, Rachel. Did you do any damage to something or someone? Did you do something you think might get you into trouble? Is that it?"

"I didn't do anything!" she shouted. "You've called me a criminal but it's what was done to me you should be thinking about. What was done to *me*."

"All right, Rachel. So Vicky drove you home, did she?"

"No, she didn't drive me back, she just took me to the bus stop and left me there, and I waited for hours before the Kingsmarkham bus came. Can I go back to Essex now or is that too much to ask?"

"You can go."

After she had gone, Wexford looked at all the collated information gathered that day. It seemed that the Devenish extended family and friends could all be cleared of suspicion. Apart from that, the most useful piece of evidence had come from the people living opposite Woodland Lodge. They were a couple called Wingrave. During the night Sanchia had been taken, Moira Wingrave had seen a car driven out of the Devenishes' drive, at about two in the morning.

Wexford blessed insomniacs, not those like Stephen Devenish but the ones who never took sleeping pills. Wakeful, Moira Wingrave had seen car lights through her bedroom curtains, had got up to look, not because she was suspicious but for something to do, something to look at, to distract her mind from those awful hours of sleeplessness. And of course she had looked at the clock, something she did at least once an hour throughout the night.

By the time she got to the window, walking slowly and carefully so as not to wake her husband, the car had come out of the Woodland Lodge drive and its headlights blazed in her face, dazzling her, almost blinding her, so that she had been unable to tell what color it was, still less its make and registration number. She couldn't tell who was driving it, man or woman.

No other neighbor had seen anything. No one had heard any sounds from Woodland Lodge. And yet a small child had been carried out of that house by a stranger, awakened from sleep, lifted from her bed, taken down a ladder, put into a strange car, all without uttering a cry. Her abductor could have covered her mouth; she would have struggled and kicked. He or she could have gagged her, carried her away inside a sack. Wexford contemplated such horrors grimly. But he didn't believe in them. "The case of the child who didn't cry in the night," he said.

"I suppose she could have been drugged," said Burden in his gloomy way. "We know Vicky uses drugs. Could she have been given Rohypnol?"

"She still had to be wakened from sleep by someone she didn't know. She still had to see a strange face looking down at her. Did this stranger clap a gag over her mouth while he injected her with something in a hypodermic? By the way, a young couple live at the Myringham address. William Street is a tarted-up former slum between the nick and the bus station. Yuppies live there in jerry-built cottages that were put up to last ten years and have lasted, more or less, for a hundred."

"Jerry-built," said Burden. "How appropriate."

"Only unfortunately it isn't. The occupiers have never heard of him or his mother, or whatever she is."

Burden, who usually left this sort of intuitive speculation to Wexford, said surprisingly, "I wonder why she picked William Street. Can there be a William Street in the entire country that isn't a squalid dump? Why choose that particular place?"

"There's a William Street in London, in Knightsbridge, that's very grand, but I know what you mean. Are you saying that she had some connection with the place? Used to live there once or her parents did or someone she knew well? And that's why she picked it?"

"A person of limited imagination would do that. It might be worth doing a house-to-house. Pity we haven't got a photo. Or the number of that car."

"If we had a photo and a car number, we'd have found her by now, Mike. But let's do your house-to-house. Or Myringham will. They've only got to cross the road." Wexford got up. "It's late and we've got that Hurt-Watch meeting in the morning."

Detective Sergeant Vine had talked to Moira Wingrave at two when she had told him what she had heard the previous night. Although not an excitable man, rather a discreet man with a deadpan face, Vine must have shown her something of what he had felt at receiving from her the single piece of real evidence he had retrieved from his afternoon's slog. For, after he had gone, from originally being angry with herself for not having seen or heard more, exasperated for failing to notice that car number, she began to feel herself an important contributor to this inquiry. With luck she might even get on to television or at least into the *Kingsmarkham Courier.*

That would take some maneuvering, she thought, as she remembered the policeman telling her that everything she said was in confidence and he would be grateful if what she had told him she kept to herself. But the disappearance of the little Devenish girl would certainly be on the radio and television news, and once it was "in the public domain"—Moira liked this phrase and repeated it to herself—she would be free to talk to whom she chose and particularly tell of the significant part she had played in the investigation of a kidnapping.

On their four television sets the Wingraves had every channel it was possible to obtain. Moira managed to find a news program at three and another at three forty-five, while one of the many radio stations produced a news summary for her at five to four. The remarkable thing was that there was nothing on any of them about the child's disappearance. This made Moira feel a mixture of excitement at being the only one to know about it—apart from the parents, of course—and indignation at the ineffectiveness of the media. When her husband came home, he'd bring the *Evening Standard* from London, but she'd bet anything you liked there would be nothing in it about whatever she was called, Sasha or Sandra Devenish.

The woman who cleaned the house twice weekly came in at four. Now that her daughters were both at school, Tracy Miller did cleaning jobs all day, starting at nine in the morning, and was so much in demand that she was unable to come to Moira till midafternoon. This was a nuisance because Bryan Wingrave always came in at six sharp and disliked Tracy being around the place, but what could Moira do about it? She had to have a cleaner, even one who had a face like Cindy Crawford, a figure like a sixteen-year-old, and wore her long black hair in a plait down her back.

Tracy was a bit of a mystery, anyway. She had been working here for six months now and still Moira had no idea where she lived, whether she had a husband or lived with a boyfriend or had children or what. This seemed to make her anonymous and belonging nowhere, an isolated woman who, for all Moira knew, might shut herself up in a cupboard after her day's usefulness was over, like the vacuum cleaner she so vigorously applied. At any rate, she seemed to be a kind of recluse, friendless, discreet, and quiet. She never spoke unless she was first spoken to, and Moira wasn't in the business of speaking to what she would have called, if she hadn't been afraid of losing Tracy, the charwoman.

But today she did speak to Tracy, beyond, that is, telling her there were finger marks on the mirrors and the coffee table hadn't come up very well. The point was that she had to tell someone, and telling Tracy was really like confiding one's secrets to a brick wall.

She merely listened while dusting, made no response until Moira was finished, and said only, "That poor mother."

"Well, yes, exactly what I said to the policeman, 'that poor mother,' I said. But if it's not in the public domain how can they possibly hope to catch whoever it is?"

"Search me," said Tracy.

Bryan came home soon after that, bringing the evening paper with him. No missing-child story—Moira had known there wouldn't be—and there was nothing on the BBC's six-o'clock news either. She paid Tracy her twenty-five pounds at seven and saw her off the premises, forgetting to tell her not to say a word. But whom could she tell, anyway? No one who counted. She was a charwoman, for God's sake.

Quiet, secretive Tracy went home to Kingsbrook Valley Drive, an address that would very much have surprised Moira Wingrave, and to a house whose purpose she didn't know existed. Domestic violence was what Mrs. Wingrave would have called "in the matrimonial domain" and therefore between husband and wife, a private matter to be hushed up.

Tracy let herself in with her key and went through the house to the play area in the garden where she had the best chance of finding her children at this hour. But there she found only Tasneem Fowler, tidying up toys after the little girls' departure. Tracy's daughters, she told their mother, were indoors watching a video and already in their nightdresses ready for bed.

"Thanks, you're a star," said Tracy, who could talk volubly to people she liked. "Hey, what d'you reckon, there's a kid gone missing up in millionaires' row. The old bat I work for told me. Little girl, under three, and from one of the biggest houses up there. Just goes to show money doesn't bring happiness."

"Missing?" said Tasneem. "A child?"

"Like I said, a little girl. She's called Sandra something. I like that name, don't you? If I ever have another one, which I'll never have with *him*, so help me God, I wouldn't mind calling her Sandra."

But Tasneem wasn't listening. She gave a loud cry, halfway to a scream. "It's that pedo! Up where my kids are. It's that pedo's taken her!"

CHAPTER 11

THE MORNING WAS BEAUTIFUL, THE SKY BLUE AND THE SUN shining through a thin veil of mist. On the Muriel Campden Estate all was still and silent but for birdsong from the park. Those few people who went to work early were just getting up. Soon after seven the milk float came around and the milkman left a bottle or two—no longer pint glass bottles but liter-sized plastic cartons—on most doorsteps. Half an hour later the sixteen-year-old Darren Meeks arrived, pushing his stolen supermarket trolley, to deliver the papers.

Maria Michaels, who was due to leave for work at eight-thirty, picked up her copy of the *Sun* from the doormat and took it to the kitchen where she was breakfasting off a cup of tea and a croissant. The phone conversation she had had with Tasneem Fowler the evening before was much on her mind, though she had said nothing about it to anyone but Monty Smith, who lived with her. There had been no opportunity, anyway, as it was ten-thirty before Tasneem had got through to her, having queued up for a long time to get to The Hide pay phone.

The missing little girl would be the *Sun*'s lead story, Maria was sure of that. But it wasn't. And it wasn't just absent from the front page, she couldn't find it anywhere. What was going on? She took a cup of tea up to Monty, who was unemployed and therefore still in bed, and asked him what he thought.

"It's not right," said Monty, taking the tea and the paper from her. "They're hushing it up. Nothing on the telly and now nothing in the paper. How would you and me feel if we'd got kids?"

"Bloody frantic, my darling. I don't blame the paper, though, I blame the police."

"They're always on the side of the criminal," said Monty. "Pedos, rapers, robbers, manslaughterers, you name it, they can't do no wrong."

"People ought to be warned. I'll just give Rochelle a phone before I go to work, my darling. My God, look at the time, better get cracking."

So Maria phoned Rochelle Keenan and, because she couldn't remember the name Tasneem had given her, told her a child called Shawna or Shana or something was missing and the police weren't doing a thing about it. After she had rung off, Rochelle phoned Brenda Bosworth, embellishing her story to make it more acceptable to that sensation-loving woman's ears, and telling her Tommy Orbe had snatched a baby from its own bedroom and taken it away in a stolen car. Brenda wanted to know why it hadn't been on the telly or in the *Mirror*, and Rochelle said the police didn't want it to come out that they'd left Orbe at large.

Brenda, at that moment, was the first to call herself and Miroslav, Colin Crowne, Joe Hebden, and the Keenans by a name later taken up by the newspapers. "It's time the Kingsmarkham Six acted," she said.

She went round in person to tell the news to Shirley Mitchell (who had already heard it from her sister), said the Kingsmarkham Six were mustering, shook her fist at the Orbes' house, and passed on to notify Hebdens, Meekses, and Crownes. Shirley went upstairs and looked out of the back-bedroom window from where she had a good view of the Orbes' back garden, but it looked much the same as usual, the rusty bedstead still there, though half-hidden now by the weeds, which had grown taller by a foot.

Her husband was about to leave for work. She told him Orbe and Suzanne had stolen a baby girl called Sarah and had her in their house.

"Orbe's not interested in girls," said Tony Mitchell. "It's always been boys with him."

"Then he's changed. Being in prison's changed him."

"Load of rubbish," said Tony. "You might as well say you've started fancying women. Don't you get involved. You want to keep yourself to yourself. If I've told you that once I've told you five hundred times."

By the time he was out of sight, heading for the bus stop in York Street, a crowd was gathering in Oberon Road, with Brenda Bosworth in the vanguard. By now the sun was hot, the mist had melted away, and the silence was broken by twenty voices chanting, "We want Orbe! We want Orbe!"

Organizing the continued search for Sanchia Devenish, Wexford was too busy to attend the Hurt-Watch meeting. Burden went in his place. Wexford had been in his office since half past eight, reviewing the progress made in tracking down Victoria Smith, or rather, the progress not made. In accordance with Burden's suggestion, Barry Vine and two officers from Myringham had carried out a house-to-house inquiry in William Street and come up with nothing. No one recognized the middle-aged woman and the young man described, no one had heard of a Vicky or a Jerry. Electoral registers going back twenty years had been consulted, but the only Victoria in William Street had been checked out and found to have died two years before.

Wexford had stopped reading and begun thinking, just sitting there with his eyes half-closed and his hands folded, reflecting on what might make someone choose a particular false address. If not because she had once lived in that street, because she had regularly walked along it on her way to work or had been to school there or had had a parent living there or a child living there, or had gone to a dentist or a doctor or a chiropodist there. Once he had found out that no doctor or dentist or chiropodist operated from William Street, and that there was no school there and never had been, he had to think again.

Of course it was more than possible, it was even likely, that Vicky had simply picked that address out of a street plan of Myringham. It was what he would do in the unlikely event of his needing a false address. But if not by this means, how else could he find her? His train of thought was interrupted by the phone ringing. It was Sylvia. She never phoned him at work, it was almost unheard of.

He restrained himself from asking what was wrong, was her mother all right, and simply said a cheerful, "Hello, darling."

"Dad, is there a child missing in Kingsmarkham, a little girl?"

Something tightened in his chest. "Why do you ask?"

"I'll tell you. One of the women at The Hide heard it at the place where she works and she told me when I came on last night. Well, not when I came on actually. Not till I'd been on quite a while. I was in the helpline room and she put her head round the door on her way to bed. It was all of eleven, otherwise I'd have phoned you."

It went against the grain with him to admit this carefully guarded secret, even, perhaps especially, to a member of his family. He said cautiously, "A little girl is missing, yes. There are reasons for not making it public. We hope to find her and then it need never be made public."

"Would the reasons have something to do with Thomas Orbe?"

"I can't answer that, Sylvia."

"Only his neighbors, all that mob that went mad the other day, they know about it. One of our women told a friend of hers on the Muriel Campden and it'll be all round the place by now."

"Oh, God. Thanks for telling me, Sylvia," and Wexford added, "You may have averted a nasty situation."

He didn't say what he wanted to, that she would certainly have averted it if she had called him at eleven the previous night. Their relationship had never been so good; let it stay that way. The only thing to do now was put a call through to Superintendent Rogers and suggest some of his people get over to Oberon Road immediately. The uniformed branch was responsible for crowd control, but Wexford might as well go up there himself—why not?

Where did that woman work, the one who had found out about Sanchia Devenish and passed on her information? He should have asked Sylvia. But no doubt it was in Ploughman's Lane or Winchester Drive, near the Devenishes'. Too late to worry about that now, he thought, as Donaldson drove him along the High Street and turned up York Street.

He expected to hear chanting or singing or even just roaring long before the Muriel Campden Estate was reached, but there was silence, or rather, a hush, as if up here even the normal busy sounds of a country town on a weekday had been subdued. The entrance to the triangle of streets was blocked by a police car in the familiar Mid-Sussex Constabulary scarlet, blue, and canary yellow, stationary across the road and at right angles to it. The uniformed officer at the wheel Wexford didn't recognize. He said to Donaldson, "I'll walk the rest of the way."

It was hot for late April, the sun blazing down by now, white on the pavements, black in the shade. He could see a crowd ahead of him, an ambulance parked halfway along Oberon Road. It pulled away and its siren sounded just as he passed the gate of No. 20. The sight of the Orbes' house almost stopped him short. The windowpanes, which the council had replaced only the day before, were once more smashed, the front door was gone, and someone, somehow, had succeeded in dislodging several tiles from the roof. Outside the gate stood Sergeant Joel Fitch and in front of the gaping hole where the front door had been a WPC called, he thought, Wendy Brodrick. The crowd, huddled together, had retreated to the green to stare.

"Who was in the ambulance?" he asked Fitch.

"Suzanne Orbe, sir. She got hit on the head with a brick. They threw the same bricks they threw on Sunday. Someone had piled them all up again and they just used them."

"Everything gets recycled these days," said Wexford.

"It's a blessing the little girl *wasn't* in there, sir. They'd very likely have murdered her."

"Where's Mr. Rogers?"

"Inside with Orbe. He's going to bring him out. Here's the van now."

The crowd, which had been silent, began a muttering. The sound of it rose and fell, rose again, and a woman shouted out, "Nobody's taking me away in no Black Maria!" It was Brenda Bosworth, arm in arm with Miroslav Zlatic, who was also arm in arm with Lizzie Cromwell.

If 16 Oberon Road had had a garage drive, things would have been much easier, but the only garages on the Muriel Campden Estate were the lockup kind, a row of them at the York Street end of Titania Road. The van driver was obliged to park against the curb, and almost before he had put the handbrake on, the crowd surged up to surround it.

"Get back there," said Fitch in his resonant voice that still wasn't quite a shout. "Go home, the lot of you. There's nothing for you here."

But the crowd wasn't going home, though it retreated a little, so that no one was any longer actually touching the van. The driver was a slender man of medium height with short-cropped golden curls. He got down and with two more uniformed men ushered the Kingsmarkham Six and their supporters back onto the grass.

"Poove," said Colin Crowne to the driver. "Look at his hair. Goes in for Carmen rollers, he does, the poove."

"And perve," said Monty Smith. "Poove and perve," and he started laughing at his own wit.

"That's why they side with that pedo," said Brenda. "They're all pooves and perves, the lot of them. Birds of a feather flock together, that's what I say."

Lizzie Cromwell shrieked with laughter, squeezing Miroslav's arm. Across the green, at her window on the second floor of the tower, Rochelle Keenan, in repossession of her camcorder, reached farther out to make sure she missed nothing on her videotape.

Wexford went past Fitch, said "Excuse me" to WPC Wendy Brodrick, and stepped inside the half-wrecked house. He pushed the door almost closed behind him. Most of the bricks had ended up in here. Broken glass was everywhere. He trod gingerly and the glass crunched underfoot. It was such a small house that to speak to those in the living room he hardly needed to raise his voice. "D'you need any help, George?"

Rogers called to come in. Wexford pushed open the door. Tommy Orbe was inside with Rogers, a tallish PC, and a shorter one. If Wexford had been asked whether he considered Orbe emotional, he would have said the man had no feeling left, either for himself or anyone else. But he would have been wrong. Orbe was crying. For his own plight or for his injured daughter? Not, surely, for his past life and his crimes. The tears rolled down his puffy brown cheeks and he made no attempt to wipe them away.

"You'd better pull yourself together," said Rogers briskly but not unkindly. "We have to get you out of here. Or get someone out."

Wexford knew what Rogers meant. "You could put a coat over—I'm sorry, I don't know your name...?"

"Dixon, sir."

"You could put a coat over Dixon's head—my raincoat, if you like. It was pretty daft wearing a raincoat on a day like this, anyway—and you and I could get him out of here between us."

"Right," said Rogers.

Impossible not to feel pity for a weeping man, Wexford would have said a week ago, but for Orbe he felt none. He looked at him and had to tense his muscles to stop himself from shuddering with revulsion. Impossible to be in his presence and, if you had any imagination, not picture the things he had done, the pleasure attached to those things that swamped all concern for others.

"He's a bit taller than you," he said to Orbe in as detached a voice as he could achieve, "but not so's you'd notice with his head covered up. Shall we give it a go?"

"What about me?" said Orbe, wiping his eyes on his sleeve.

"This is for your benefit." Rogers wasn't pleased. "With luck they'll take their departure once Dixon is out, and you can slip away quietly in one of the cars."

"Slip away where?" Orbe looked uneasily from one to the other.

Rogers said they would come up with something. He had managed to cut his hand on a piece of broken glass and it was bleeding. Wexford, who sometimes thought he was the only man left in the world who still used handkerchiefs, handed Rogers his clean white one. He took off his raincoat and they draped it over Dixon, covering his head and face and shoulders so that he was unrecognizable. Starting to cry again, Orbe stared hopelessly at the man disguised as himself.

Wexford and Rogers were both big men so that Dixon, sandwiched between them, looked less than his five feet eight inches. As soon as the front door was pushed open, howls went up from the crowd, a bit like the baying of hounds on the scent, Wexford thought. He and Rogers and Dixon stepped down onto the path and WPC Brodrick stood back to let them pass.

Policemen with linked hands, eight of them, held the crowd back but couldn't stop the baying. The banner had reappeared while Wexford was inside, as well as the two boy and girl sandwich boards, one worn by fat Carl Meeks, whose belly held it out almost at right angles, and the other by Joe Hebden. The crowd started chanting, "Pedo out, pedo out..."

Wexford and Rogers with Dixon between them made their way down the path while the crowd strained and pushed against the linked hands and the broad backs, finally breaking through just as Dixon was shoved into the van. Rogers jumped in beside him, and as Wexford stepped back, the driver was already pulling away from the pavement.

Wexford had wondered for a moment if they intended to attack him and if he would be obliged to struggle with them, but it was soon clear that no one was interested in him. He might as well have been a gatepost or a lamp standard. Brenda Bosworth, Monty Smith, and John Keenan, and others whose names he didn't know, had all attached themselves to the van, grabbing hold of the door handles, hammering on the windows, and shrieking at the occupants. The driver had to stop while Fitch and two PCs pulled them off, Fitch getting Monty Smith's fist in his face, for which assault on a police officer Monty was promptly arrested by PC Dempsey, shouting a triumphant, "You're nicked!"

The van moved again, gathered speed, and headed for York Street. Wexford sent Wendy Brodrick into the house, told her he would have a car come round and to bring Orbe out once the coast was clear. For his part, he didn't want to see Orbe again. Being in his company was a depressing experience, for this was a man and he was a man too. Probably, being a woman in his company would be easier. On the other hand, women were mothers…

He walked across onto the green, glad to have found a useful way of dispensing with his raincoat on what promised to be the warmest day of the year so far. Only Brenda Bosworth, Miroslav Zlatic, and Lizzie Cromwell remained standing on the grass, and when they saw him approach, they too moved off, still arm in arm, Lizzie giggling and thrusting forward her swelling stomach. He decided to follow them and see them safely to their homes. It was unlikely there would be more arrests. Prosecuting these people would be a hopeless business since it was highly unlikely anyone would give evidence against anyone else.

The remaining police officers were departing in cars, taking Monty Smith with them. Wendy Brodrick had disappeared into No. 16, and when Wexford next looked over his shoulder, he saw the red, yellow, and blue car that had blocked the entrance road pull up outside. Not the wisest move, he thought, not the best way to avoid attracting attention, and he stopped, exasperated. Fortunately, no one remained on the green, and the woman with the camcorder had gone in and closed her window. For a moment he had been distracted from watching the three people ahead of him. A shriek made him turn around and start to run in their direction. Brenda Bosworth and Lizzie were rolling on the ground, locked together, half on the pavement, half in the council's newly planted flower bed, Lizzie whimpering and Brenda growling, clutching a handful of the girl's blond hair in her fist. Miroslav stood back, his arms folded, shaking his head.

A lot of things became clear to Wexford in that moment; several mysteries were solved. He grabbed hold of Brenda by the arms and tried to pull her off as Lizzie hugged herself, doubled up to protect her swollen belly. Brenda kicked Wexford, but ineffectually, and he put a stop to that by holding her in a fireman's lock. Set free and not much hurt, Lizzie got first to her knees, then up to a squatting position. Her knees were grazed and she had earth on her face. Perhaps she expected aid from Miroslav, for she held out her hand for him to help her to her feet, but he was looking the other way, pretending an interest in a new motorbike parked in the front garden of No. 42.

"Go on home, Lizzie," said Wexford, still holding Brenda. "I'll come and talk to you in five minutes."

He relaxed his hold on Brenda and propelled her to her gate, Miroslav following sheepishly behind. Brenda, turning to face Wexford once she was inside her own garden, gathered spittle in her mouth.

"Don't do it," said Wexford.

Instead of spitting, she spoke. "That was indecent assault, the way you were holding me. I'll have the law on you."

"I am the law," said Wexford, "so shut up and get inside."

The way she slammed the door after her made the house shake. Left outside and apparently without a key of his own, Miroslav looked to Wexford for help much as Lizzie had looked to him. Wexford shrugged and walked off, leaving him hammering on the front-room window. The flower bed was wrecked, a mess of crushed pansies and snapped-off primulas. Wexford picked up a purple-and-orange pansy and stuck it in his buttonhole.

The Crownes' door was open and on the latch, so he rang the bell, walked straight in, and found Lizzie with her mother, who was washing the blood off her knees with a facecloth and a bowl of soapy water. "You'd better have her see the doctor," he said. "I doubt if there's harm done, but it's best to be on the safe side."

"That bitch," said Debbie Crowne. "That slag. Fighting like a bloody animal. I'll kill her, I'll poke her bloody eyes out."

"When you've finished washing Lizzie's wounds, Mrs. Crowne, I'd like a word alone with her, if you please."

Surprisingly, Debbie went off without another word. Wexford shut the door after her, though he couldn't stop her listening at the keyhole. Lizzie was giving him one of her truculent, lowering looks, her underlip stuck out and her brows drawn together in a heavy frown.

"You're getting on for four months pregnant, aren't you, Lizzie?" he began. She nodded, still frowning.

"Miroslav Zlatic is the father, isn't he? You used to meet him in that old house outside Myringham, it was the only place you could be alone together. That's how you knew about the blanket. No doubt it was useful. Brenda found out when you were all walking back, did she?"

"I don't know how," Lizzie said innocently. "He sort of touched me when he didn't think she was looking, but she must have been looking. It must have been that. She went bonkers. Will I lose my baby?"

"I shouldn't think so for a moment. Babies aren't lost so easily. Is he going to leave Brenda and set up house with you when it's born?"

Lizzie shook her head. "He can't talk, can he? All he ever said was 'Leezee, Leezee.' How would I know what he's going to do?"

Wexford reflected that Miroslav had got it made. Who knew how many other young women he had taken to the derelict house and made love to in silence? No doubt he had no intention of ever learning English. "And now we know all about you and Miroslav and your baby, perhaps you'll tell me what really happened in the pretty white bungalow you liked so much at Sayle. Did you do those people's housework? Sew for them and cook for them?"

She nodded, looking down again, apparently contemplating the scratches on her knees.

"Vicky and Jerry. They said to you that if you told what had happened to you, they'd seek you out and punish you. Is that right?"

Again that slow nodding. But he could tell that his guesswork and the conclusions he had drawn had deeply impressed her. How had Brenda intuited what had happened between her and Miroslav? How, equally, had he, Wexford, got it all so effortlessly right? As if he had been there, as if he, alone of all men, could speak Miroslav's own language. The look she gave him now was wondering, even respectful. Innocent, naive, and slow, she was unlike most of her kind in that she admired, and admired reverently, intelligence in others.

"They won't punish you, Lizzie, they can't. I won't let them. The best way you can help me to stop them is by telling me everything you can remember."

She said nothing, but the admiring look didn't change.

"There's a little girl missing, Lizzie. You know that, that's why you were out on the green with all the others, but perhaps you don't know that she's not yet three years old. Tommy Orbe hasn't got her, that was all nonsense that someone made up. They made it up because they were afraid of him. He's gone away now and the little girl is still missing. Do you think Vicky and Jerry have got her?"

"She couldn't do housework," said Lizzie.

"True. But that wasn't all you did, was it?"

"He never did any of that to me, not like Miroslav did."

"No, all right. I understand that. Why did they let you go?"

"I wasn't right. I didn't do any of it right. I can do hoovering but I can't cook or mend things. Vicky said, 'You're stupid, you won't do.' And she brought me back in her car."

"What did she mean, 'won't do'? Won't do for what?"

"I don't know. Nobody said."

"Tell me what she looked like."

He expected her to say "Just ordinary" or "Just an old woman," the normal reaction of an unobservant person. Instead he was discovering that Lizzie was in some ways more perceptive than Rachel Holmes. "She hadn't got any hair. She was bald. She had a wig, a big gray wig, but I saw her without it. I saw it hanging on a stand in her bedroom and I saw her head without any hair."

"What happened at the meeting?"

"Not much," said Burden. "When does anything ever happen when Southby's in charge? That woman Griselda Cooper made some helpful suggestions about how to distribute the mobiles, but our ACCD wasn't having any of it. He's set up a committee"—Burden made a disgusted face—"to, and I quote, *consider and review the domestic-violence victim communication project.* And guess what? I'm on it."

Wexford laughed. "How about this unit they're setting up at Myringham? Twenty officers to have special training is what I heard."

"I'm not on that," said Burden, "too senior, thank God, but Karen is, so we're going to be without her for the next three months. Any more leads to Vicky and Jerry?"

"Lizzie Cromwell gave me an interesting piece of info." Wexford described his morning briefly, then told Burden about the wig. "Rachel said Vicky seemed ill, she had a cough. Now what sort of illness results in a woman going bald?"

"Alopecia," said Burden promptly.

"Yes, but where does the cough come in? Isn't it much more likely she'd had chemotherapy? She's got cancer and been treated for it with chemotherapy, which resulted, as it often does, in complete hair loss."

"Maybe, but I don't see how it helps. You can't go along to Akande or the Royal Infirmary and ask them how many of their patients have had chemotherapy in the past few weeks. Or rather, you can but no one will tell you."

"Let's go and have lunch, Mike. It had better be the canteen for quickness. Then I want to go back to those Devenishes and maybe you'll come with me."

The canteen, on the top floor, had much improved in the years since Wexford had first been there. In those early days, to avoid it, he had mostly eaten out or, when particularly busy, sent out for sandwiches and later the various kinds and nationalities of take-away available. On the canteen menu today were pasta, curry, and risotto.

"You never see an old-fashioned steak-and-kidney pie these days," said Burden wistfully. "Have you noticed?"

"Of course I've noticed. I'm not supposed to eat it, anyway."

Mention of the diet he seldom followed reminded Wexford of his doctor and thus of the other GPs in the practice. Carrying his tray of tagliatelle and salad, and a small crème caramel, he went up to DS Vine, who was sharing a table with WPC Wendy Brodrick.

"May we join you?" Wexford sat down and told the sergeant his theory. "I don't think you'll get any joy out of those GPs, Barry, but there's just a chance when it's a matter of a young child at risk."

"I'll give it a go, sir. I don't know if you've seen what the lab has to say yet, but they've been over that ladder in the Devenishes' garage and they're as certain as can be no one's shifted it, let alone climbed it."

"How can they be?" asked Wendy Brodrick.

"It's a brand-new metal ladder, which was bought in plastic wrapping. Devenish removed the wrapping and simply laid the ladder on the garage floor. You can see the outline of it in the dust, and there's no doubt it's never been moved. Devenish's prints alone are on it and only on the top rung."

"Exactly. That ladder wasn't used, though another may have been."

"What, brought there in an ordinary saloon car? Impossible, surely. We have to see what more we can get out of Moira Wingrave." Wexford turned to Wendy Brodrick, who was eating a glutinous gray mass he supposed must be the risotto. "What did you do with Orbe?"

"I packed a case for him, sir, and made him a cup of tea, and when the coast was clear we left. Mr. Southby told me to take him to headquarters at Myringham."

"Have they accommodation for him?"

"They've a room with bath. Putting him in a police cell doesn't seem fair, does it, sir? After all, he's paid his debt to society."

Wexford ignored Vine's snort and Burden's humorless "Huh!"

"He'll join the other one hundred and ten thousand convicted pedophiles living in this country. After all, only four percent of them are in jail. It doesn't bear thinking about, does it? So most of the time we don't. What did you do? Bring him back here and await instructions?"

"I drove round the back and he didn't even have to get out of the car. Mr. Southby was just coming out of his meeting and he said take him to Myringham. Well, actually, sir, he said to get shot of him as fast as I could."

Wexford nodded. That was just like Southby, an expert at passing the buck. Send the domestic-violence issue into a committee and the child-killer ten miles up the road. "Were you seen bringing him here?"

"I'm sure not. I was careful and there weren't many people about. He was sitting in the back. Apart from that lot up at the Muriel Campden, there aren't that many who would recognize him, sir."

Telling Tracy Miller about the missing baby had seemed an innocent enough thing to do at the time. Only afterward, in the night when she couldn't sleep, did Moira Wingrave's guilt begin. And those pangs of conscience continued to bring her twinges throughout the morning, pinpricks made sharper by the sight of Stephen Devenish opening the gates to his driveway, so that when she saw the two policemen coming up her drive toward her front door, she was sure they knew all about it. They had come to reproach her, or worse. Yet there had been nothing on the news about it and nothing in the paper this morning…

She had to open the door, there was no help for it. The big policeman she recognized, the other one she had never seen before, but she supposed that he too was a detective, in spite of his elegant suit in a tiny dogtooth check and his dark green silk tie. It was all she could do to stop herself saying, "It was me, I did it, I *told.*"

But they seemed uninterested in that. All they wanted was for her to tell them about the car she had seen come out of the Devenishes' drive at two in the morning, and she'd already told them everything, or she thought she had. The big one, whose suit wasn't nearly so nice, but baggy and probably in need of cleaning and in a shade she always called "men's suit gray," told her to close her eyes and try to recapture in her mind that car and what it looked like, and what color it was and what sort of a person was driving it.

Shutting her eyes in their presence made her feel uncomfortable. Vulnerable, really. It was as if they could see so much more of her when she couldn't see them. A bit like taking off one's clothes. And with her eyes tight shut, Moira blushed. She couldn't see anything but redness and little black floaters, but suddenly, though the car wouldn't appear on the screen she was trying to create, she *remembered* two things.

"I thought it was going to hit the gatepost," she said. "I nearly opened the window and shouted out to be careful. I nearly did, only my husband was asleep."

"So you didn't think this was a stranger, an intruder, say?" said the green-silk-tie one. "You didn't suppose it was someone who had no right to be there?"

"Well, I didn't know. I knew it was a strange car. I mean, I thought it was some friend visiting them. Not that they've got many friends."

The big one nodded. "So what was the other thing?"

"The other thing?"

"That you remembered. You said there were two things."

"Well, that was it. That I thought it was a friend of theirs."

Green tie said, "Who was inside the car?"

"Only the driver. Well, I think so. I couldn't see into the back."

"And the driver was a man or a woman?"

Moira tried the eye-shutting method again. It felt less embarrassing this time. A picture actually appeared. She wouldn't have believed it possible. Perhaps it was because she was relaxed. But was it a man or a woman? Just an outline, a silhouette, a faceless head. "I don't know. I just don't know. I think it was a man, but it might have been a woman."

"Was there a ladder in the car, Mrs. Wingrave? To accommodate a ladder either the boot or one or both rear windows would have had to be open. Did you see anything like that?"

Moira shook her head. "The baby was on the backseat, wasn't she? There wasn't room for a ladder."

"You mean you saw the baby on the backseat?"

"I don't know." She felt rather huffy now. "You *told* me the baby was on the backseat, so she must have been."

They crossed the road and walked up the drive under the overhanging tree branches. Stephen Devenish opened the door and, standing aside to let them come in, asked if there was any news of his lost child.

"We are following up a number of leads," said Burden.

He knew how inadequate this must sound to the bereaved father, but what else could he say? It had the merit of being true. Devenish, he thought and Wexford thought, looked a lot less distraught than Rosemary Holmes had when her daughter disappeared. Even the Crownes, in his situation, had been nearer the panic edge than this calm, courteous man who took them into the study where his wife lay on the hide-covered sofa, covered by a car rug. The room was such an abode of maleness and somehow so stern that Wexford fancied a woman might feel uncomfortable in it, but Fay Devenish had apparently chosen to relax and rest here.

"Darling," her husband said gently, "we expected to see Chief Inspector Wexford this afternoon, didn't we?" He turned to Burden. "And you are?"

"Inspector Burden."

"How do you do. We don't want to pester you, but naturally we are anxious."

The woman on the sofa looked ill. Her face was not so much white as gray, and she was shivering in spite of the blanket that covered her. She struggled to sit, while pulling the blanket up to her chin. The hands that clutched its border were the pathetic little hands of a monkey clinging to the bars of its cage.

"Don't try to sit up, Mrs. Devenish," Wexford said. "It's best for you to rest. Has your GP seen you?" These days he seemed to be always recommending that people seek medical attention.

She shook her head, then nodded.

"Of course the doctor has seen you, darling," said Devenish, and he gently prized open the thin, gray fingers, laying them on the blanket. "Try and relax, that's better." He stroked her cheek, smoothed the hair back. "You've nothing to tell the chief inspector that I can't tell him."

Wexford nodded. "Mr. Devenish, it is impossible that whoever took Sanchia away could have used your ladder to climb up to the window of her room. And highly improbable that he or she brought a ladder along. Our investigations have shown it to be equally improbable that entry was effected to Sanchia's room from the outside. Whoever took her did so from the inside. Now, there were no signs of a break-in or a forced entry. Who, besides yourselves, has a key to this house?"

"No one at all," said Devenish.

Burden, who had difficulty taking his eyes off Fay Devenish, he was so shocked by the sight of her, said, "No cleaning woman, sir, no gardener?"

"The gardener never comes into the house. My wife does the housework herself." The surprise that showed in their faces communicated itself to him, for he said hastily, as if in defense, "She'd be the first to tell you that since she has no profession, running our home is her job. It suits her and she has never wanted help."

Protesting too much, thought Wexford. And what, for God's sake, was Devenish's own *profession?* He was the managing director, or something like that, of an airline.

"Your sons?"

As if on cue, after the sound of a door somewhere opening and closing, the two boys came into the room. Came tentatively and stood in the doorway, as if they expected to see something inside that no one would wish to see. The younger, Robert, looked at his mother and quickly away. The elder, Edward, who was as tall as a man but with a child's soft, vulnerable face, turned his eyes on Stephen Devenish and, curiously, unexpectedly, closed his hands into fists. As if he were going to hit him, Wexford thought. No, as if he would give it a year or two and then hit him.

But Devenish was smiling benignly at the boys. He went up to them and put an arm around each. "They don't have a key. Big they may be, but they're not quite old enough for a key to the door, are you, boys?"

Fay Devenish spoke for the first time. Wexford saw that she had a lisp and talked with difficulty. "One of our neighbors fetched them from school and they came in by the back door. We don't lock the back door in the daytime."

"But you do by night?"

"Of course. Always." She sounded more than normally emphatic, almost as if she were afraid to open a chink of doubt.

The children had wriggled out from under their father's arms and retreated from the room. Devenish smiled ruefully. "They grow up too soon as it is."

"If no one has a key now," said Burden, "has anyone ever had one? Keys can be copied, you know."

Fay Devenish turned her face into the cushion on which her head rested. Her husband drew the blanket up over her shoulders and said to the policemen, "I'd like my wife to be left to rest now. Let us talk in the living room."

Unwell she might be, but she had maintained her high standards. The beautiful room had been dusted and the furniture polished, and fresh flowers were in the vases. The air was scented with the white and purple lilac that filled a huge Chinese urn. Her little daughter had vanished, but still she made flower arrangements and cleaned the silver ornaments and plumped up the cushions.

"Do sit down," said Devenish. "I'd offer you tea, but as you've seen, my wife is hardly in any condition to make it."

And you can't? Wexford didn't say it aloud. "I had the impression, Mr. Devenish, that you brought us in here to tell us of someone who once did have a key. Am I right?"

"Yes. But I'm feeling rather...well, I should have told you before."

"Are you saying that this person wasn't on your list of relatives and friends?"

Trying to make light of it, Devenish gave a light, deprecating laugh. "I'd better come clean, hadn't I? She's a friend of my wife's, this woman, and frankly, to be absolutely honest, I can't stand her. Well, used to be her friend, only after several very unfortunate incidents—I don't think I need say more—I..."

"Put your foot down, Mr. Devenish?"

"Oh, come." For the first time Devenish showed irritation. "I was going to say I persuaded my wife that she wasn't a very suitable person for a friend, especially round the children. We only had the boys then, but even so…"

"What's her name?" Burden asked.

Having gone so far, Devenish had to tell them. "She's a Miss Andrews, Jane Andrews. She lives in Brighton. I don't have the address, but she'll be in the phone book. She had the key because quite a long time ago, when Robert was only three, she came to stay here and look after the place while we went away on holiday. It was my wife's idea, of course. We had a cat then and she took care of the cat as well. It was soon after that that my wife agreed with me the best thing to do would be to break with her. I asked for my key back and naturally she gave it to me, but that's not to say she didn't have another one cut, is it?"

Wexford nodded. He would see this Jane Andrews, follow it up, but he interpreted Devenish's remarks as paranoia. And they made him see the man in a new light. Does a normal person with a good adjustment to life suspect a friend of deviously having keys cut to his house?

Wexford changed the subject abruptly. "I don't suppose you've had any more of those threatening letters, have you, Mr. Devenish?"

"Oh, those. No, I'd have told you."

"Well, you didn't tell us before, sir."

"I couldn't see why they'd be important," Devenish said.

"I think you know why now," Burden put in. "They mean you've an enemy, don't they? Now do you think the writer of those letters would be capable of abducting Sanchia? Did any of them threaten to get revenge on you through a member of your family?"

"Several of them threatened to make my wife a widow and my children orphans, if you call that getting revenge through my family. They said nothing about harming *them*."

Extraordinary terminology, Wexford was thinking as they were shown out of the room. The phrases had a biblical ring, as if they came from a psalm. One of those nasty, savage psalms that were full of fire and brimstone, and whole tribes put to the sword. Distantly, from some nether regions, he heard the sound of a cuckoo clock, cuckooing five times.

CHAPTER 12

THE STREETS IN THE CLUSTER WERE ALL CALLED AFTER GEOmetric shapes, Rhombus, Oval, Pyramid, and Rectangle. It seemed odder than flower names or girls' names or battlefields. No one knew why, and since the streets had been built and named more than a hundred years ago, it was unlikely anyone would ever know now. Pyramid Road had nothing to do with Egypt or mountain peaks or the tombs of kings. Like its fellows, it was a mean little street of mean little houses without front gardens or trees, originally constructed to accommodate workers in the chalk quarries.

Such backstreets may be found in all English country towns, but photographs of them never appear in guidebooks or on postcards. This one was now on the route of the Stowerton one-way traffic system, linking a roundabout to the beginning of the shopping area. Heavy-goods vehicles rumbled along it from dawn till midnight. During the hours of darkness it was brightly lit for the benefit of the traffic and against the wishes of residents, but no lights were on now in the early afternoon of a sunny day in April.

The house Trevor Ferry lived in was almost identical in shape and size to that owned by Rosemary Holmes and only two streets away, but still there was all the difference in the world between them. Hers looked as if she had begun improving it when she moved in, perhaps ten years before, and those enhancements continued; it was comfortable, nearly luxurious, there were books and flowers and the means of making music, and the best possible use had been made of restricted space. When he entered Trevor Ferry's house, Burden, who had watched the film with his wife on Sunday evening, quoted to himself the opening line of *Who's Afraid of Virginia Woolf?*: "What a dump!"

Although, as he was to tell Burden, Ferry had been living there for nearly a year now, the living room was still piled with the crates and boxes moved from his former home. The few pieces of furniture—fireside chairs and a wooden-armed settee, a gateleg table and cane stools—seemed set out solely for the purpose of the maximum viewing of television. At two in the afternoon, Ferry had been watching it. Not some sports fixture of international interest, not politics, not even a quiz game, but a cheerful young woman demonstrating the mixing and baking of croissants. He had the look of the long-term unemployed: dull-faced, perpetually tired, always at a loose end.

"I haven't worked since Seaward Air said they 'had to let me go,'" he said. "Nice expression that, don't you think? 'We'll have to let you go,' as if I'd been begging to be released. That was getting on for two years ago, and d'you know how many jobs I've applied for in that time? Three hundred. Well, three hundred and twenty-one, to be precise."

"So you've no reason to be very fond of Stephen Devenish?"

Ferry switched off the television just as Burden was about to ask him to do so. He was a small man and overweight, with the unhealthy fat of the drinker of stout and eater of junk food. But his face was pale and puffy, and he had adopted the balding man's unwise trick of combing strands of longer hair over the naked pate in an attempt to disguise it. The eyes that fixed Burden in a disconcerting stare were a pale toffee-brown, the white blood-spotted. Burden thought he knew what the man's reply would be and was astonished when Ferry said, "Why? What's he done now?"

Burden hesitated. "What would you expect him to have done, Mr. Ferry?"

"I only meant, who else has he given the boot to? Or, come to that, been bloody to or lost his temper with."

"You wouldn't describe him as a charming man, then?"

"He can be."

"To women?"

"He's not one of those, what these days they call sex addicts. I'll give him that, he's devoted to his wife. I suppose he's got some good in him. I asked you what he'd done."

"I know you did, Mr. Ferry," said Burden, who wasn't going to be spoken to like that. "I heard you. It isn't what he's done but what's been done to him." It was still too soon to mention the missing child to Ferry or anyone else. "Someone's been sending him threatening letters. Anonymous letters."

"No kidding," said Ferry, and he looked happier than he had since Burden arrived. "Threatening what?"

Burden didn't answer. "He's got a little daughter. She's nearly three. Have you ever seen her?" He knew at once from Ferry's expression, his obvious lack of interest, that this man had nothing to do with the kidnapping of Devenish's child.

Ferry said, "His wife brought her into the Kingsmarkham office once—you know they've an office there, and one at Gatwick and another in Brighton. I happened to be there. I can't say I'm much of a child-lover, and as for babies…"

"I suppose you draw unemployment benefit, Mr. Ferry?"

"Yes, I do, if it's any business of the police. And I'm likely to draw it as far as I can see till it's replaced by the old-age pension. Fortunately, my wife has a job." Ferry's voice had taken on a scathing edge of sarcasm. "Fortunately, we have no children, no *little daughters.* She went back to teaching when Devenish 'let me go.' Didn't want to, of course. Who would when they've been a lady of leisure living in Kingsbrook Valley Drive? And she has to work in the private sector, which means less pay."

"You mentioned just now people Mr. Devenish had been unpleasant to or with whom he'd lost his temper. Can you give me the names of any of those people?"

Ferry gave a harsh laugh. "There'd be too many of them. The answer's practically everyone he came in contact with."

Jane Andrews was out shopping but her mother was at home, a garrulous and highly articulate old woman who, in the space of ten minutes, had told Wexford she was seventy-two years old, a widow who had lived in this Victorian villa for forty years (and intended to die in it), that she had two daughters, Jane and Louise, that Louise too was a widow and that Jane had been married twice and divorced twice, circumstances that Mrs. Probyn spoke of as if they were symptoms of a life-threatening disease.

"My daughters haven't had very happy lives, Chief Inspector. Poor Jane is one of these career women, so-called, who's sacrificed married happiness to the demands of the job. She's something in PR, which my late husband always said meant 'proportional representation' but nowadays seems to mean 'public relations,' whatever that may be."

"She has always lived with you?"

"My goodness, no. One flat after another she's had, and what you might call one husband after another, I suppose. But when my husband died—I firmly believe the balance of his mind was disturbed, poor man—he left a very curious will." Mrs. Probyn said this in the manner of an old-fashioned storyteller about to relate, before an audience, a tale of mystery and suspense. She paused dramatically, then went on, "My daughter Louise is a rich woman. Her husband left her extremely well off. She, at least, doesn't have to work. You might say that her only misfortune—apart from losing him, of course—is her failure to have children. Well, that's my view of it. But I digress. Quite reasonably, my husband felt he need leave her nothing, as he might also have felt with regard to poor Jane, whose troubles I must say have been largely of her own making. But alas, no. Under the terms of his will, this house, my home for forty years, was left to Jane, giving me only a life interest. In other words, I was to live here for the term of my natural life but in point of fact it belongs to Jane. There! What do you think of that?"

Wexford had no intention of saying what he thought of it, his principal reflection being that if he had been Jane Andrews, he would have gone on occupying one of those flats rather than move in here with this loquacious harpy. But he was saved from some anodyne reply by a newcomer's arrival.

At first he thought this was a man, and the illusion lasted a few seconds. A rather feminine-looking man, certainly, with tip-tilted nose and full lips, but quite tall enough, not far short of six feet, and flat-chested. Then he saw her hands and noticed the absence of an Adam's apple. She spoke to her mother, held out her hand to him, and said hello. The voice was deep and rather harsh. She was no more dressed like a man than the average woman, her jeans and white shirt and trainers were almost a uniform, and her hair was simply fashionably short. The illusion faded.

She seemed to be in her late thirties, slim and quite good-looking. Makeup would have improved her, for her skin was poor, pitted on the cheeks with pinprick acne scars. Her face shone with the exertion of carrying two heavy bags up the hill. She dropped them on the floor and sat down, sprawled in an armchair. He told her who he was and asked her about her friendship with Fay Devenish. He believed she was still in possession of a key to Woodland Lodge. Before answering, she suggested that her mother leave them alone.

"She does have her own sitting room," she said as the old woman left the room with an offended air. "And it's not this one. This is a big house, plenty of room for two women to live in without actually meeting all that often." She smiled to soften the harshness of her remarks. "I expect you think I'm being very mean. Sorry. I've only myself to blame for moving in here. I should have stayed where I was or taken my sister's offer to share with her. She doesn't live far away."

Having no comment to make, Wexford said nothing.

"What was it you asked me about Fay?"

"I said I believed you were a friend of hers."

"I was once, but no longer."

"There was a quarrel?"

"Not between her and me, if that's what you mean."

"Then between you and her husband?"

"Let me put it this way. He doesn't like her to have friends. He told her to stop seeing me and stop—well, communicating with me. He's jealous. He's even jealous of his own children. And that's absolutely all I'm going to say."

No policeman worth his salt takes much notice of that frequently uttered statement. "Jealous how? Are you saying he dislikes his children? How about the little girl?" Wexford purposely used the present tense. "Does he dislike *her?*"

"I never said anything about dislike. I said he was jealous. And I've never seen Sanchia. I just about know she exists, that's all. I haven't seen the boys for years."

Wexford could tell she was unaware of the slip she had made. He looked at her thoughtfully. "What became of the key, Miss Andrews?"

"What key?"

"The key the Devenishes gave you when you stayed in the house to look after their cat."

"That was years and years ago."

"About seven years." Wexford was watching her carefully and he saw that a muscle in the corner of her left eye had begun twitching. It was slight, a mere flicker, but she put up her hand and touched it with one finger to hold it still. "Was there some reason for you to have the key copied?"

She said too quickly and too indignantly, "That would be dishonest, and I'm not dishonest. I really don't want to say any more about the Devenishes, so if you don't mind..."

"Do you own a car, Miss Andrews?"

"Of course I do."

She sounded exasperated, but more than that. Nervous too? Most people were nervous when questioned by the police. Innocent or guilty, they were apprehensive. He tried to imagine her driving to Ploughman's Lane in the middle of the night, parking her car on the Woodland Lodge drive, entering the house and going upstairs, picking up out of her bed a child she had never seen before, preventing that child from crying out—he tried to imagine it and failed. But there was still one odd thing...

"Miss Andrews, something puzzles me, I'm bound to say." He looked at his watch. "I've been questioning you for the past fifteen minutes yet you've never asked why, you've never asked the reason for our coming here. I find that very strange, don't you?"

She answered quickly, with no hesitation. "I didn't need to ask. It's because the Devenishes' baby's missing, because Sanchia's missing."

"But how did you know that?"

"It's been in the papers, it's been on television."

"No, it hasn't. Come to that, how did you know her name was Sanchia if you have had no contact with Mrs. Devenish for seven years?"

The muscle beside her eye jumped again. She closed her eyes for a moment and, opening them, looked straight into Wexford's face. It was the way, he thought, that no one in ordinary social intercourse ever looks at anyone else.

"Well, Miss Andrews?"

"Fay told me, of course. She phoned and told me."

"So, in spite of what you've said, you do keep in touch?"

Jane Andrews's hands clenched in her lap. "Stephen doesn't know it, but we do phone each other. Once upon a time she used to tell me *everything*. Stephen hated that. He told her I was a lesbian and—and had designs on her. It would be funny if it weren't so stupid and false. I've been *married*, actually I've been married twice. I'm likely to have done that if I were a lesbian, aren't I?"

She was more animated than during the whole rest of their talk. Color had come into her pale face and her eyes were so bright they seemed full of tears.

On his way home he stopped off in Ploughman's Lane. The house Sylvia had once lived in, before she and Neil and the boys moved out into the real country, was next door but three to Woodland Lodge, if you could use such an expression about a neighborhood in which properties were fifty yards apart. He had always liked the house, one of the smallest in this neighborhood, its unpretentious, comfortable Arts and Crafts ashlar and gables, its simple garden with strategically placed trees. The people who had bought it had added a double garage and a glazed porch. The planning department must have allowed it, he supposed, regretting past simplicity and spaciousness. Short of cutting them down, no one could do much to spoil the beauty of the trees up here, the copper beeches at their loveliest golden red in April, the horse chestnuts in flower, the oaks just coming into amber-green leaf. That place had been called, was still called, Laburnum House. The trees after which it was named were still in bud, their yellow blossoms due to appear within days. He had never liked laburnums since Sylvia, aged three, had been rushed to hospital after eating a seed pod in her grandmother's garden.

The curious thought came to him that in a case like that the parents knew almost from the start their child's fate and future. Within minutes he and Dora had been told that Sylvia's stomach had been pumped, she was fine, she would *be* fine. The Devenishes knew nothing of their daughter's whereabouts, her well-being, the state of her mind, not even if she was still alive.

At Woodland Lodge the older boy, Edward, answered the door. He said, without waiting to be asked, "My mother's asleep and my father's in the garden."

"I'll walk round and find your dad," Wexford said, wondering, as he took the path that led around the back of the house, why a boy of twelve referred to his parents so formally instead of using his own gentler diminutive.

How did people get their lawns like that? This one was like green felt, closely shaven. Stephen Devenish was standing in the middle of it, clipping the edge of the turf around a large rose bed with a pair of long-handled shears. Strange thoughts seemed to be dodging in and out of his mind today, Wexford reflected as he walked toward him, speculations and unprecedented fancies. Why on earth, for instance, did he feel that he would have much preferred to encounter Devenish when he wasn't armed with a dangerous implement? The man was charming, gracious, courteous, patient, and civilized, wasn't he? Not always. Not when he talked about Jane Andrews.

And as if he read Wexford's mind, it was to her that he immediately reverted as he laid the offensive weapon on the grass. "I'm afraid I spoke a mite roughly about Miss Andrews when I talked to you earlier." He smiled, that ever-present smile apparent even in the worst adversity. "She meant well. No man likes to see an outsider come between him and his wife though, does he? An intervener, wouldn't she be called?"

"That was in divorce cases, Mr. Devenish," said Wexford. "She was the female equivalent of a corespondent."

"Really?"

"As to outsiders, as you put it, most women have women friends apart from the couples they and their husbands or partners call their friends."

"We don't," said Devenish. "We have each other. We don't need anyone else. Come into the house."

Wexford followed him. They went in through the back door into a kind of boot room and thence into a large, well-appointed, immaculate kitchen. In a dining or breakfast area, the table was laid for an evening meal for four, a white cloth instead of place mats, silver instead of bone-handled cutlery, flowers in a vase. Again Wexford thought how peculiar it was that Fay Devenish did all this on her own without help, and apparently still did it while her baby daughter was missing, while she was distraught and while her doctor had evidently sedated her and told her to rest.

He wanted to say something like this, that frankly he was troubled, that he was like someone in a dark wood, confused and disoriented. No one could have got into this house without breaking in, but on the other hand, no one could have brought in a ladder. Most significantly, no stranger could have taken Sanchia without the child's crying and disturbing her parents. He wanted to say it, he had begun to say it, when, unexpectedly and dreadfully, Stephen Devenish burst into tears. He flung his arms across the neatly laid table, lowered his head, and sobbed. He shook with sobs, his shoulders heaving, his hands clenched.

Taken aback, Wexford sat opposite him patiently. There was nothing he could do, he hardly knew why he had come. Perhaps just to see this man again, this house again. He looked about him, studying his surroundings. The counters were laden with equipment of the steamer, rice-cooker, pasta-maker variety. A knife block of some dark hardwood held seven or eight horn-handled knives. The walls were hung with blue-and-white porcelain plates, Royal Copenhagen and Delft. There was a calendar of the Highlands and a cuckoo clock. Last time he was here he had heard it tell the hour, but distantly. Now, suddenly, a jaunty painted cuckoo popped out and, flapping its break, cuckooed six times.

At the fourth cuckoo Stephen Devenish raised his face. He had been drumming on the table with his fists and had knocked over the pepper pot and the flower vase. One of the glasses fell over and rolled onto the floor. Wexford got up and filled another with water from the tap. He said quietly, "Here, drink this, come on," and wondered why he couldn't lay a hand on the man's shoulder, why his reluctance to touch Devenish amounted to revulsion.

"I'm a fool," Devenish said, sitting up, taking the water. "I couldn't help it. I keep thinking I'll never see her again, she's dead." His face was dry. He had cried without shedding tears. "I'll never see her again in this world, those are the words that go round in my head."

"While there's life, there's hope," Wexford said in a cliché he didn't normally use.

"Yes, but is there life? Isn't it much more likely there's death?" Devenish drew in a long, shuddering breath. "I'm sorry I broke down like that. I love my little girl, you see. I want to see her grow up."

Wexford didn't stay long after that. Incongruously, his last thought as he left that kitchen was that when Fay Devenish woke up, the first thing she would do—or would be expected to do?—was straighten, refresh, and relay that crumpled, finger-marked cloth.

So often late home that Dora no longer reproached him or even commented, Wexford nevertheless expected some kind of reproof from his elder daughter. Sylvia had called in on her mother on her way home from work at Kingsmarkham Social Services and was sitting next to her on the sofa, the two of them drinking white wine. But instead of admonishing him she seemed anxious only to defend herself. "I'm driving, Dad, so I'm positively only having one glass."

He said, smiling, "You know, my dear, I can't imagine you ever willfully breaking the law."

She flushed with pleasure. "Can't you? That's nice."

"If you've a moment, I'd like to ask you something you might call in the field of child psychology."

Dora sprang up. "I'll just put your dinner in the microwave."

"No, don't. I will. In a minute." He felt a sudden distaste for the idea of expecting any such service from her. "Sit down. Stay."

Sylvia finished her wine and set down the glass. "I'm not a psychologist, Dad, child or otherwise, though I must say people are always taking me for one. I just did a course in it for my degree."

"You'll do," her father said. "Darwin said, I hope I can get it right, 'Man has an instinctive tendency to speak, as we see in the babble of our young children; while no child has an instinctive tendency to bake, brew, or write.' Tell me at what age you'd expect a child to start talking."

She shrugged. "I don't know—eighteen months? If you mean real words and phrases. Robin was over two but Ben was talking a lot well before. I suppose it was because his brother was always talking to him."

"You were a very early talker, Sylvia," Dora said. "By eighteen months you could say anything. Sheila was later."

"Funny how a mother remembers that. I don't, it's completely gone out of my head. So what would you say are the reasons behind it when a child is talking hardly at all at thirty-three months?"

"Thirty-three *months?* That's nearly three years old." Sylvia looked dubious. "We're discounting brain damage, I take it?"

"Oh, I think so."

"He or she could be deaf. That's a real possibility, but these days I'd think that would have been checked out by thirty-three months. Or, of course, it could be some sort of emotional disturbance. Tasneem Fowler at The Hide told me her older boy stopped talking for two months after the younger one was born."

"But he'd been talking before?" said Wexford. "He was jealous of the newcomer and that inhibited his powers of speech?"

"Probably. You must have some particular case in mind, Dad. What sort of a home does this child of yours come from?"

"Middle class, maybe upper middle class, plenty of money, nice home, and that's an understatement, natural parents living together and apparently devoted, two older brothers. I would say a much loved, much wanted child."

"Then I haven't a clue," said Sylvia.

"I remember reading somewhere that Einstein didn't talk till he was three," Dora said.

"And what on earth is that supposed to prove, Mother?"

After Sylvia had gone he watched the nine o'clock news, then a program about a new kind of activist, the eco-warrior. A group of these people, fighting their war against genetic engineering, had uprooted a field of wheat in Shropshire and poisoned an orchard in Somerset. The wheat had been genetically altered to create a springier kind of bread and the apples were redder than normal and had no cores. He was looking at a section through a coreless apple when Dora came in and said she was taking winter clothes to the dry cleaner's in the morning and she couldn't find his raincoat.

"Oh, God," he said, "I lent it to a chap called Dixon to put over his head and pretend he was a pedophile."

Dora gave him a strange look. "Get it back. You don't want to lose it. It's a Burberry."

She switched off the television and they went to bed. He often had interesting dreams but seldom nightmares. This dream, into which he seemed to fall at once, took him and Dora years back to when they were young and their children very young. He was sitting with Dora, admiring her appearance as she brushed her long dark hair—an ordinary enough romantic cliché—when she turned around and told him quite calmly that Sheila, their baby, had disappeared, had been stolen out of her cot. She had been into the room and found the cot empty.

His grief and terror had known no bounds. He had run through the house, calling to Sheila, begging her to come back, rushed into the street, wakened the town, the world. And then the dream shifted, as such dreams do, and he was in a television studio, being interviewed by a demonic character played by Peter Cushing. He was begging for a message to be sent to the kidnappers, offering a ransom for Sheila, and the ransom—

this was the worst part, the positively most dreadful, shame-making part—was his elder daughter, Sylvia. Take her, he heard himself saying, and give me back Sheila. Then he woke up, sweating and trembling.

At midnight Lynn Fancourt, who had spent the evening at the cinema and afterward had had a drink in the Rat and Carrot with her boyfriend, got into a car that stopped for her at the north end of York Street. In fact, it had stopped for a red light. Lynn tapped on the passenger window and asked for a lift. The driver was a woman someone very young might describe as middle-aged and the passenger was a man of about thirty. They were going, the man said, to Myringham, but could drop her off in Framhurst if that was what she wanted.

From the conversation Lynn soon knew something funny was going on, and it wasn't the something funny she was on the lookout for. When the man suggested they stop for ten minutes in a lay-by on the old bypass, she thought it was drugs and was of two minds what to do if controlled substances made their appearance. Nick them for possession? Call the station on her mobile? But she was wrong. The car stopped and both of them got in the back with her, amorously inclined. Lynn's discouraging tactics led the woman to say she quite understood and it would be best to go straight home where they could have their threesome in comfort.

It occurred to Lynn then that they had taken her for a prostitute, a new phenomenon in Kingsmarkham but not unknown. She had only herself to blame for that, tapping on car windows—and at a red light, that was an irony. They were quite nice people, pleasant and gentle, and when she said she had changed her mind, they took her to Framhurst just the same and gave her their phone number in case she had second thoughts.

For more than a year now Wexford had stopped taking his local paper. The *Kingsmarkham Courier* had caused him more irritation with Brian St. George's coverage of the bypass hostage-taking than he thought within the bounds of anything a man should suffer over the breakfast table. He would not go through that again, so the paper had been given up. Neither the *Times* nor the *Independent* could ever bring him so much rage, so he would stick with them.

But since his happy relinquishment of the *Courier*, his newsagent had taken on a series of new paperboys, most of them inefficient. When it rained, they let the papers get wet, and if they couldn't find the right one on top of their load, they delivered anything that came to hand: a tabloid, maybe, or the *Financial Times*. Any of these would have been infinitely preferable to Wexford than what he saw lying faceup on his doormat. Under the masthead of an eagle with a scroll in its beak, on which the *Courier*'s name was lettered in Gothic script, the lead story leapt out at him.

He closed his eyes, but of course he had to open them again. We always do have to. WHERE IS SANCHIA? the headline read in the largest Roman type available to the *Courier*'s printers, and underneath, only slightly less bold and huge, ORBE IN REFUGE WITH COPS. What the story beneath would say he guessed before he read it. The gist had come into his head the moment he saw those headlines: a baby girl had disappeared, the news had been suppressed while Orbe was spirited away, a huge cover-up was in progress. He hadn't, though, anticipated St. George's statement—his was the byline—that Henry Thomas Orbe was currently accommodated in a refurbished cell "with all mod cons" at Kingsmarkham Police Station.

Two photographs were inserted in the text, the classic one of Orbe taken on his release from prison and featured everywhere, and a portrait of Sanchia Devenish he had never seen before. It had evidently been taken when she was about six months old, for this was a baby, her round, almost hairless head resting on a lacy pillow. A fuzzy picture, probably much enlarged. An adult's hand could be seen in one corner—Fay Devenish's?—and what might be the side of a pram or pushchair.

Growling to himself like a cross bear, Wexford took the paper with him into the kitchen and put the kettle on for tea. His instinct, like most people's these days when astounded, delighted, shocked, or appalled, was to phone someone. But whom? Southby, of course. He had as little contact with the ACCD as he could achieve. Superintendent Rogers? The desk sergeant at the station? In the end, when he had taken up Dora's tea, when he had observed that it was raining again but had not reverted to the subject of his missing raincoat, he fell back on the old faithful and phoned Burden.

"I've seen it," Burden said.

"I thought you'd given up that rag."

"I have. They delivered the wrong papers."

"You and me both. St. George must have seen Wendy Brodrick bring Orbe in. He was doubtless prowling about outside or loitering in a parked car. They were only there five minutes."

"Long enough. Where did he get that picture of Sanchia?"

"God knows. Those Devenishes hadn't a photo to give us, but St. George gets one. Not that we'd have been interested in this, a child of six months looks nothing like how it will two years later. That photograph of St. George's would no more help find Sanchia Devenish than a shot of you or me."

Burden said thoughtfully, "Maybe the Devenishes didn't give it to him. You know how the *Courier* organizes all those contests, allegedly for charity—the guy with the biggest feet, some ghastly ferret competition, Miss Kingsmarkham till the feminists stopped it—well, I've been wondering if Sanchia was ever in a baby show, if maybe she *won* a baby show and they took the picture. She was a pretty baby, wasn't she?"

These words, uncharacteristic of Burden, moved Wexford so profoundly, driving away all his anger in a moment, bringing him instead an ache of sadness at that past tense, that he was silent. The poor little girl, he thought, please God or Fates or Furies, let whoever's got her be kind to her.

Burden said, "Are you still there?"

"I'm here." Wexford cleared his throat. "The Devenishes aren't the sort of people to let their daughter compete in a baby show, are they?"

"God knows what sort of people they are. Don't ask me, you'd better ask St. George."

"I mean to," said Wexford; then he added, with atypical relish, "I mean to think of a way of punishing him."

CHAPTER 13

This time the trouble began in Stowerton, in Rectangle Road, not far from the homes of Trevor Ferry and Rosemary Holmes, where Joe Hebden's brother lived with his girlfriend, two children of hers, and two children of his. David Hebden drove the van that delivered new copies of the *Courier* fresh off the press to every newsagent in Kingsmarkham, Stowerton, and Pomfret, and his round began at 6 A.M. Reading was not among his skills, though he was able to decipher the headlines on the sports pages. What drew his attention to the *Courier* this wet morning was a name, one of the few he could read, being that of his girlfriend's younger daughter.

David Hebden was fond of little Sanchia. She was not his child but he liked her better than his own children, whom he saw as coming between him and his ex-wife. For a fearful half hour he thought something dreadful had happened to her. Why otherwise would her name be in the paper?

Asking other people to read things to him was something he avoided whenever he could, so he said nothing to any of the newsagents, simply growing more and more anxious and frustrated each time his eye lighted on that beloved name in that horrible huge print. When he got home, everyone was still asleep. He rushed upstairs to look for Sanchia, found her in bed with her mother, where she must have come after he left, and woke up the whole household with his whoops of joy.

Sanchia's mother, Katrina, took the paper from him and read the story. After a while the other children came in and sat on the bed, seeing in this break from routine a prospect of excitement.

"The police are a disgrace," said Katrina. "This little kid's been missing since Monday and what do they do? Not look for her, or her body more like, oh, no, they turn the police station into a hotel with all mod cons to keep that pedophile in luxury."

"What's a pedophile, Mum?" said Georgina, aged six.

"Ask no questions and you'll get no lies. I'm going to give Joe and Charlene a phone, Dave. Or you can, it's your duty, they've a right to know."

Since the departure of Orbe from the Muriel Campden Estate, all the excitement and most of the heat had simmered down. Another event had convulsed the residents of Puck, Titania, and Oberon Roads: Colin Crowne's assault on and destruction of Jodi the virtual baby. It had happened on the day before Lizzie Cromwell was due to return Jodi to the Social Services. After her fight with Brenda Bosworth and acknowledgment by everyone except Miroslav himself that he was the father of her child, Lizzie had seemed to lose interest in Jodi. From nursing him and feeding and changing him, putting him in his cot, lifting him up again, and constantly cuddling him, she had rapidly passed to total indifference, and Jodi, unattended for the first time in his short life, for he had been newborn when he came to her, began to cry. He cried and sobbed and wailed, and when the crying mechanism ran out, his tape rewound and he began again.

"You can't just put him on the back burner, you know," Debbie scolded.

Colin said nothing. Nor did he make any attempt to immobilize Jodi by removing his batteries or even smothering him. At nine at night when the robot had been crying for six hours, he picked him up by the legs and smashed him against the bathroom wall. Bits of Jodi, his limbs and his mechanism and his fine handsome head, fell into the bath where Colin stamped on them.

Lizzie didn't care, she was bored with the whole thing, but she had to explain to the social worker. Colin wasn't there, it was his day at the Job Centre for signing on. The social worker said such a thing had never happened before and what sort of a mother would Lizzie make when she had a real baby? Of course she or her mother or her stepfather would have to pay for a replacement for Jodi, and did she realize how much a virtual baby cost?

Colin came home and said over his dead body would they make him pay for breaking a fucking stupid doll, and Debbie said she wouldn't either, on principle. It would probably be his dead body, anyway, Colin said, he'd already started coming out in a rash all around his waist and down his bum. No one appreciated the stress he'd suffered through having that thing in the house, and God knew what it would be like with a real baby.

News of this unjust claim on the part of Kingsmarkham's Social Services Department spread around Muriel Campden like a bushfire. Almost everyone took the Crowne-Cromwell side with the exception of the Mitchells, Monty Smith, and Maria Michaels. Monty Smith had been put on probation and required to pay an unimaginably large sum (which he had borrowed off Maria) for hitting Sergeant Fitch, and his view was that if he had been unfairly fined, why should others get off scot-free?

"How d'you make a petrol bomb?" Colin Crowne had said to Joe Hebden in the Rat and Carrot the night before.

"You what? You're barking."

"No, I saw it on the telly. It was somewhere like Algeria or Iraq, some place like that, and this lot was throwing petrol bombs at the government. I thought to myself, 'They ought to do that to the council, make them sit up.' "

A man neither of them had ever seen before said, "You fill up a bottle with petrol, like a milk bottle."

"We don't get milk bottles no more," said Colin.

"Right. You don't. Any bottle so long as it's not plastic. Fill it up and stuff the top with a bit of rag. You put paraffin on the rag, pink or blue paraffin, don't matter, and you light it with a match and throw it. You throw it right away, mind, no hanging about or you'll go up in flames. But you don't need the hassle. You want one, I can supply it. There's a market for them things."

"It was a joke," said Joe.

The man only laughed and said he'd buy them a drink, then he'd like to show them something.

Joe's wife, Charlene, took the call from her brother-in-law at seven-thirty next morning. That the child was still missing didn't much concern her. She knew that, everyone on Muriel Campden knew it, if the media didn't. But Orbe in hiding at Kingsmarkham Police Station! In luxurious accommodation! Charlene was fond of saying that the world was divided into those who don't and those who do, and she was a doer. She got dressed, grabbed an umbrella, and went out into the triangle, knocking on every door.

There are fat men who are solid like Carl Meeks, men with big shoulders and bellies like convex drums, taut as if corseted but corseted in vain, and there are fat men whose obesity seems liquid, seems to slosh around inside a thin membrane, so that a pinprick would reduce them to a collapsed balloon. Brian St. George, editor of the *Kingsmarkham Courier*, was of the latter sort, and his liquidity was currently flowing over the arms of Wexford's chair and seeping like a tide against the edge of the desk. His shirt was meant to be white but looked, as usual, as if it had been put through the wash in company with a pair of black jeans and a red T-shirt. If he had a tie with him, it must have been in his pocket. Since becoming bald, he had grown his remaining hair long so that if you eyed him from above, as Wexford was now doing, his head looked like a big white daisy with a pinkish-yellow center.

He had come to the police station when summoned, perhaps not much fancying the chief inspector's presence in the *Courier*'s offices, sat down in this chair, and suffered a grilling. St. George put up a spirited defense, half whining, half aggressive, and insisted he was obliged to "improvise" because Kingsmarkham police never told him anything.

"'The Kingsmarkham Six,'" said Wexford disgustedly.

"I didn't think it up," Brian St. George said as if in mitigation. "It's vindictive, it's revenge. You know you don't treat me fairly, Reg."

"Don't call me that."

"Sorry, I'm sure. I'd been under the impression we were all old friends here. You Reg, me Brian. It's formality gone mad the way you call me 'Mr. St. George.'"

"Call it what you like, but we'll keep to formality under this roof. If you believed Orbe was hidden here, what stopped you phoning your old friend and checking? No, don't bother to answer. You'd have got a denial and a denial was the last thing you wanted. You'd have had no story."

St. George shifted his floppy bulk an inch or two. A gap opened between two of his shirt buttons to reveal a circle of hairy pink skin. Wexford tried not to look at it. The editor of the *Kingsmarkham Courier* took a packet of Marlboros from his pocket, looked around for an ashtray, but in spite of not seeing one, lit his cigarette.

"This is a smoke-free zone."

"It never used to be," St. George protested. "Since when?"

"Since nine this morning." Wexford looked at his watch, which showed three minutes past. "Put that fag out, come on now."

Slowly and with an expression of bitter regret, St. George stubbed out his cigarette. "The story's in all the nationals," he pleaded. "It's the *Mail*'s front-page lead."

"Only because you told them. Apparently there have been calls coming in from them all night. Everything has to be denied. Orbe is not here. Orbe was here for precisely five minutes, sitting in a car in the car park. I suppose you saw him brought in."

"Guilty, my lord," said St. George, managing a boyish grin.

"And passed on your think piece to the media but too late for them to upstage the *Courier*."

"Well, what would you have done in my place, Reg? Sorry, I mean, Mr. Wexford."

"Behaved like a responsible citizen, but that's an alien concept to you, I know. It's too late now to do anything about it. We must hope there's no harm done. Where did you get the photograph of Sanchia?"

"I can't reveal my sources, you know that."

"I'm not talking about your sources, I'm talking about a photograph you must either have got from the child's parents or have taken yourself at some earlier time."

"It was when her dad got a big salary increase, a hundred K or whatever, and we ran a 'fat cats' story. You know, 'Can Airline Tycoon Justify Massive Pay Rise?'"

"What had that to do with Sanchia?"

"Human interest, you know that. Family values. Our photographer happened to see Mrs. D. out with the baby. As a matter of fact, that's how we knew her first name, going through the picture archives. They were calling her Sasha and Sarah and all sorts."

Wexford looked at him in disgust. "We shall not be offering any information to your newspaper in future on any subject whatsoever, so you will please instruct your staff that reporters who normally come in for the twice-weekly press release will no longer be welcome."

St. George got to his feet, his whole body on the wobble. "Now look here, you can't do this. This is outrageous, I'll go to the chief constable." Echoing Dora's words, he said, "That's like the Stasi, it's like the KGB."

"It may be like the Taliban for all I care."

Any further comments he might have made were cut off by the noise of breaking glass from below. It sounded as if something had struck one of the windows on a lower floor. Wexford went to his window and looked out. He stood there quite still for a moment, then he turned around and beckoned to Brian St. George. "Come and see the result of your handiwork."

By eight-thirty most of the population of Kingsmarkham and the villages knew that a child was missing and a notorious pedophile was under police protection. The rumor that Orbe had killed Sanchia Devenish, confessed to her murder, and been given refuge in Kingsmarkham Police Station to save him from being torn to pieces by all right-thinking local parents was started by a woman in Glebe Road. She was herself the mother of two, the elder of whom had been the victim of an indecent assault by a man from Stowerton. With her half sister Jackie Flay, Jackie's daughter Kaylee, and half a dozen of her neighbors, she set forth on foot—it wasn't more than a quarter of a mile—and halfway there encountered a contingent from the Stowerton end of the town. This band of protesters all carried paper banners, rapidly improvised, bearing the legends WE WANT ORBE and SAVE OUR BABIES. If it had only continued to rain, as Wexford said later, the whole demonstration might have been avoided, as many of these people would have been reluctant to get wet. But the rain had stopped at a quarter to eight, giving place to an angrily blue sky, bright sunshine, and a strong northwest wind.

The two groups met, by chance, outside the Job Centre where they paused to muster their forces. Truants from Kingsmarkham Comprehensive, the usual dispirited teenagers, were already sitting on the wall outside. They were half-asleep on account of being got up early by their parents and sent to school. Nothing ever happened in this dump, according to them, so they were delighted to be asked to join the protest. Just as they were all on the march again, turning into the High Street, the bus from Stowerton stopped outside the Olive and Dove and David Hebden got off it with Katrina, her daughters, Georgina and Sanchia, and his sons, Grant and Jason, the children having been kept from school for a more important activity.

Recognizing their purpose from the sandwich board worn by Grant (a cutout of two children holding hands with SAVE THE LITTLE CHILDREN on the front and ALL PEDOS FOR THE CHOP on the back), the Glebe Road group welcomed them with open arms, and the whole party, now thirty strong, marched up the High Street past St. Peter's Church. They were such an orderly group that WPC Lydia Wingate and PC Leslie Wilson, out on the beat, held up the traffic at the Kingsbrook bridge to let them cross the road.

Meanwhile, a bigger crowd was streaming out of the Muriel Campden into York Street. Missing for various reasons such as pregnancy, simple cautiousness, genuine illness, and fear of paying more fines or even imprisonment, were Lizzie Cromwell, Sue Ridley and Pete McGregor, and Monty Smith. But Brenda Bosworth was there with Miroslav Zlatic in the lead followed by Hebdens, Keenans, Carl and Linda Meeks, Maria Michaels and Shirley Mitchell, and Tasneem Fowler's Terry with Kim and Lee. Many of them were carrying what looked like full shopping bags, but there was nothing particularly suspicious about this, and when Lydia Wingate saw them, she even failed to notice that they were the Muriel Campden residents she had encountered the previous weekend.

They joined up with the Stowerton and Glebe Road protest outside the Heaven Spent shopping mall. Joe and David Hebden were each overcome with emotion at the sight of his brother and fell into one another's arms, embracing and patting backs, both having reached their midthirties without doing such a thing in their lives before. This show of fraternal love put heart into the fifty or so people who had assembled, and they cheered before marching on toward the police station.

But orderliness had ended with the arrival of the Muriel Campden cohort. Here was the contrast between the effete and weary old town and the vital and energetic new, and it was as if the old had received a stimulating injection that put fire into their veins, for they began to sing as they walked, their voices low at first but rising in a steady crescendo.

To the tune of "Stand by Your Man" they chanted, "Stand by your kids, and tell them that you love them..." Who had been responsible for this inspired translation of Tammy Wynette's song no one seemed to know, but later the consensus was that it had been Brenda Bosworth.

So they proceeded along the east end of the High Street, a troop of people all between the ages of two and forty, a company of the young, the youngest in pushchairs and the oldest with a balding head and incipient belly, all singing that perhaps best known of country songs, if an old-fashioned one to most of them. They carried their bags and their banners, and the bright sun shone on them and the wind blew the women's hair all over the place, and just after nine o'clock they came up to the railings outside Kingsmarkham Police Station. The gates were open, the car park, which could just be glimpsed around the side, was full of cars, and there was no one about.

The protest hesitated. Carl Meeks, questioned later by the police, said that they had been taken aback to see no one. The emptiness of the place was uncanny. And even the big double doors were shut. If someone had come out, some "responsible officer," they could have put their case to him or her. They would have told the officer, said Carl Meeks, to take Orbe elsewhere, anywhere so that he was finally removed from Kingsmarkham. As it was, no one came out. But for the cars, there might have been no one inside.

Who led them on to the outer courtyard where stood just one police car and one unmarked car? Again it was suggested it must have been Brenda Bosworth, though nobody could remember. One thing was certain. Once they began to pass through the gateway, they stopped singing and a silence fell. It seemed to Shirley Mitchell that the whole town was hushed, traffic became soundless, and even the blackbird in the maple tree on the forecourt ceased his song. In silence they walked to within a few yards of the steps and the double doors, and there they stopped to allow the woman they called their spokesperson to pass through. This was Brenda Bosworth, who had somehow uncharacteristically found herself at the back of the crowd and had to make her way to the front of it.

While she was doing so, a window in the police station opened and Sergeant Joel Fitch put his head out. What he would have said, how he would have admonished them, advised them to go home or take themselves off elsewhere, was never known, for the sight of him to Maria

Michaels was like the lighting of a fuse. At once she recognized him not so much as the author of Monty Smith's troubles as the cause of his borrowing everything she had in her Co-operative Bank account to pay his fine. She plunged her hand into the Marks & Spencer bag she was carrying, pulled out a brick, and hurled it at Sergeant Fitch.

Maria had been in her early youth the County of Sussex Women's Putting the Shot Champion of 1984, and she could still throw farther and better than most men. Luckily for him and for her, she failed to hit Fitch, but only because he ducked. The brick went through the casement to the left of where his head had been. A short, shocked silence was succeeded by loud cheers, and the chant was taken up with renewed vigor.

"We want Orbe, we want Orbe, Orbe, Orbe!"

The tune this time was that of "Colonel Bogey" and it brought every passerby to a halt outside the gates. Perhaps this audience stimulated them, for a hail of cans and stones followed that first brick, but only one missile struck a window and broke the glass. The rest hit brickwork and fell harmlessly into the bed of overblown wallflowers at the foot of the wall. But they had the effect of bringing half a dozen police officers running out of the double doors toward the crowd. At the same time Superintendent Rogers opened the French windows in the middle of the front of the building and stepped out onto the balcony, holding a loud-hailer. He was accompanied by two other officers, one on either side of him.

"We want Orbe, we want Orbe, Orbe, Orbe!"

When the police station was designed in the early sixties, the balcony was tacked on for just this purpose: for a senior policeman to stand on and admonish, harangue, or reassure a deputation. Jokes had been made about it, references to palaces of justice in small South American states, places where revolution might be expected. It had never been used until today, and George Rogers had to seek assistance from the nearest help available, in this case DC Archbold, to get the window open. When he finally stepped out, he saw a much larger crowd than he had expected, as many as fifty people, all held back by his own officers straining against them with linked hands. No more missiles had been thrown, and at the sight of Rogers, with Fitch on one side of him and Archbold on the other, the chanting fell to a low mutter, an angry buzz like that of swarming bees.

On the floor above, at the window, Wexford stood with Brian St. George. He had opened the window, having heard what had happened below and being anxious not to be hit by flying glass. The last person he wanted with him in this situation was St. George, but he could hardly send the man out of the building into, so to speak, the jaws of the protest and certainly not leave him to roam the police station, picking up whatever he might devour.

Once, Rogers, or his equivalent, would have read the Riot Act. Instead, he said into his loud-hailer, "Those persons who have thrown missiles will be dealt with accordingly. Arrests will be made. The rest of you must go home. Orbe is not here and has never been here. No child has been killed. You have been misled by false rumors in newspapers. Orbe presents no threat whatsoever to your children. Your children are perfectly safe."

"Where is he, then?" called someone from the crowd.

"I'm not at liberty to tell you that," said Rogers.

"He's in there with you! You're protecting him!"

"We want Orbe, we want Orbe, Orbe, Orbe!"

"How would you like it if a child murderer and rapist came and lived next door to your kids? Is that right? Is that fair?" This was Brenda Bosworth. "How would you like it if the police protected him and made the mums and dads criminals?"

Much as he disliked her, Wexford had to concede that she had a point. How would he have liked it when his daughters were small? Come to that, how would Rogers feel himself, he who had married late and had two children under ten? Rogers had handled it badly. Wexford wouldn't have said that aloud to anyone but Burden and then in the strictest privacy, but Burden wasn't there; for some reason he was late in this morning. Imagine the results of criticizing Rogers to St. George! Rogers should go inside now, he thought, leave it now. Make his arrests, if he could find the guilty parties. He thought what a ridiculous word *missile* was, that it had lost its original meaning of something sent by throwing and was now irretrievably associated with a kind of rocket, a projectile bomb, nuclear or otherwise, wielded in war situations. It was strange, he reflected afterward, that he had been thinking this at that very moment and stranger still that he and he alone witnessed what happened next.

He heard from below Rogers's parting shot, a somewhat feeble, "I repeat, Orbe is not here. He is no longer living among you and he is not in this police station."

The men on the forecourt coaxed the crowd back, easing them through the gates and out onto the pavement. The chanting had stopped, had died away to a low muttering. Rogers went inside, followed by Fitch and Archbold, and the door to the balcony closed. Wexford was about to shut the window. Instead he opened it wider and looked down.

DS Ted Hennessy had come out of the double doors and was crossing the forecourt toward the gates. To make the threatened arrests? Or simply because at that moment, previously out of sight and earshot in the back of the building, he had come out in all innocence for some quite other purpose? Afterward Wexford bitterly regretted having taken his eyes from the protesters to look at Hennessy and thus having missed seeing what he was later told had happened. He saw the thing loop out of the crowd, though, saw it leave an unidentifiable hand, and he cried out, too late, "Watch out! Get down on the ground!"

The bottle was alight, he saw the thin sheet of flame as it flew and, although it was well below him, ducked, dragging St. George with him to the floor. If he hadn't, the explosion would have knocked him off his feet. It was thunderous, deafening, a roar rather than a crash, a great hissing sound like a tornado sucking up air. But not loud enough to drown the scream from the forecourt. A horrible cry it was, scarcely human, the noise you imagined an animal dying by violence might make. Wexford rolled over onto his back. He reached for St. George but the man was up, craning out of the window, crying at the top of his voice, "I saw it! I saw it all!"

Wexford got to his feet. Broken glass was everywhere, crunching under his shoes. The window was gone. Below him a car on the forecourt was burning, a column of flame hissing up into the blue air. The crowd had shrunk, people squatting or even lying on the pavement. Wexford saw Burden come in from the street, come in on his way to work and, his hands up to his face, walk slowly across the now empty forecourt. Behind him, their presence perhaps unknown to him, streamed the press pack with their cameras and their microphones.

It was too late to do anything for the man who had been close to that car. He had disappeared. He was in that inferno, burning along with the metal and the chrome and the leather, somewhere inside that hissing blaze, that eddying spiral of white smoke and black smoke, and the breath-snatching stench of burning petrol.

A groan rose from the crowd. The chain of officers continued to hold them back. Wexford found himself speechless, incapable even of making the mourning, regretful moan that came from the people on the pavement. He watched the press approach, cameras flashing, heard in the distance the sound of the fire engines' sirens, and then, turning to St. George, did something he had never done to a man before—grabbed him by the collar of his jacket as one might take a disobedient dog by the scruff of its neck and propelled him toward the door.

"I saw it all!" gasped St. George, half-strangled. "What a piece of luck!"

CHAPTER 14

The death of Ted Hennessy had done nothing to inhibit the media. Their cars filled Ploughman's Lane and Savesbury Road and Winchester Drive, and they set up camp in the front garden of Woodland Lodge. Wexford held an impromptu press conference and did his best to answer questions on the lines of "Why have you been keeping this disappearance dark?" and "Can you be certain Thomas Orbe has nothing to do with the missing child?"

In vain he repeated the simple truth: that Orbe had never, in the course of his miserable career, been known to show interest in girls. He had convictions for abusing boys and had been imprisoned for the manslaughter of a boy. In the original meaning of the word he was truly a pedophile.

"He got married, didn't he?" one young woman from a national tabloid asked. "He's got a daughter."

"His victims have always been male," said Barry Vine, who was on the platform with Wexford. "Orbe has nothing to do with the disappearance of Sanchia Devenish."

Those of them who weren't laying siege to the Devenishes or on Hennessy's widow's doorstep, directed their onslaught to Suzanne Orbe, convalescent at 16 Oberon Road. An unfounded rumor had got about that Suzanne was one of her father's early victims, Suzanne must have been an abused child, wretched copartner in incest. Her head still swathed in bandages, she came out from the boarded-up house through the makeshift door and screamed at them. "He never laid a finger on me, you filthy buggers! Poor old sod'd have never touched those dirty kids if my mum hadn't gone off and left him. That was what done it, that was what turned him bonkers for dirty kids. You fuck off the lot of you and leave us alone!"

Up in Ploughman's Lane, Fay Devenish had picked up the local paper off the doormat at seven-thirty. Even before Stephen Devenish had seen it, reporters were ringing his doorbell, pounding on his door, and his phone had started ringing and went on ringing nonstop. He knew better than to answer the door. One of the media people climbed up onto the garage roof and tried to get in through a fanlight. He should have had Kaylee Flay with him, as Wexford remarked when told about it.

Devenish called a taxi to take him to the police station. If he got his own car out, the pack would descend on him and maybe gain entrance to the house. The cab company was called All the Sixes and its vehicles regularly plied between Kingsmarkham town, Kingsmarkham Station, and the villages. The driver couldn't get through the media people and the parked cars. He left his cab and went on foot. Reporters surrounded him and some clung to him, begging to know who his fare was to be, where was he taking him, and to give them a moment to talk to Sanchia's father.

The cabdriver felt as if he were in a film. He thought of asking the reporters for a considerable sum to hold Mr. Devenish captive, then he thought of losing his job as a result, and besides, the hero—sheriff or principal witness or driver of the stagecoach—must behave heroically, keep silent, be strong, and stride boldly to the rescue. So he did his best to ignore them, marched up to the front door, and rang the bell. First Devenish put his head out of a window, then he came out. The cabdriver said soothingly, "Now you keep close to me, sir, and don't say a word and you'll be okay. I'm going to take your arm and get you through this bunch of paparazzi—you won't mind that, will you?"

Devenish said he wouldn't mind that, or rather shouted that he wouldn't, for everything he said was drowned by the press pack's questions, their running feet and the clicks and flashes of their cameras. The cabdriver took charge, not neglecting to get his own scowling face into the pictures as he masterfully steered Devenish to where the cab waited.

Shivering, Devenish sank into the back, said, "Thank you. Thank you very much. Frankly, I don't know what I'd have done without you."

The pack followed but the driver managed to lose them. When they got to the police station, Devenish gave him an enormous tip. After

Devenish had gone in through the damaged double doors, the driver drove twice in a circle around the forecourt to get a good look at the broken windows and blackened front of the police station. If he got the chance later in the day, he'd come back with a camera.

Stephen Devenish asked for Wexford. No, the chief inspector wasn't expecting him but Devenish thought he'd see him and there was no way he was going out there again like a fox running into the jaws of a pack of hounds. The desk sergeant sent him up in the lift and said Wexford would come out to meet him. The first press cars arrived on the forecourt by the time he reached the second floor.

In Wexford's room Devenish didn't complain about media intrusion, but he shouted just the same and Wexford saw for the first time signs of that famous temper. Devenish crashed his fists on the desk. "Has that pedophile got my child?"

"Please try to keep calm, Mr. Devenish."

"Just answer me!"

"Sit down, please. That's right. I understand your anger. I would feel the same myself in the circumstances. But, no, Orbe has not got your child."

"How can you know that? How can you possibly know?"

"We kept her disappearance a secret because we feared the very thing that has happened. It's an unfortunate coincidence that Orbe was present in the neighborhood at the time she went missing, but that's all it is. There is no connection—I hope you understand that."

"Where is he now, then?"

"I can't tell you that. I'm sorry. But he is not in this building, or indeed in this town." Wexford was tired of telling people that boys had been Orbe's quarry, but he repeated to Sanchia's father what he had said so many times before. "Thomas Orbe isn't interested in girls. He's a homosexual pedophile."

"How disgusting! It makes you sick to your stomach."

Too bad, Wexford thought, you can't have it both ways. "We're doing everything we can to find Sanchia," he said, "and I can tell you, which I hope may be a comfort to you, that she is not in the hands of any known pedophile on our lists. I'm talking nationwide. No pedophile has her. In these cases, the culprit is very often a disturbed person, usually a woman, who has recently lost her own child or who cannot herself have children.

That is why I was so anxious to get from you and your wife the names of all your friends and acquaintances, on the chance that such a woman might be among them."

Wexford thought he detected a faint difference in the man's expression, no more than a flicker, a tiny change in the iris of his eyes, a barely perceptible tightening of the mouth. Rather than pursue it, Wexford changed the subject from the possible kidnapper of Sanchia back to the situation in Woodland Lodge on the night she was taken. "It's not quite a question, Mr. Devenish, of who might have a key or who might otherwise gain entrance to your home but rather of how anyone could do so without disturbing you or your wife or your sons and without Sanchia making a noise. Can you really tell me that any stranger could take your little girl out of her bed in the night, wake her and lift her up, and she not cry out or call to you?"

"I don't know."

Wexford didn't want to ask it but he had to. He had to establish once and for all just how impaired Sanchia's intelligence and faculties were. "She can cry out, I suppose? You have said she talks very little, but she *can* speak?"

"Of course she can," Devenish said, quite hotly for him. "She's not dumb. What are you saying? That she's some sort of idiot?"

"No, Mr. Devenish, I'm not saying that. But you must admit yourself that the whole picture is a very strange one. Has any doctor or psychologist given an opinion on why Sanchia isn't talking at the age of two and three-quarters? Has anyone offered an explanation?"

"We haven't asked." Devenish was calm now, the color had receded from his face, and the charm was back. He spoke lightly, with his habitual half-smile. "We never thought it necessary. She's a late developer, that's all. Forgive me, but is this to the point? Finding out why she doesn't speak isn't going to find *her.*"

"I like mysteries to be solved," Wexford said simply. "I should like to solve the mystery of these threatening letters you've received. Envy makes enemies and there are plenty who must envy you. For instance, when you secured your present job and later when you received a very large salary increase, there must have been people who were passed over to make way for you. Perhaps there are those who feel they have a grievance against the airline for some real or imagined shortcoming. They might transfer this grievance onto you as the airline's representative. I'm sure you understand what I'm saying."

"Oh, yes, of course I do. But there's nothing."

On Devenish's transparent face, lying or truth-telling immediately showed. Now he was lying. Wexford was sure of it. And there was a stubbornness, too, revealed in those dark eyes. It wasn't just a matter of lying but of a decision not to expand on what he had said. There was nothing, he had no enemies, and that was it. There could be no room for argument or persuasion.

"You hardly seem to realize," Devenish said, but perfectly politely, "that the people who send this sort of letter are mad. They don't have to have a reason. They read something in the paper and that's enough to trigger them off. They're mad."

"I realize it, sir, I realize that this is often, though not invariably, the case. And now I'd like you to tell me something you may find similarly irrelevant but I assure you it isn't." Wexford paused, looking steadily at the other man. "Do you have a second home?"

"What, a cottage in the country, d'you mean? We live in the country. And we don't have a flat in London either."

"And it would be even less necessary to ask you if an obviously devoted husband such as yourself has, or has ever had since his marriage, a relationship with another woman?"

If Devenish noticed the edge of irony to Wexford's voice and his uncharacteristic use of the third person, he didn't show it. "Chief Inspector, you must be joking." Devenish smiled, at the same time shaking his head as at an incredibly tall story. "You can't be serious."

"I'm perfectly serious, sir," Wexford said in a hard voice. "I don't find any of this amusing. A man has died a horrible death here this morning. You'll excuse me if I concentrate on that for the time being."

The remains of Ted Hennessy lay in the mortuary. He had been thirty-four years old, for four of those years attached to the Regional Crime Squad at Myringham. Married, with two children, as the media put it. The notice of his death in a national newspaper, not the front-page story but the announcement in the Births, Marriages, and Deaths columns, said that he had been the adored husband of Laura and father of Jonathan and Kate.

Someone in that crowd had thrown the petrol bomb that killed him. He wouldn't have been in Kingsmarkham at all in the ordinary course of events. He was a reinforcement for Wexford's beleaguered team. You could say Orbe and the Devenishes were responsible for his being there, which was an irony if you like.

"I don't see any irony," said Burden.

"No, maybe not," Wexford said. "I really meant he wasn't here for anything real. He was here through people making a nuisance of themselves."

He didn't explain what he meant. He had a date with Brian St. George at midday. The editor of the *Kingsmarkham Courier* had failed to turn up for the press conference and Wexford thought he knew why. At any rate, he guessed or hoped he knew why. St. George had "seen it all" for himself. He had had a piece of luck and seen the petrol bomb thrown.

"I'm not saying I actually saw it, Reg," St. George began. He looked nervous. "Not to say *saw* it. That's not exactly what I meant."

"What did you mean, then?"

"Well, I saw it hit its target."

"By its 'target' I suppose you mean Detective Sergeant Hennessy," Wexford said, barely suppressing rage. "For a journalist you've a singularly unfortunate way of expressing yourself. Is that what you're going to write in that rag of yours?"

If it was possible to hurt St. George's feelings, this could only be done by impugning his writing skills. He winced a little. He put his hands on his head, on the daisy-center bald spot, and looked at Wexford loweringly. "I never saw who threw it. I never meant that. If I had," St. George added recklessly, "I wouldn't tell. I don't want to be a marked man, not in my position I don't, Reg."

"Don't call me Reg."

Hennessy's widow, Laura, when told of his death, said, "I always knew the job would kill him, but not like this, not like this."

By next morning the police station forecourt had been cleaned up, the burnt-out car—once the property of DC Archbold—removed, and the broken windows boarded up. Several arrests were made, and half a dozen people, including Brenda Bosworth, Maria Michaels, and David

Hebden, appeared in court on charges of causing criminal damage. Barry Vine and Lynn Fancourt were obliged to give up the hunt for Sanchia Devenish and, with two members of the Regional Crime Squad, track down whoever among the crowd on the pavement had thrown the petrol bomb that killed Hennessy.

It was one thing for no witnesses to come forward when throwing a brick and breaking a window was in question, quite another when a man had died as a result. Not everyone was as chicken, as Wexford put it, as Brian St. George. People were anxious to talk, and volunteers with information came from all over Stowerton, Kingsmarkham, and the Muriel Campden Estate. The difficulty was that no one could be exactly sure who had the petrol bomb, still less who had thrown it. Hennessy's killer had been in the midst of them, was one of them, had marched with them up the High Street, talked to them and chanted "Stand by Your Kids" with them, that everyone knew. It must have been so, but there they stopped and looked helplessly at Barry and Lynn. They couldn't absolutely say it was so-and-so, they wouldn't swear to it if it came to swearing, it was just that they *thought*...After all, you don't want to say something's absolutely certain when it could end with the person getting life imprisonment.

Andy Honeyman, landlord of the Rat and Carrot, was profuse with his information. As Barry remarked later to Michael Burden, you'd have thought he'd been there, seen it all, and taken notes and photographs. In the end it came down to a conversation he had overheard in his saloon bar. "So this guy says, 'How d'you make a petrol bomb?' I ask you, you wouldn't take it seriously, would you? And this other guy, he didn't take it seriously. 'You what?' he says, 'You're bonkers' or 'You're barking' or something. And too right, I thought, never imagining what would come of it. And then another guy comes up."

"Wait a minute," said Vine, "I can't sort out all these guys. You don't know their names, I suppose?"

"Of course I know their names," said Andy Honeyman. "The first guy, he was Colin whatever, Cromwell—no, Crowne. Her ex was called Cromwell, this one's Crowne. And the other guy was Joe Hebden. Both of them come from that blot on the landscape, the Muriel Campden Estate. Well, as I say, another guy comes up—"

"What was *his* name?"

"Don't ask me. I never saw him before. I don't know who he was, but I know what he said. He told them how to make a petrol bomb—get a bottle, fill it with petrol, I leave it to your imagination. He said there was a market for the things, meaning folks would buy them, I reckon. Then he said making them was a hassle when he could supply them. There was dozens listening. I mean, there was that chap Fowler, the one with a blackie wife who's left him and gone to that bunch of slags down the road here, The Hide they call it. I know what I'd call it."

Barry interviewed Colin Crowne and Joe Hebden and Terry Fowler. Colin said where would he get petrol, he hadn't got a car, as if possession of a motor vehicle were the only criterion for access to a fuel pump. He didn't remember the conversation in the Rat and Carrot, which he believed was an invention of Andy Honeyman. Anyway, he hadn't been with the protest, he'd been in bed with shingles, from which he was still suffering as anyone could see with half an eye. Joe couldn't remember the conversation, and Terry said he had heard the word "bomb" but he couldn't recall any guy coming up and giving advice how to make one. But Colin's rhetorical question gave Barry an idea, and next day he began making inquiries at every petrol station in the town and its environs.

Lynn drove home, left her car, and out on the Savesbury Road, waited, looking forlorn, until she accepted a lift from the fourth driver and first woman driver who offered. She hadn't gray hair, or rather she had but it was dyed red, she was thin rather than thickset and certainly no more than forty-five, and she drove Lynn back into Kingsmarkham, leaving her where she asked to be let down, outside St. Peter's. Lynn had to get a taxi home and wondered if she could get the fare off expenses.

The inquest on Ted Hennessy was opened and adjourned. Wexford and Burden came away from it together, and Wexford put on the thin plastic mac he had bought many years before for a holiday in Ireland. "I don't seem to be able to think of anything but that poor chap," he said. "It's what his wife said, not so much his death, though that's bad enough, but the manner of it. To be burned to death—you can't imagine much worse."

"We'll get him," said Burden, looking askance at the mac. "No doubt about it. Him or her, we'll get them."

"I'm afraid I don't find revenge much consolation, Mike."

They walked down the High Street, where the sun shone brightly on wet pavements, on puddles, on lakes of water half across the roadway. A car, passing too fast, sent up a sheet of spray that just missed Burden's trouser legs. The driver, for no known reason, leaned across the passenger seat at the red light and shook his fist at them.

"Let's go in the Europlate and have a coffee," said Wexford.

The Europlate had opened six months before. Its name had nothing to do with European Monetary Union but referred solely to its menu, a suitably eclectic offering of the so-called principal dishes from the cuisine of every country in the EU. You could have Swedish meatballs, Spanish omelette, Greek salad, Irish stew, German sausage, *croque monsieur*, and the Roast Beef of Old England. The trouble was that everything tasted of stir-fry. The cook was reputed to be Chinese, though no one claimed to have seen him and verified this. Last time he was in there, preferring the place over the police station canteen, Wexford had asked if they did Turkish delight and got a rather surly negative response.

The place was done up in yellow and blue. Tablecloths were dark blue and every table napkin had in its center the ring of stars that is the emblem of the Union. They ordered coffee and were each offered a complimentary Danish pastry. Burden refused with an incredulous smile, but Wexford had difficulty in resisting this sugary, nut-sprinkled, apricot-jam-filled confection and eventually succumbed. "I'm going to have it," he said. "I know I shouldn't, but I need the comfort. It's been such a bloody week, hasn't it? There'll be an inquiry into what happened last Friday morning, and the outcome will be a resigning matter for poor old Rogers."

"No one could have foreseen that petrol bomb. Who'd imagine petrol bombs in this place? It's not Seoul, it's not"—Burden hesitated, trying to think where else it might not be—"Jakarta."

Wexford started on his Danish pastry. It was the first of its kind he had eaten for more than a year and would probably be the last for another year. "I went to Seaward Air yesterday, as you know. The headquarters at Gatwick, not the Brighton one or the office here. I talked to Devenish's PA and his secretary—two different women, by the way, he's very grand—and to the present general manager. They all like him, they all say he's a good employer, very fair, pleasant without being too matey."

"And?"

"Well, yes, there's an 'and.' The secretary talked about his bad temper, of which I saw some signs myself the other day. She's seen it directed at others, though not at her. Apparently, there was an incident when he threw some chap out of his office. Fellow forced his way in, making complaints about some relative of his being badly treated by Seaward. It was two or three years ago and before her time, but she'd heard he physically threw the man out—neck and crop, as they say. The rumor was that the chap broke a rib. But it's all very vague. She doesn't know his name and I couldn't find anyone there who did."

"You make him sound popular," said Burden. "You paint a very different picture from Trevor Ferry's."

"As you said yourself, it's understandable Ferry hasn't got a good word for him." Wexford finished his Danish pastry and picked up in his fingers the last crumbs off his plate. He said quietly, first glancing over his shoulder, "I believe Devenish abducted his own daughter."

Burden looked at him and didn't say anything.

"I don't know why he did or where he took her or where she is now, but I believe she's safe and that he's hidden her."

"I suppose I've been thinking the same thing," Burden said.

"He blusters too much, he *cried.* Maybe it was pretend crying, as the children say. I didn't see any tears. Sometimes he seems upset about his daughter's disappearance and at others he doesn't seem to care."

Burden nodded. "Hidden her with someone? You must mean that."

"First of all," Wexford said, "I considered a girlfriend. He's good-looking, he's young, he's well-off. His wife looks older than her age and she looks tired. And he goes on too much about his happy marriage. The existence of a girlfriend wouldn't have surprised me."

"You mean he was planning to leave his wife for this girlfriend but wanted to keep the child? The child is hidden with her in some secret hideaway he can afford because he's rich?"

"Something like that. But there is no girlfriend, Mike. Someone among the dozens we've talked to would know of it if he was having an affair. I know everything there is to know about him, I even know he met his wife at a staff Christmas party when he was chief executive at Southern Cross Rail Link and she was the chairman's PA. There's not a breath of scandal about him. He's never even been known to have lunch with a woman. One of the ticket-desk managers at Seaward was sure that if he spent a night a year away from his family, that was the maximum and then only because he was absolutely obliged to attend a meeting in Brussels or Frankfurt.

"He goes to sung eucharist at St. Peter's on Sunday mornings, the whole family goes. He never misses parents' evenings at the boys' school, and he frequently takes them to sports events. He gave his wife a sapphire-and-diamond eternity ring on her thirty-fifth birthday and a car on her thirty-sixth a week or so ago. She may look old and tired—sorry to sound so callous—but he loves her." Wexford wiped his mouth on the EU logo. "He seems to be one of those rare men who are totally monogamous, not from necessity or prudence but by inclination."

"I assure you I'm monogamous by inclination," said Burden hotly.

"You know what I mean. He wouldn't even fancy a woman he saw in the street. In other words, he doesn't commit adultery in his heart. He's a devoted husband. Do you want another coffee?"

"May as well. But this saint you're describing kidnapped his daughter, who is incidentally also his beloved wife's daughter?"

"He's not a saint. Saints aren't arrogant and superior and insensitive to the feelings of others, and he's all those things," Wexford said. "The kidnapper, as you call him, was well enough known to the child for her not to cry out when she saw him. He knew exactly where she was. He had no need to break into the house because he was already in it." Wexford signaled to the waitress, holding up the empty blue-and-yellow coffeepot. "He drove her away in a car Mrs. Wingrave opposite didn't recognize and therefore assumed to be a stranger's. She didn't recognize it *because it was the car Devenish had given to his wife only two days before.*"

Burden looked unimpressed. "Right, and where did he take the child in his wife's new car?"

"Not to a relative or a friend. Not to a girlfriend. That car's being gone over now. Peach and Cox went up there first thing and brought it back here. According to Mrs. Devenish, it hasn't been driven since it was given to her. She hasn't been out of the house since Sanchia disappeared. So we shall soon see." Wexford filled their two cups with fresh coffee. He picked up a Danish pastry crumb with a nut on it off the plate and put it in his mouth. "Sanchia would have sat up in that car, she wouldn't have been lying in a cot, she's nearly three."

"In which case she should have been strapped into a child seat."

"I dare say he didn't bother about that. God, how irrelevant can you get? It doesn't matter whether she was in a child seat or not, she was *there* and must have left traces of herself behind—hairs, fluff from her clothes, fingerprints. Now, he wouldn't dare be away from the house for long in case his wife woke up. He's the one who takes sleeping tablets, not she, though I don't suppose he took one that night. So I think he only drove Sanchia a short way and was met by someone else in a car, an accomplice, who took her from him and drove her to wherever she now is."

"Not in the river or a grave, we hope," said Burden.

"Who knows? He came down here in a taxi and he came in rage and despair. He put his head down on the kitchen table and wept. People weep from rage and despair and remorse though, don't they? Not simply from grief."

Entering the police station, they met PC Dixon, whose golden curls had been even more rigorously trimmed since the smuggling out of Orbe. He had been much embarrassed by the taunts of Colin Crowne and Monty Smith, even more than he was by the inquiry frequently put to him as to how were things in Dock Green. He said to Wexford, who was taking off the plastic mac, "I've been looking for you, sir. I think you wanted to know the whereabouts of your raincoat. It never left the estate. I gave it to Jim Donaldson while he was parked in Titania Road waiting for you."

Just before midday Barry Vine called at the last petrol station on his list. This tiny place in the middle of the village of Bredeway was designed to blend in, insofar as this was possible, with its rural surroundings. Its two pumps were painted green, there were tubs of azaleas and pansies on its forecourt, and the building itself had a thatched roof. The proprietor, who was inside at the till, presiding over a counter filled with Snickers bars and Polo mints at one end and CDs and Disney videos at the other, asked Vine if he liked the setup and described it as environmentally friendly. Vine hadn't much hope of the place but he said he was looking for someone who might have come in on the previous Friday, quite early in the morning, before eight at any rate, and brought a vessel to be filled with petrol, some sort of can, perhaps, or bucket.

"You mean their car had run out of juice on the road somewhere?"

"Maybe. That would be the reason they gave."

The proprietor asked a lot of questions, called to his wife, who was around the back, asked her questions, offered Vine a selection of theories, and finally said that it couldn't have been the Bredeway Garage because they didn't open before eight-thirty in the mornings.

Vine went back to Kingsmarkham and picked up DC Archbold. The two of them started on the second phase of the project, calling on hardware stores that sold paraffin.

The doors of the big double garage stood open. Both cars were gone, Devenish's and his wife's. The front lawn was covered in red petals, the blossoms fallen from the chestnut tree. Wexford rang the bell and, when no one came, rang it again. A casement opened upstairs and Fay Devenish put her head out.

"May we have a word, Mrs. Devenish?"

She didn't want to let them in, you could tell that, but she didn't know how to refuse. The inability of most ordinary middle-class people to say no was an enormous advantage to the police, Wexford often thought. One of the claims of psychotherapy was that it taught patients that it wasn't necessary or desirable for their egos and their peace of mind always to accept. Saying yes was propitiatory, a weak desire to placate and ingratiate. He sometimes wondered what would be the effect on police work if a generation grew up briefed to turn down requests and invitations.

Fay Devenish manifestly wasn't one of them. She didn't quite say how nice it was to see them, but she hovered on the brink. Her husband had gone in to work just for the morning. Would they care for coffee or tea? Would they mind sitting in the study because she hadn't yet "done" the living room? She was in housewife's garb to the extent that Wexford hadn't seen for forty years. An old-fashioned wraparound overall covered her blouse and skirt, and her head was tied up in a turban made from a red-checked duster.

Her face was pale and shiny, untouched by makeup. Presumably, the lipstick and powder and mascara would go on after the housework was done and her husband due home. Yes, she would dress and paint, and set her hair like a wife in a fifties magazine advertisement. ("Always be fresh and neat for him, and put on something pretty when he comes home after a hard day's work.") Then he reminded himself that her little child, her only daughter, her three-year-old, was missing, and it gave him a shock; all this was so *inappropriate.*

They went into the study where, at his last visit, she had been lying on the leather sofa. Now she sat down on the edge of it and looked at them expectantly. She so nearly fitted the description he had given of her to Burden, tired and looking older than her age, that for a moment he had asked himself what on earth a clever, handsome, wealthy, and successful man like Devenish saw in her. Her face was prematurely lined and her eyelids drooped. What would she look like at fifty?

"Mrs. Devenish," he began, "I believe you know we're examining your new car, subjecting it to certain laboratory tests. You haven't driven it yourself, but could anyone else have done so?"

"I wouldn't lend my car to anyone," she said in her soft, almost childish voice.

"Not even to your husband?"

He thought she winced—but why would she? "My husband has his own car. He wouldn't need to drive mine."

"I think you have a friend called Jane Andrews," said Burden.

She hesitated. "I used to have."

"But not any longer?" Wexford watched her face for a sign of dismay or concealment, but there was none. "What broke up the friendship? Do you mind telling us?"

"We grew apart. Friends do."

"How did you meet in the first place?"

Her sudden distress was unexpected. "Why do I have to tell you all this? What's it got to do with my little girl?"

"When did you last see Miss Andrews, Mrs. Devenish?"

"Years ago. Six or seven years." Suddenly she grew voluble. "You ask how we met. We did a business studies diploma at the same time. Seventeen years ago now. The fact is that my husband dislikes her. He disapproves of her; she's been married twice and divorced twice, you know." She must have become aware of their puzzled looks. Was a friend's complex marital history a reason for breaking a friendship? "I don't think it's possible in a marriage to keep a friend if the other one doesn't like them," she said, sounding confused, "not whether it's the husband or the wife, do you?"

"I'd like to go back to the night Sanchia disappeared, Mrs. Devenish."

Wexford looked at her in silence for a moment. With her old-fashioned ways and her antiquated ideas of marriage, her housewife's uniform and her nervousness, a fear of an unspecified something that seemed to pervade her, she was a mystery, and as he had said to her husband, he liked mysteries to be solved. Fear, when it is lived with daily, abates only to a certain extent and then not for long, eats up its victim, ages her and wears her out, may drive her mad, kills her before her time. He had seen it happen before.

"You don't strike me," he said, "as a person likely to be a heavy sleeper. Of course I don't know, I'm not a doctor, but I would say you were rather tense, very often on edge, while your husband presents on the whole a picture of a calm, steady man under his own control. Yet you and he tell me that he is the one who takes sedatives at night, not you."

She tried a laugh. It was a pitiful, strained sound. "I may not look a sound sleeper, but I am."

"He was drugged and you're a sound sleeper, so neither of you heard your little girl taken from her room and brought down the stairs, necessarily past your door. Remember that we know now there was no question of her being carried out through the window. She was brought along past your door and down the stairs."

"Most mothers," put in Burden, "well, most parents, become light sleepers through being habituated to waking in the night when babies cry or children call out. It takes years to change that and maybe only changes after the children are grown up if at all."

"But you're not one of those parents, though you've had three children?"

"I heard nothing. I slept."

Leaving, Wexford turned back and said almost casually, "What age is your older son, Mrs. Devenish?"

"He's twelve."

"Ah, yes. He looks older. So many of them do these days. Long way off driving a car yet, then?"

She hesitated. "He's tried driving a car—well, round the front here and in the drive. That's not illegal, is it? On private land?"

"No, that's not illegal, Mrs. Devenish."

"They all want to drive, you know, and Edward's so big."

As they were leaving, she said suddenly, surprising them, "It was dreadful about that poor man, that policeman, it was such an awful way to die."

The report on the white VW Golf, Devenish's birthday present to his wife, confirmed most of what Wexford had expected. No fingerprints were on the steering wheel, which still held shreds of the polythene wrap that had protected it when new. The prints of five people, Devenish's, his sons', Fay Devenish's, and those no doubt of the man who had delivered it to the showroom, were all over the interior. There was nothing remarkable about that.

Explicable only if Sanchia had been in the car was the presence of baby fingerprints and three fair hairs from the head of a small child. But did this mean she had been taken away in it on the night of her disappearance? Sanchia too had doubtless been among the admirers of the new car, had clambered all over the backseat while her brothers sat in the front and played with the gadgets, her mother uttered her pleasure and gratitude, and her father stood benignly by.

"Can you think of a single reason why Devenish would abduct his own child?" Burden asked over a quick drink in the Olive and Dove. "What's his motive? What could he possibly get out of it? I mean, if there was another woman involved and he saw himself as having a future with this other woman, I could just about imagine him putting the child into her keeping so that when he and and his wife divorced and Fay got custody of the kids, he'd have Sanchia. I can just about imagine it, but even so it's full of holes."

"Besides, if he did all that, what chance would he actually have of getting away with it?" said Wexford. "Precious little. If Sanchia wasn't found beforehand, once he moved in with this woman, she would be. And there is no woman, or if there is, he and she have been to such elaborate pains to conceal her existence as is only compatible with their having been planning this abduction since the affair began."

Burden stared into the sparkling creamy head on his bitter like a clairvoyant looking into a crystal ball. "You know something? I don't believe in those threatening letters. I think Devenish invented them in a clumsy effort to put us off investigating him. If he'd had them, why not keep them? Why not, at any rate, keep one? All that stuff about the letters being particularly literate, the biblical-sounding bit, that was just put in to make us think him a discerning person who'd know good prose when he saw it."

"You may be right. If we only knew why Sanchia was taken, we'd be a long way toward finding her. There's no motive for taking her nor for hiding her. No reason for taking the child from her home and torturing his wife in the process. I can see how, the mechanics of it I mean, but no matter how hard I try to imagine it, I can't come up with why."

"And can you come up with why some villain would want to kill Ted Hennessy? For nothing. For simply refusing to understand facts that had been explained a hundred times. Can you? I can't."

CHAPTER 15

When her car broke down on the old bypass, Lynn had given up thinking about her entrapment of Vicky. After all, she had made several more attempts after the strange experience with the threesome couple, and all had come to nothing. Vicky, she now believed, had gone to ground, had abandoned this curious plan of hers to recruit young women to do her housework—if that had been her motive—and settled down to life with or without Jerry in her own home wherever that might be. Besides, Lynn was starting to feel guilty. She shouldn't have embarked on this enterprise without permission.

On her way back to Framhurst home from work she had called in on Laura Hennessy. Laura wasn't a friend of hers and Ted hadn't been a friend, but they had worked together and Lynn had liked him and, besides, it was such an awful tragedy and, as she put it to Laura, such a *waste.* Two small children were left fatherless, there was a big mortgage outstanding on the house, and if that would be covered by the compensation, it was still a worry. Lynn left the semidetached house in Orchard Road in a dismal frame of mind, thinking what a hazardous occupation hers was, what risks she and her fellows daily ran and how little thanks, or indeed respect, they got for it.

There is no moment convenient for one's car to break down, but some moments are less maddening than others. It shouldn't happen on a dark, wet night when one's boyfriend is away on business, one's contemporary and fellow officer has been burnt to death, and there seems no one in the whole world worth talking to. A consolation was that when the engine simply died, the Fiesta wasn't in the fast lane but far over on the left and no other traffic was on the road in either direction. It died, the car slowed down and seemed to collapse hopelessly, though of course it was all in one piece and all that had happened was that it refused to go. Lynn tried everything to make it start, but it wouldn't. She wasn't mechanically minded. She blessed the absence of traffic on the road—a lorry passed her and then a motorbike—because she didn't want help from others. The only thing to do, the obvious thing, was to call the special number she had for the RAC. They would come as soon as they could and that might be very soon, in no more than ten minutes.

The rain had stopped and a misty orange moon appeared. Afterward Lynn blessed the fact that she hadn't dropped her mobile onto the seat before she got out of the car. It was the merest chance that she didn't do this because she couldn't imagine needing the phone while simply standing outside the car to breathe the fresh night air and waiting for the RAC man. Probably it reflected her police training never to be separated from her phone.

The hazard lights on the Fiesta still worked though the motor didn't. They flashed on and off, on and off, in the darkness. The trees, the dense woods along both sides of the dual carriageway in this section, made it dark and mysterious and, strangely on a wet road at night, beautiful. For the endless rain, the torrential or drizzling or misty or steady rain, the relentless daily rain, had fed these beeches with their feather fronds, these long-leaved chestnuts, these limes and hornbeams and oaks, so that they were greener than Lynn had ever seen them, greener and lusher and fresher and more luxuriant. It took her car breaking down to make her appreciate trees, she thought, and she moved to the woodland edge to look down the aisles between the trees where the rain dripped from glossy leaves, brilliant emerald in the pale moonlight.

A car drawing up made her turn around. She thought it was the RAC man, but it wasn't. A white car and a woman at the wheel, leaning across and out of the passenger window to ask her if she needed help. Lynn nearly said she had already called the RAC, thank you very much, and he would be along any minute, but then she noticed that the woman was middle-aged and thickset, with unusually luxuriant gray hair. Tension gripped her, tautening her stomach muscles, and she forgot about not doing things on her own initiative.

"I don't really want to wait here for them by myself, though. If you would just take me to a garage. I'm a stranger round here but I've been told there's an all-night one at the Myfleet exit. That would be very kind."

Lynn had never before heard herself sound so naive and sweetly girlish. The woman pushed open the door and she got in, praying that the RAC man wouldn't come until they were on their way. Then, sitting next to the woman who could be Vicky, who surely was Vicky, feeling really bad about the poor RAC man on his way to going off duty, maybe, and home to his family and his dinner, and who would come and find her gone, the car abandoned, and wonder what on earth had happened to her.

This he wouldn't guess, though. She burbled a little more to the woman about how kind she was and how awful it would have been if she hadn't come along because she, Lynn, was terribly nervous about being out alone on a lonely road in the dark, one read such awful things. It was getting more likely to be Vicky by the minute, for she hadn't even turned around to face in the direction of the Myfleet exit but was speeding up the bypass toward the Myringham turn. Lynn didn't want to show anxiety yet, it wasn't in keeping with her trusting and girlish pose. She had studied Vicky's head, quite sure now that that thickly waved, dense coiffure was a wig, had had a good look around the car, had actually said what a lovely car it was, and now she was watching where they were going and telling Vicky the scenery was quite beautiful around here, she'd had no idea.

Then Vicky said it, what Lynn had been waiting for: "By the way, my name's Vicky."

"Lynn."

"Soon be at this garage of yours. Turn left up here."

Vicky turned left, squeezing the car down a lane about as wide as Lynn's double bed. The fronds on the high bank, hart's-tongue ferns and dog's mercury and lords-and-ladies, brushed wetly along the side of the car. Now was the time, Lynn thought, to say this didn't look much like the way to the garage, that would be the authentic remark to make and utter in an increasingly nervous tone, but she didn't make it and Vicky didn't seem to notice.

Where were they? On the way to Myringham by a tortuous back route? Certainly they were nowhere near Sayle and the Chorley bungalow, but by now a good fifteen miles away. But Vicky made her living house-sitting for people, didn't she? There had been other Sunnybanks since Rachel Holmes, at least one other Vicky had cared for and in which she had entertained Jerry. She was going to one of them now, Lynn thought, with that little inner gasp and catching of breath that denotes excitement. She looked at her watch. Ten to ten. God, she didn't want to have to stay the night, but if there was no help for it...

The car crawled through this narrow, wet, green tunnel of a lane, came out into a slightly wider road with a little spurt like a sigh of relief. The car turned left and Lynn saw in its headlights a signpost pointing to Myringham as five miles away and Upper Brede as three. Now was the time, she thought, to express anxiety: "This isn't where I saw the garage."

"It was closed," Vicky said. "There's an all-night one at Upper Brede."

Lynn didn't want to sound too intelligent. On the other hand, excessive stupidity might arouse suspicion. "Will they have a mechanic, do you think, or just petrol pumps?"

"They've a mechanic. Don't worry. I've used them many times." She smiled as if she were looking at Lynn and not at the road ahead. "Now amuse me. Tell me about yourself. After all, I've put myself out to give you a helping hand, haven't I? The least you can do is talk."

Vicky sounded suddenly quite cross and indignant. It must be a cue, Lynn thought, for her to start being frightened. But she did as she was told, or an approximation to what she was told, and gave Vicky an account of an entirely fictitious young woman who lived with her parents in Stowerton, had been driving their car home from an evening spent with an old school friend—a girl, of course—in Kingsmarkham. She was nineteen years old and maybe Vicky would find it funny, but she hadn't got a boyfriend. She worked as a veterinary assistant in Kingsmarkham, but that wasn't nearly as grand as it sounded. It mostly involved clearing up messes and scrubbing floors! Lynn was proud of herself for managing to put a quite audible exclamation mark at the end of that sentence.

"Exciting life," said Vicky.

She had changed entirely in the short space of ten minutes. From friendly geniality she had passed through brusqueness to barely concealed sneers. And now, as they entered another lane and turned almost at once into the front drive of a large, well-lit, newish house, she said, rather in the tone an ill-disposed prison officer might use to a recalcitrant inmate, "All right then, get out. Don't get any silly ideas, I'm right behind you."

Lynn wasn't much of an actress and didn't know how the girl she was pretending to be might react in these circumstances. So she did nothing at all but obey. Like a bemused sheep she scuttled out of the car and up to the front door, which at the moment of their arrival was opened from the inside. Vicky gave her an unexpected push, and she stumbled over the doormat and nearly fell. Nearly but not quite. It was a funny thing to recall at that moment, but she remembered Wexford saying a miss was as good as a mile and adding that he was quoting the Duke of Wellington when someone took a potshot at him in Hyde Park.

She only stumbled. She looked up and found her eyes meeting a pair of stony, flat, gray eyes in a curiously blank face. At first she thought the face was lopsided, heavier about one cheek than the other, but it wasn't, it was an illusion. The man was a little taller than she was, thin, with receding dark hair and wearing a rather shabby pin-striped suit. He looked sad and as if he never smiled, never could, didn't know how to make the requisite muscles work. Lynn looked over her shoulder at Vicky, who was just standing there, then back at the man who must be Jerry, and said what the nice little veterinary assistant would surely have said: "What am I doing here? What is this place?"

"It's useless asking," said Vicky, "because I'm not saying. Why should I? You don't have a choice. You're here and here you stay until I decide if you'll do."

"Do?"

"Do for my purposes. Say hello to Jerry. Haven't those parents of yours taught you any manners?"

Lynn said hello to Jerry, who gave her a blank, silent stare in return.

Among the hardware stores that sold paraffin none opened before nine-thirty in the morning. Vine had to revise his ideas about one of the troublemakers buying his paraffin on the morning the bomb was thrown. He began to think he was on the wrong track altogether, for petrol and paraffin were such common and generally used commodities that certainly 50 percent of households would have either or both accessible.

But he had spent the day calling at ironmongers and hardware shops just the same in the hope, which turned out to be vain, that an assistant might tell him of a regular customer and frequent purchaser of paraffin.

By the evening he was back in the Rat and Carrot, talking once more with Andy Honeyman. Vine found it hard to understand how someone could remember what another man said and recollect the circumstances in which he had said it without being able to describe that man. Honeyman must either be lying or totally unobservant, or forgetful to the point of amnesia, for he steadily denied any knowledge of the customer in the Rat and Carrot who had told Colin Crowne how to make a petrol bomb. Nor could he remember who else had been present, apart from Colin and Joe Hebden and Terry Fowler. Heavily pressed by Vine, he finally said that there had been a woman there he knew by sight. She lived in Glebe Road and he thought her first name was Jackie. None of this was of much help to Vine, who went back to the Muriel Campden Estate and began questioning Colin Crowne and Joe Hebden and Terry Fowler once more.

Colin had taken to his bed before the bomb throwing and the death of Ted Hennessy. What with the pain from his shingles and Miroslav Zlatic's refusal to listen to him or even give any sign that he understood when Colin asked what the Serb intended to do to provide for Lizzie's child, the stress had been too much for him, contributing to his malaise. On the following day he had been told by Kingsmarkham Social Services that their virtual babies were valued at £1254.80 apiece, that Jodi must be replaced, and they intended to recover that sum from him by whatever means were in their power. Colin knew that meant the County Court and maybe the bailiffs in. He didn't want to get up when Vine arrived, but Debbie said he had better, so he came down in tracksuit pants and a T-shirt.

Vine made him go through it all again, how he had only asked about making a petrol bomb out of natural curiosity. He was personally too law-abiding to have any inkling of these things, but he'd seen this bit on telly, throwing bottles that blew up and set fire to cars, and naturally he'd wanted to know how it was done. Putting in a good word for his neighbor, he said that Joe Hebden was of the same way of thinking.

"But your natural curiosity didn't take you so far as to find out the name of your instructor?"

"My what?"

"The guy who told you how to do it?"

"I never asked him, did I? He put his spoke in. I never said to him, how d'you do it. I said it to my mate. He come along and put his spoke in."

"What did he look like?" said Vine, who had asked this question before.

Colin Crowne gave the same answer. "Just a bloke. Twenty-something, maybe a bit more, I don't know. I wasn't to know I'd have to remember, was I?"

One of Terry Fowler's sons opened the front door. The other was sitting with his father on a sofa, watching *Crimewatch* and eating taco chips. The Crowne home was far from immaculate, but this place was among the dirtiest and least cared-for Vine had ever seen. No one had cleaned it since Terry's wife left him. Something was on the floor behind the television set that Vine, quickly looking away, hoped was dog turds but feared might be from a human source.

But Terry was able, this time, to offer a scrap of help. He knew this Jackie woman through her sister, whose son went to school with his two. The sisters lived next door to each other in Glebe Road, but more than that he couldn't say. The little Fowler boys then began talking without a trace of diffidence or shyness about another school friend, cousin of someone or other, a boy of six who had his own computer and who had been to Florida on holiday and visited Disney World. Vine thought this a long way from the point—they seemed to be traveling through the ramifications of a whole cluster of Kingsmarkham families—and tried to get back to the subject of Jackie. Terry said that he had once seen her in the company of Charlene Hebden, but beyond that he couldn't help.

The six-year-old Kim Fowler accompanied Vine to the door. He was what Vine's grandmother called an old-fashioned child and he apologized for the dirty floor and the dust that covered everything. "Mum used to do it," he said, "but she's gone away and left us so there's no one done it. Dad says cleaning is for ladies, not guys."

"Well," said Vine, "there are some guys called New Men and they do cleaning."

"We haven't got none of them round here." Kim stretched upward to open the door and just made it. "That Jackie's got a girl called Kaylee, and do you know what her dad did? He put her through a cat flap so she could steal things. Only he didn't go to jail because they couldn't prove it."

Tasneem came into the helpline room just as Sylvia was putting the phone down after her fifth call of the evening. It was half past ten, a pitch-dark night and raining hard. Sylvia hadn't pulled down the blind and the rain hung on the window like a shifting, glittering veil of silver. By this time, and after all those disquieting or upsetting calls—one had been from a man with a fanatical manner and an Irish accent who had threatened to come and get her and do to her "what they did to the blessed martyred Saint Agatha"—she was always glad of a visitor, Tasneem or Tracy or the black woman with a name she hadn't learned to pronounce correctly, or the newcomer, Vivienne.

Tasneem stood at the window and gazed out through the water-drop veil at the wet, black night. Tonight, especially, there was nothing to be seen, but Tasneem often stared out there, looking, Sylvia knew, in the vague direction of York Street and the Muriel Campden Estate where Kim and Lee were.

"You don't happen to know anything about Saint Agatha, I suppose?" Sylvia said.

"Moslems don't have saints, Sylvia."

"No, I suppose you don't. It's prophets you have."

The phone rang. Sylvia said, "The Hide helpline. How may I help you?"

"It's my boyfriend," a voice said breathlessly, "we moved in together last week—well, I moved in with him. He's always been so lovely, he's a really nice guy, everyone says so, and he's always been so gentle. Well, last night I was half an hour late home from work, the bus never came, and I didn't phone him—are you there? Can you hear me?"

"I'm here," Sylvia said. "I'm listening. Go on."

"Like I said, I was half an hour late, and when I came in, he acted like I'd done something terrible, committed a crime or something, and he grabbed hold of me and said where had I been and who had I been with—it was only six-thirty in the evening, for God's sake—and then he slapped me hard on both cheeks, wham, wham. I was so shocked, I could hardly believe what had happened except that I've got a really bad bruise on the left side. He said he was sorry, but then he said I ought to understand he did it because he'd been so worried."

"Where are you now?"

"At home, at my own place. I'd kept it on, thank God I did. He's gone out for the evening, so I found this number on a card in a call box and came in here and phoned you. Look, I can understand he was worried about me—well, up to a point I can—but you don't hit people because you're worried about them, do you?"

"Some do, as I'm afraid you now know. You said it all when you told me thank God you'd kept your own place on."

"You mean I ought to stay here and not go back to him?"

"You know it without my telling you."

"If that's what happens after I've lived with him for one week, what's it going to be like after six months, is that what you mean?"

Sylvia said that was what she meant and repeated that the caller knew the answers already, she just very naturally wanted reassurance and support. Putting down the phone, Sylvia told Tasneem what she had just heard.

"Terry was like that, a really nice guy and gentle and all that. From a distance, that is. It's when you get together it starts, when you're all shut up inside alone with them. I'd like to do your job, Sylvia, it'd be doing something I really know about. Terry used to call me stupid, he said I was ignorant about everything but cooking and cleaning, but if there's one thing I'm an expert in, it's domestic violence."

Sylvia took Tasneem's hand and squeezed it. "You could train to go on the helpline, Tas, but it's not paid and you've got your degree to do. Besides, once you've got your flat, you won't want to come near The Hide again."

"And I'll get my boys back, won't I?"

"I'm sure you will," Sylvia said, though she wasn't all that sure, but she couldn't say any more because the phone was ringing again.

The threatening Irishman once more. She cut him off before he had got more than three words out, but they were three offensive words and her hand on the phone was shaking. "Silly, I ought to be used to it."

"There are some things you never get used to," said Tasneem with feeling.

"No. I think I'll tell my dad about this one, see if we can track him down."

Griselda Cooper put her head around the door and said the roof was leaking in the northwest corner of the house with rain coming in through the ceiling. She'd had to move Vivienne into Tasneem's room, it was only temporary, and she hoped that was okay with Tasneem. Tasneem said she'd like the company, and Sylvia asked Griselda what it was they did to Saint Agatha.

"Don't ask me. Put her on a grill or tied her to a wheel, I expect, something disgusting, anyway. Why? Does one of our charming callers want to do it to you?"

It was because she had made a bargain with her captor, Lynn thought, that she was spared the Rohypnol-doctored drink that had been given to Lizzie Cromwell and Rachel Holmes on their arrival. Lynn didn't struggle or even protest much, she said her parents would be anxious and she became a little tearful, but if Vicky would promise to let her go in the morning, she would agree to spend one night there. Could she phone her parents?

That made Vicky laugh. She didn't even bother to answer but, looking Lynn up and down, said, "Those trousers you're wearing won't do. We'll have to get you into something else tomorrow."

But Vicky didn't search her or even look in her bag where the mobile was. Vicky seemed to accept Lynn's meekness and acquiescence as behavior only to be expected from an independent girl of nineteen, for Vicky, as Lynn soon saw, was an egomaniac of gigantic proportions. She didn't observe or question or even have suspicions because she saw only herself, and saw herself as a figure of strength and power and rectitude. And, of course, she saw Jerry.

Set down in a chair opposite him—literally set down by Vicky, a hand on each shoulder pushing her into a sitting position—Lynn felt she owed herself congratulations on not being afraid of him. She just made it, just managed to resist and turn back the finger of fear that crept up her spine. It was his eyes as much as anything, his eyes that seemed to have more white around the irises than most people's, and his silence, so that he made her doubt if he was able to speak. If he made a sound, what kind would it be?

Ever since she had come into the house, she had been thinking of the missing little girl, listening for child noises and looking around the room for child signs. But there had been no sounds. Whoever had furnished this room had no interest in their surroundings beyond requiring them to be comfortable and insulated. Beige was the predominant color, and those people had no interest in toys, either for children or grown-ups. Sanchia wasn't here, unless Vicky was cleverer than Lynn thought.

After staring at her, those eyes apparently unblinking, for ten minutes, Jerry got up and began walking about the room, picking things up and putting them down again, a book, an ashtray, a brass ornament in the shape of a tortoise. From an arrangement of flowers in a basket he took a blue iris, brought it to his nose, sniffed it, dropped it on the floor, and trod on it. Not a simple treading underfoot but a concentrated, manic stamping and crushing. Then he passed on to the window and stood there with his back to the room, although the curtains were drawn.

Vicky bent down and scraped the remains of the iris off the carpet, where it had left a dark blue stain. "You can clean that off in the morning," she said to Lynn. "When you've had a good night's rest."

All the time Jerry was staring at Lynn and later roving about the room, Vicky had been talking, giving some sort of explanation, or as much of an explanation as she thought fit for Lynn to know. This wasn't her house, she was house-sitting for the owners, who were away on holiday. She and Jerry had only been there for three days so far. The owners liked their place to be immaculate, as Lynn could see. Keeping it that way would be her job, but first, early in the morning, she, Vicky, would show her how to get Jerry's breakfast.

"Time for bed now," Vicky said. "My goodness, look at the time, it's after eleven."

At that, as if time had a particular fascination for him, Jerry spun around. He was wearing a shirt of khaki-colored cotton buttoned up to the neck, and at his sharp turn the top button came undone to reveal two strips of plaster covering a lint pad on his upper chest. Vicky went up to him and buttoned his shirt. She did it quickly as if she didn't want Lynn to see the plasters. He allowed her attentions but, when she was finished, sat down cross-legged on the floor with his back against the curtains. His eyes closed, his head nodding, he looked as if he was about to fall asleep in that position.

Lynn was glad to get away from him. She went upstairs, taking careful note of the geography of the house. From outside, in the dark, that it had a third story wasn't apparent, but now she was being urged to mount another flight. Vicky was behind her, telling her to hurry up, she hadn't got all night, which seemed a strange thing to say in the circumstances. At the top Vicky showed her into a bathroom, doubtless mounting guard outside, for when Lynn came out, she almost bumped into her. The door to the room that was to be hers Vicky opened from behind her. Everything happened quickly after that, and when it was too late, Lynn realized how much she had underestimated the woman, for as Lynn stepped into the room she heard a click and a snip and felt her bag slide from her shoulder. Vicky had cut the strap with scissors. Lynn twisted around and made a grab for her, but what she clutched was Vicky's hair and the gray wig came away in her hand. The door was slammed in her face and the key turned in the lock, Vicky on the outside and Lynn on the inside, without her mobile.

The scenario she had created in her mind had been quite different. Vicky would bring her to a bedroom and stand over her while she undressed and put on the nightclothes provided. With her back turned, of course, like the puritanical wardress she resembled. Her own clothes would be taken away, the door locked on her, and she left to make her phone call. Things had not happened like that.

Wexford would be cross. He became a different person when he was cross—cold and stern and rather contemptuous, if never unfair. He would say she was too inexperienced to mount an operation of this kind with herself as decoy. She should have told him or Barry Vine first, she should have *asked.*

Police officers in TV sitcoms knew how to pick locks or, if they were the brute-force type, break them down with a running kick. Lynn knew that if she tried to break the door down, she would make so much noise that Vicky and Jerry would come and between them they could overpower her. Besides, she very much disliked the idea of a hands-on struggle with Jerry. Though stoutly determined not to be afraid of him, she thought she might scream if he so much as laid the tip of one finger on her skin.

She went to the window and pulled back the curtains, having first switched off the light. At first she could see almost nothing beyond that the rain had stopped. She opened the window, which was a casement. The lamps were still on in the room below, quite a long way below, about twenty feet, as she appeared to be in some third-story extension built on up here perhaps only a few years back. The light down there showed in the parting between the curtains and as a thin yellow line across the wet, black paving. A long way down, too far to jump, much too far when she'd be jumping onto concrete. Sheets, curtains, blankets, Lynn disliked the idea of any of those. She looked inside the cupboard. It was full of women's clothes, old clothes or the clothes of an old person, smelling musty and of camphor spray. Two of the dresses had self-belts, but she could see they were too flimsy for her purpose.

She sat down on the bed. She listened. The house was silent. Her watch told her the time was twenty-five past eleven. Up here it was doubtful if she would hear them go to bed, but she would see the light go out. Did they share a bed? She didn't care for that idea either. It wasn't much use to her knowing if they were in bed unless she could find a way out. Somehow she must use the room, she must use what was in the room. It hadn't been designed as a prison, it was the owners' guest room. Visitors slept here, used the bathroom next door, probably enjoyed their semi-isolation at the top of the house. And if the owners weren't keen on color and adornment, they evidently were on comfort. There had been soft, fluffy towels in that bathroom, new, unused cakes of soap, and a jar of expensive bath essence.

Vicky and Jerry hadn't taken Sanchia, that was certain. Unless they had taken her but she was no longer here now because...No, she wouldn't even think of that, it wasn't her job or her place to think of it. She went to the window once more. The light was still on down there. She hated to think of Jerry near a child or a child in his presence. Vicky's wig still lay on the floor, inside the door where it had fallen. Well, Vicky could come and get it after she was gone.

If you want a thing badly enough, said Lynn to herself, you can do it. Pity there wasn't a phone. People never do have phones in guest rooms, no matter how hospitable they may be, but they do have television sets, and the one in here had an aerial of zigzag metal plates standing on the top of it. There were two bed lamps, one on either side of the bed, and another standing on the dressing table. Lynn got on her hands and knees and crawled under the bed. Two double sockets each held two plugs. What appliances did the others serve? She followed the lead of one of them up into the bedding and found an electric blanket. The other belonged to a radio.

Each lead was about two meters long, say six and a half feet. Lynn looked about her. She opened drawers in the dressing table, but all were empty, neatly lined with white-spotted beige paper. Back to the window to check if the light was still on. It was. There was a drawer in each bedside cabinet. The one on the left-hand side contained the television remote, the one on the right an unopened box of tissues, a packet of throat pastilles, a container of nasal spray, and a tiny pair of nail scissors.

Better than nothing, much better. It was no good longing for a sharp knife. The leads on the bed lamps and the aerial were thin—though, Lynn hoped, strong—and they responded well to the snip of the small, fairly sharp scissors. The heavier electric cables on the blanket, radio, and television set were a different matter. She worked on them until her right forefinger was sore and bleeding, and she realized she would never get through the television cable.

From somewhere far below her she heard a stair creak. She went back to the window and saw that the light was out. Lynn began to feel rather excited. Then she had a thought she at once condemned as silly. Kingsmarkham police were going to have to replace all these cables, mend everything she'd destroyed in here, not the owners, still less Vicky and Jerry. What did all that matter when she'd found them?

She set about tying the cables together. Reef knots, that was the way. The knots took up a great deal of lead. At first she had thought she had an enormous length to play with, something like eighteen meters for a drop of something like six, but the knots took it up, and when it was done and firm and looked safe to use, it wasn't more than maybe five meters long. And she still needed a length of it to tie on to something.

Tie on to what? The farther away from the window the more of those five meters would be used up. Underneath the window was a radiator. Lynn examined it and saw that it was fastened to the wall by two metal brackets and to the floor by the pipes through which the water or oil or whatever passed. It felt firm enough. It would have to do. She passed the cable through the flanges on the top of the radiator and made it fast with another reef knot, a double one this time.

Again she listened to the silence of the house. Then she switched off the light. It would be harder in the dark but safer. If only she had gloves! She put one leg over the windowsill, blessing the trousers Vicky so disliked, then the other. Sitting on the ledge, her legs dangling, she realized that this was going to take some resolution, the very letting go and depending on that thin cable. Even the thick blanket and radio leads looked weak now. She turned herself over, still holding on to the sill, and lay on the window ledge on her pelvis, her legs outstretched.

The darkness was deep, inside the room and outside. She took hold of the cable in her right hand, eased herself away from the window, still holding the ledge with her left hand, and brought both feet onto the wall. It had a rough surface, as if the rendering had been worked on with a pargeting tool. The pattern was formed in a kind of bas-relief in which none of the raised portions protruded more than half an inch, but it was enough to get a better foothold than on an absolutely flat surface. Lynn tried to grip with her toes, but her shoes were stiff and had leather soles.

She climbed back into the room, took her shoes off, and hung them around her neck by their laces. Her socks came off too and she tucked them into her shoes. Back on the windowsill, she went through the same process and found it much easier this time. Perhaps going back and starting again had been a good idea. Now she could grip the protrusions in the bas-relief much more satisfactorily.

The worst part, as she had known it would be, was letting go, taking her left hand from the sill onto the cable and depending entirely on it. She hadn't foreseen how the cable would stretch and swing, and the radiator give a long, groaning creak. But it held. Gripping the cable as firmly as she could, she moved her right foot down a few inches, then her left, then her right. Her hands slipped on the cable then and she began to slide, desperately trying to walk down the wall, running instead, until her feet slipped off it, she swung in the air about ten feet up, and from above came a crunch, a clatter, and a grinding, wrenching sound.

Lynn dropped then, the cable running through and burning her fingers, to land on her feet, her legs wide apart. But she was upright and she was sound. Up above her she couldn't see much except a whitish thing on the windowsill with the cable still attached to it. She weighed only eight and a half stone, but her weight had pulled the radiator away from the wall. Would the pipes have gone too? Was there any water or oil in there when the heating was off? She wasn't going to stay to find out, and with pictures of pipes spouting water and the house flooding passing through her mind, she put on her socks and shoes and fled.

Through the side entrance, around to the front. Not a light on in the house, not a light anywhere. Only those who have lived in the country, better still in a house outside a village, know how dark the countryside can be at midnight. Without a torch it is virtually impossible to go for a walk. But after a while you get used to the dark as Lynn did. Absolute blackness becomes black and gray, then gray and black, then the varied shades of monochrome, like an old, dark film.

She was walking along the lane by which they had arrived. At the crossroads she went close up to the signpost but was still unable to read it. But she had noted where she was on the way here and she would find it again. Left here for Bredeway and the bridge over the river. Suddenly, ahead of her, on the right-hand side, she saw a light, and she made her way toward it, keeping close up against the hedge. She hadn't got her bag with her, nor her mobile, but her warrant card she had. Carry it *on* you, Barry Vine had once told her. Not in your bag or your overcoat pocket but on you, in an inside pocket. So she had and it was there, against her heart, really, though that was a dramatic way of putting it.

The light was upstairs in a thatched cottage by the bridge. It must have been generally brighter here, for she could read the name Bridge Cottage and she noted it as another pointer to where she was. She rang the doorbell. No one answered. She rang again and again, banged on the door, using the knocker and her fist. She even thought of throwing stones at the window, but she might break it and she didn't want to be responsible for causing more damage.

No one was home. They left that light on to make people like her, or more dangerous people, think someone was there. She turned away, closed the gate behind her, and walked on over the bridge. If Vicky had heard the noise wrenching the radiator off the wall had made, would she come after her? It was likely enough. But Lynn knew she would be more than a match for Vicky on her own. A sign on the left side ahead said something, that this was the beginnings of a village, Bredeway probably. Close up, she could just read it: BREDEWAY. DRIVE CAREFULLY THROUGH OUR VILLAGE. Chance'd be a fine thing, thought Lynn. Her car was still up there on the bypass, unless someone had nicked it or driven into it.

The village was mostly in darkness, though lights were on in two of the cottages and one biggish house was ablaze with light. That was the one, thought Lynn. She could hear the noise from the place before she was inside the gate, music, shouting, laughter, and as she entered the garden, she could see people dancing in the brightly lit front room. Her warrant card in her hand, she rang the doorbell, then knocked. They might not hear the bell.

A girl of about eighteen opened the door. She didn't wait for Lynn to explain. "Oh, God, I'm sorry. The people next door rang and said they were phoning the police and we promised not to make so much noise, but, I don't know how it is, you get carried away, don't you? It's my boyfriend's eighteenth birthday party. I didn't think the police would actually come. Oh, God, I feel so terrible..."

"All I want," said Lynn, "is to use your phone, if I may."

"Of course you may, of course. Come in. Have a drink. There's only Football Red and Football White, we've drunk the champers. Look, we'll be as quiet as mice while you're phoning, I promise."

CHAPTER
16

AT SOME TIME DURING THE NIGHT SHE HAD GONE UP INTO that room and retrieved her wig. A complicated structure of blue-gray puffs and whorls and curled wisps, it sat on top of a grim face, in which the crags and cracks had appeared early, if the age she had given was a true one. She looked a lot more than fifty-five. Her neck was thick but her face drawn and pinched. The ringless hands looked swollen and her ankles bulged above the tops of her lace-up shoes.

In a gruff, mannish voice, she kept saying she hadn't done anything wrong. She had been trying to help Jerry, that was all, caring for him as she always did. Wexford said nothing. He was waiting for James Beamish to arrive. The solicitor representing Jerry had turned up ten minutes before and was in the next interview room with his client and Burden and DC Cox. Jerry Dover, his name was, according to her. *She* was Victoria Cadbury, and his late mother's sister.

Both of them had been up when the two squad cars arrived at 1:30 A.M., Jerry sitting cross-legged on the hall floor, swaying from side to side and keening softly. Vicky had been on the top floor, trying to pull a heavy metal radiator off the windowsill but lacking the strength for it. Neither of them had gone in pursuit of Lynn Fancourt. Jerry Dover looked incapable of being left on his own, though Vicky must have left him when she went for her interviews, for the night she had spent at Mrs. Chorley's house, and later to seek her prey. Wexford had only caught a glimpse of him when he arrived at the station himself this morning, but that was enough to define Jerry as mad, or to put it more correctly, severely schizophrenic, the kind of person they used to describe as "unfit to plead."

The house in Upper Brede had been searched and the garden

inspected. Of course there was no sign of Sanchia Devenish and no evidence that she had ever been there. It seemed that no child had lived there or been there for many years. The house belonged to a couple called Jackson. Vicky Cadbury had been house-sitting for them while they were on a Greek island. They were due home tomorrow to find their spare bedroom's electrics dismantled and its radiator torn off the wall. Wexford had to give grudging approval to Lynn Fancourt. After all, she had caught this pair on her own initiative, but at the cost of a good deal of the taxpayers' money—unless the householders' insurance would pay up—and in some ways it served her right that her car, which she had left on the old bypass, had been vandalized during the night and its radio stolen.

At first he had thought he would have liked to have been there and seen her snatch off Vicky's wig, but already he was beginning to feel pity for these two. A tragic, if ludicrous, story would emerge, and coincidentally with that thought, came James Beamish, brisk and cocky as ever.

Karen, none too pleased to have had to postpone her domestic-violence training owing to pressure here, spoke into the recording device: "Present are Victoria Mary Cadbury, Chief Inspector Wexford, and Sergeant Malahyde. Mr. James Beamish has just entered the room. The time is nine thirty-two."

"Ms. Cadbury," Wexford began, "or is it Mrs.?"

"Miss, Ms., or Vicky, I don't care, call me what you like. But not Mrs. I've never been married."

"At some time in April, did you abduct a young woman called Elizabeth Cromwell and take her to your home and keep her prisoner against her will? And did you a week later abduct Rachel Holmes and keep her a prisoner against her will?"

Vicky shrugged her shoulders. They were heavy shoulders, such as people develop who have been on anabolic steroids. "So what? It wasn't my home, I've done nothing wrong, I didn't hurt them, I fed them, I saved them off the street. God knows what would have happened to them, out there on the street. I made them dress decently, in a skirt instead of those trousers." She shook her head. "It's them that's done wrong to us. That Rachel girl stuck a penknife in Jerry. She found a knife in a drawer—you never know what's about when it's not your house—and went up to Jerry, who's harmless, who wouldn't hurt a fly, and stuck it in his chest. I thought she'd got the lung, I thought he'd bleed to death. I drove her back after that, of course I did, once I'd dressed Jerry's wound. I'd been a nurse and it's just as well, isn't it? Jerry might have died."

So that was what had made Rachel Holmes lie, Wexford thought. She was afraid of the trouble that might ensue if it was known she stabbed Jerry Dover, so she invented a house with shingled walls and a big conifer in the front garden.

"So you did abduct these two young women?"

"My client has just said she did, Mr. Wexford," said Beamish.

"Very well. For what purpose?"

"You need not answer that," said Beamish.

"I want to answer it. I want you all to know I wasn't doing anything wrong, I was doing a kindness. I did it for my nephew." Vicky looked defiantly from Wexford to Karen and from Karen to James Beamish. She seemed not to understand that Beamish was on her side, although his function had been explained to her. "I love that boy. D'you understand that, any of you? D'you understand you can just love someone without sex and stuff being involved, and when they're not your own kid? His mum and dad are dead. I've looked after him since all that started. You've seen him, you know what I mean."

Beamish, who hadn't seen Jerry Dover, looked puzzled. No one enlightened him.

"He's been in and out of those places, psychiatric wards, they're worse than the old Bedlam was, so for the past ten years he's been with me. He lives with me. I give him his drugs and his meals, he doesn't eat much. I'm not saying he's not a bit destructive, he is, but he's harmless." Vicky said in a different, shriller tone, "I've got cancer."

No one said anything. Wexford nodded.

"I don't say I've *had* cancer, I say I've got it. Because I have; once a cancer patient, always a cancer patient. I know, like I said, I've been a nurse. But it's worse than that, I'm going to die. It's breast cancer I've got; you always say you've got the cancer where it started, but it's in my lungs now. They say they don't know, but I know. I've got a year at best."

"What has this got to do with the abductions, Ms. Cadbury?" Karen asked.

"You were looking for someone to look after Jerry, weren't you?" said Wexford. "A kind of wife for him, am I right? A young woman to cook and clean and mend his clothes? Someone to care for him?"

"Not for sex," said Vicky sharply. "Jerry doesn't know what sex is and he doesn't want to know. But they'd have got married, to be on the safe side." She didn't explain what she meant by the "safe side." "And there was plenty in it for the lucky girl. Her and Jerry, they'd come in for my house when I'm gone, nice modern house with a washer and a spin dryer, and all the linen and cutlery and whatever."

"Did you explain that to these young women?" Wexford asked dryly.

"I would've if I'd found a suitable one. I'd have taken her to my place in Guildford and shown her what she'd be getting. I couldn't do that with the wrong sort, or the first one to complain; you'd have found us and then there'd be no more getting Jerry a wife. Like you have now, like you've knocked all that on the head."

Her delusive state grew more and more apparent as she talked. Schizophrenia can be genetic, Wexford knew, perhaps always is. Back in the sixties and seventies those Victorian theories of inherited madness, of whole families afflicted, had been derided. Today it was seen that the nineteenth-century writers were not so far wrong.

"But the girls didn't suit," he said gently. "They weren't quite what you were looking for, and you were afraid you'd die and leave your nephew alone without anyone to care for him?"

"Really, Mr. Wexford," said Beamish, "I can't have this."

But Vicky said, looking calmly into Wexford's eyes, "Yes. Yes, that's exactly right."

Burden came out, then Wexford. "Barking mad, that Jerry," Burden said, casting up his eyes. "He shouldn't be allowed out alone."

"He's not."

"False imprisonment," said Burden in a severe tone, "is a very serious offense."

"I know. I've been telling you that for the past three weeks. And it's no good saying no harm was done. They'll appear in court tomorrow and both will be remanded for psychiatric reports." Wexford sighed. "Rachel Holmes stuck a knife in Dover's chest."

"Ah, so that's the answer. I asked him what the plaster was doing there. He didn't answer so I asked him a second time and then the poor devil did speak. He put his hands over it and said, 'Hurt, hurt.'"

It was all pathetic, Wexford thought, a sad, ridiculous story. When Vicky Cadbury was dead, who would look after Jerry Dover? The state? More likely was his release "into the community," only there was no community, just neighbors who would be afraid of him or regard him much as people in times past had regarded the village idiot, and he would end up, at the beginning of the twenty-first century, a crazy beggar on the street. "There's nothing more I can do in there," Wexford said, "so I'm going to pay another visit to Miss Jane Andrews, and since there's nothing more you can do in there, you may as well come with me."

"My daddy said I wasn't to tell."

Sitting on her mother's knee, playing with her mother's long hair, Kaylee Flay smiled virtuously. She took hold of a lock of Jackie Flay's hair and twisted it around and around her forefinger, while giving Vine a coy sideways glance.

"You told Kim Fowler," said Vine.

"That's different. He's a *boy*, he's not a grown-up."

He thought how intelligent she was, this four-year-old who had come out of the lowest stratum of society, almost the socially excluded. Somewhere he had read that, for all the claims that every child of today had an equal opportunity for education and betterment, those from her group were the least likely to avail themselves of it. It made him angry when he looked at her bright face and keen eyes and knew that she was using that intelligence, which should have been channeled into the right paths, to deceive authority. That was the real crime, to pervert a child like this one, to corrupt her into becoming a criminal's aide and to make stealing a game, in which success was rewarded.

Jackie Flay hadn't said a word once she had told him she didn't mind him questioning Kaylee. She sat there apathetically, her arms around the child's waist, turning her head slowly around and around to make her hair more accessible to Kaylee. She seemed to enjoy this rough caressing and pulling. Vine asked her about the evening she had been in the Rat and Carrot. Had she been alone or with Patrick?

"I don't like you and my dad going out in the evening," said Kaylee.

"Now you know Auntie Josie was only next door."

"I don't like Auntie Josie."

"Yes, you do, Kaylee. You do like Auntie Josie. You're a naughty girl to say that."

"And you're naughty to go out and leave me on my own. I could get burnt up in a fire or that pedo could come and take me."

"Mrs. Flay, I asked you if you and your partner were together in the Rat and Carrot that evening?"

"What if we was? Leave off pulling, Kaylee, you're hurting me."

"Did you hear someone in that bar describe how to make a petrol bomb?"

"I don't know what you're talking about," said Jackie.

Kaylee got off her mother's lap. She slid to the ground, climbed up onto another chair, and sat there with her legs dangling. "My daddy," she said conversationally, "got two bottles and he put this stuff in them and it smelt awful, pooh, and he stuffed up the tops with socks, they was my socks what I've grown out of, and he took some more stuff out of the heater that's in my bedroom and put that on the socks, and he said they was petrol bombs and they was for killing the pedo, so there!"

Jackie Flay let out a loud scream. She made a dash for Kaylee, one arm upraised, but the child dodged her hand, and Vine, wondering what he was letting himself in for, snatched her up in his arms and held her high in the air.

Mrs. Probyn was seeing someone out when they arrived. The woman who was leaving was so like Jane Andrews, was a more feminine version of her, that there was no doubt this was her sister. Although it was a surprise visit, Mrs. Probyn seemed delighted to see them and introduced her daughter on the doorstep. "This is my daughter, Mrs. Sharpe. These are the policemen I was telling you about, Louise, the ones that had some important business with Jane which I, of course, was not permitted to hear."

Mrs. Probyn smiled brightly to show the good child that this treatment was only to be expected from the troublesome child. Louise Sharpe was plumper than her sister and less stylish, only her expensive jewelry—a huge diamond in the engagement ring above her wedding band, diamond earrings, and a Cartier watch on her left wrist—giving any indication of her affluence. Apart from these, she wore a longish floral skirt and a cotton sweatshirt bearing the logo of a well-known sportswear manufacturer. Her dark hair was untidy and in need of a good cut, and her pale face was bare of makeup but for some smudged black stuff circling her eyes.

She gave her mother a kiss that was just a peck in the air two inches from her cheek and remarked that she must get back as she didn't care to leave "new staff" on their own for too long in the circumstances. Saying to Wexford and Burden, in the ludicrous expression often uttered when no words have been exchanged, that it was nice to have met them, she went down the path to her car, a new red Mercedes.

"Your daughter has a big house?" Wexford asked as Mrs. Probyn ushered them into the living room she was discouraged from occupying.

"Louise? Oh, yes, huge house, six bedrooms, three bathrooms—well, she's very well-off, as I believe I told you." Mrs. Probyn laughed merrily. "*Noblesse oblige*, you know." Like most people, she seemed to have only a muddled idea of what the phrase meant, Wexford thought. "I think it's important to keep up appearances, don't you? I will say for poor Jane, she does make the best of herself. She used to have lovely long hair, you know, but she would have it cut off. Said it was too much trouble, if you please. Louise looks a ragbag most of the time, but her carelessness in that regard doesn't extend to her home, I'm glad to say. She has a truly beautiful home, a real abode of bliss for a child—what a pity, as I always say, she had no children of her own."

"She never thought of adoption?" Burden hazarded.

"Well, yes, she did try to adopt a baby from one of those countries, Romania or Albania, one of those places in the *Eastern Bloc*, as the powers-that-be call it. She had all the papers, but something went wrong, don't ask me what, and then of course poor James died, her husband that is." Mrs. Probyn giggled and put her hand over her mouth like a schoolgirl. "But I'm not supposed to talk about it. Jane says I gossip too much and not to talk about family things. But what I say in response to that is, what else can I talk about? What else do I know? I'm not exactly out in the great world, am I? I'm not in the corridors of power or the—the Weather Centre, am I?"

They were saved from replying by the entry into the room of Jane Andrews, alerted no doubt by the sound of her mother's giggle and raised voice. She was well dressed today in a short black dress and yellow jacket, the male image discarded, but she looked aghast. She turned white under the heavy makeup. Wexford had thought cosmetics would improve her looks, but now he changed his mind. Her face was a painted mask. This time she made no attempt to expel Mrs. Probyn from the room. "I was upstairs working. I didn't hear the bell."

"They didn't ring the bell, Jane. They arrived just as Louise was going and the door was open."

"Oh, was Louise here?" Jane Andrews looked as if she wanted to say more but bit back the words. "I didn't hear her come," she said instead.

"She came to see me." Mrs. Probyn's unconcealed gratification made her seem senile. "Not everyone who comes to this house wants your company, you know, my dear, hard though that may be for you to grasp."

Jane turned toward Wexford. "What did you want to see me about?"

Burden answered her, saying quietly, "Miss Andrews, we know your relationship with Stephen Devenish isn't a sexual one. But there is some kind of relationship with him, isn't there?"

The effect on her was startling. She burst out laughing. The laughter had no amusement in it, only incredulity and wonder at the folly of human assumptions. It held relief too. "I never would have expected that. Even from the police I wouldn't. What can I do to make it plain to you how much I loathe and despise Stephen Devenish? How can I explain to you what a bastard he is?"

"Language, Jane," said Mrs. Probyn.

Wexford ignored her. "You've already done so, Miss Andrews. Or, rather, you've given a strong impression of doing so. Perhaps you'll fill in the details."

She hesitated. Her own vehemence seemed to put a check on her. "He is an absolute bastard," she said more quietly.

"So you said. But is there a reason for your saying so? Or is it a case of Dr. Fell?"

"Of what?"

Unexpectedly, Mrs. Probyn intervened and recited:

I do not love thee, Doctor Fell.
The reason why I cannot tell;
But this alone I know full well,
I do not love thee, Doctor Fell.

Wexford thought it would anger her daughter. To his astonishment, it made her laugh, it made her human. "I've never heard that before, Mother," she said, and to Wexford, "I certainly don't love Stephen, I dislike him awfully, but of course I can tell you why. He's a sexist tyrant, he makes Fay his slave, he rules that house like the despot he is and I loathe him."

"And perhaps you've said as much, Miss Andrews, which is why your friendship with his wife was broken off? Perhaps she is a loyal wife who doesn't care for criticisms of a husband she is obviously very attached to?"

She shrugged. "Perhaps. I don't suppose she did like it. They have no friends now, either of them. Well, he may have at work, cronies, business acquaintances, if you can call those people friends."

"Or perhaps none of this is true. Perhaps his declared dislike of you and your unquestionable dislike of him are a blind to conceal a friendship and an alliance." She leaned forward, tried to speak. Wexford held up his hand. "No, one moment, let me finish, please. I am not suggesting, as I've already said, that there is or has ever been any sexual relationship. You might be useful to him and he to you. That's all I'm saying. And that, if we had recorded this conversation and were able to play it back, even you might say that you protested your dislike of him too violently to be credible."

"If you're suggesting, and I think you are," said Jane Andrews, once more aggressive, "that I, or I and Stephen Devenish together, have abducted his daughter and are keeping her here, then you are mad."

"Oh, Jane," said her mother.

"Oh, Mother, yes. That's what they mean."

"But you don't like Mr. Devenish. That's why we never see that nice Fay anymore, isn't it? Because you and Mr. Devenish don't get on."

The wake of Ted Hennessy took place the following day. The chief constable and the assistant chief constable were there, as well as Wexford and his entire team, and the members of the Regional Crime Squad, a junior minister in the Home Office, and Hennessy's cousin who happened to be a famous television comedian. Not on account of the minister but owing to the presence of the comedian, coverage of the whole thing was shown on the BBC's evening news.

As he was leaving, Mitchell came up to Wexford to say how sorry he was about Hennessy. "We're having a whip-round at Muriel Campden, collecting for the poor guy's widow." Mitchell gave Carl Meeks a baleful look. "Well, some of us are."

Returning to his car, Wexford remarked to Donaldson that it was the thought that counted, and did he know what had become of his raincoat.

"A Mrs. Hebden came up to me in the car, sir, and said you were in her house and you wanted to walk back, it being such a nice day for a change, and to give her your raincoat to take in to you."

"And you did?"

"Yes, I did, sir. I hope I did right."

Wexford didn't answer. He went upstairs where he had been due to see Lynn Fancourt five minutes before. She was waiting for him in his office, tense, her shoulders hunched, picking at her nails. Allowing none of the amusement he felt and none of the underlying approbation to show in his face, he gave her a five-minutes-long lecture on the inadvisability of showing this kind of initiative, of taking matters into her own hands and pursuing secret personal goals as if she were some kind of private eye instead of part of a team. That was not the way to look to promotion. This was amateurish, not enterprising. Lynn squirmed at "private eye" and again at "amateurish," but she said nothing, though frequently nodding her head in an earnest fashion.

Petrol bombs and nail bombs. Patrick Flay admitted that he had made both in his kitchen in Glebe Road. In an interview room at Kingsmarkham Police Station, when asked why by Barry Vine, he first said that it was just a matter of interest, to see if he could, but later confessed he made the bombs for sale.

"Who were you going to sell them to?"

"You'd be surprised." Flay was becoming increasingly confident that he had done nothing wrong, or rather, that he had committed no indictable offense. "There's a market for weapons. It's an industry. Don't you watch no TV? Supplying arms is big business worldwide."

"That's tanks and guns and missiles and whatever," said DC Archbold, "not your piddling petrol in a Ribena bottle."

"Not so piddling," said Flay, "when you think what it can do. It's a funny thing, you know, how it's getting harder all the time just to get hold of a glass bottle. All cans it is these days and plastic."

"You were going to tell me who you sold your petrol bombs to," said Vine.

"Was I? Pardon me, but I don't think you asked. As a matter of fact, I never *sold* none of them. I *give* one of them away, for a sample like, and one of my nail bombs. Then"—Flay assumed a pious, caring expression—"on account of the tragedy what happened here, I destroyed all my stock. Search the place if you want, be my guest."

"We will, you can be sure of that. So you didn't make a profit on them. Who did you give the sample to?"

"Colin Crowne," said Flay.

"So you've said before. Crowne was ill in bed with shingles."

"I can't help that. I don't know what he done with it. I give it to him in the Rotten Carrot, that's all I know. And it's no use asking me if I saw who threw it—*if* it was one of mine—because I wasn't there. You got all this out of my Kaylee, didn't you? Don't trouble to deny it. You got it out of Kaylee when her mum was out of the room, you wormed it out of her, she's only four years old and that's illegal what you done."

"Mrs. Flay was present throughout the interview," Vine said stiffly.

"You can tell that to the judge," said Flay, "when I've writ about you to the chief constable."

A warrant was obtained and the house of which Jackie Flay was the tenant was searched. Nothing was found, neither petrol nor nail bombs nor stolen goods.

CHAPTER 17

BOTH BOYS RESEMBLED THEIR FATHER, BUT IN DIFFERENT ways, each favoring a different aspect of him, so that Edward had his height, his dark, wavy hair, high forehead, and straight nose, while Robert shared his eye color, sensitive, rather full mouth, his high cheekbones, and his grace of movement. Their mother seemed to have contributed nothing to their genetic makeup; not a trace of her could be seen in either young face. Did the little girl look like her? Wexford had no means of knowing. The people on the Muriel Campden Estate and in the Glebe Road area had records of their children not only filling albums but on film. The Devenishes of Ploughman's Lane had one picture, and that taken by a newspaper when Sanchia was a baby, out in her pram.

"We don't take photographs of people," Edward explained, if it was an explanation. "We take them of places."

Wexford was questioning each of them individually, in the presence, of course, of their mother. He asked Edward first to cast his mind back to when Sanchia disappeared, to close his eyes and attempt to re-create that night, beginning with the exact time he had gone to bed, if he had read in bed, when he had put the light out, and how soon he had fallen asleep. The boy followed this procedure, or Wexford thought he did, and said he didn't read much and never in bed. He had been playing a computer game and left it on by mistake, so that it was still on when he woke in the night and he had to get up and turn it off.

"What woke you?" Wexford asked him.

The boy said he didn't know and added, with the first sign of perception he had shown, "You don't ever know what wakes you because by the time you're awake, it's stopped." He hadn't known what time it was either. It might have been the sound of someone coming up or going downstairs.

"That wouldn't wake you, Edward," Fay Devenish said. "Dad or I often go up- or downstairs after you're in bed and you don't wake up."

"Then I don't know," the boy said, and he gave his mother a look Wexford couldn't interpret. It seemed resentful yet puzzled. "I said I didn't know and I don't."

"Are you fond of your sister?"

"Of course I am. She's my *sister.*"

Fay Devenish began to cry. Most boys of twelve, brought up as these had been, in this environment, would have gone up to their mother and put an arm around her shoulders, at least told her not to cry, in some way comforted her. Edward sat stony-faced. He looked away. She dabbed at her eyes, seemed to be making a stoical effort at controlling herself.

Wexford went on, "Did you ever think you would have been happier *without* your sister? If, for instance, your sister had never been born?"

Fay made a little murmur of protest, the sound a woman might make if she cut herself or was stung by an insect.

"I'm sorry, Mrs. Devenish, but I'd like him to answer."

She nodded, rather hopelessly.

"Edward?"

The boy, whose expression hadn't changed, said, "I don't know. I got used to having her around." He hesitated. "I suppose I thought it was funny, I mean it was strange, having her when me and Robert were so old."

"But you never thought of harming her in any way?"

"Chief Inspector, I'm sorry, but I can't have this." To his knowledge, Fay had never been so assertive. Color had come into her face and her eyes were bright. "I can't sit by and hear you ask him things like that."

"Very well, Mrs. Devenish. That's all, Edward."

"Can I go now?"

"You can go. Tell your brother I'll see him next."

He was smaller than Edward but would probably attain his height in two years' time. Many children, especially boys, have inquiring or mystified expressions, not surprising, Wexford thought, when you considered the state of the world they lived in. But in the eyes of these two was something more than that, something they shared but he had seen in few others, a look of bitter bewilderment. It was particularly evident when they looked at their mother.

He asked Robert about that night, but the boy could remember even less than his brother. To the question as to whether he had been fond of Sanchia, he replied that he supposed so: "I liked her all right."

Wexford noticed this past tense if Fay Devenish did not. But she gasped when Robert said, "She's dead, isn't she? The kids at school say she's dead."

"Do you know a friend of your mother's called Jane, Robert? Miss Jane Andrews?"

Before the boy could answer, Fay said quickly, too quickly, "She's not a friend of mine."

"Robert?"

"I think so. A long time ago. We never see her anymore."

Wexford said he had nothing more to ask him. The child went away and his mother began crying again. "She's not a friend of mine, she's not. You shouldn't have said that in front of my children."

"It's understandable that you're upset, Mrs. Devenish, but there are one or two more things I must settle while I'm here."

"That's all right, but you shouldn't have... Oh, what's the use?" She pulled tissues out of the box on a side table, dried her eyes, and blew her nose. "I won't cry anymore. What is it you want to know?"

"It's not so much what I want to know as what I want to have. When I asked you for a photograph of Sanchia, you offered me only a family group. I refused it then, but I'd like it now. It's better than nothing."

"My husband will be home in a minute."

"That's fine. It's best for you not to be alone too much. But it's not a reason for your not finding a photograph for me. All we have at present is a poor, smudgy shot taken by the *Courier*, and we don't even have the original."

"I saw that picture in the paper," she said, as if answering him, as if explaining. "The person who took it, I didn't even know they were taking it."

"Perhaps you'll have a look now." A conviction that Devenish's homecoming would put an end to everything useful he could accomplish here made him urgent. "Please, Mrs. Devenish."

She went reluctantly. They had been in the living room and he heard her go into the study, then upstairs. Once more he asked himself why the missing little girl wouldn't or couldn't speak, why those boys' eyes were so troubled, and a fresh question, also to be unanswered, was why their mother had cried when he had simply asked her elder son if he was fond of his sister. And did she now dislike Jane Andrews so much that she wept at the imputation the woman might be her friend?

She came back and he noticed changes in her. She had powdered her face and made up her eyes and mouth, put on perfume and changed her shoes for a more elegant pair. Something had been done to make her hair look thicker, and the resulting arrangement had been sprayed with lacquer.

"Here," she said, "I'm afraid that's the best I can do."

Two snapshots. He could see at a glance that they were pairs or groups of people, not a single one of the child alone, but now was no time to take a closer look. Fay Devenish jumped at the sound of her husband's key in the lock.

Wexford said quickly, "May I take these? They'll be returned to you, of course."

"Yes, take them."

She might have been a spy passing the plans to an enemy agent, so low and urgent was her voice, more a hiss than a whisper. She stood up, running her hands down her dress as if she could smooth away weariness and pain and anxiety.

"I was just leaving," Wexford said as Devenish came into the room.

The man kissed his wife. Not a casual kiss but passionate, the kind of kiss, Wexford thought, a little embarrassed, that should never be bestowed and received in the presence of others. Devenish's lips lingered on Fay's passive, half-open mouth, then he drew slowly away. To Wexford he extended his hand, smiling, warm, said, amazingly, that he was afraid they were giving the police a great deal of trouble. Wexford resisted saying, as he always did resist, that he was only doing his job. Walking back to his car, he asked himself if it was his imagination that Mrs. Devenish had wanted him to stay longer, would have been content for him to sit down and talk it all over once again. Yet she had dressed up for her husband's homecoming and responded gratefully to his kiss.

"I've been wondering about the older boy, Edward," Wexford said to

Burden later in the Europlate. "They don't give much away, those children. They're cagey and secretive, their eyes are puzzled. I have even wondered if they were abused children."

"The father?" said Burden.

"One would suppose so. There's no evidence. It may be that this whole affair of Tommy Orbe put the idea into my head, and it's hardly an idea, it's more a thought without foundation."

"The fact is," said Burden, "that child abuse is the fashion. You can't open a newspaper without reading of some fresh terrible case somewhere. It's ghastly but it's not that common, and I can't see Stephen Devenish in that role."

"I'm not so sure. He looks capable of violence and we know he has a bad temper. What are you going to eat? Three kinds of herring with new potatoes—that's Swedish—or maybe Hungarian goulash. Is Hungary in the European Union?"

"God knows," said Burden. "I'm reading the blackboard. Sparkling water to drink, inevitably?"

"When we find that child, we'll have a bottle of the Widow."

Wexford ordered the herring and potatoes and Burden bacalao from Portugal. "Dried salted cod with something done to it. We had it when we were in the Algarve last year."

"It sounds disgusting. I got some photographs from Mrs. Devenish. D'you want to see them? They're not up to much, just out-of-focus family groups really."

Burden gave the pictures Wexford laid on the tablecloth a fleeting glance. "Worse than useless, I'd say. I don't know why you're bothering with them. Either Devenish took her or one of his sons."

"If it was one of those boys, Sanchia is dead."

Burden looked at him. "You mean Devenish could have hidden her somewhere, he may even have engaged a nanny and set her and the nanny up in a rented flat somewhere, that's a possibility. But if one of her brothers took her, he must have killed her. He'd have nowhere to hide her and no wish to hide her, as far as I can see. He'd have taken her because he was jealous of her position in the family, killed her to get her out of the way—and then what?"

"Hidden the body." Wexford poured mineral water for both of them. "And hidden it somewhere nearby. His mother says he can drive. Perhaps he can. He may be able to drive a car in theory, but I doubt very much if he could maneuver it out of that drive by night. They're both big boys, either of them could have carried her, and probably she wouldn't have cried if either had lifted her out of her coat. So if Edward did it—or, come to that, if Robert did it—he killed his sister somewhere in the garden, possibly by strangling her, and back we come to your point."

"What then? Either is strong enough to carry a three-year-old some distance, but dig a grave and bury her? How long would it have taken? Would they even know how to set about it?"

Their food was brought by the Europlate's proprietor, a fat man who for some reason always wore a starched and spotlessly white apron, though he was not the cook. In the opinion of some of his patrons it was done to give him a French appearance. He combined in his looks supposedly typical features of many of the Union's members, being black-haired and mustached like a Spanish bullfighter, with the regular thin-lipped profile of the Scandinavian, the olive skin of the Greek, and the high cheekbones of the Slav. Some said his name was Henri, others Henrik or Heinrich, and he was called by all these. But his English was spoken in the pure accent of the Lowland Scot, and now, as he set each plate down, he expressed the opinion that a wee bi'o'fish would set them up for the day, as it fed the brain.

"I can do with some of that," Burden said when Henri had returned to the back regions. "We know it wasn't one of the boys, though, don't we? It has to be Devenish, or according to my as yet unfed brain, it has to be. Why he took her and where he put her we don't know, but we can be pretty sure if he took her, she's alive."

"Fathers do kill their children, you know that."

"Sure, and it's a monstrous crime but it's usually accidental, the result of violent abuse. Devenish had no reason to do it."

"No reason in your estimation, maybe. How about jealousy? How about seeing her as the one person with the power of coming between him and his wife? Of separating him from his wife? He looks as if he's in love with his wife. He greets her as passionately as if they've known each other a year and been parted for the past six months. We know a lot about these people by now, Mike, but we know very little of their feelings. What do we ever actually know of anyone's feelings, come to that, even when they're our nearest and dearest? Devenish may have disliked and resented Sanchia. Sanchia may have been her mother's favorite, preferred over her sons—preferred over *him?*"

"I sometimes wish," said Burden, "that we had ordinary, normal people to deal with."

"Are there any? Do you realize, Mike, that you've contrived a possible scenario for Devenish? I don't think you meant to, but you have. He's sexually abused all his children and now turned to the little girl. This happens in her bed during the night. He doesn't in fact take a sleeping pill, he only tells his wife he does. That night he paid his usual visit to her, accidentally killed her, carried her body downstairs, and buried her in the garden."

"How about the car, then?"

"Not in the garden. No, you're right. He took the body away somewhere and buried it."

Burden put down his knife and fork. He wiped his mouth on a dark blue napkin with the EU logo in its center and picked up the menu. Suddenly he said, "I don't feel like eating anymore. I was going to have the Olde English Summer Pudding or the zabaglione, but all this talk of what Devenish may or may not have done has rather put me off. Silly, isn't it? I'm not usually like that."

"I shall have a pudding," said Wexford stoutly. "I shall have something called *rød grø*, which I am certain I'm not pronouncing correctly. As Henri said, I have to feed my brain."

"Are you going to arrest him?"

"Henri?"

"No, Devenish, of course."

"Not yet," said Wexford. "He won't run away, you know. He's absolutely confident he's safe. I'd say he always is, in everything he does. He knows best, he is right, Devenish rules okay. Doubtless it's the secret of his success, total confidence in himself."

"I'd like to see what happens to this famous confidence," said Burden viciously, "when we get him in court."

"I'm dining with a client—remember?"

Once upon a time, when her husband made that remark, and made it ten minutes before he was going out to his engagement, Sylvia would, in his words, have laid into him. She had been known to lean against the front door, holding it shut, while she lectured him on her rights as a woman and told him that the children were his as well as hers. But she had spent half the day at a seminar entitled "Psychological Abuse in Relationships," and it was either this or, more likely, her experiences at The Hide that affected her, so that she asked herself if today's lecturer would have on many occasions accused her of verbal abuse. It chastened her, she liked to think of herself as virtuous, upright, and politically correct, and she forced out pleasant words: "That's all right. I'm on a short shift, the eight to midnight, so I'll ask Mother to have Robin and Ben, shall I?"

"It might be best." He said it abstractedly, then, "Do as you like. I'd better go, I'll be late."

What had she expected? That he'd go down on his knees? A good-bye kiss, even a good-bye? The front door closed after him. She phoned her mother, packed the boys' pajamas and clothes for the morning. It was still half-term, so her father wouldn't have to take them to school.

Could she keep it up, being nice to Neil, if most of the time he behaved as if she weren't there? Would they ever have sex again? Would *she* ever have sex again, since she couldn't imagine it with any other man?

She got her sons into the car and drove to her mother's. It was strange, but often she worked so hard she didn't notice the weather, and at six in the evening she saw for the first time that it wasn't raining and was going to be a fine night. The sky looked different, hazy rather than clear, and the massed clouds had split into a delicate feathering. A full moon, such as was due to rise tonight, always made working on the helpline less stressful. After a particularly disturbing encounter with a woman on the helpline, she liked to stand at that window, watch the sailing moon, and look at the gardens bathed in its pale, cold light.

Therapy, really. Her father did it too. Perhaps she had picked it up from him. Modeling herself on the parent of the opposite sex, a bad thing, said the psychologist inside Sylvia. She could have sworn that night that the moon moved—well, it did of course, but not fast, not so that one could see it move. Counselors sometimes suggested their clients alleviate pressure by watching the tranquil movements of goldfish swimming in circles. Well, the moon was her goldfish.

It would be a long time before night fell. The sun came out palely just as she arrived. Her father came out to meet her and welcome the boys. She knew he was trying hard to be nicer to her, just as she was trying to be nicer to Neil, and if she felt a certain resentment that her own father had to *try*, she didn't show it. She kissed him back and asked herself, but only herself, what was wrong with her that comparative strangers such as those people at The Hide all liked her, while her own family…

"Stay a little while?" he asked her. "We were outside in the garden. It's almost the first chance we've had this year. I'll wait till after you've gone, then I'll take the boys down to the river."

She used to get angry because her mother did the garden as well as the housework and cooking. That kind of feminism seemed old hat now. That her mother enjoyed the things she did and was very well suited to housewifery had never seemed to enter into Sylvia's calculations. She sat down in a cane chair, and her mother brought a tray of homemade lemonade, ice-cold with lemon slices and sugared rims to the glasses.

"You've got some new photos." Sylvia hadn't really looked at them beyond seeing that they were photographs, but as soon as she picked them up, she did.

"They're your father's, something to do with work. He emptied his pockets onto the table." Dora laughed. "You know how he does."

Keys, change, a perfectly ironed white handkerchief—another cause with her in the past for pontificating against male supremacy—and these photographs. She picked up the top one. It showed a family group: man, woman, two boys a bit older than her own children, a baby in the woman's arms. They were standing in a garden in front of a house, and Sylvia recognized the place at once. It was Ploughman's Lane. She had once lived just down the road, though in a rather more modest house. This one was called Woodland Lodge. In her mind's eye she could see the nameplate by the gates at the entrance to the drive. One of the finest houses up there, this was. She had been inside once, collecting for something, and she remembered the elegant, broad staircase and the carved woodwork.

These people weren't there then, or if they were, she didn't recognize them. The woman who had left her in the hall and went away to find a five-pound note had been elderly. But that had been several years ago when her own boys were very small and she was very young, and she and Neil were still getting along….

She turned to the next photograph and the next. The baby was older here, maybe a year older. Impossible to tell if it was a boy or a girl; the hair was short, the child's expression a blank, and his or her clothes the uniform of the modern infant: tracksuit pants and sweatshirt. Mother and child were alone, and Sylvia looked closely at this one, laying it down with a sigh.

Wexford came out of the house and sat down opposite her. He picked up the picture she had already looked at and watched her while she studied the remaining two. In neither of them could the child be clearly seen, for he or she had turned away from the camera. The father of this family was by far the most striking member of the group, dwarfing the woman and her sons, his grin broad compared with their tentative smiles.

"Tell me something, Dad. How did St. Agatha die?"

"Don't ask me. There's a dictionary of martyrs in the living room." He thought about it. "It's on the third shelf from the bottom with all the other dictionaries."

Sylvia went indoors and came back with the *Oxford Book of Martyrs*. She didn't open it but once again picked up one of the photographs.

"I don't suppose you're going to tell me who these people are?"

"Is there any reason why you want me to?"

"Only that the woman is a victim of domestic violence. Oh, you can't see any bruises, you can't see healed fractures, but that's what she is and no doubt that grinning idiot is what you'd call the perpetrator."

Taken aback, he asked her how she could tell. He had been with Fay Devenish half a dozen times, and in her company and that of her husband together, and had seen nothing. Of course he had noted that she was a thoroughgoing old-fashioned housewife and that Stephen Devenish expected a high standard of cleanliness in his home; he had noticed they kept to themselves and had few friends, but that surely was a far cry…

"How can I tell? Hard to say. I just can. You get to know when you're always meeting women in her situation. There's a vulnerable look, a cowed look, and something worn that comes into these women's faces, especially when the abuse is sustained over a long period. Look at her now, Dad, in the light of what I've said."

He looked. He looked particularly at the picture in which she was alone with her little daughter, standing in the garden, smiling diffidently, a cautious, shy, self-deprecating woman who seemed here to wish to efface herself entirely if only she were allowed to. Her body language expressed a reluctance to be photographed at all and as if she were submitting only under pressure. The child had her back to the camera, her face pressed into her mother's long skirt.

"There's no bruise you can see," Sylvia said. "He's careful to hit her where the bruises won't show. If he's careless and he happens to leave marks on her arms or her legs, she'll cover them up with long sleeves and long skirts."

"I should have known," Wexford said. "I should have seen for myself."

"Maybe you have to be trained to recognize it. You know, Dad, I can't only see it in her, I can see it in him. The arrogance, the grace, the charm, the smile. He's the type. Oh, there are many types, but he's one of them."

Wexford sat silent for a moment, thinking of the implications. What did this mean for Stephen Devenish? Suddenly he had become a different person, a monster, as much a criminal as the thug who punches a bystander in a pub brawl. If it was true, if Sylvia was right. He thought of how hard it would be to ask Fay Devenish and how much harder for her to answer.

"Do you remember a couple of weeks back I asked you why a child of nearly three was apparently mute? And you gave me several possible reasons?"

"Dad, are you saying that this child is the missing little girl Sanchia?"

He nodded. "This is the Devenish family."

"Then the reason's plain. She doesn't speak because she's witnessed her father beating up her mother. I'm not saying it's direct, I mean, like, 'My mother talks and you hit her, so I won't run that risk, I won't talk,' though it's something like that. But it's more complex, it's protective behavior all right—look at the way she's hiding herself in her mother's skirt. How about the boys? How has it affected them?"

"God knows, Sylvia. Now you've told me, I can say what in fact I did think at the time, that the older one looks as if he's biding his time until *he's* old enough to hit his father."

"Maybe, or maybe the father's encouraging them to hit her too. Oh, you needn't look like that, Dad. It happens. And don't ask why she puts up with it, will you? Where can she go? Where can she take her children? She can't keep herself—at least, I suppose not—so who will keep her? And she doesn't tell people because, believe it or not, she's ashamed. *She's* ashamed. She dreads the neighbors knowing, friends knowing. She's ashamed because *real* women, women who are beautiful enough and clever enough, and really good about the house, they don't get abused. They get admired and cherished. If she were like that, if she could only come up to her husband's standard, she wouldn't get beaten either. "Probably no one knows about it, or maybe she's told her parents, if she has parents, and they say she's exaggerating, he's a good provider, he's faithful, she's making a fuss about nothing. Or she tells just one girlfriend, and the friend tells her to leave him but won't take her and her children in, so what's the use?"

Jane Andrews, Wexford thought. She would be that friend and confidante. But there had been a quarrel and she had been sent away—because she knew and Devenish couldn't bear anyone to know? Or Fay, like many a person who entrusts to another the deep and painful secrets of the heart, could no longer tolerate the company of the woman she had confided in?

Sylvia was leafing through the *Martyrs* book, stopping, making a face and flinching. "God, she had a kind of double mastectomy, they cut her breasts off. I wish I hadn't read it!"

"It was a long time ago," said Wexford gently, "and maybe it never happened."

"It was in people's minds, though, wasn't it? They must have done things like that or it wouldn't—it wouldn't be in here."

"Violence and cruelty are always with us, Sylvia. By telling me what you've just told me about the Devenishes, you may have put a stop to some of it. Think of that instead of St. Agatha."

After she had gone he understood that she had also shown him the way Sanchia's abduction had been planned, the way it had happened, the despair and last-ditch remedy, the complicity of others, the final painful but necessary sacrifice. It was as if a whole panorama of revelations, causes, consequences, and seemingly endless cruelty unrolled before his eyes. He saw the paradox of the innocent victim declared guilty and the ruthless perpetrator emerging guiltless. And what on earth was he going to do about it?

CHAPTER 18

A GLASSY LAKE OF FLOWERS HAD COVERED THE POLICE STATION forecourt since the previous week. People who had never known Ted Hennessy, even those whose only knowledge of CID work came from television serials or who hated the police, all these had brought flowers and left them lying in their slippery sheaths of cellophane under the falling rain and now the blaze of the sun. Many names on cards were those of Muriel Campden residents.

Wexford, returning to the place from Hennessy's funeral, wondered not for the first time at the current passion for mourning with flowers still in their wrapping. When had it begun? Probably when the custom began of placing bouquets on the site where someone had died by violence or tragic accident. Ten years ago? Not much more. It was almost always when the person who had died was someone you didn't know or hardly knew. Perhaps it was a sign of a more caring society and he was all for that, and he asked himself why no one ever thought of taking the flowers out of their wrapping and throwing away the plastic, so that all these roses and carnations might not bloom unseen.

He had been to the funeral but played no active part. Forbidden to be a bearer by his doctor, on account of his weight and his age, he had watched Burden, with Vine, Donaldson, and Cox, carry Hennessy's coffin on their shoulders from the grim black undertaker's car up the aisle of St. Peter's Church. The wreath from the Mid-Sussex Constabulary crowned it, a huge, gaudy thing of delphiniums, gazanias, and stephanotis, chosen by the assistant chief constable, while Laura Hennessy's knot of white mock orange and her children's pathetic twin pink roses lay at its head.

The giving of the address had been left to Southby, who had said all the usual things about gallant officers and exceptional devotion to duty, and laying down one's life for one's friends, than which man has no greater love. But poor Ted Hennessy hadn't really laid down his life for anyone. He had only been in the wrong place at the wrong time.

Funerals depressed Wexford, not only for the obvious reasons, but because they brought out in men and women so much hypocrisy and false piety. Just looking at Southby, half-sitting, half on his knees, with his hands over his eyes, mouthing prayers he hadn't uttered since primary school, sent up Wexford's blood pressure. The rest of them could go back to Laura's house for sherry and Dundee cake if they liked. He wouldn't and he was pretty sure Burden wouldn't either.

Pressmen and cameras were everywhere. A flash went off in his face as he came down St. Peter's steps and for a moment the world went black. He squeezed his eyes shut and stood still in the sudden panic we all feel when threatened with blindness, real or imagined.

Burden touched his arm. "Are you okay?"

"I think so. Do you ever dream there's something badly wrong with your eyes? You're going blind or will if you don't do something about it fast?"

"Everyone dreams that," Burden said surprisingly. "Everyone I've ever talked to at any rate."

"Do they? I find that curiously comforting."

A crowd had gathered in the High Street. As Wexford put it, God knew what they hoped to see. But perhaps it was in the same category as bringing the plastic-wrapped flowers and it made them feel they belonged, that they weren't left out, but part of this drama, this human tragedy.

"Any man's death diminishes me, is that why they're here?"

"Bit high-flown, isn't it?" Burden said. "They just want to see themselves on television."

They walked back, stared at by passersby as if they were policemen from Mars and not the familiar faces any of them could have seen any day. Wexford was silent, thinking about Fay Devenish. He must see her but not yet. A strange reluctance to meet her again had taken hold of him and he asked himself if all abused women had this effect on others. They weren't wanted, they must be ostracized; in becoming victims of this kind, they put themselves outside ordinary human intercourse.

These passive creatures were the ultimate objects of demonization. It was a terrible attitude and he confronted it only for a few seconds before thrusting it out of his mind. He was avoiding seeing her because he had to see someone else first.

"Come upstairs." He and Burden picked their way through the lake of flowers. "I want to tell you a story, see what you think." Under the plastic glaze, roses and fuchsias and zinnias were dying now, petals curling up, brown at the edges, their scent undergoing strange chemical changes. "Lilies that fester smell far worse than weeds."

"I don't see any lilies," said prosaic Burden. "But I know what you mean."

"An amazing number of people want to adopt children, don't they?" Wexford said when they were in his office. "They get obsessed about it. Even normally law-abiding people, women particularly, though I hardly dare say it, they forget their principles and the rules by which they've lived and break the law in all kinds of ways."

"What, you mean like going to Romania and bringing back orphan babies, forging passports and birth certificates, that kind of thing?"

"That kind of thing. Do you remember Mrs. Louise Sharpe?"

"No. Should I?"

"For God's sake, Mike, it's only a couple of days ago. Jane Andrews's sister."

"Oh, her. What of it? And what about this story you're going to tell me?"

"Wait a little. Would you be surprised to learn that Mrs. Sharpe has a record?"

"The life we lead," said Burden, "I wouldn't be surprised to hear anyone had a record. I wouldn't be surprised to hear *you* had."

"Thanks very much. Louise Sharpe is a widow…"

"Not a criminal offense unless she murdered her old man."

"I've no reason to think she did that. He had a heart attack two years ago. He was a few months under forty, but he had a heart attack and it killed him. His name was James Michael Sharpe, and he was an accountant who had gone into computers in a big way and made a fortune. She was thirty-eight when he died and pregnant. The child, a girl, had to be kept on a life-support machine and finally only lived two months. She and her husband, believing themselves infertile, had been trying to adopt a child for five years before she finally conceived. A home study was done, two babies were candidates—or whatever the term is. In both cases the mothers changed their minds at the last moment. Then Louise Sharpe became pregnant..."

"How do you know all this?"

"Thanks to our wonderful computer system, a lot of info is available on anyone with a criminal record."

"You haven't said what the criminal record was for yet," Burden grumbled.

"I'm coming to it. Her husband died and she lost her baby, a double tragedy. I don't know what happened next because I only got facts, not emotions. That part I have to imagine. Anyway, at some time in the following year she renewed her application to adopt, but the situation was very different now. She was three years older, she was no longer in a long-lasting and stable marriage. Her chances of being acceptable as a potential adoptive parent were practically nil."

The heavy throb of a diesel engine brought Wexford to the window. He looked down on the white-and-green truck owned by the local authority's contractors and the green-and-white-uniformed men with Day-Glo armbands as they began gathering up the flowers. "Which today are," he said, "and tomorrow are cast into the oven. Only they're cast into that monstrous chewing machine."

"What are you talking about?"

"Nothing," said Wexford. "Ignore me. Back to Mrs. Sharpe. The first child was called Nicola and she was dead. Sharpe, as I've said, had made a lot of money and he left his widow very well-off, as the loquacious Mrs. Probyn has told us. Not being short of cash, she went off and bought a baby. To Albania, in fact, where apparently you can buy Gypsy babies. She was fortunate not to be caught there as God knows what would have become of her. I don't imagine an Albanian prison is a very pleasant place to spend a couple of years in. Instead, she was caught here, having tried to use the passport she had for the dead child, Nicola."

"She had a passport for a sick baby that only lived two months?"

"Rich people are always taking their children out of the country. Maybe she planned to go abroad with the baby when she was better, only she didn't get better, she died. Louise Sharpe was lucky not to go to prison for buying the Albanian child. They had a psychiatrist in court who said she was badly mentally disturbed, so she got off with a heavy fine and Nicola the Second went back to Albania."

"I'm beginning to see your drift," said Burden. "Here was a ready-made adoptive mother, a woman who longed for a child, even had a name all ready for her and a birth certificate and passport."

"I think so."

"Are you saying this woman, this Louise Sharpe, got into Woodland Lodge by night and abducted Sanchia Devenish? Where does Devenish himself come into all this? And what about Jane Andrews?"

"I can tell you all that too, I think."

Once more Jane Andrews was in her "unisex" attire, scrubbed face, trainers on her feet. She had willingly come to Kingsmarkham because, Wexford suspected, she was anxious, now the whole scheme was over, to tell the rest of it. Her boats were burnt, she could recant nothing, and now she had to do the best she could for the friend she felt she had betrayed and the sister she had perhaps irrevocably injured, albeit with the kindest intentions. The solicitor she had at first demanded she no longer wanted. In fact, as she said to Wexford, she hoped that not more outsiders than absolutely necessary would be involved in this. Instead of an interview room, he took her upstairs into his office. Barry Vine and Karen Malahyde had gone to Brighton to confront Louise Sharpe.

"And take Sanchia-Nicola away with us?" Karen had said.

"You must. The Social Services have been notified and a woman from Kingsmarkham Adoption Department will go with you. Sanchia must be restored to her parents as soon as possible."

Wexford repeated this to Jane Andrews when he was seated at his desk and she was opposite him. She looked down.

She said quietly, "He will kill her."

"Stephen Devenish will kill his own daughter?"

"He will kill Fay. You said you knew why Fay gave Sanchia away. Maybe you've an idea, but you don't know the extent of it. You're like all men, you think it's okay for a man to give his wife a little tap. That's the expression, isn't it? 'A little tap'? Well, that wasn't the way it was with them. If he'd done to a man what he's done to her, systematically, over the years, on and on and more and more violent and brutal, he'd have been put in prison for life."

Choosing to ignore her placing him in much the same category, Wexford said, "Go on, please."

"All right, I'll go on. It'll be a pleasure to go on. He hit her for the first time on their honeymoon. He caught her talking to a man who was staying in the same hotel. Just talking and maybe daring to laugh. Stephen asked her to come up to their room with him, she thought he wanted to make love, and when they were inside, he slapped her face so hard she fell over. In other words, he knocked her down. She wasn't to be alone with another man, he said, and now she knew what would happen to her if she was. She cried so much, she couldn't believe he'd do it, you see. It was, she thought, so unlike him that she cried and cried until he said he was sorry, it wouldn't happen again, but he loved her so much he was insanely jealous, he couldn't help it. Well, of course it happened again. Too many times to go into. Even I haven't been told how many times or all the details. Her mother and father haven't, though it wouldn't be much good. Her mother never wants to hear about anything she calls 'unpleasant' and her father asks her what she does to provoke her husband.

"He's broken both her arms. He hit her so hard in the eye once they thought she'd lose her sight. He cuts her. He'll take a knife from the kitchen and see to it she sees him take it, then he'll call her into that ghastly study—it's always for some imagined or invented misdemeanor—and he'll tell her to hold out her hand, and he doesn't smack it like teachers used to smack schoolchildren's hands, he cuts it across the palm with the knife.

"He's all contrite and sorry afterwards, of course, and he always says it won't happen again, but at the same time it's always her fault, she makes him do it. She's got a lover he overhears her talking to on the phone, or her skirt is too short, or she's flirtatious. That's why they haven't any friends. He beats her if she talks to a man and he's even jealous of women she likes. At the same time he says she's mad. I don't know how many times he's accused her of being a lesbian. She's never had a job because she might meet other people, men and women, at work. Besides, she has to keep the house spotless and do all the cooking, that's her function, and if she's not perfect at it, or he *decides* she's not perfect, he's giving her what he calls 'a little smack,' which in fact means knocking her down and kicking her."

Jane Andrews paused to draw breath. Her color had become high and her eyes glittered. Wexford saw that she was holding her fists clenched as if ready to strike someone, and he had no doubt who that someone would be.

"All right, Miss Andrews, take it easy. I'm beginning to understand. Where do the children come into all this?"

She didn't reply. "It was quite funny, really, you thinking he might have a girlfriend. Stephen Devenish is the most faithful husband on earth. He *loves* his victim, she's the one woman he can beat to death." Her bitter laugh was unpleasant to hear. "She phoned that Women's Aid helpline, you know, not long ago actually—well, it wasn't Women's Aid but one of those. He was in the garden with Sanchia, but he came in and accused her of talking to a lover. He hit her so hard she lost consciousness and she was out for five minutes." She relaxed the fists and let her hands go limp, looked at him tiredly. "Don't ask why she stayed, will you? Don't ask why she didn't leave him, call the police, whatever. I used to ask her that. Once."

"Where do the children come in?"

"They're *there*, aren't they? He doesn't stop because his sons are there. I don't know what he tells them. That that's what you have to do to women to keep them in line, I suppose. Or Mummy's been naughty again. Something like that. Of course you can tell it's affected them, they're both disturbed in different ways."

"And Sanchia?"

"Sanchia was the result of rape. We're permitted to use that word now, aren't we, about men forcing themselves on their wives? It's not their right anymore, is it? Well, Stephen raped Fay when she was ill in bed because he'd beaten her so badly. She was in pain and she begged him to leave her alone but he didn't, he was a man, he said, and he needed sex or his health would suffer. So she got pregnant. When she was four months pregnant he kicked her in the stomach. He didn't want another child, he said. Fay would love the child more than him. Well, his kicking her didn't have the desired effect and Sanchia was born. Undamaged too, which was a piece of luck. Fay begged him not to hit her anymore, she went down on her knees to him. If you behaved yourself like a responsible, grown-up woman, I wouldn't have to punish you, he said. Kneeling to your own husband, what kind of behavior is that? And he kicked her over."

Wexford interrupted her. "He beat her like this in front of the child? In front of Sanchia?"

"Of course he did. She and I were no longer allowed to be friends, but, as I told you, we spoke on the phone. I was all she had and that wasn't much." Jane Andrews cleared her throat, as if she feared the sudden hoarseness of her voice betrayed an overwhelming emotion. "I couldn't confront him with this. All that would have happened was that he'd have taken it out on Fay. I knew that. I'd spoken to him before, when she first told me, which was about seven years ago. I'd told him I'd call the police, and d'you know what he said? He denied it, he said it was all in Fay's imagination, that she was neurotic or worse and was lucky in that she had a husband who understood her. He wasn't rude to me or angry or anything, he was quite calm and charming as ever, soothing really, almost paternal. He just took it out on her afterwards."

"But finally you were banned from the house?"

"That was when I found out he was beating her in front of Robert. Robert was only three then, the same age as Sanchia is now. It was almost as if he did it on purpose, so that the child could *see*. Well, no, not almost, he did do it on purpose. He'd take the child out of Fay's arms and lay him down, then he'd start on Fay with Robert watching. Now he'll learn what happens to women who are stupid and disobedient, he said.

"Well, I went for him, I told him it couldn't go on, I'd take Fay and the children away and have them live with me, God knows how, but I did mean it and he knew it. So he told me I wasn't wanted around his family anymore. That wouldn't have stopped me seeing Fay, but he took his revenge on her, he took it out on her and I couldn't stand that. We kept up our friendship on the phone, that was all we could manage, and even so Fay was afraid all the time that somehow he'd find out about the calls. I usually made the calls, and when that one-four-seven-one system came in—you know, the number you dial and get the number of who made the last call—she was terrified he'd try that and find out if I'd made a call when she was out. She got me to promise only to phone at set times when he couldn't be in and she wouldn't be out."

Wexford, who for the most part had sat silent, listening to this catalog of suffering, now said, "Whose idea was it to remove Sanchia?"

Jane Andrews said quickly, "Fay's. Not mine. I never even thought of it. She told me it was either that or she'd kill herself."

"And by 'that' you mean the giving away of Sanchia for adoption so that she might not see her mother constantly abused by her father? So that she might grow up in a happy home even though this meant Mrs. Devenish would never see her daughter again?"

"That's what I mean, yes. When she first suggested it, I thought it was madness and I didn't see how it could work out. Then I thought of my sister, Louise. You have to understand this was months ago, it took a lot of planning. Louise had had a bad experience trying to adopt a baby from Eastern Europe, and I thought she'd given up all ideas of adoption, but far from it. She told me she was as keen as ever, keener, desperate in fact. And the problems I'd foreseen but Fay hadn't, like getting Sanchia a birth certificate and a passport and whatever, that would all be taken care of because Louise had kept all the documents she'd had for her baby that died."

"Was your mother in on this—this plot?"

"My mother knows nothing about it. She doesn't even yet know that Louise has got a child—Louise has a nanny and a live-in maid—and now she won't have to know, will she?" Jane Andrews paused, looking suddenly horror-stricken. "Oh, poor, poor Louise," she cried, "this will kill her, to lose this one after all she's been through…"

"Miss Andrews, the fact is you should have known this whole operation was bound to fail. It was wrong of you to raise Mrs. Sharpe's hopes and encourage her in this way. You must know that."

"I don't see that. It could have worked, it *nearly* did."

"And the effect on Sanchia has to be damaging."

"Not half as damaging as living with a violent criminal." An upsetting thought struck her. "She won't have to go back, will she?"

"Of course she will have to go back," Wexford said with a sigh. "I understand, I appreciate the circumstances. But whatever Mr. Devenish may have done, he is her natural father, who is living in an apparently stable relationship with her natural mother." He held up his hand as Jane Andrews started forward in her chair. "Just a minute, Miss Andrews. I hear what you say and I believe you. But if Mrs. Devenish makes no complaint to us about her husband, there is nothing we can do. And if she was going to make a complaint, she would have done so already, wouldn't she? According to you, this has been going on for about thirteen years."

"He has to know what Fay did? I mean, that she took Sanchia away herself?"

There was something in the way she said it that sent a chill down Wexford's spine. He wanted to be unaffected by her, to maintain detachment, but he was unable to control his body's response, the shiver that ran through him.

All he could do was conceal it and tell her as coolly as he could that of course Devenish would have to know, adding to himself that the man should already have been told, just as Sanchia should by now have been reclaimed and returned to her parents. These things had to be done at once. He didn't want to look into Jane Andrews's white, frightened face, but he had to.

She repeated the words she had spoken before: "He will kill her."

Restoring a missing child to her parents should be one of the pleasantest of a police officer's tasks. Wexford had found missing children before; taking them home, seeing the bereft mother's face, the father's joy, had been enough to warm his heart. This time would be different and a happy occasion transformed into...he hardly knew what. Horror? Dismay? Perhaps fearful danger. But it had to be done and he had to do it.

It was useless Jane Andrews telling him she wanted as few people as possible to know of this. They had to know. Charges would have to be brought against Jane Andrews and Louise Sharpe, but it was a puzzle to know what charges. At any rate, there was no great hurry. Neither of them would run away. As for Fay Devenish, he couldn't bring himself to think of punishing her further, and of her husband he couldn't bear to think at all. Giving himself an unusual injunction, to play it by ear, he had Donaldson drive him to Ploughman's Lane and Woodland Lodge.

It was the first time he had been there since Sylvia's, and then Jane Andrews's, revelations. In the light of them, the idyllic place looked different, not a peaceful sylvan corner of Kingsmarkham lying snugly between the old market town and the downs, but sinister, covert, the beautiful trees there for the purpose of hiding what went on beneath their shelter. Yet no one would imagine, looking at the house that seemed on this fine sunny afternoon to nestle comfortably in a leafy dell, that inside it a continuous crime was perpetrated, an ongoing, perpetual assault on a defenseless creature. So delightful was the picture and so peaceful the atmosphere that for a moment he doubted. Jane Andrews had invented it, imagined it, contrived this story to cover the truth. There had been some other motive for Fay Devenish giving away her own child. But as soon as he saw her, for it was she who opened the door to him, he knew it was all true, and he was almost at a loss for words.

At least Stephen Devenish was away from home. He was at Seaward Air in the Brighton office. She told him so, as if he couldn't possibly have wanted to see her—it must be her husband he was in search of.

"I'm glad to have the chance of seeing you alone, Mrs. Devenish."

"My sons will soon be home."

Did she think she needed protection from *him?* "I want to talk to you without your sons. On your own. I have something to tell you."

She knew. She read it in his face and she went as white as the ivory linen blouse she wore. For a moment he thought she was going to faint and he wished he had brought Lynn with him or Wendy Brodrick. But she recovered, even managed a dreadful strained smile, and he thought how recovering from pain and shock was her life, she was used to it.

He was going toward the study where, once before, he had talked to her as she lay on the hide sofa, her face marked and swollen, her speech impeded, but she laid a thin, light hand on his arm, said, "No, not in there. Please don't let's go in there."

He remembered what Jane Andrews had said about that room, that male place, darkly paneled, leather-furnished, with the swords and the dagger on the wall, as the scene of many of her injuries. Instead, he followed her into a room designated her province, the kitchen.

On the refectory table where Devenish had wept stood a large wooden bowl brimming with fruit, pale yellow apples, dark green pears, gleaming oranges, golden bananas, and grapes like jade beads. Everywhere was spotless, as if newly spring-cleaned. Two of the casement windows were open and the fresh white curtains fluttered in a breeze that ruffled the leaves of the herbs, basil and sage and savory and marjoram, in glazed earthenware pots on the sill. The little painted doors on the cuckoo clock were shut.

He motioned to her to sit down at the table and he took a chair opposite her. It was an immense relief to him, a comfort almost, that she had no bruises on her face, no marks or scars, so that he could tell himself that perhaps it wasn't so bad after all, perhaps there had been exaggerations. Her eyes met his and she looked away. And then he told her. He told her that Sanchia was found, that she was safe and content in the home of a Mrs. Louise Sharpe, but that Mrs. Sharpe had not abducted her.

"You did that yourself, Mrs. Devenish." It was a statement, not a question. "You need not tell me why. I know why."

The whitening, the threatened fainting, was past. She only sighed. "Someone is bringing her back?"

"In about half an hour's time."

She hesitated. She dreaded saying it but she was obliged to. The words were forced out painfully, like something stiff squeezed from a tube. "What am I to tell my husband?"

The hard rejoinder would have been that she should have thought of that before. He wouldn't have dreamt of saying it. "We'll come to that in a minute. Your friend Miss Andrews has told me a lot of things about you and Mr. Devenish. I expect you can guess what they are. If they are true and you have been the—let's say the victim of repeated assaults..."

She stopped him and now the words poured out. "You're going to say I could call you, the police that is, and bring charges against him and have him in court, and I could leave—but where could I go? And it wouldn't stop, it wouldn't, he would just be angrier, and wherever I went, he'd find me, I know he would. He says so, he says he'd find me wherever I went. There isn't any escape, not while he's alive and I'm alive, no escape at all."

She put her fingers up to her eyes, touched her temples as if stimulating thought, then said, looking at him with pathetic bravery, with a forlorn hope, "The only thing is that he may change. I thought he was changing a year ago when he hadn't...well, done anything to me for a whole four weeks. I mean, it didn't last, but it wasn't quite so bad for a while and then it started again, but I know he was stressed-out, there was trouble at work, and I'm—I'm not always—well, the wife he expected, the wife a man like him deserves, if you like. I know all that. He may change, do you think?"

Not believing it for a moment, Wexford said, "The temporary loss of his daughter may make a difference; it may have shocked him into changing his ways." Can the leopard change his spots? "But Mrs. Devenish," he tried again, "there is no need at all for you to put up with this treatment. What your husband does to you is just as much assault as when a man knocks down another man in a street fight."

"I know. But *he* doesn't. He says he loves me, I'm the only woman he's ever loved. It's his duty to...well, chastise me. He says I need it or I'd go completely to pieces. He really believes that." Her voice, low as it normally was, rose suddenly to a shriek as her control vanished. "What will he do when he knows it was me took Sanchia? What will he do?"

"Please try to keep calm. I do understand. I understand your predicament. I will be here, I will tell him. And the other officers will come with Sanchia and stay here." It all sounded so feeble, such a wretched compromise. He put strength and firmness into his voice. "Please remember what I've said. You aren't obliged to put up with this. Next time he strikes you, get into your car and come straight to the police station. Will you do that?"

She was crying now, shaking with sobs, as she had never cried when her child was missing. Wexford fetched her a glass of water. She sipped it, then took the glass back to the sink, rinsed it, dried it on a tea cloth, and put it away. The back door opened and the two boys came in from school. Their entry made a physical change in her. She sat up straighter, seemed to brace herself, managed a smile. But they didn't speak to her and she didn't speak to them. She got up and put cans of Coke from the refrigerator onto the table for them with a plate of biscuits and two packets of crisps. Would Wexford like tea? He shook his head. Both he and she jumped when the doorbell rang and she gave a little scream of fear.

Edward said, "Come on, Mum, get yourself together."

Robert went to the door and came back with Barry Vine, Karen Malahyde, a young child-care officer, and Sanchia. Both boys were shocked and silent. Fay Devenish said, "Sanchia," as if she were uttering an exclamation of despair. The child stared, put her fists in her eyes, turned her back on her mother, and buried her head in Karen's skirt.

"Someone make a cup of tea, will you?" Wexford said to the company, not daring to single out the young women.

But the child-care officer complied.

"Where has she been?" Edward said to his mother.

"Don't ask."

"You and Dad, you're crazy," said Robert.

He took one of the crisp packets and walked out of the room. Barry handed round the teacups. Sanchia turned her head slowly, looked at her mother, stuck her thumb in her mouth, and squeezed her eyes tight shut. No one seemed able to think of anything to say. There was no conversation apart from Karen's remarking that it hadn't rained for a couple of days and the child-care officer's saying in her bright social worker's voice how much she liked the cuckoo clock and had it come from Switzerland. At that moment the doors opened, the cuckoo came out, flapped its beak, and said "cuckoo" five times.

Another half hour went by and they had all had two more cups of tea before Stephen Devenish came home. Fay was the first to be aware of his car; she seemed to hear it before it could possibly be heard, as if some extra sense abuse and fear had developed in her picked up inaudible sound across long distances. She stiffened, sat rigid, then began to shiver visibly.

"All right," Wexford said. "Stay there. Leave it to me."

He reminded himself that the man didn't know, no one had forewarned him. No doubt, strange as the whole concept was, monster that he was, he loved his child. Human beings were beyond belief strange creatures. Wexford didn't wait for Devenish's key to enter the lock but went outside onto the forecourt. Sanchia's father was standing beside the black Jaguar he had just stepped out of, and when he was aware of Wexford, he turned and gave him his charming smile.

"I have good news for you, Mr. Devenish," Wexford said in a low, steady voice. "Your daughter is found. Sanchia is home again with her mother."

There was no mistaking Devenish's joy, his unfeigned delight. He crowed with triumph, punched both fists in the air like some sportsman who has scored a goal or won a set. He took Wexford's hand and pumped it up and down. He laughed with pleasure.

"Where was she? What happened to her?" A less pleasant thought seemed to strike him. "Is she all right?"

"She seems fine. Shall we go inside?"

"But what happened to her?"

"I'm going to tell you that. In a moment. And I am going to ask you to be very understanding and patient and tolerant, Mr. Devenish. Shall we go into your study? I want to speak to you alone. I'm sure you can postpone seeing Sanchia for ten minutes."

Devenish listened with his back turned. He stood at the window, apparently looking out, while Wexford talked. Then, when he could stand it no longer, Wexford said, "Please sit down, Mr. Devenish."

The man turned to him a face suffused with blood. Dark veins stood out on his forehead. He sat down on the edge of the leather sofa. "She's not sane. She's quite mad. I didn't know she was mad when we got married, but I soon found out. It's a blessing for her she's got me or she'd just go to pieces. She's a nymphomaniac, for one thing. Not with me, I may add, with everyone else but me. Still, what can you expect. She's mad."

Wexford was in a dilemma. He had no proof of Devenish's violence, though he believed in it absolutely. But he couldn't tell the man to leave his wife alone when Devenish would only deny he had ever assaulted her. "It's not a matter of insanity," Wexford said at last, "but she certainly needs to see a psychiatrist…"

"What are you going to charge her with? Kidnapping? Abduction? She ought to go to prison for life. I couldn't bear that, I love her, she needs me."

Instead of answering, Wexford said, "As much as anything, your wife is going to need your sympathy and your support, sir. Now you had better come and see her and your daughter."

By this time Karen had told Fay Devenish that a woman officer trained about domestic violence would be visiting her and a child-care officer would be making regular calls. Fay said that after they had gone, her husband would kill her. Offered a mobile for getting rapidly in touch with the police or the Social Services, she said they already had three mobiles in the house and there was no point in having another. Sanchia crawled under the table and sat there sucking her thumb, but after about ten minutes she came out and climbed onto her mother's lap.

"What have I done to her?" Fay said. "Have I traumatized her?"

"I shouldn't think so for a moment," the child-care officer said. "She'll be fine." But when Devenish appeared with Wexford, Sanchia started to cry. It wasn't ordinary crying but sustained screams, pumped out hysterically. Fay sat with her head bowed, holding Sanchia around the waist but making no attempt to quiet her. Her husband walked over to Fay, stood beside her chair, laid a hand on her shoulder. Fay didn't move. The child continued crying, sobbing now.

"All right, darling, I know all about it," Devenish said. "It's not so terrible. We've got her back and that's all that matters."

Fay looked at Wexford and asked if he was going to arrest her.

"We'll have a talk about that tomorrow," he said.

There was nothing more to be done, but he had never before left a situation with such reluctance. He told himself not to be melodramatic; above all, not to imagine he was leaving her to her death. Devenish would be chastened, he would know he was being watched. It was absurd to feel that the moment Wexford, Vine, and the two women were out of the house, Devenish would turn upon his wife and strike her, knock her to the ground.

On the other hand, it wasn't over, the man would never change. Fay would again have her face punched and her eyes blackened, perhaps her bones broken, maybe not tonight or tomorrow, but next week or the week after. It would never cease until she left him or he killed her. And if she left him, he would pursue her. Wexford had never felt so powerless.

Next day he went back as he had promised and he did see her without Devenish. The woman officer from the Regional Crime Squad had called earlier, she told him. Fortunately, her husband had left at eight-thirty for the Brighton office. DS Margaret Stamford had offered her a pager as well as a mobile, which she had refused, presented her with all sorts of options for accommodation and support if she left her husband, and told her about The Hide helpline. Nothing more had been heard from Kingsmarkham Children's Department, and that Fay Devenish felt was a relief.

"They won't take Sanchia into care, will they? I don't know why I say that, really, it might be the best thing for her if they *did* take her into care."

"Mrs. Devenish," Wexford said, "you are not to be charged with any offense. Indeed, the only offense you could be charged with is wasting police time, and preparing such a case"—he smiled reassuringly—"with all the paperwork would waste more police time. I would just like to reinforce what DS Stamford said to you. We can't prosecute your husband unless you are prepared to give evidence against him, and you've said you aren't. I would urge you to think again, and if there are any more assaults, to be in touch with us as soon as possible. You can phone at any hour of the day or night. Do you understand that?"

She nodded. "Of course," she said, "of course I will," and he knew she didn't mean a word of it.

So he went away and left her, but his thoughts refused to abandon her. She was with him all the rest of that day and the next, and the next. He kept thinking of ways he might act to stop it, post a man to watch the place by day and another by night, lurk outside the windows to catch Devenish when next he attacked her. It wasn't practical, it wasn't possible, he hadn't the manpower. He waited for a phone call, not from her—that he was sure would never come—but from someone, even one of her sons, who had found her mutilated or dying or dead.

It was beyond his imagination to picture what scenes ensued after he had gone and she was alone with Devenish. Or perhaps it was only that his mind flinched from it. She was so small and frail, and Devenish such a big, burly man who must be twice her weight. And the terrible thing was that Devenish had a *right* to be angry with his wife for what she had done, taking away his child, deceiving him, lying to him and her sons. But no one had a right to vent his anger against someone else with savage treatment and blows.

"When we found Sanchia," Wexford said to Burden, "we were going to have champagne—remember? I don't feel much like it now, do you?"

"Not much," said Burden.

Had he beaten her again? Wexford had no means of knowing. As time went on, he asked Margaret Stamford to call at Woodland Lodge again and she did call. This time Fay Devenish didn't even let her get past the front door. She came out onto the step, almost closing the door behind her, and whispered that she was sorry but nothing profitable could come out of another interview. Her husband was indoors, she said, and she would have to explain who her visitor was and what she had come for. Only she wouldn't explain, she would invent something, God knew what.

It sounded as if Devenish's violence toward her was continuing. And of course it was; Wexford had never really doubted that it would. Everything he might do, every action taken to support or help her, would only exacerbate his violence. Brian St. George carried a story in the *Courier* of the proceedings in court where Jane Andrews and Louise Sharpe appeared on a charge of wasting police time and obstructing the police in their inquiries. Wexford wondered then what would happen to Fay when Stephen Devenish read it. A much more serious charge against Victoria Cadbury, that of abduction of three women and falsely imprisoning them, made bigger headlines. Would that also incense Devenish and thus endanger his wife? Perhaps, but he heard nothing.

He even asked Sylvia if, while operating The Hide helpline, she had ever had a call from Fay Devenish or from someone who might be Fay Devenish, but there had been nothing. If there was violence at Woodland Lodge among the high trees and in the deep peace, Fay suffered in silence.

And then, after two months, the silence and the peace came to an end.

CHAPTER 19

Down in Brighton, Louise Sharpe twice attempted suicide. The first time, she left her six-bedroomed, three-bathroomed house with its swimming pool and its staff of resident Filipino couple but no-longer-resident nanny, went down to the beach, and walked into the sea until it covered her head. She was seen by a swimmer and rescued. A month later her housekeeper found her unconscious, having swallowed a packet of sleeping pills and half a bottle of gin. The psychiatrist who saw her when she came out of hospital called her actions a cry for help, but Louise said she didn't want help, she wanted to die.

No. 16 Oberon Road, now no longer the Orbes' home, had been seriously damaged by the Kingsmarkham Six and their supporters, all the front windows broken, the door panels kicked in, and tiles knocked off the roof. Weeks passed before the local authority's contractors moved in, and during those weeks the windows and front door were boarded up and the roof covered in a big sheet of blue plastic. One night, while the Muriel Campden Estate slept, a graffitist had moved in and decorated the entire facade with pictures of bleeding corpses, decapitated torsos and their separate heads, open-mawed animal faces, and such words as *pedo*, *filth*, and *killer* in the bright colors of spray paint—pink, yellow, emerald, Prussian blue, and scarlet.

The *Kingsmarkham Courier* ran a story on the appalling situation of the homeless sleeping on the streets of Myringham while accommodation stood empty in that town and particularly in Kingsmarkham. Not to mention the shameful situation of Kingsmarkham Police Station being restored to pristine condition within three weeks while 16 Oberon

Road still stood derelict. On their front page they used a photograph in full color of the graffiti.

Speculation was rife on the Muriel Campden Estate as to whom it would be allocated when the repairs were finally carried out. Debbie Crowne hankered after it for her daughter Lizzie, and Miroslav Zlatic and their child. As to marriage, she cared little about that, whatever Lizzie might feel. Debbie just wanted, as she said to Maria Michaels, to see them in a stable relationship with family values. Unfortunately for her ambitions, Miroslav was still with Brenda in a partnership that seemed happier than formerly, and it was reported that her sons called him Dad.

Lizzie was nearly six months pregnant and what her mother termed "as big as a house." The social worker called occasionally, urging Lizzie to attend parenting as well as antenatal classes, but she said she was still thinking it through. It was an awkward situation, seeing that Kingsmarkham Social Services were bringing an action against Colin Crowne in the County Court for the cost of replacing Jodi the virtual baby.

Tommy Orbe and Suzanne, his daughter, had been rehoused in a flat on the outskirts of Peterborough. The accommodation was in a bungalow block designed for pensioners and the disabled, and a long way away from any families with children. But the pensioners' families soon discovered Orbe's identity. They stopped bringing their children to visit their grandparents, with the result that the other occupants of the bungalow block ostracized Orbe and Suzanne and sent them obscene letters. Suzanne's fiancé never returned, and after a time she became engaged to one of the men who came to collect the tenants' recycling.

The police are particularly assiduous with their investigations when one of their own has been killed or injured. Burden and Vine, with Cox and Lynn Fancourt, had spent uncounted man- and woman-hours pursuing inquiries to find Hennessy's killer. All they had succeeded in doing was eliminating Colin Crowne from the inquiry. Patrick Flay recalled that he had seen Miroslav Zlatic "holding a missile." Vine found a Serbo-Croat speaker who taught Balkan studies at the University of the South to interpret for him, but Miroslav still said nothing, being apparently as disinclined to his own language as to English. And there the matter stood, though Burden and Vine pressed on, determined to find Hennessy's killer, not to think of giving up until they had.

Frustrated by Fay Devenish's disinclination to have her husband indicted for assault or to give evidence against him, Wexford nevertheless refused to let the Devenish affair disappear into that great recycling bin of unfinished business into which unresolved family troubles were cast and came out the other end as "in the domestic, not police, domain." Instead, he kept an eye. DS Karen Malahyde, while undergoing a three-day-a-week training in the handling of domestic violence, had visited Fay, taking care to do so in her husband's absence. With things back to normal, Stephen Devenish had returned to his former commitment to Seaward Air and spent between eight and ten hours a day at the Gatwick, Brighton, or Kingsmarkham offices. With the boys at their preparatory school in Sewingbury until the end of July, it was easy enough to see Fay alone.

Karen soon became at home in Woodland Lodge and managed, while with Fay, to subdue her own feminist inclinations, her loathing of housework and contempt for those who did it. After all, as she remarked to Lynn, whether the poor woman polishes the floor right is the least of her worries. Having first arranged for a babysitter for Sanchia, Karen set up a meeting for Fay with Griselda Cooper, and the three women had lunch together at the Europlate, Fay having ascertained that it was her husband's day at Gatwick for a trial flight to Brussels and back in one of the new Flyfast 355 Stratoslicer aircraft Seaward had bought.

The lunch was profitable only in that it brought color into Fay's face and a light into her eyes. She hadn't had a meal out with friends since Stephen stopped her seeing Jane Andrews. Griselda tried to get her to wear an alarm device around her neck, but Fay said Stephen would spot it in five minutes, smash it, and probably smash her as well. One good thing had come out of all this, Karen said, and that was that at last Fay felt able to talk quite freely about what went on at home. It was no longer a dark and terrible secret, to be whispered only to one intimate friend.

The neighbors knew. Operation Hurt-Watch's policy was to alert residents in the vicinity as to what went on. Karen had herself told Moira Wingrave and met with a nervous not-in-my-backyard response. Moira said she couldn't possibly think of interfering between husband and wife, especially in a select area like this one, but other dwellers in Ploughman's Lane were more accommodating and less shocked.

"Not that any of them will know," Karen said to Wexford. "It's not exactly a housing estate with paper-thin walls. He could beat her to death and they wouldn't hear her screaming. Not through two hundred yards of dense rain forest."

Wexford himself, when not busy tracking down and prosecuting eco-warriors, speculated as to what currently went on at Woodland Lodge. He talked to his wife about it and to Sylvia. When he mentioned it to his younger daughter, Sheila, all she said was that if any man she'd ever been with hit her, he'd wonder what had hit *him*. Wexford knew it wasn't as simple and straightforward as that. The Devenish affair was Karen's responsibility, but he sometimes called on Fay himself, talking quietly to her, trying to discover what the situation now was and looking for signs of the abuse Sylvia had taught him to recognize.

He looked for other signs too. No bruises had shown on Fay's face since the return of Sanchia, but many an abusive man is crafty and inflicts physical damage where the results of it won't show. That too he had learned. And he observed what Karen had not, that although it was high summer, Fay wore dresses with long skirts and long sleeves. She was only just thirty-six but she never showed off her arms or her shoulders, and all her clothes were high-necked. This might mean not only that the covered parts of her body exhibited bruises and contusions but also that Stephen Devenish demanded the excessively modest dress of a Shaker woman or an Irvingite. Wexford sometimes asked her if she was all right, and she understood perfectly what he meant, simply replying yes and he was not to worry about her.

So he ran to earth (in more ways than one) the well-intentioned, earnest people who broke the law by uprooting fields of genetically altered oilseed rape and linseed, arrested them and had them charged with causing malicious damage, and he thought about the Devenish family. Was Stephen Devenish still receiving those threatening letters? Or had there ever been any threatening letters? Wexford hadn't much belief in the onetime existence of obscene or anonymous letters the recipient declares he has thrown away. Probably they existed only in Devenish's paranoid imagination.

Nor had he ever discovered exactly what had happened when Stephen and Fay were alone together after Sanchia's return. She wouldn't tell him and she wouldn't tell Karen beyond saying that Stephen more often accused her of being a "mental case" than he formerly had. He had also frequently told her she was unfit to look after his children, but whether this accusation was accompanied by blows she never said.

Sanchia had begun to talk. At the beginning of July she became three years old, and by then she was forming sentences and developing a large vocabulary. Children who are late talkers speak fluently once they begin. Knowing his reasoning was unsound, Wexford nevertheless saw her speech development as a sign that she had witnessed no further violence by her father against her mother.

"It doesn't work that way, Dad," said Sylvia. "She was bound to start talking sometime. What will happen is there'll be other traumas, she'll be hyperactive or absolutely not, or spectacularly badly behaved or too quiet, but there'll be something."

"If he's still doing it."

"Dream on. He's still doing it. Why would he stop?"

"What amazes me," said Dora Wexford, "is that these are middle-class people—well, upper-middle-class if you go in for all these gradations. They're very well off, he must be earning a couple of hundred thousand a year."

"Three hundred and seventy-five thousand, to be precise," said Wexford.

"Well, there you are, then. If they got divorced, she'd still get a huge allowance. She could keep that house and he could buy himself something just as nice to live in. I don't understand it."

"No, you don't, Mother, so you might as well not air your opinions. Domestic violence occurs in all classes, it's absolutely not just a working-class thing, which is what you're saying. You don't know what you're talking about."

"That's me crushed," said Dora.

Wexford laughed. "I really ought to say, 'don't talk to your mother like that,' only as someone or other said, Lord Melbourne, I think, 'Those whose behavior requires admonishing are seldom wise enough to profit by admonition.'"

A view he had no reason to change when he went to Woodland Lodge to see her a week later. Unusually for her, her face was heavily made up, some kind of pancake foundation coating the fine pale skin but not entirely concealing the black bruise that covered her forehead, her left cheek, and her left temple. Her left eye was ringed in purple and the upper lid thickly swollen. Wexford found himself in the rare situation of feeling deep embarrassment. She answered the door to him, giving a little gasp when she saw who it was.

Sanchia was with her, clinging with both hands to her skirt. Once he had observed that the sons weren't in the least like their mother, but this little girl resembled Fay, even to the wide-eyed, fearful look. He glanced once more at Fay's damaged face and hardly knew what to say, but he had to say something and that pertinent to what he was seeing. She walked ahead of him into the living room, her hand up to the bruises, an inadequate mask for that awful evidence.

"I know you haven't walked into a door or fallen against the mantelpiece," he said. She shook her head. It might have meant a denial or simply a dismissing of the subject. The little girl was holding a long strip of cloth, a piece of cotton material, one end of which she stuffed into her mouth, while staring at him with her mother's flying-fox eyes.

"I can't talk about it in front of her," Fay Devenish said. "And she's here with us and I can't send her away."

"You can at least tell me if she witnessed it."

Another nod. All the time that hand remained pressed against the damaged flesh, the half-closed eye.

"Mrs. Devenish, I've said it before, DS Malahyde has said it, everyone would say it, you must no longer tolerate this treatment. You surely have tolerated it once too often. Next time you must come to us. You must."

Her heavy sigh seemed to raise and sink her whole body in a wave of suffering. "I wish I spoke another language so that we could talk in that. I wish I spoke French—well, proper French. Do you speak French?"

He nodded his head.

She made an effort, an effort that was both ridiculous and moving. "*Il me cherchera et eligne tuera.*"

He understood that. Or he understood enough. Her husband would hunt for her and, when he had found her, kill her.

Never had he felt so impotent and helpless. He imagined arresting Devenish, talking to him with his solicitor present and the man denying everything, Fay refusing to give evidence, coming up instead with one of her ready stories, the walking-into-a-wall one, the accident-prone one. At the same time he wished he understood the man's raison d'être, that he could begin to understand a philosophy of life that decreed a large, heavy man beat with his fists and his feet a small, vulnerable woman, for an unreal and manufactured cause. Because she couldn't always maintain the standard of perfection he desired in her household, because she lost control over the behavior of her children. It made no sense. It denied all human decency, kindness, and civilization. Of course Devenish was a sadist, and not one content with a masochist partner or one who merely pretended pain.

But how would he, Wexford, feel if the man killed her? Wouldn't he then look back with bitter regret that he had failed to do more?

But do what?

Make sure Karen kept up her visits to Woodland Lodge. Alert Hurt-Watch and its newly trained operatives to this classic situation in their midst. Make certain the Social Services were aware and attentive. Visit there himself whenever possible and whenever safe. Never forget her.

Never let her disappear from his thoughts.

He and Dora went away on a fortnight's holiday to Portugal in July. When he found that the travel agent Dora used had booked them on a Seaward Air flight to Lisbon, he felt a momentary dismay. But why on earth shouldn't they fly with Seaward Air? Even if it meant putting money in Devenish's pocket—which it did not—Fay and her children would benefit as much as the chief executive of the airline himself. Burden often said he allowed himself to become obsessive. Now he was overemotional as well.

At Gatwick, waiting for their flight to be called, he was nervous of seeing Devenish. It was unlikely, he knew. A man in Devenish's position was hardly to be found wandering among the economy-class passengers or chatting to them about how they liked the service. The trouble was that if Devenish did appear and did see them, he would almost certainly invite them into some private room or sanctum of his own and produce drinks. He might even offer to upgrade their seats. Wexford would of course refuse, but the refusing would in itself be unpleasant. However, there was no sign of Devenish and they boarded the plane uneventfully.

Estoril and Sintra were enjoyable, the sun shone but not too blisteringly, the food was good, the hotel comfortable, and they returned in the last weekend of July, rejuvenated and tanned. Wexford immediately phoned Burden to find out what had happened, what new developments had there been, and how, in general, were things.

"We've got no one for Hennessy's murder, if that's what you mean," said Burden.

"That's only partly what I mean. Anyway, if you had, it'd have been in the English papers, which I read every day like a good citizen."

"Vicky Cadbury will never come to trial. She's dying. They say any more treatment would be useless and now it's only a matter of administering morphine to kill the pain. Jerry Dover's gone barking mad and been sectioned."

"I don't suppose my raincoat has turned up?"

"Not that I know of. Charlene Hebden denies knowing anything about it and says she's never seen Donaldson in her life."

Wexford faced up to something much more important. He drew breath. "And Fay Devenish?"

"Nothing new. Karen's called on her while you were away. I gather she's found out exactly how Devenish took revenge on Fay for attempting to get his child adopted. Karen will tell you herself. It's not pleasant. Otherwise it's snafu."

"You're picking up bad language from the Muriel Campdenites," said Wexford, making an attempt to lighten the atmosphere and failing.

He went back to work. The newly refurbished police station had a white and glaring look in the strong morning sunshine. The whole facade had been repainted and the windows renewed in new frames. He thought of Ted Hennessy, who would never see it but might have admired it. Wexford remembered, from a conversation they had once had while on a case, the man's fondness for modern, innovative architecture.

Karen Malahyde had started her holiday, so whatever horrors she had to tell him would have to wait. Instead, he was obliged to face a mountain of papers relating to the arrests, offenses committed, and damage caused by fourteen eco-warriors in the arable country between Flagford and Sayle. Burden came in and said he had just heard that Vicky Cadbury had lapsed into a coma from which she was not expected to emerge. He sat on the edge of Wexford's desk and Wexford remarked on his suit, obviously new lightweight and in a fetching shade of dark caramel. His tie was caramel and black stripes. Wexford said it would be fifty pee to speak to Burden now and he was sorry he still hadn't done anything about getting a mirror put up in here.

The paperwork took till the next morning, till halfway through it. Vine was questioning Flay yet again, WPC Brodrick had been sent off to Muriel Campden where all the council's recycling bins had taken to disappearing during the night and their contents of paper and card, bottles and cans, scattered on the triangular lawn, and Wexford was starting to think about lunch, when his phone rang for only the second time that morning.

"There's been a murder, sir," said Vine. "It's just come through. Up in Ploughman's Lane. Woodland Lodge."

Afterward Wexford could have sworn that his heart had stopped. His heart stopped, his breath suspended, and his voice lost. Time ceased.

Vine said, "Are you still there, sir? Can you hear me?"

Voices come back and time goes on. Healthy hearts miss no beats. It only seems as if they do. Wexford found a voice from somewhere in the depths of him, said, "I was afraid of this. Oh, God, I was afraid of it. Where's her body? At the house?"

"In the study, and it's not Mrs. Devenish who's dead, it's her husband, it's Stephen Devenish."

CHAPTER 20

THE GREAT TREES WERE DARKER IN COLOR AND THEIR FOLIAGE heavier. They were like middle-aged people, handsome enough, vigorous and voluptuous, until set beside the flawless freshness of the young. The trees had no such comparison to bear, for they were all growing old, all beginning to get tired, their leaves dry and browning at the edges. Again like aging humankind, they were fine when seen from a distance, less delectable in close-up.

Wexford looked at the trees as he got out of his car and thought how the first time he had come up here to interview the Devenishes they had been in green bud. Stephen Devenish would never see them turn brown and fall. He would see nothing ever again. Wexford believed it was wrong to feel satisfaction at anyone's death, but except for the circumstances, he would have felt positive pleasure and gratitude at Devenish's. Except for the circumstances...

He would have given a lot to find out that she was somewhere else when her husband met his death, far far away out of reach and traveling distance. But Fay never went away. She was always here and she was here now. In the kitchen, according to Lynn Fancourt, who opened the front door to him and Burden. She was in her domain, the kitchen, sitting at the table, drinking tea.

"Where is he?" Wexford asked, saying "he" because it seemed too soon after the death to say "it."

"In the study, sir. The scene-of-crimes team is there as well as the pathologist."

Photographs were being taken. Perry, the scene-of-crimes officer, was busy taking measurements, and the pathologist Sir Hilary Tremlett (elevated to the House of Lords in the resignation honors as Lord Tremlett of Savesbury) was squatting on the dark brown rug, studying the dead man's wounds. He turned his head when Wexford came in but he didn't get to his feet.

"He's been stabbed in the chest. There are three wounds, one of which was made when the knife passed clean through the heart. Another may have punctured a lung. You can take him away when you like and I'll have a better look at him in the morgue. I don't want to get blood on my shoes. They're new."

The body lay half on the rug, half on the hardwood floor. It appeared as if Devenish, when attacked, had sunk to his knees, then tumbled over backward. His handsome features were so white in death that they looked like the face on a marble bust. He was dressed as became a professional man leaving for the day's work, in a dark gray suit of perfect cut, a pearl gray shirt, and a pink silk tie with a gray horizontal stripe. Or, rather, this was the appearance he must have presented when first dressed that morning. Now suit jacket and shirt were dark with blood and the pink tie spattered with it in a pattern like a bunch of roses.

"I can't be sure yet," said Lord Tremlett, "but I'd say whoever did this was a lot shorter than he. Wouldn't be difficult, though, he was a big chap." Staring up at Wexford, Tremlett said as if height were a disadvantage, "Like you."

"When did he die?" Wexford asked.

"I knew it! I was waiting for that. You want me to say, 'At precisely twelve minutes past eight, give or take a second or two.' That's what you want, isn't it? Well, I can't. No one could. I can *guess*."

"Go on then, guess," said Wexford, bored with the man's posturing. "Break the rule of a lifetime."

Tremlett didn't like that. "I didn't get into their lordships' House on guesswork but on my reputation for accuracy and thoroughness."

Some say with a hundred thousand pounds, said Wexford silently. "All right, when was it? Approximately."

"Approximately between seven-thirty and eight-thirty this morning. I hope you won't twist my arm, I'd take a very dim view of anything like that, but *if* you did, I might say between seven-thirty and eight-fifteen."

Wexford left the room, went into the hall, and asked Barry Vine who had found the body.

"She did, sir. She phoned us."

"When?"

"Just after nine. She thought he'd gone to work and she went in there to clean the place."

"Where were the children?"

"The boys had gone to school. It's their last day of term. I suppose the little girl was with her." Vine hesitated. "She says someone called on Devenish at eight this morning. Devenish let him in himself and took him into the study. She didn't see him but she heard a man's voice."

"Mrs. Devenish did?"

"That's right."

"She told you that?"

"It was almost the first thing she said."

"I see. No sign of the weapon, I suppose?"

"There was no knife in the study, sir. Plainly, a knife was used. There are knives in a block in the kitchen and no one's touched them. That is, no one's touched them since I got here. Lynn's in the kitchen with Mrs. Devenish."

Wexford remembered the knife block. It and the cuckoo clock were to him symbols of that kitchen, and in a curious way symbols of Stephen Devenish too.

"Right. I'll go and see her now."

He found her where Vine said he would, said good morning to her and that this was a dreadful business, and motioned to Lynn to come out into the hall. There, with the living-room door shut, he asked her if the clothes Fay was wearing, a long button-through dress of white-spotted blue cotton and blue straw-soled espadrilles, were what she had on when she found her husband's body.

"I asked her, sir. She said they were."

"We'll start a search of the house immediately."

He walked back to the kitchen. It was as immaculate and neat as before. Fay Devenish looked stunned—literally so, as if someone had given her a blow to the head and felled her. Perhaps Devenish had. She sat on one of the Windsor wheel-back chairs, pulled somewhat away from the table, bending forward, her head bowed, her knees and feet pressed close together. Her lank, pale brown hair hung across her cheeks. She looked up when he came in and he saw that her face was as white as if the blood had drained out of her rather than her husband.

In similar circumstances, when a woman has lost a husband by murder, Wexford would have begun with condolences as a preamble to the questions he had to ask. Here, sympathy seemed inappropriate. "You found your husband's body."

She lifted her head again and looked at him, straight in the eye. "Yes." It was plainly all she wanted to say. She had nothing else to say, but she perhaps recognized that he would want more, much more, and she burst out in a hoarse, half-strangled voice, "I can't believe it, you know. I find it quite unbelievable, it *can't* be true. I was the one who'd die, I'd be killed, that's what I thought..."

Wexford's own sentiments too, his own fears.

"But Stephen's dead. He's been killed. I can't believe it. I couldn't when I—when I saw him. He was so big and strong and—and full of life. I still can't believe it."

"It's true."

"There was so much blood. How could anyone have so much blood in him?"

His own blood ran cold. It was Lady Macbeth's phrase, the grotesque and inappropriate comment that stems from the shock of looking on horrors.

"What time did you find your husband's body, Mrs. Devenish?"

"It was nine this morning. Just before nine. I went in there...to...to do the room. I only thank God, I thank God, Sanchia wasn't with me. I'd left her in the playroom. She had a video on. *The Lion King* it was. She was watching a video, thank God, thank God!"

"Tell me about this man you say called on your husband at eight."

She didn't like that "you say" and she frowned. "You mean you don't believe me?"

"I don't mean that." But perhaps he did. "Tell me about him."

"I heard his voice, I didn't see him. I thought—I thought it was one of our neighbors. I suppose my husband let him in. My husband was—well, he was going to the Brighton office and sometimes this man gets a lift with him. That's who I thought it was."

"What is his name, this neighbor?"

She said she didn't know. "He lives at Laburnum House."

Sylvia's old home. He tried to remember the name of the people who had bought it from Sylvia and Neil. Paulton? Poulson?

"I see you've cut your hand," he said.

"*I* haven't cut it." She looked at her hand with a kind of wonder as if she had never seen it before. Across the palm, diagonally, where the life-line ran, was a long, deep cut. "It bled a lot at the time."

"How did that happen?"

"Stephen did it." She began to laugh hysterically, madwoman laughter, almost operatic, running up and down scales. Backward and forward she flung herself on the chair, against the table, laughing and shrieking, beating on the tabletop with her hands. "He did it, he did it," she shrieked, "but he'll never do it again, never, never, never!"

Lynn came in, alerted by the noise. "Get her a glass of water, will you?" Wexford said to her.

By the time it came, Fay Devenish was sobbing. Lynn held the water to her lips, and to the surprise of both of them, she drank greedily. She drew a long breath and expelled it on a deep sigh. Then she did something that was all the more shocking because it was performed under absolute control and quite calmly. She got up and, showing surprising strength, seized hold of the cuckoo clock and struggled to pull it off the wall. She tugged at it for a moment before succeeding, then flung the clock on the floor with all the force she could muster. It smashed in pieces. The pert little cuckoo, defeated at last, its flapping beak silenced, rolled out from the wreckage and lay on its back under the table.

Violent activity had set her hand bleeding again. She seemed not to notice the blood that poured from her palm and dripped onto the floor.

Wexford said, "That needs treatment. It should probably be stitched."

She shrugged. "He bought that clock when we were on holiday in Lucerne. I always hated it. I used to feel it mocked my…my sufferings."

Lynn got down on her knees and started picking up the pieces.

Fay said, "You must be the only person apart from me who's ever done anything like that in this house."

"You shouldn't be alone," Wexford said. "Is there anyone we can call on to be with you?"

"Jane. I can see Jane now."

The body had been taken away. Peach, Cox, and Archbold had searched the house in a quest for bloodstained clothing and found nothing of interest. Wexford went into the utility room where a pile of clean washing, folded but not ironed, lay on a counter. Among the items, as well as half a dozen snow-white shirts belonging to the dead man, he could see what looked like a cotton skirt, several T-shirts, and another button-through cotton dress. The portholes on the washing machine and the dryer both stood open. The utility room communicated with the kitchen where Fay Devenish still sat and Lynn Fancourt with her. He looked around him, saw the knife block, and noticed that each of its slots but one was occupied by a knife. Seven knives. On the day Stephen Devenish had cried in this room, his arms flung across the table, had there been seven knives or eight?

"Bag that knife block," he said to Cox, "and we'll send it to forensics." Then he inquired of Fay Devenish if a knife was missing from the block.

"I don't think so. Let me see. No, they're all there." She looked fearfully up into his face. "You think that one of these knives...?"

"I'm not thinking anything much yet, Mrs. Devenish. I wondered because while there are eight slots in the block, there are only seven knives."

"There never have been any more." She spoke flatly, her hysteria over. "There's a reason for that. It's made to take eight knives, but if you put eight in, they're crowded together and when you try to pull one out, it brings the next one to it with it. Do you see what I mean?"

"I think so."

He waited for her to say that one of her kitchen knives couldn't have been used to kill her husband. She had been in the kitchen all the time and the man who killed Stephen Devenish had never entered it. He expected her to say it but instead she said, "The knife my husband cut me with, I don't know where that came from. It wasn't one of these."

He said no more. They would soon know, forensics would tell them.

In the hallway he encountered Burden. "Where's the little girl, Mike?"

"I had her taken to a neighbor. The Wingrave woman. It's not ideal but better there than here. And I've phoned the boys' school; it's the Francis Roscommon School in Sewingbury. I said I'd go over there and talk to the head teacher, but he sounds a sensible man. He said he'd tell them when he found a suitable moment. And he'll bring them home."

"I don't want them brought home, Mike."

Burden looked at him.

"Or, rather, I want them brought here but not left alone with their mother. I don't want her to have a chance to talk to them or they to her. Some other arrangement will have to be made."

"You're thinking of the mysterious stranger she says called here this morning? She thought that up on the spur of the moment, didn't she?"

Wexford shrugged. He went into the study and stood at the window. From here, because the room was in a block or wing of the house that jutted forward, you could look to your left and see the front door. Had Devenish been in here to watch this man arrive? Was there a man? Or was he a desperate woman's invention? Wexford looked ahead of him again and saw Jane Andrews's car approaching along the long, green tunnel of the driveway. Her arrival obscurely cheered him. It was better that she was here.

This, Stephen Devenish's death chamber, was also the room where so much of the regular meting out of violence to Fay Devenish took place. It had been searched, but he set about searching it himself. In a desk drawer he found a whip. It was the kind of whip he supposed a jockey might use, though not being familiar with this means of coercing horses he couldn't be sure. One thing was certain, Devenish hadn't used it on a horse. Another drawer held nothing but a pair of nutcrackers and an instrument that might have been pincers but whose purpose he couldn't define. It was a relief to find that the top drawer contained only paper, much of it letters in envelopes.

All this would have to be gone through. Later, though, not now. He was closing the drawer when the writing, or rather the printing, on the top envelope caught his eye. It had been torn open, the contents no doubt read and then replaced inside. Addressed to *Stephen Devenish Esq., Woodland Lodge, Ploughman's Lane, Kingsmarkham KM2 4ZC*, the lettering had been produced by a computer and printer. Hardly believing himself so competent in this area, he recognized Word for Windows, the program they used at the police station—and in millions of other locations, of course. The postmark was Brighton, the date July 24. He took out the letter. Same computer- and -printer-created text.

Dear Mr. Devenish:

I often wonder if you know what a monster you are. A psychopath, not a human being at all. Evil like yours is, in fact, quite rare. Thank God. But God won't have His revenge on you till

> after you have died a natural death in your comfortable, luxurious bed, so He has appointed me to carry out retribution. I shall kill you. In the next few days, perhaps, or weeks or even months. But it will happen. And it will be painful, as painful as the cruelty you have inflicted on your poor wife. I will make her a widow and your children orphans and laugh for joy, as they will.

There was no signature. It often amused him to note how, without a thought, we address people we dislike, despise, or distrust with the endearment *dear*. It was even done by writers of anonymous letters. In his time he had seen many of them but never one like this. It seemed, for one thing, the work of an educated person. There was something evangelical about that last sentence, almost like a line from a psalm, and a suggestion in the mention of God and the capital letters for the deity pronoun that the writer might be religious.

He changed his mind about not going through the drawer now. Two more letters in much the same vein came to light. Both began *Dear Mr. Devenish* and both mentioned Devenish's "cruelty" to his wife, while the second referred to his habit of cutting her with a knife. One was dated early July and the other mid-June. So perhaps Devenish hadn't lied when he said in April that he had had such letters but had destroyed them. Perhaps there had been many and they had come regularly.

When Wexford returned to Woodland Lodge in the afternoon, not two but three women were in the living room. Jane Andrews, neat and smart in a long-skirted, cream linen suit, was sitting with her friend on one of the sofas, holding her uninjured hand, while in an armchair was a woman Fay surprisingly introduced as her mother, Mrs. Dodds. Thin, worn Fay in the blue cotton frock that hung on her bore no resemblance to this tall, well-built lady in bright green dress and matching high-heeled shoes, her "big hair" a carefully teased golden helmet, her face skillfully painted. Cakes were on a table, with biscuits in a silver dish, and someone had made a pot of coffee. They offered Wexford a cup but he shook his head.

"Mrs. Devenish, I'd like to speak to you alone, so perhaps you can spare your mother and your friend for ten minutes."

Shepherding them outside, he called to Lynn to sit with Fay Devenish. He was thinking quickly, seeing a way to seize his chance.

The study was obviously out of bounds. However much Jane Andrews had loathed Stephen Devenish, she would probably balk at going into the room so soon after he had met a violent death there. But it was a big house of many rooms. Opening a door, he looked into a playroom where the television set was still on, though *The Lion King* was long over, and where toys lay scattered everywhere as Sanchia had abandoned them. With his next attempt he was luckier. Here was the dining room. A table big enough to seat twenty—had the poor woman been obliged to hold dinner parties for Devenish's business associates?—still left room for a sideboard, drinks cabinet, and occasional chairs.

He asked the two women to sit down, then said, "Mrs. Dodds, your grandsons will soon be brought home from school. I don't think it a very good idea for them to be here, do you? Your daughter needs to rest. I'm wondering if you'd have them for a few days, just to—"

She cut him short. Her eager smile and rapturous voice changed the image he had of her as far from grandmotherly. "I'd *love* to have them. What a splendid idea. My husband and I are always saying we never see enough of them. I wouldn't mind keeping them for a month. And they love being with us."

"That's fine, then. If you could"—his glance took in Jane Andrews as well as Mrs. Dodds—"just make it appear the invitation came from you in the first place? It would... well, come better that way."

"Of course I will."

"You and Miss Andrews could pack some clothes for them while I'm talking to Mrs. Devenish. I'm sure you know what they'll need."

Fay was sitting quietly, contemplating her left hand, now bandaged. Perhaps she was thinking this was the last wound she would ever receive at Devenish's hands. Or of what she had done? Or what her rescuer, this stranger, had done?

"What time was it when you heard this man's voice, Mrs. Devenish?"

"I told you. About eight. I was in the kitchen, clearing away the breakfast things. The boys were with me, waiting for their lift to school."

"I should like to get the sequence of events right, if you please. I won't keep you longer than I can, I appreciate what a strain this must be on you."

Fay cleared her throat. She glanced across the room, and for a moment Wexford thought she was going to ask if it was necessary for Lynn to be present, but she didn't.

She sighed. "Sanchia was awake by six-thirty. She always is. I got up when I heard her and got her dressed and downstairs. By that time my husband was up and having a shower. I went into the boys' rooms at seven and got them up. I had to go back and tell them again, but I always do have to. I was helping Sanchia with her breakfast when my husband came down. I gave him his breakfast. He always has—had—a cooked breakfast. Then the boys came down for their cornflakes and toast. I'd…I'd run out of oranges to make juice from, it's a bad time of the year for oranges, so I used some frozen juice but it wouldn't thaw out—you don't want to hear all this."

"I want to hear everything," said Wexford. "Go on."

"My husband finished his breakfast and went into the study. That was about a quarter to eight. He called to me to come in there…I—oh, I don't…"

Her face crumpled in distress. There were no tears, rather a twisting of her features into a grimace of dismay and pain. It was as if—and Wexford thought he read it plainly—she was asking herself, as she had always asked herself, why this man of hers had felt the need to hurt her over and over and on and on. Why? Had she really been so bad that she deserved this?

Wexford said gently, "Your husband called you into the study to punish you, didn't he, for failing to supply fresh orange juice?"

She sucked in her lips, bent her head, said an almost silent, "Yes."

"He had a knife but it wasn't a knife from the kitchen? It was a knife he happened to have with him in the study?"

No more than a nod this time.

"He told you to hold out your hand—your left hand because he had no wish to interfere with your ability to do housework—and cut you across the palm."

"Yes."

Unsuitably and uncharacteristically, Wexford found himself exulting in his heart that the man was dead, had died by violence, had been *punished.* He said nothing.

Fay said in a voice that trembled, "He was much, much worse to me after that—that business with Sanchia. Every day there was—there was—something, beatings or cutting me or kicking. Edward and Robert saw it, Sanchia saw it."

"It's over now," said Wexford, adding silently to himself, whatever the truth of this, whatever the outcome, there would be no more of that. "Tell me what happened after your husband cut you."

"I went back to the kitchen. No, I went into the downstairs cloakroom first and tied my hand up in the towel that was in there. The boys didn't see the cut, but they saw my hand was tied up. They were just leaving for school. On the days I don't take them, they walk about a hundred yards down the road and get a lift with a woman who's also got children at their school. I sent them off—"

"Excuse me—do you mean you went to the front door with them?"

She looked at him, puzzled at first. "Did I... oh, I see what you mean. No, I just told them it was time to go and said good-bye to them, and they went out of the kitchen into the hall and out of the front door. I didn't actually see them leave the house, but I know they did. And then, almost immediately—well, a couple of minutes later, the doorbell rang. It was this man. I heard his voice and my husband's voice, talking to him."

He noticed that she never referred to Devenish as Stephen, but always as "my husband," as a slave might say "my master." "That would have been at eight o'clock. Did you hear him leave?"

"I don't know. I thought I heard the front door close, but that could have been my husband going, only it wasn't."

"Weren't you surprised, Mrs. Devenish, that your husband said nothing to you before he left? That he didn't say good-bye to you?"

Her shaky laugh rang shockingly in that quiet place. "Would you be surprised if someone didn't say good-bye to you when he'd just slashed you with a knife?"

"Perhaps not. Perhaps not."

Suddenly she sprang from her chair, looked around her wildly. "Where's my little girl? Where's Sanchia?"

"With Mrs. Wingrave."

"I want her, I want her back! Oh, God, d'you realize, I never need fear for her again!"

"Of course you can have her back."

"I'll go and fetch her," said Lynn.

Across the road and down another driveway, Moira Wingrave was alone in the cushiony, flock-wallpapered room she called the "lounge," reclining on a sofa with her feet up, a long glass of something beside her that might have been virgin tomato juice or a Bloody Mary, and the television on. Sanchia was somewhere about, she said, probably upstairs with Tracy. "Oh, yes, she's taken a great fancy to Tracy. Those simple people are always a hit with children."

Lynn asked her if she had seen a man enter the driveway to Woodland Lodge at about eight that morning.

"What man? You don't mean poor Stephen Devenish?"

"No, not him. Maybe a neighbor who lives at Laburnum House?"

"Oh, Gerry Paulton. No, why would I see him? He doesn't even know the Devenishes, does he?"

"I'd like to take Sanchia back to her mother now."

"Please do. Be my guest. I'm not used to children, and frankly I never know what to say to them."

Tracy Miller knew. She was playing a game with Sanchia called "around and around the room," of which Moira Wingrave would certainly have disapproved, since it consisted in the child's clambering around the master bedroom on the furniture without putting her feet to the ground, jumping from little gilt chair to Louis XVI reproduction commode, ending up on the ivory-silk-festooned dressing table, and leaping off it into Tracy's arms. Articulate now, Sanchia said she didn't want to go home, she wanted to stay with Tracy, and began to cry. Eventually Lynn persuaded her with a bribe of Smarties, which she found by a lucky chance in the bottom of her bag.

Back at home, her mother gave Sanchia a smothering hug and covered her face and head with kisses, treatment that Sanchia struggled under. She had been back home for ten minutes when Edward and Robert arrived at the back door, driven by their head teacher in his car. They looked as children of their ages always do when caught up in tragic events, awkward, embarrassed, lost, and helpless.

Edward muttered something in response to Jane Andrews's greeting. Robert said nothing. He shuffled his feet, then asked his mother if there was anything to eat. From force of habit Fay got up and fetched cans of Coke out of the fridge, bread and butter and Marmite from a larder, Mars bars from somewhere else. But when their grandmother came in, both showed more enthusiasm than Wexford had ever seen from either of them. He felt content with his plan and said he must go.

Outside he met Vine, who had been paying a routine call at Sylvia's old home where Gerald Paulton, just home from work, told him that he always drove himself to Brighton. It was true that he had once had a lift from Stephen Devenish when his car was having its electrics overhauled, but that had been more than a year ago.

"What a dreadful thing. I was devastated when my wife told me, just devastated. He was the nicest chap, one of the best."

"So you didn't call at Woodland Lodge at about eight this morning?"

In fiction people questioned by the police take interrogation in their stride or are merely annoyed by it. Reality is different. Gerald Paulton was shocked and frightened by Vine's question. What on earth did he mean? What was he insinuating?

"I'm not insinuating anything, sir. I'm making a routine inquiry."

"You've got me on your list of suspects!"

"We don't have a list of suspects, Mr. Paulton. This investigation has only just begun."

"Well, I didn't go there this morning. I left for work at half past seven. Ask my wife, ask my kids, the au pair, anyone."

At home, Wexford read and reread the copies that had been made of the anonymous letters he had found in Devenish's desk. The originals had gone to the lab for testing. He thought how much harder the universal use of computers had made the identification of anonymous letter writers, but probably policemen had said much the same thing when typewriters were invented. These letters were plainly the work of someone with more than a grudge against Devenish. He must find out more about this man Devenish had allegedly turned out of his office and thrown downstairs. One thing particularly struck him: Why had Devenish kept these letters, that is, those that came in June and July, but not the earlier ones?

Could it be because only these specifically mentioned his abuse of his wife? Of course Wexford didn't even know if this was so, it was just guesswork. The others might have mentioned it too.

And what need, anyway, to look farther afield for Devenish's killer than his own home?

CHAPTER
21

CONCILIATORY TACTICS APPEALED TO WEXFORD NOT AT ALL and he hoped to get through this interview with Brian St. George without using any. On the other hand, he wanted information from the editor of the *Kingsmarkham Courier*, which could only be obtained from St. George. If necessary, he would have to make a concession and restore to the *Courier* its old press rights with Kingsmarkham Police.

But as it happened, when he met St. George in his High Street office, the editor was anxious to be helpful, even obsequious, and prepared to say and do anything in order that the status quo might be restored. "The 'fat cats' story, Mr. Wexford? When we took that photo of Sanchia? I can't tell you precisely when it was, nor off the cuff. But my PA will do so in the twinkling of an eye. Our computer system here is quite excellent."

St. George's PAs were constantly changing and none seemed more than sixteen years old. The last one had been a plump blonde who wore a micro-skirt that barely covered her buttocks. Her successor was black, six feet tall, with long, gold-beaded extensions to her dyed-red hair.

"See if you can find the Devenish 'fat cats' story, will you, Carly-Jo? Try two years back. And bring me a printout."

Wexford said, "Did you interview him?"

"Sure we did. It's all in the story. We'll be using extracts, I expect, in this week's account of his murder."

Rather taken aback, Wexford said, "You will? Why is that?"

"He had quite a bit to say about enemies. He made enemies in his job, he said. For instance, the airline manager was sacked soon after he got this salary increase. It was for incompetence, and he *was* incompetent, according to Devenish. He'd been hopeless from the start, lost the company untold business."

Trevor Ferry. "You won't be running a story about that, I trust," said Wexford rather severely.

"Certainly not." St. George assumed an expression of extreme rectitude. "I hope we're more responsible than that."

"So do I."

"We didn't use it in the 'fat cats' story. I'm simply telling you what he told me. Very nice chap he was, very easy to get on with, open and honest. In his position he met with a lot of envy, he said. You know, great job, megabucks, lovely wife, smashing kids, beautiful home..."

"Yes, all right. I do know."

"I was only going to say, Reg, that people don't like it. They resent it. I mean, why should he have it and me not have it, that sort of thing. They don't think it's fair. Oh, here's our story."

Carly-Jo came back with the printout, put it in front of Wexford in a sweet, heavy wave of perfume. Afraid from the tingling in his nostrils that he was going to sneeze, he pressed his forefinger against his upper lip, a sure preventative. The story, he saw at once, offered little help. It was the usual thing, beginning with a word picture of Devenish's lifestyle, then leading into a long quote from him, justifying a salary of nearly £400,000 per annum. Not a line about enemies, still less threats. Nothing about the sacked manager.

"Since you were aiming to bring the chap into hatred, ridicule, and contempt, I suppose you were scared of libel." Wexford laid down the printout.

"I don't think that's altogether fair, Reg. It's not as if we were a national daily. Most of us have to live among the people of this town. *We* don't want to make enemies either. Besides, there's something to be said for goodwill, keeping up a happy relationship with one's contributors."

"Why did he mention enemies at all? Don't tell me, I can guess. You or your reporter asked him if he had them, if he got threats, if this so-called envy took positive form."

"As I recall it," said St. George uncomfortably, "he did mention threatening letters he'd had. And of course I said there was no question but that he should take the matter to the police at once."

"Naturally," said Wexford dryly. "You would."

"He laughed it off, said he'd thrown them away. They were garbage and the best place for garbage was the dustbin."

"How original. I'm not surprised you couldn't make a story out of it. Apart from Trevor Ferry, I don't suppose he named any of these enemies, did he? He hadn't any idea who sent the letters, for instance?"

"There was some guy made a nuisance of himself that he had to put out of his office once, he said that, but he didn't name any names."

To Burden the Devenish death was merely a nuisance that distracted him and took officers away from the hunt for Hennessy's killer. Finding the wielder of the petrol bomb and bringing him or her to court was enormously more important in his eyes than running to earth whoever had stabbed Stephen Devenish. In his customary fashion he had long since dismissed Devenish as a villain and a brute, unfit to exist. He wouldn't go so far as saying good luck to his killer, for justice mattered to him, but he resented having to surrender good men and women to the inquiry when there was still so much to be done to track down the petrol bomber.

"I suppose she did it, anyway, didn't she?" he said to Wexford over a snatched lunch at the Europlate. "These wife-beaters who get their comeuppance, it's always the wretched, abused woman who's done it. The worm has turned, that's all."

"The fact is that only two percent of all homicides involve abused women killing their partners."

"Oh, come on, Reg. She's stuck it for years, he's bashed and kicked her to kingdom come, and one day it's the last straw. She breaks, she picks up the knife or whatever he cut her with and gives it to him. Tit for tat and then some."

Wexford, who was eating Italian pasta with German asparagus, shook his head, then, seeming to think better of it, nodded. "There's a lot more I want her to tell me. But I want to talk to the boys first. Then there's this business with the weapon."

"You haven't found the weapon, have you?"

"The funny thing is that I don't know. I say I don't know because there were seven knives in that kitchen. Of course, one could say that there should have been eight."

"I can't say I follow you."

"No, well, is it true what Fay Devenish says and there never were eight knives? Or were there eight and one is missing? Or was one of the seven others used? Or is it true what Fay says that none of the kitchen knives was used? If it was one of the kitchen knives, three can be discounted because they're too small to inflict those sort of injuries and one is a saw. That leaves three."

"We'll know more," said Burden, "when the noble lord, Lord Tremlett, gives you his postmortem results. No doubt it'll be quite a simple matter to match the knife to the wounds."

Wexford said, and to Burden his remark sounded irrelevant, "She's got a dishwasher."

"She's what? So have I. So have you. What's that got to do with it? The way I see it is, they have that absurd contretemps with the orange juice, he summons her to be punished, cuts her, and somehow she gets hold of the knife and stabs him. Blood everywhere, lashings of it. She puts her clothes in the washing machine and has them in the dryer before she phones us. Her only witness is a child of three who wasn't even there, thank God, when the killing took place. Clear as crystal, no problem."

Burden pushed away his plate and drank some water. All this talk of stabbing and blood had started putting him off his food. It never seemed to have much effect on Wexford, and yet, if Burden absolutely had to say, he'd call himself more callous than the chief inspector.

"When he called her into the study," Wexford said slowly, "the boys were still in the house."

"So she says."

"They very likely were if he summoned her, as you put it, at seven forty-five. But they can't have been in the house when Devenish was killed. You're not saying he submitted to having a knife stuck in him three times without a murmur? He probably shouted and screamed the place down."

"So she didn't kill him straight after he cut her," said Burden, taking the pudding menu from Henri. "She went back into the study after the boys had left to walk down the road for their lift and did it then. That need have been no later than five past eight, which left her ample time to get those clothes washed. She was probably wearing the pink dress we found among the clean wash. When you come to think of it, she was in an ideal situation to stab someone and get away with it, having the means of getting rid of bloodstains right there. As for the knife, she could have buried that anywhere in all those acres they've got. Are you going to have a pudding?" Wexford shook his head. "Nor am I," Burden said.

Catherine Daley, the mother of a son of eleven and a daughter of ten, told Karen Malahyde that three days a week she drove her children and the Devenish boys to school in Sewingbury and fetched them back two days a week. Fay Devenish drove all four children to school two days a week and fetched them on three. On the morning of Stephen Devenish's death it had been Catherine's turn to take all the children to school, and as was their habit, Edward and Robert Devenish had come to her house, Braemar, Ploughman's Lane, at about five past eight. It might have been nearer ten past, but they were never late, Fay saw to that, knowing that Catherine Daley would leave in her car at eight-fifteen. The drive took twenty minutes and both mothers liked to have the children there in plenty of time for an eight forty-five start.

"How did the boys seem?" Karen asked Catherine.

"What exactly do you mean?"

"Were they normally behaved? Excited? Frightened? Subdued?"

"I really don't know. Perhaps Edward was rather quiet. But then he is the quieter of the two. Robert can be rather boisterous."

"Was he boisterous yesterday?"

"Not really. No, he wasn't. They were both quite normal."

Wexford spoke on the phone to the sacked manager, Trevor Ferry. At eight on the previous morning, the day of Stephen Devenish's death, he had still been in bed, he said. Could anyone substantiate that? His wife could, Ferry said. Anyone else? There had been no one else in the house, Ferry said rather sullenly. What did Wexford think? That they had an au pair?

"Mr. Ferry, this is a far more serious matter than that which we had to deal with when I last spoke to you. If you remember the names of any of these people you seemed then to think had reason to quarrel with Mr. Devenish, will you get in touch with me, please?"

Wendy Brodrick had stayed at Woodland Lodge overnight and Lynn Fancourt was in the house now. If Fay thought this surveillance strange, she said nothing about it. She was in the playroom with Sanchia, another Disney video running but the child ignoring it and playing instead with a convoy of camouflage-painted toy army vehicles that must surely have once belonged to her brothers.

Not the original but a photocopy of the threatening letter was what he showed Fay. No, she had never seen it before but she knew about these letters. Stephen had had plenty of them. He had never shown her any but he had described them to her.

"I thought he'd accuse me of sending them," she said. "But he never did. They were done on a computer and he knew I couldn't use a computer. He thought them well written and I expect he thought I was too ignorant to write them. He was always saying I was ignorant." She changed the subject. "My sons went to stay with my mother. Did you know that?"

"She said she was going to invite them."

Fay switched off the television by means of the remote. Although Sanchia wasn't watching the video, hadn't watched it since Wexford came into the room, she immediately set up a howl of protest: "Put it on, put it on, put it on!"

If she had been wordless and silent before, she had made up for lost time. She came up to her mother and began hitting her with a toy jeep.

"Oh, all right," Fay said, "but you're to *watch* it. I don't feel I could cope with the boys at the moment. She's bad enough, but I don't want to be separated from her just the same."

"You won't have to cope with them," Wexford said. "Where does your mother live?"

"My mother and my dad. He's not dead. Did you think he was? They live in Myringham." She gave him an address. "Are you going to ask them to keep the boys a bit longer?"

"Possibly. If you like. I want to talk to Edward and Robert, Mrs. Devenish. Do you have any objection?"

She looked surprised at being asked. Then she looked defeated. As if she had been found out? Or was about to be found out? "No, I don't think so," she said in a weary voice. "No, I don't mind. Would it make any difference if I did?"

He wasn't going to answer that, not when she had consented. "I will, of course, speak to them in the presence of your mother or your father."

As if she hadn't heard him or didn't care, she said almost dreamily, "I never told them anything about what was going on till...well, last year,

I suppose, then I told my mother what Stephen did to me, and do you know what she said? She said, 'You must have done something to provoke him.' And my father said, 'There's not much in that. They used to say it was all right to beat your wife with a stick as long as it wasn't thicker than your thumb.' And he laughed and said it was a lot of fuss about nothing. That's why I've been...well, a bit distant from them lately. The children love them."

He nodded. Sometimes there is absolutely nothing to say. Lynn came out from the kitchen and met him in the hall. "She's made no phone calls, sir, and the phone's been put onto the answering machine for incoming calls. Not that there've been any. I checked."

"You've done well," said Wexford, pleasing Lynn more than she would have thought possible.

He went into the study and sat there, trying to imagine the scene of the morning if what Fay Devenish said was true, if a man had come to the front door at eight o'clock and been admitted by Stephen Devenish, a man who brought a knife with him. In a briefcase? In a carrier bag? Or had he found a knife there, ready to hand? And did Devenish know him? Devenish had been in the study, scene of the recent latest wounding of his wife, and had seen a man he knew come to the front door. Presumably, he had believed he had no reason to fear this man.

They went into the study where, fifteen minutes before, perhaps only ten minutes before, Devenish had punished his wife for the heinous offense of failing to buy oranges by slashing her across the palm of her hand with a knife. What knife? The *same* knife? And where was it now? One thing was for sure, it wasn't the dagger hanging up on the wall. The blade of that was corroded with rust, he saw when he took it down.

What had happened in this room, the male room that Fay so hated, the leather-padded, sword-hung room, between this man and Devenish? Threats? Demands? Refusals to comply or pay or what? Then out comes the knife and the man gives Devenish three stabs to the chest. Covered with Devenish's blood—he would be covered with blood—he had left the house, taking the bloody knife with him, and run off down the street, seen by no one.

Who could believe such a story? Still, Wexford had heard of odder things. He must delay no longer but take himself to the Doddses' home and talk to Edward and Robert Devenish.

The call came through to him on the car phone as Donaldson was driving him northward through the villages and along the Sewingbury-to-Myringham road. At first the line was fuzzy and the tone blurred, and he couldn't make out who was speaking to him. Then suddenly the voice of Trevor Ferry came on clear and almost too loud. "I've remembered something. You know you asked if I could think of anyone who might have a grudge against Devenish? Well, there is someone."

"Really?"

"Oh, and before I forget, my wife has gone along to Kingsmarkham Police Station to tell them I was definitely at home and still in bed at eight this morning. Providing an alibi is what you call it, right?"

"That's what we call it, Mr. Ferry," Wexford said, wondering why these people were quite so quick off the mark and if they had something to hide. "Who is this someone with a grudge?"

Wexford's heart dipped a little when Ferry said, "I don't remember the name," leapt when he went on, "but I can tell you the story. This guy said Devenish caused his brother-in-law's death."

"I'll call on you, if I may, early tomorrow morning."

"How early?" said Ferry.

"Don't worry, you'll be up. It won't be before nine-thirty."

Trevor Ferry, saying good-bye and ringing off, sounded disappointed that Wexford wasn't coming at once, rushing to him at top speed, to hear earthshaking revelations. But a hundred sensational tales of Devenish's misdemeanors or provocations of injured fellow workers and dissatisfied customers couldn't alter that Fay's version of events remained incredible. Only corroboration of her story could make it believable, and what corroboration could there be?

The three-story town house was almost in the center of Myringham. Fay Devenish could hardly have grown up here, it was too recently built. Everything about it looked new, from its fresh white facade, bright paint, and gleaming glass to the young, struggling plants in its window box of a front garden. Even the car on the garage drive was new, an S-registered, two-door saloon in the latest shade of rose-pink.

There seemed nothing in particular here to interest boys of twelve and ten. Perhaps their grandparents took them out a lot. But not long after Wexford was inside, admitted by Fay Devenish's father, a skinny, little old man whom she strongly resembled, he found himself revising his opinion. For the whole house seemed a boys' paradise, and since this could hardly have been spontaneously contrived, merely on the chance of his asking Mrs. Dodds to invite her grandsons to stay, he supposed it must be like this all the time. One room they passed before ascending the stairs contained, indeed was entirely given over to, a train set. Most adults with a passion for trains have their railway hidden away on the top floor, but Mr. Dodds had his downstairs. He had armies on mantelpieces, toy menageries on windowsills, a video library of monsters, horrors, and outer space on the landing, and as far as Wexford could see through open doors, a television set in every room.

"And a video," said Mr. Dodds. "Not much point without a video, is there? We've not long moved here, used to have a bigger place, but I've managed to squeeze all my stuff in. We've four bedrooms and the fourth's entirely for my model aircraft. I used to have dogs and cats too. Can't be done here, but we've fifteen guinea pigs in the back garden and the gerbils live in *our* bedroom."

The two Devenish boys were in the room Mr. Dodds called the lounge, each with a computer—"I've got six," their grandfather put in—Edward playing patience on his, Robert concentrating on a soccer game in which, from the colors the players wore, France seemed to be competing against Brazil. Mrs. Dodds, dressed in scarlet today with a short skirt, sat placidly by, reading *Vogue*. Wexford greeted her and said hello to the boys, who took absolutely no notice of him.

How had Fay reacted to this setup? The dogs and cats, guinea pigs and gerbils, were all right, but how about the toy soldiers and the trains? Perhaps it had been different when she was young and the Dodds family lived elsewhere. Dodds might have turned to these juvenile artifacts only as he entered his second childhood. Whatever it was, Edward and Robert obviously relished it all, and Wexford had some difficulty not only in persuading the boys but in prevailing upon Mr. and Mrs. Dodds to "exit from" or "shut down" the computers or whatever the jargon was. Mrs. Dodds even said it was a shame when they were enjoying themselves so much. Wexford couldn't help thinking of Fay, who had told him her parents had dismissed her complaints of Devenish's behavior as fussing about nothing.

One thing to be thankful for about this room was that, apart from the computers and the huge television with video recorder, there was no sign of Mr. Dodds's preoccupations. Neither boy could be distracted by Lego, Godzilla, or a miniature motorway. Both grandparents elected to stay while Wexford talked to the boys and he was thankful for it. Afterward, no one should say that he had acted improperly. The tall, older boy sat in an armchair beside his grandmother, the younger on a sofa next to his grandfather. There was something uncanny about their resemblance to the dead man. Edward already had the face of a young Lord Byron, handsome, shapely, dark-eyed, with strong, full mouth and firm jawline. And then, as Robert turned to look at his grandfather for reassurance, Wexford caught in the angle of his head and the tilt of his nose a glimpse of Fay, and somehow this tiny flash of likeness, soon probably to fade, was the most saddening of all things...

"I want you to tell me what happened yesterday morning," he began, "when you first got up and when you left for school to have your lift from Mrs. Daley." He waited until Edward nodded and Robert followed with a vigorous nodding. "Now, you got up and came downstairs for your breakfast. That would have been about half past seven. What did you have for breakfast?"

"We always have the same," Edward said. "Orange juice and cornflakes—well, he has Shreddies—and toast." He looked from one to the other of them, as if for approval. *Am I doing it right?* was unspoken but it was there. "My dad has—I mean, he used to have—a cooked breakfast. Eggs and bacon, and maybe a sausage and fried bread, and sometimes mushrooms." A shadow seemed to pass across Edward. Wexford saw, perhaps for the first time, what is really meant by the phrase *his face fell.* "Mum hadn't got any oranges for the juice and Dad got furious, though she'd got frozen. He ate his breakfast and went into the study, he said he was going into the study and he did go in there." Edward looked at his grandfather and, getting an encouraging smile, went on in a way that elderly child had not perhaps expected, "Dad called Mum into the study and I—I shut the kitchen door, I..."

Wexford said, "Go on, please, Edward. I understand what you're saying. It's all right for you to go on."

The child was desperate and Wexford felt for him to an extent he had never empathized with his own grandchildren; he had never needed to do so.

But it was Robert who butted in and saved his brother. He said almost harshly, "He was going to start bashing her around. I mean, Dad was. Beating or kicking her, he's always doing it."

His grandmother gave a little scream. "Robert, you naughty boy, how dare you tell such wicked untruths!"

Robert shrugged. Suddenly he looked decades older than his age, a little old man like his grandfather. "I'm glad he's dead," he said flatly.

More shrieks followed this statement. Mr. Dodds shook his head sorrowfully. "They've got powerful imaginations at that age," he said.

Wexford intervened. "Perhaps we'll let Edward continue now. Just one thing, Edward. Did your father take a knife with him from the block in the kitchen?"

"I don't think so. No, he didn't."

"While your mother and father were together in the study, did you hear either of them cry out?"

Had Wexford imagined that faint flash of alarm in Robert's eyes? Edward said, "No. Nothing."

Then Robert said, "I didn't hear anything."

"Then please go on, Edward."

"Mum came back," the boy said, more confident now, "with her hand wrapped up in a towel. It was the towel from our downstairs toilet and it was quite big, but the blood was coming through. He'd cut her. It's no good making that face, Gran. I'm not telling lies and you know it. You don't like hearing the truth, that's all. D'you think we liked it?"

Edward didn't wait for Mrs. Dodds's reply. "She got a cloth and tied it up, then she told me and Robert it was time to go down to Mrs. Daley's. Mrs. Daley does the school run when Mum doesn't," he explained for the benefit of those who might not know it. "We went out into the hall just as someone rang the doorbell. I opened the door and it was someone to see Dad, a man. I told him to go into the study and he did, and Robert and I went off to Mrs. Daley's house."

"Right," said Robert.

CHAPTER 22

The two boys were both staring at him, then Robert looked away. If you witness your father repeatedly beat your mother, will you, in your turn, beat your wife when the time comes? They say such cruelties form a chain from generation to generation. Did Stephen Devenish's father beat his mother? Wexford dismissed these ugly thoughts—there was no point in dwelling on them—and asked Edward if he could describe the man he had admitted to the house.

The boy frowned. He looked as if he were concentrating. "He was just a man. Not as tall as Dad. He was wearing jeans and a jacket, and a shirt. And he was wearing a tie."

"He had a briefcase," said Robert. "The dagger was in the briefcase."

His brother rounded on him. "How do *you* know? You can't see through leather. You don't know what he had in the briefcase."

"Can you make a guess at how old he was?" Wexford knew this was unlikely, almost hopeless. To a child of twelve everyone over twenty-five is old.

But Edward said promptly, "About the same age as Dad."

"I don't suppose you saw what color his eyes were? Or his hair?"

Robert started laughing, throwing himself about in his chair and kicking his legs. "His hair was blue and his eyes were red!"

"You're stupid," said Edward. "No one would think you were ten." He said to Wexford, suddenly very grown-up, "I don't remember about his hair, and his eyes I didn't notice. I mean, I didn't know I was going to have to remember. He was just a man who came to see Dad."

Apparently, it had never occurred to either Mr. or Mrs. Dodds that their daughter might have been suspected of her husband's murder, so they showed no signs of relief. Rather, they were bemused. Who would have thought the day before yesterday, they seemed to be saying to themselves, that the whole of life could be overturned like this so quickly and with no warning?

Mrs. Dodds appeared to be looking about her for some means of distraction, some way of lightening the atmosphere or removing the seriousness, and she came up with an idea commonplace enough, the universal panacea for the British, but she brought out her offer with an air of triumph. "Shall we all have a cup of tea?"

"I don't like tea," said Robert.

And Wexford said, "Not just now, Mrs. Dodds, if you please. It's important I ask Edward a few more questions." He turned to the boy. "Your mother was out in the kitchen when the man went into the study to see your father?"

"I suppose so. We left her there. She might have gone into the garden, but I don't reckon she did. She was trying to stop her hand bleeding."

"Where was Sanchia?"

"In the kitchen with Mum. Mum has to help her eat things or she gets them all over the floor."

"Did this man come in a car?"

Robert starting laughing again. "He came in a high-speed train. It came up our driveway at a hundred and fifty miles an hour."

The child's laughter was manic but without mirth or joy, or even amusement. It was the cackle of a parrot or a mynah bird. He opened his mouth, but unsmilingly, and the sound rattled out.

Wexford remembered uneasily how Jane Andrews had said all the children must be damaged by what they had witnessed and heard at home, not the little girl alone. "Edward?" he queried.

"He must have walked," the boy said. "I didn't see a car. Or he could have left it in the road, I didn't see. People don't always bring a car up our drive, they don't know if they'll be able to park it."

"What did he say to you?"

The boy thought. "Something like 'I've come to see Mr. Devenish' or 'I've come to see your father,' one of those, I can't remember."

"And you heard nothing from the study after he had gone in there?"

"I told you. I told him to go into the study, and then we went, my brother and me. I shut the front door behind us and we went down the road to Mrs. Daley's."

"Daley, waley, scaley," sang Robert, and suddenly babyish, stuck one finger in his mouth and whined, "Can we go now? I want to go and play with the aeroplanes, Granddad."

"You can go," said Wexford.

When he got back to the station, he found Burden waiting for him, sitting in his, Wexford's, office at his, Wexford's, desk, drinking tea and eating, fastidiously and with the help of a paper napkin, a chocolate éclair.

"You won't believe this, but that villain Monty Smith says someone videoed the whole of that bomb-throwing affair on a camcorder."

"The Mitchell woman—where does she live? Oberon Road? Next door to Orbe? Somewhere down there—she's got a camcorder," Wexford said.

"She hasn't now. She says she got rid of it and I can't prove she didn't. Anyway, she says she was in the middle of the crowd outside here and couldn't have filmed it and she's right. Monty Smith says he didn't recognize whoever was filming the whole show. It was no one he knew. Colin Crowne is sticking to his story that he put Flay's petrol bomb in a skip outside twenty-one Oberon Road—and there was a skip there. The builders had it, the ones that left the pile of bricks about for the Kingsmarkham Six to hurl through Orbe's windows. If what Crowne says is true, someone found it there and helped himself."

"I doubt if Crowne would *give* anything away or, come to that, throw anything away if he could get money for it. Is there any more tea? No? Okay, I'll phone down for some." Wexford sat down. He made his phone call. "We were wrong about Fay Devenish. This is the one case where the unknown assailant really did come to the door." He told Burden what had happened. "It's a funny thing, when Fay told me about the man at the door, about hearing a man's voice, I scarcely gave it credence. It was such a cliché thing to come up with. 'No, it wasn't me, it was a mysterious stranger at the door.' I *knew* we weren't going to get confirmation, but we did."

"And you separated those boys from their mother, lest she get at them and tell them to lie for her."

Wexford grinned. He was feeling inexplicably happy. "I like your use of the subjunctive, Mike. Must be the effect of Mensa membership.

Sure, that was my reason for separating them. I'm very glad I did. Robert confirmed it too. He said the man was carrying a briefcase."

"Containing the weapon and maybe a raincoat?"

"Presumably. So what I thought would turn out a waste of time, trying to discover who sent those threatening letters and whatever revelation Trevor Ferry has for us, is actually essential stuff. Someone had it in for Devenish, and that someone accomplished his revenge or whatever it was."

"Let's go and see him now. I'll come with you."

"I do't suppose there's anything in it," Ferry said.

That phrase, or versions of it, always alerted Wexford. It invariably seemed to be used when the reverse was true and there was plenty "in it." He was far less anxious to hear accounts that were vaunted as sensational, hair-raising, or calculated, in the storyteller's estimation, to lead to immediate arrests. He said what he always said in these circumstances. "We'll be the judges of that."

It was three in the afternoon and they had been admitted to the house by Gillian Ferry. Burden asked her if she had got home early from work, and she said her school had broken up two days before. She was a thin, stringy woman with a prematurely lined face and silvering blond hair, in all respects ordinary but for her large, angry green eyes. Once she had shown them into the living room, where her husband was again enjoying culinary banalities on television, she left them, shutting the door rather too sharply behind her.

The slam had made Ferry wince. He shook himself as if coming to, returning to the real world from Bolognese kitchens and Tuscan feasts. "You want to know about the guy Steve Devenish had the tussle with? I'll tell you. It was about two years back. More than that, because I was still there and it was around the time Steve Devenish got that big raise. Mind you, I don't reckon anyone would ever have heard of him if they hadn't put that piece about him in the paper with all those photos."

"The *Kingsmarkham Courier*, you mean?"

"The local rag, yes. They called him a fat cat and had pictures of him and his house, and they even had one of his wife and baby—that was the baby that went missing, right? Well, round about the same time as that there was this chap flying on Seaward to Amsterdam—I think it was

Amsterdam—only when he got to Gatwick he was told along with a couple of others that the flight was overbooked. We'd got more passengers than we had seats. It was the sixteen-ten flight, four-ten P.M. to the layman.

"Now this doesn't very often happen, not with Seaward, but it does sometimes, especially on the popular flights. The point about Amsterdam—Schiphol, that is—is that you can get a cheap flight from there to the U.S., I mean cheap*er*. Well, this chap wasn't going to do that, he was going to Amsterdam for a dirty weekend or whatever, or he thought he was, only we were overbooked and something had to give, if you see what I mean."

Ferry looked expectantly at the two policemen, apparently awaiting approval. Wexford gave it with an encouraging nod.

"So we started making offers to the passengers. You know the sort of thing: give up your seat on this flight and take the later one—say in three hours' time—and we'll give you a free dinner at the Holiday Inn and a complimentary bottle of wine. Now one passenger accepted so we were left with two. Of course we upped the ante, and the other guy, not this chap, he accepted. But we were in trouble because, for some reason—plain inefficiency, I'd guess—we'd issued two tickets for the seat this chap thought was his.

"I was called in—I was the Seaward manager then, of course—and I talked to this chap, privately like, took him into a room and gave him a drink. Everyone else was on board, waiting for takeoff. I knew there'd be trouble, he didn't want the air miles, so off my own bat I offered him a hundred and fifty quid to take the later flight. Well, the upshot was that he accepted, he said he'd take the cash and have the price of his ticket refunded, so I agreed, but he didn't take the flight, he used the cash to hire a chauffeur-driven car to take him to Harwich and go on the ferry over to the Hook of Holland."

"Why didn't he drive himself?" Burden asked. It was irrelevant but he wanted to know.

"Liked the idea of the luxury. That was what he called it, 'the luxury.' Apparently he'd never in his life been in a car with a driver, not even a bloody minicab, or so he said. Well, he got his car and his driver, but he never got to the Hook. The car was in a pileup on the M25 near the Dartford crossing, and him and the driver were both killed."

Ferry looked at them with more animation than usual in his face, evidently proud of his dramatic tale.

Wexford said, "Where does the threat or the menace to Devenish come in?"

"I'm coming to that," said Ferry with the storyteller's talent for suspense. He looked much brighter, less hangdog, and color had come into his grayish face. "This chap had a sister and she was—is, I suppose—married to a very aggressive guy. Lives round here, this guy does."

Wexford thought he could manage to sort things out fairly satisfactorily, provided Ferry categorized his principal characters as a "chap" and a "guy." "Go on."

"Well, this guy knew the story; it seems the chap rang up his sister from Gatwick and told her the tale. I mean, he was full of it, over the moon, how he'd got this money out of the airline. I mean, I reckon he put it across as if he'd practiced some kind of deception."

Ferry paused as his wife came in with three mugs of tea on a tray. The milk came in a quarter-liter carton and the sugar in a half-empty packet. There were no spoons so it was just as well none of them took sugar. Gillian Ferry left as quickly as she had come in. Handing out the mugs, her husband looked around for something to stand them on, but looked in vain, shrugged, and gave up.

"Please go on, Mr. Ferry," said Burden.

"Right. Where was I? Oh, yes. Now you understand there's no question it was anything to do with Seaward, what this chap decided to do with the money. He chose to spend it on a chauffeur-driven car and the car crashed and he was killed. There was no way Seaward was responsible. You might as well say the airline caused the driver's death. But this guy, the brother-in-law, and his wife, the sister, they didn't see it like that. For some reason they picked on Steve Devenish and put the blame on him."

"Because Mr. Devenish was, you could say, the boss of Seaward?" Wexford asked.

"Exactly. The way this guy saw it, or the way I suppose he saw it—if you can say an animal like that sees anything—was that Steve Devenish made the company's policy—which was only partly true—and that the company's policy was to overbook flights and—well, 'bribe' was the word he used—and put temptation in the way of people like his brother-in-law by giving them large sums of money that went to their heads and they couldn't handle it."

"Bit over the top, wasn't it?" Burden said.

"Out in the stratosphere," said Ferry. "But this guy came to Seaward's office in Kingsmarkham first of all and Steve happened to be there. He made a big scene and threatened to sue. Steve didn't think much of it and he even tried to ignore it when the guy forced his way into his office at Gatwick. That time he said he'd call the police."

"And did he?"

"Not so far as I know. He didn't have to, Steve threw him out himself. He was a big chap, was Steve, as I dare say you know. Then he got a solicitor's letter from this guy's solicitor, whoever it was, saying this guy's wife had a right to substantial compensation. Rubbish, of course. Seaward's own lawyers soon put him in his place."

Ferry took a mouthful of tea and set the mug down, making a wet ring on the coffee table. "Of course, when the death threats started coming, Steve should have got on to you, but for some reason he didn't. D'you know what I think? I think he didn't want any more hassle."

"What d'you mean by hassle, Mr. Ferry?"

"Well, he'd thrown the guy out of his office, hadn't he? I mean, literally thrown him out. And when a great big bloke like Steve, in what you might call the prime of life, picks up a little guy like this guy and throws him onto his back onto a marble floor, if he doesn't do lasting damage, he definitely causes pain. The guy said he'd broken one of his ribs. I don't know, I wasn't there. But it was why Steve didn't want you lot called in."

It might be the Rachel Holmes story all over again, Wexford thought. You are attacked, physically or verbally, certainly illegally, but in repelling your assailant you injure him and, fearing repercussions, keep silent, or as silent as you can, about the original assault. There ought to be a name for it—how about the Kingsmarkham Defense? He looked up at Ferry and nodded just as Gillian Ferry came back into the room. She kicked open the door because her hands were full with books and papers—schoolchildren's work to mark in the holidays?—but it seemed to Wexford as if she kicked in anger.

"You mentioned death threats," he said. "You mean letters?" The tea was thin, weak, and tepid, and he wished a potted plant were nearby in which secretly to tip it, but there wasn't. No green leaves flourished here. "Did you see any of them?"

Ferry shook his head. "Steve told me about them. That was just before he told me Seaward were 'letting me go.' Nice expression that, isn't it? It's what they call a UFO-something."

"A euphemism," Gillian Ferry said in a rather sharp, schoolmistressy tone. It told Wexford a lot about her relationship with her husband. She felt she had married intellectually beneath her and it rankled still. Had Ferry attracted her only because once he was well-off and successful? And, finding this not enough, had she been trying to improve him ever since? Wexford said to Ferry, "Your contention is that the brother-in-law wrote these letters?"

"Who else? Maybe it was his wife who actually wrote them. The guy could barely write, or so I'm told. Steve laughed it off. Well, whether he went on laughing it off I couldn't say. I wasn't there, was I? I'd been *let go*. The guy made phone calls too until Steve had his number changed and went ex-directory."

It interested Wexford that of all the people he had talked to about Stephen Devenish, Trevor Ferry was the only one to call him by a diminutive of his given name. No one else, apparently, called him Steve. Yet this man, in spite of what he professed, had particular reason for bitterness against Devenish and could never have been intimate with him. Wexford found it hard to believe Ferry bore him no grudge. "You refer to him as 'the guy' because you can't remember his name?"

"Oh, didn't I tell you I remembered? His name's Carl Meeks."

This was no special cause for surprise, but Wexford was surprised. He remembered Meeks from the various disturbances that had taken place at Muriel Campden, an undersized but fat man with a round face and loose lips, his wife one of those grossly fat women until recently rarely seen in any British communities. Burden had interviewed them in the hunt for Hennessy's killer and Wexford recalled murmuring to him, in a paraphrase, "It is such fools as you make the world full of ill-favored children." But aggressive? Violent?

That this man and this woman might be capable of the literate letter he had found in Stephen Devenish's desk seemed questionable. The language used would scarcely have been available to them.

"When exactly did you leave Seaward, Mr. Ferry?"

"I like 'leave,'" said Ferry with an unamused laugh. "It's almost as good as 'letting go.' I *left* in July, exactly two years ago, struggled to keep up the payments on my house, which, incidentally, was in Kingsbrook Valley Drive, Kingsmarkham—a nice part if you know it—failed, sold it for a lot less than I gave for it, and bought this dump."

"So you don't know if the threats went on coming after July two years ago?"

"No, and he can't tell you, can he? Maybe his widow can."

At least we know he had a letter very recently, Wexford thought. He was rather surprised to hear Burden ask the name of the private preparatory school where Gillian Ferry taught.

"The Francis Roscommon in Sewingbury."

"Quite a distance," Burden said. He was remembering the plastic-hooded bicycles in the passage outside. "You no longer run a car?"

"She gets the bus," Ferry said shortly.

Fay took him out into the garden. It was one of the rare mornings of that cool, wet summer when sitting outdoors was just possible. When the sun was out, it was almost too hot, and when the clouds surged up once more and covered it, too cold. Three wicker chairs were arranged around a wicker table on the broadest area of lawn, under a mulberry tree, so that it looked as if they were expected. But Fay said the neighbors kept coming in. She made them tea and they gave her their condolences, though what sympathy they felt was due to her she couldn't imagine, as most of them had been alerted by the police and the Social Services under Operation Hurt-Watch of her situation with her husband.

The little girl, Sanchia, had a blanket on the grass, on which stood a glass of orange-colored liquid (or so it appeared from its dregs) that she had managed to knock over, an opened can of Coke, a packet of custard-cream biscuits and another of chocolate-chip cookies, and a welter of toys. It was a happy, comfortable mess and one that, Wexford was sure, Devenish would never have tolerated. Passing through the house with Fay, he had noticed that on only the third day after the man's death it was already less immaculate, less tidy. At ten-thirty in the morning two wineglasses with wine dregs in them stood on a table in the living room, had certainly been drunk from the evening before and left there.

"Jane's gone back to Brighton just for the day," Fay said to him. "She was here last night and we drank—oh, nearly a bottle of wine between us. I'm getting sloppy, I haven't cleared up." It was still necessary for her to make excuses for untidiness. "I don't know what I'd do without Jane. I had to do without her for so long."

She looked a lot better. It was strange; to anyone who hadn't known what went on in that house it would have been monstrous. Her eyes were brighter, her color better, she even looked younger. Somehow he guessed that the clothes she wore, a short denim skirt, a top that was rather low-cut, had long been banned but never disposed of, had thankfully been put on now the censor and brutal judge was gone.

"My boys are coming home today. I've missed them. It'll be good to have them back."

"They both go to the same school, I think you said?"

"That's right. In Sewingbury. Edward will be leaving next year to go to Oundle."

"Don't let them tire you out."

"I don't think I shall get tired the way I used to. The only thing is, I cry all the time. I just start to cry for no reason."

"I think you've plenty of reason," he said, then, "Mrs. Devenish, do you remember the threats made against your husband by a man called Carl Meeks? Do you remember how he came to the Kingsmarkham office of Seaward Air, then to Gatwick? And your husband threw him out, allegedly injuring him?"

She said, but without bitterness, "He was great at injuring people."

"But you remember these incidents?"

"He never said much to me about them. He didn't talk about his work, but he did tell me about this man Meeks. He was proud of hurting him."

"Do you think Carl Meeks could have sent these threatening letters? They threatened your husband's life, didn't they?"

"He said he'd kill him, yes." She spoke dreamily, almost as if with a longing for some wished-for event. Then she said, in quite a different tone, "I loved him so much once. When we were engaged, he was so gentle and thoughtful. He hit me while we were on our honeymoon, but that was because he was jealous of me talking to a man in the hotel, and he was so sorry afterwards. Only even then, you know, he said I'd made him do it, it was my fault for being—for being flirtatious."

Her eyes filled with tears. She made a little sound that was between a gulp and a sob, and Sanchia came over to her with the biscuit packet, an offering of comfort. "Mummy not cry."

"Mummy won't cry, darling," Fay said, and it was true, she had stopped crying. She put her arms around the little girl and kissed the top of her head. "I'm so lucky. Look what I've got, all my lovely children, and my health and I'm free, but somehow I keep crying. You see, I always loved Stephen, somewhere the love I had for him was still there. He tried to beat and kick and knock it out of me, and in the end he nearly did, but when I think of the love I once had, I cry. And it was true I was the only woman for him, the only one he ever loved, it was *true*. It was just that he had...well, a funny way of showing it..."

CHAPTER 23

THE BUILDERS WORKING ON THE RESTORATION OF 16 OBERON Road were sitting on the front step, having their midmorning coffee break. So far, all they had done was put back the tiles that had come off the roof during the fracas led by the Kingsmarkham Six. The graffiti still remained, *filth*, *pedo*, and *killer*, among the decapitated bodies and the snarling animal faces, all done in red and pink and blue and yellow. The builders would leave repainting till last. Later in the day, unless it rained, which it looked likely to do, they would set about replacing the glass in the upstairs windows.

They finished their coffee and were just having their second smoke when a van drew up outside from Kingsmarkham Borough Council's Domestic Environment and Landscape Department. The logo on its side was of a female doll holding a spade and a male doll with a bunch of flowers. This reversal of what some would call the accepted order of things had taken place in response to the demands of the militant feminist element on the council. The driver of the van, who had long red hair like a teenage girl, and his mate, with an open mouth and protruding tongue in much the same sort of red tattooed on one wrist, got down from the cab and went around the back to size up the situation.

Daunted by the now waist-high grass, the giant hogweed, and man-height thistles, not to mention the iron bedstead, they came back to have a cigarette with the builders. The driver said it was a job for a JCB. All the department's mechanical diggers were in use, so it would be at least three months before one could be spared to start on this garden, and in his opinion they would be lucky if they got it done by Christmas. There was the added problem of getting a JCB around the back of No. 16.

From her second-floor window in the Muriel Campden tower,

Rochelle Keenan was filming the four men on her camcorder. Kingsmarkham Council had just banned all its employees from smoking in public places, and Rochelle intended to produce her film as part of her revenge campaign against the driver of the van. She had had a brief affair with him a couple of years back while her husband was in Stowerton Royal Infirmary (about to be renamed the Princess Diana Memorial Clinic) having a hernia operation. He had been the one to end it, and now when she saw him, he pretended not to know her. She watched him light another cigarette before sitting down on a camp stool one of the builders had produced from inside the house.

John Keenan didn't know about the affair, but he suspected something, largely owing, Rochelle believed, to the youngest Keenan child, Winona, having red hair. He said that as soon as he could raise the £300 it cost, he was going to get one of those home DNA-testing kits and find out for sure. To make certain of getting it right he had already tried taking a swab from the inside of Winona's mouth, only the enterprise had come to nothing because the little girl had swallowed it. Rochelle didn't know which of them was Winona's dad and she didn't much care. She was far more interested in her video and in getting the redheaded driver the sack or at least a severe reprimand.

A stone's throw away in Titania Road—"a stone's throw" at Muriel Campden being more a fact of life than a figure of speech—Maria Michaels had a date with Miroslav Zlatic. He admired powerful women and had somehow managed to make her understand with signs but without words that he had fallen in love with her when he saw her put the shot that broke the police station window. Their meeting planned for this morning was to be in the derelict house on the outskirts of Myringham, where Miroslav had taken Lizzie Cromwell and perhaps other young women as well. Leaving the despised Monty Smith in bed, Maria was off to catch the Myringham bus at the York Street stop.

Wexford saw her as his car entered the approach road but he ignored her cheerful wave. Although not one of the Kingsmarkham Six, she was almost certainly responsible for a great deal of the criminal damage caused on the day of Hennessy's death. The difficulty was that, along with other people's involvement, he couldn't prove it. Donaldson drove him the long way around, up Titania and along Puck, for the purpose of assessing what was going on, if anything. On the street sign the name of this latter road had once more been defaced. "I don't know why they don't rechristen it another name from *A Midsummer Night's Dream,*" he said to Karen Malahyde. "Call it Bottom or something."

"I'm not sure that would be a wise choice, sir."

"What? No, I suppose not."

The first few spots splashed against the windscreen, then the rain came in torrents. Donaldson put the wipers on at fast speed, but still he felt it wiser to stop until the heavy shower had passed. Someone in No. 2 Oberon Road shut an upstairs casement with a slam. Wexford rubbed at the steam on the window but could still see nothing out there, not even the graffiti on No. 16, beyond glassy streams and dazzlement.

"This Meeks, sir," Karen said. "I suppose he's on the benefit?"

"He's unemployed at any rate."

"Living on our taxes, and from what I hear they're both obese."

"Being overweight has nothing to do with affluence," said Wexford. "It's not so much a matter of you can't be too rich or too thin as you have to be rich to *be* thin."

"Cheap food makes you fat," said Donaldson sagely, "all those pies and chips." He switched on the ignition and they were off once more, the rain having subsided into a drizzle.

Wexford put on the plastic mac. "I suppose I shall have to buy a new raincoat," he said to no one in particular, but Donaldson's shoulders hunched a little.

No one had blamed him for Wexford's loss, but he sometimes felt he had been negligent. He was thinking how, if he chanced to see Charlene Hebden while he was up here, he would confront her and get the truth out of her, when he found himself outside 24 Oberon Road and Wexford was telling him to stop and let him and DS Malahyde out.

Karen Malahyde never seemed to notice rain. Her clothes had a rainproof look to them, even skirts and blouses, and on a man her hairstyle would have been called a crew cut. She stood on the front path, surveying the house, leaving it to Wexford to find shelter under the diminutive porch and ring the bell.

Linda Meeks was immediately recognizable, an often-seen figure in those riotous assemblies. She should have been in the hierarchy, he thought, important enough to enlarge it to the Kingsmarkham Seven, though she had never been one of the ringleaders. A large woman, soft and cushiony, she looked as if her plump, dimpled flesh, mottled pink and white, would hold the impress if a finger was dug into it. It was evident from a flicker of alarm in her pale blue eyes that she expected these two police officers to question her on the subject of DS Hennessy's death. It wouldn't be the first time. Just the same, she had hoped the first time would also have been the last.

Wexford had a feeling he had set her mind at rest when he said he wanted to talk to her and her husband about her brother-in-law who had died in a car crash on his way to Harwich.

"My brother," said Linda Meeks, "not my brother-in-law." She looked relieved, positively cheerful. "Come in. You want a cup of tea?"

Wexford said no, thanks, and Karen said no, not now, which for both of them was a way of saying that this matter was too serious for sociable cups of tea. Both expected Meeks to be in front of the television with a can of something and a bag of crisps, which behavior, as Barry Vine, a golfer, put it, was par for the course at Muriel Campden. Instead, he was out in the garden, in a shed, doing woodwork. He appeared to be making a table, for the legs and base were finished and he was planing what appeared to be the top. When he saw them, he laid the plane down carefully on its side and came out, putting up an umbrella.

The garden was exquisitely neat. Vegetables grew in it where others might have flowers. That is, they were not planted in rows as on an allotment, but in clusters as in an herbaceous border: lettuces making a nice contrast with beetroot, and runner beans in full scarlet bloom climbing up the fences instead of clematis.

Meeks spotted a tiny plant that shouldn't have been there and, in spite of the rain, pulled it out. "Never pass a weed," he said philosophically.

He was a little man, shorter than his wife, and with his fatness, as is often the case in middle-aged male beer drinkers, concentrated on his belly. This area of his body was so large and protuberant as to make an onlooker feel uneasy. It looked as if its possessor must be uncomfortable, embarrassed by what was almost a deformity, ashamed of such grotesqueness. But if Meeks felt any of this, he gave no sign of it. He walked very upright, carrying all before him, as he led them back to the house where he dropped the weed into a waste bin.

In the living room, the boy Scott had the television on, playing a video game in which the player won points if he could steer a surfer through a stormy sea without bumping into islands, ships, and other obstacles. His father was going to leave it—keep him quiet, it's harmless—but Wexford asked him to switch it off and leave them. Scott Meeks, who had never been spoken to like that before, gave Wexford a glowering look, his underlip stuck out, but he did as he was told and departed, slamming the door behind him.

"I'd like to talk to your wife as well, Mr. Meeks," Wexford said, "but not till after I've had a word with you. Tell me about this trouble with your brother-in-law. For a start, what was his name?"

"Jimmy—well, James, I suppose, James Crabbe."

If Meeks was surprised to find the police at last taking an interest in his brother-in-law's wrongs, he gave no sign of it. Rather, he seemed pleased to have a chance of talking about what had evidently become an obsession, and before Wexford could ask him anything else, he had launched on a muddled account of the fateful happenings at Gatwick.

"They was all dead against him from start to finish, don't tell me they don't make no difference between passengers and whatever, they was set against letting him on that plane from the start, and it's my belief it was on account of he was wearing shorts, shorts and sandals, and that got up their noses, so they was set on making him a victim, it's my belief they paid those folks to—what do they call it—overbook and then—"

"Just a moment, Mr. Meeks," said Karen. "Would you tell us how you know all this? You weren't there, were you?"

"He gave us a bell, Jimmy did. Him and Linda, they was very close. I mean, they was twins. It hit her very hard, him dying like that, I can tell you. I mean, it upset me, but her, she was devastated, it knocked her for six, they thought she was going to have a mental breakdown. Well, like I was saying, he gave us a phone. He was over the moon, like out on cloud nine, bubbling over he was, how he'd got this money out of Seaward and he was going to spend it on a chauffeur-driven car to the ferry."

"What was he going to Amsterdam for?" Wexford asked. Jimmy Crabbe wasn't gay, he thought, or was he? He wasn't going to buy cheese or porcelain or look at *The Night Watch*. "Was it just a holiday?"

"It was his girlfriend. She'd got a job as a nanny over there. He was going to have the weekend with her while the folks she worked for was away. But he never made it. The car he hired crashed on the M25 soon after it come out of the Dartford Tunnel. Big truck jackknifed and went smack into it."

"But surely that was no one's fault," said Karen. "Well, maybe the truck driver's fault or the hire-car driver's fault but not Seaward Air. All they did was give him the money."

Whose side are you on? Meeks may have been thinking. "They shouldn't put temptation in a poor man's way," he said sententiously. "Folks like Jimmy, they need looking after, they need to be protected."

"Your brother-in-law wasn't"—Wexford sought about for something reasonably PC and failed lamentably—"he wasn't mentally afflicted, was he?"

Meeks jumped up. "What are you insinuating? That Jimmy was backward, is that what you're saying? I never said that, I never meant that. I mean he'd never been nowhere or done nothing, he said as much, he had that car because he'd never been in a chauffeur-driven car. He was thirty-six years old and he'd never even had a girlfriend before this one. Those Seaward folks put temptation in a poor man's way when they should have been putting him on that plane and looking after him, and the air hostesses bringing him beer and a sandwich. D'you know, he'd never been on a plane before? Well, he never went on that one, did he? Thanks to them. Thanks to that bastard Stephen Devenish, he was the one made the rules, he was the one said what they all had to do."

Linda Meeks put her head around the door. "I heard you shouting, Carly. You all right?"

"Of course I'm all right. I just got a bit aerated."

"Leave us for a while longer, Mrs. Meeks, will you?"

She retreated without argument, and as the door closed, Wexford changed tack completely and asked Meeks in an abrupt tone where he had been on the previous Tuesday at eight in the morning.

Meeks looked astonished but he apparently failed to make the connection. "Out with my dog. I'm always out with my dog at eight in the morning."

"I don't see any dog."

"He's in the kitchen with Linda."

Wexford asked if Meeks had a car and then if anyone saw him while he was out, got a "No" to the first and an "I don't know" to the second, qualified by "I go out at half-seven and there's not many about then.

Folks round here may have seen me. I go in York Park or out in the fields and there's no one there so early." Either he was acting or the purpose of these inquiries hit him, rather late in the day. "He's dead, isn't he? That Stephen Devenish? He was murdered." More light dawned, an unpleasantly searching light. "You think I done that? I murdered him?"

"We don't think anything, Mr. Meeks," Karen said. "We'd just like to eliminate you from our inquiries. You threatened Mr. Devenish, didn't you? You made threatening phone calls and wrote threatening letters and went along to Seaward Air and threatened him."

Carl Meeks was shaking his head. "I never wrote no letters." He seemed to be making up his mind to come out with a confession, he even closed his eyes briefly, screwed up his face, said in a rush, "I'm not much at writing and reading, never seemed to get the hang of it, I reckon it's not up my street." He brightened a little. "The wife can write and read."

"I think we'll have Mrs. Meeks in now," said Wexford.

"And bring Buster with you," Carl Meeks called out.

Linda had changed out of leggings and T-shirt into an all-enveloping check dress like a tablecloth with sleeves. For their benefit? Or because she was going out? But it wasn't her appearance that made the impact. She was pulled into the room, as a bowfront carriage might be pulled with a frisky horse in harness, by the biggest dog Wexford had ever seen. It seemed to be a Great Dane, of a slate blue color, and it slipped its lead, making straight for Carl, placing its paws on his shoulders and licking his face with a huge, slimy, dark blue tongue.

"Down, boy, down! Get off me! That's enough now. Get down!"

"I think I've seen enough," said Wexford dryly, "to know you genuinely do possess a dog. Perhaps you'd remove Buster to the kitchen, Mrs. Meeks. Thank you." He waited until she came back, panting from her exertions, and said nothing until she was sitting down, catching her breath. "You didn't much like Stephen Devenish, did you, Mrs. Meeks?"

"I didn't mind him," she gasped. It took her a few moments to be able to speak. Then she said, "I didn't know him—well, only by sight. It wasn't just him. It was all of them Seaward people." Once started, she was voluble. "That driver was drunk, they found I don't know how many pints of whatever in his blood, and it was those Seaward people told Jimmy to go to them, they said to him what's 'is name was a good driver, they recommended him, and what did he know? He just did what they said and it killed him, *they* killed him. You said, did I like Stephen Devenish, and I say, what d'you expect when someone throws your husband down the stairs?"

"We heard he'd thrown him out of his office," Karen said.

"Well, you heard wrong, then. He kicked him out of the office and then he picked him up by his coat collar and dragged him to the top of the stairs and threw him down."

"Is that how it was, Mr. Meeks?"

Meeks nodded. He seemed less than pleased, though, that his wife had shown him in such an abject light, as a man who could be thrown hither and thither, wherever his attacker's fancy took him. "He was a bastard," he said at last. "It's a blessing he's dead."

"But you didn't kill him?"

That made Linda Meeks give a thin shriek. Her husband said, "Do me a favor. He was about twice as big as me."

Compounding her offenses, Linda Meeks said, her expression quite serious, "He wouldn't have let Carl kill him."

"There's a lot in that," Wexford said to Burden later. "We know that whoever stabbed Devenish was shorter than he, so there's your question, why did he let whoever it was kill him?"

"I suppose he was taken by surprise."

"Well, he wouldn't have been taken by surprise by Meeks. If Meeks was the stranger Edward Devenish saw and his mother heard, he was no stranger to Devenish. The moment he was let into that study, Devenish would have known who he was and that he meant to do him harm. Are you saying that after Devenish cut his wife's hand he left the knife he used, the certainly bloodstained knife, lying on his desk or a table? And that when Meeks came in, he continued to leave it there for Meeks to pick up and use?

"Because the knife must have been there, Mike. God knows where it came from, perhaps he kept a knife in a drawer. Why not? He had a whip. He maybe kept it for the express purpose of chastising his wife, used it that morning, and then what? It wasn't in the study, he didn't throw it out of the window—why would he?"

Burden said thoughtfully, "He could have cut her and then handed her the knife and told her to take it away and wash it."

"D'you know what that reminds me of? It reminds me of that directive in the Jewish law. 'Thou shalt not seethe a kid in the milk of its mother.' It's adding insult to injury."

"But he was capable of it."

"I believe he was." Wexford sat silent for a moment, reflecting with no great pleasure on human iniquity. "We've had the report on the knives that were in the kitchen. They're expensive knives with horn handles. No traces of human blood on any of them. Her fingerprints on all but two, his on none."

"Does any of them have a blade that fits those wounds?"

"Two do. But you needn't look like that. These blades are—well, a standard size. Thousands of knives in people's kitchens and on sale in shops are that size and would fit those wounds. The evidence we need is Devenish's blood on a knife, and as I say, there was no blood. Perhaps it was one of those knives, but more likely it wasn't and the knife that was used was taken away."

"By Carl Meeks?"

"Maybe. I don't know. The sequence of events is that Devenish's killer either brought a knife with him and that knife happened to have the same size blade as one of those in the Devenishes' knife block or that he used the knife Devenish had left lying on the desk after he cut Fay. It has to be one or the other. If it is as you say and he gave the knife to Fay to wash, could she wash it so thoroughly as to remove all trace of its previous use? But why would she want to? So the likelihood is that the killer used that knife and took it away with him."

"Unless there were eight, not seven, knives in the knife block."

"I don't think there were, because what Fay says is true, and though there are eight slots in the block, if you put eight knives in, they jam up against each other. I know, I've tried it."

"And Meeks?"

"We've a house-to-house going on at Muriel Campden to see if any of the neighbors saw him out with his dog at eight that morning. His dog is an enormous Great Dane, a bluish-gray thing, name of Buster. It's not the kind of animal you'd miss. Once seen, never forgotten."

"The way things are going," said Burden, "we shall soon know that Muriel Campden lot better than our own families."

It was a fine evening if rather muggy. The residents of Oberon, Titania, and Puck Roads, and of the tower, sat on their front doorsteps if they had them or in deck chairs on the tower green if they didn't.

"Like a bloody caravan camp," said Tony Mitchell, who thought it was common, the kind of thing people did who lived in tenements.

They gossiped. They had been talking for weeks about who might or might not have thrown the petrol bomb that killed Ted Hennessy, and all of them had different views, depending on the side they took in personal vendettas or the degree of their paranoia. Now they had Carl Meeks to talk about, a subject made even more enthralling by the arrival on the scene of three police officers doing a house-to-house.

Maria Michaels said she was sitting outside to save them the trouble of ringing her bell. She had just seen her old friend Tasneem Fowler go into her own house accompanied by a woman called Tracy something, and Maria had called out to them and said to come over and have a drink when they'd done their business or whatever with Terry and the kids. Maria went into the house and fetched two chairs, which she put on the bit of grass in the front garden, and she was going back for a third when she met Monty Smith coming downstairs, carrying all his belongings in two Tesco carrier bags.

"For two pins," said Monty, "I'd smash your face in."

"You wouldn't do it twice, my darling. I'm not like that poor little cow Tasneem." Memories of glorious shot-putting days came back to her. "When I get going, you wouldn't know what hit you. Don't shut the door, I'm bringing another chair and a table out."

Despised, rejected, and expelled, Monty Smith went off down Oberon toward the York Street bus stop. Halfway down he met Detective Constable Archbold, who asked if he could have a word. The word was to ask where Monty was at eight on that Tuesday morning and if he had seen Carl Meeks out with his dog. Monty said Archbold must be joking as he never got out of bed before ten, or that had been his habit, but God knew what the future held.

Shirley Mitchell was on the green, picking up litter by hand and dropping the beer cans, crisp packets, cigarette ends, fish-and-chip paper, and take-away and hire-car flyers into a shopping trolley she had lined with a plastic bag. Archbold asked her about Carl Meeks, and she burst into a long diatribe about dog owners whose pets fouled the pavements. That Buster was one of the worst offenders. She had personally offered to supply Mr. and Mrs. Meeks with a dustpan, rake, and hygienic bags for the disposal of the Great Dane's waste, but they had laughed in her face. No, she couldn't say if she had seen Carl Meeks out with the dog on Tuesday morning, but she saw him every morning, or almost every morning, and it was just as well she did, for she was able to run outside and clean up the mess before her unfortunate neighbors trod in it.

One of the few Muriel Campden residents who wasn't sitting outside was Terry Fowler. He and his sons were watching a video he had made of the France-Brazil final in the World Cup. They had seen the match live, and since then they had looked at the video twice. This was the third time, but Terry, Kim, and Lee Fowler never tired of football, especially international matches of this caliber. France had just scored their first goal when a key was heard in the front door lock and Tasneem walked into the room with a strange woman.

She had only got up the courage to come because Tracy had egged her on and promised to go with her. On the way they were stopped by Lynn Fancourt and asked about Carl Meeks. Both found this quite exciting but, regretfully, had to say they didn't know because they didn't live here, they were just visiting. The idea of "just visiting" her own home brought tears into Tasneem's eyes, and the marks of the tears were still there when she entered the house and confronted, after many months, her husband and her children.

"What are you doing here?" said Terry, ignoring Tasneem's timid introduction of her friend. "You reckon you can go away when you want and stay away for a fucking year, do you, and then walk in here as bold as bloody brass like you've just been round the shops?"

Kim and Lee hadn't even looked at her. They were watching France go on to score their second goal.

Tracy Miller glanced about her and said, "This place is filthy, I bet it wasn't like this when Tas lived here."

Tracy crossed to the set and turned it off. A great wail went up from the boys. Terry leapt to his feet and there ensued what Tracy's dad used to call a slanging match, beginning with Terry calling Tracy a slag and an interfering bitch, and her calling him an animal.

A string of name-calling ensued, Terry dubbing Tasneem with epithets of such richness and obscurity that Tracy had never heard of half of them. The boys both burst out crying and Tracy's heart bled for them. She thought Terry was going to hit Tasneem and she was wondering whether to get between them—as if she hadn't had enough of that in her own married life—when Tasneem said, "Okay, I'm going, and that's it, I've had it up to my eyes."

They got out into the hallway and heard the television go on again. Terry and Lee sat down once more but Kim came running after them, got hold of Tasneem's trousers—she was wearing the *salwar kameez*—and sobbed, "Don't go. I don't want you to go."

Tasneem set up a wail of grief but Tracy said quite firmly, "You stop crying now, love. You and your brother's going to come and live with your mum and everything'll be *fine*."

God knew whether it was true. Tracy got Tasneem out of the house and more or less dragged her down to Maria Michael's. Maria was sitting on a chair in the front garden with an elegant little table in front of her, on which were a tray with glasses, a bottle of Scotch, a bottle of gin, two cans of ginger ale, and two of orange crush. She said hi to Tracy, that she was pleased to meet her, and what was it to be, my darling, whiskey or mother's ruin? Tasneem, being a Moslem, asked for orange crush, but Maria insisted on something stronger to "put some lead in her pencil."

"Come on, that's men," Tracy said, but Maria said, so what? And hadn't Tracy ever heard of the equality of the sexes?

Both women put their arms around Tasneem, and Tracy held the whiskey to her lips like a nurse with a feeding cup. Then Maria said she'd something to tell them that would cheer them up, a real bundle of laughs. She'd thrown Monty Smith out, the lazy bugger, and—how about this?—she'd got somebody else. Maria was telling them how Miroslav Zlatic had been a freedom fighter in Sarajevo, had had to flee with a price on his head, and how great he was in the sack, when DC Kevin Cox opened the gate, came up the path, and asked her about Carl Meeks.

Maria was only too happy to help. She offered Cox a drink, but Cox, who had been looking longingly at the gin, was obliged to refuse. Carl Meeks, she said, was a regular out with his dog at eight in the morning. That is to say, she often saw him when she was on her way to work, and that dog was more the size of a horse, but not *every* day, my darling, not this morning, for instance. This morning she'd had the day off and she smiled dreamily, remembering.

"What about last Tuesday morning?" said Cox.

"Well, I saw him, but whether it was Monday or Tuesday or Wednesday or what, I couldn't say. As I say, I don't see him every day. Some days he goes down the fields. He goes in the park."

"I'd like a dog," said Tasneem. "When I get my boys back, we'll have a dog."

"Of course you will, my darling, and a cat and a rabbit and a bloody alligator too if you want."

Cox went off, drew a blank at the remaining houses in Titania Road where the occupants were out, and called on the Crownes and Sue Ridley, and the people next door and the people next door to them, but three sets of them didn't know Carl Meeks, not even by sight, or they said they didn't, and the Crownes got up too late to see him out with the Great Dane. At the Meekses' house in Oberon Road, Lynn Fancourt was questioning Darren Meeks. Darren was still doing his paper round, so Lynn thought he of all people might know where his father had been that Tuesday morning, but Darren didn't know, he left for his round three-quarters of an hour before eight. Still, he reckoned his dad must have taken Buster out. The dog made so much racket, whining and howling for his walk, that you took him out just to get a bit of peace.

"So what's new up in millionaires' row?" Maria wanted to know after Tasneem had told her Tracy worked for a lady in Ploughman's Lane.

"That bastard as was murdered," said Tracy, "he was another of them, used to beat her up something disgusting. Nobody knew till she kidnapped her own kid to get her out of his clutches and then it all came out. The neighbors was warned to keep an eye on him. Talk about bloody useless when those great places up there are all about ten miles apart."

"Good riddance to bad rubbish, then," said Maria. "I suppose she did it."

"I don't know. It doesn't look like it, not with them asking us all that about what's 'is name."

"Oh, I reckon she did it, my darling. I would have."

Lord Tremlett's medical report showed that Stephen Devenish had received three stab wounds to his chest, and in Tremlett's opinion, these wounds had been inflicted in a frenzy. The one that killed him had pierced the left ventricle of the heart. A woman could have inflicted them, but it was impossible to say whether the perpetrator was a man or a woman. He or she was probably shorter than Devenish, because the dead man had been so tall.

The murder had been committed between seven forty-five and eight-thirty, the original estimate. Tremlett was unable to narrow the time down further. The weapon used was a kitchen knife with a blade two inches wide at its widest point and between eight and ten inches long. Devenish, prior to his death, had been a healthy man in his midthirties, of an exceptionally powerful physique, a well-made man without bodily flaws or scars. The inquest was opened and adjourned.

Wexford, who had attended the brief proceedings, went to see the widow and told her the funeral could take place whenever she chose.

Jane Andrews was at Woodland Lodge, was apparently staying there, and Fay's two sons were back home. It might have been Wexford's imagination, but he felt that Sanchia was already a calmer, quieter, and perhaps happier child. For the first time he noticed that she was also pretty, looking, perhaps, as her mother had at her age, pink-cheeked with satiny skin and regular features, big, gray-blue eyes, and fine, shining hair. That hair was much longer than when the family group photograph was taken, and now there would be no confusing her with a boy. It was a feminine, delicate face. She looked up at him and smiled. And he thought how dreadful it was that anyone could die, and moreover die by violence, and leave behind him so much relief and thankfulness.

The whole family—for Jane Andrews fitted in like a family member—were in the big living room where the French windows were thrown open. The children ran in and out of the garden, bringing grass clippings from the lawn on their shoes and onto the white carpet. There was no one to stop them and no need to stop them now. But when she had shown him in, Jane Andrews suggested to Sanchia that she might like Jane to push her on her new swing, and the child took Jane's hand and pulled her outside, leaving him alone with Fay.

Fay said in a cold, practical voice, "Am I allowed to cremate him?"

"Of course. The undertakers you use will see to the formalities. I think it's only that you have to have two doctors sign the certificate instead of one."

He couldn't read her expression. There's no art, he thought, to find the mind's construction in the face. Burn him, destroy him, scatter the ashes, be rid of him forever—was that what she was thinking? Or, more likely, I loved him once, he seemed different once, if only he could have been the way I believed him to be when we were young…

"How do the boys seem?" he asked her.

"They're fine."

"I'd like to talk to them again, especially to Edward, about the man who called here at eight last Tuesday morning."

Fay nodded, apparently neither shocked nor gratified. "I'm going to sell this house. I shall put it on the market when all this"—she used an extraordinary phrase in the circumstances—"has blown over."

He could find nothing to say.

"He left everything he could to the children, you know. The house is in my name, I don't know why he did that, some tax dodge, I expect. He always said I wasn't fit to manage money. Shall I call Edward in now?"

"I think he's coming of his own accord, Mrs. Devenish."

A little color came into her face. It was almost a blush. "Please don't think I'm correcting you, you don't have to remember it now, but I'm going to call myself by my maiden name. I'll be Ms. Dodds in future."

Edward came in from the garden. Wexford could have sworn he had grown in the past few days. He was entering puberty and looked like a teenager.

"Sit down, will you, Edward?"

The boy glanced at his mother and at a nod from her sat down in the least comfortable chair nearby, sat upright, and looked straight at Wexford.

"The man you admitted to this house on the morning your father died, you described him as 'just a man.' Can you be more specific?" Seeing that the boy was unsure of what he meant, he amended that. "Can you try to describe him to me? Close your eyes and try to get a picture."

Edward closed his eyes but opened them again almost immediately. Again he looked at his mother, said, "He was just an ordinary man. About Dad's age, I told you that." He screwed up his face as if in an effort to remember. "I think he had jeans on and maybe a jacket. Oh, and he was carrying a case."

"What kind of a case? A briefcase?"

"A big briefcase."

"Now, the doorbell rang while you and Robert were out in the hallway, heading for the front door. The door to your father's study is on the right. Was that door closed?"

"I think so. It might have been just—well, pulled to."

"I see. Now you answered the door and saw the man with the briefcase there. What did he say? And what did you say?"

"I don't think I said anything. He said, 'I'd like to see Mr. Devenish.'"

"Deep voice, high voice, what kind of voice?"

"Quite deep. Just an ordinary man's voice."

Fay Devenish had attempted to seem uninterested in all this, had turned her eyes toward the garden where Jane Andrews, Robert, and Sanchia were slowly strolling toward the house, but now she turned to Edward and watched him inscrutably.

As if on cue, he said, and said with the snobbery of which only the privately educated child of wealthy parents is capable, "He had the local accent. Like yours, only more so."

Wexford allowed himself to react to this not at all. Inwardly, he smiled. Impossible even to feel angry with this poor child. "Was he fat? Thin? Dark? Fair?"

"I don't know. I didn't notice."

"You'd have noticed if he'd been a big fat man, wouldn't you?"

"He wasn't like that. He was just normal size."

"Now, did your father come out of the study or did you open the door and show the man in?"

"I opened it. I just said to him 'in there,' then Robert and I went. We closed the front door after us like we always do. We had to go to Mrs. Daley's and we'd have been in trouble if we'd been late."

"Did you close the study door after the man?"

Suddenly Edward looked bored, as if he had lost interest. "I don't remember. Can I go now?"

"Yes. But I want to talk to your brother."

This was a hopeless task. Robert was as childish as Edward was—if not altogether pleasantly—mature.

"He looked like Batman."

"Can you remember what he said, Robert?"

"He said, 'Trick or treat,' and I said, 'Where's Godzilla?' and he turned into a bear, black fur grew all on him, and he roared and showed all his big teeth. I said, 'You're not Godzilla, you're the Beast.'"

Robert collapsed in helpless laughter. To Wexford's astonishment he rolled on the floor, laughing and shrieking. Jane Andrews came in, prodded Robert with her toe, said in a teacher's tone, "Get up. Come on, don't be crazy."

It was effective, but only up to a point, for the boy's laughter was succeeded by a storm of tears. Fay put her arms around him and he sobbed against her shoulder. Her eyes met Wexford's above Robert's head, but Wexford could see only blankness in them and dismal resignation.

Jane was in jeans and sweatshirt, but today her face was made up and she wore earrings, a long silver chain necklace, and a big watch with a black-and-silver face. She looked pleased with herself, glad to be busy and useful, the heroine's friend, her mainstay and support. "I'll be staying here for as long as Fay wants me," she said, "as long as I'm needed," and she bent down to pick up Sanchia.

But the little girl, seeing her brother in their mother's arms, was immediately jealous, pushed Jane away, and climbed up beside Robert. The almost adolescent Edward, not hesitating for long but unable to find a corner in Fay's chair for himself, stood behind it and leaned his cheek against her hair.

Wexford and Jane Andrews looked at each other and Jane smiled. "Love-bombing, as the psychologists put it," she said.

CHAPTER
24

A NEEDLE IN A HAYSTACK IS NOT TOO DIFFERENT A CONCEPT from a knife in a hundred acres of woodland, interspersed with gardens, with shrubberies and hedgerows, and a drainage system branching underneath it. The drains had been investigated for that knife, and an unpleasant task been assigned to PC Peach and WPC Brodrick: that of sifting through the rubbish collected that Tuesday morning from Ploughman's Lane by Kingsmarkham's contracted refuse collectors, Agate PLC.

From only one household had a knife been put into the wheelie-bin. But it was just a knife, quite the wrong sort, short and serrated. All the knives taken from Woodland Lodge were returned to Fay Devenish, though before they went back, Wexford looked at them closely, probably for the twentieth time, at their long smooth or serrated blades and their horn handles, dark brown horn or, in two cases, a lighter bleached shade. He looked especially at the two, one with a dark handle, the other with a light, whose blades matched Stephen Devenish's wounds.

"He must have brought the knife with him in that briefcase," Burden said. "Brought it with him and took it away. Young Edward says it was a big briefcase. How big, d'you reckon? Big enough to carry something to cover that jacket and those jeans? Say a raincoat?"

"Don't talk to me about raincoats," said Wexford. "Dora's taking me to London on Saturday to buy a new one. Another Burberry, she says. God knows what they cost now." He sighed. "What you're saying, I presume, is that this guy brought a raincoat with him to cover up the bloodstains on his clothes. Maybe it was mine. It was at Muriel Campden it went missing."

"Be serious, will you? He would have had to conceal his clothes."

"Doesn't seem to matter whether he did or not," Wexford grumbled. "No one saw him."

"No, but he couldn't know that, could he?"

Wexford didn't answer. "No one saw Carl Meeks either. Of course the trouble with checking up on someone who performs some regular task at the same time every day, like dog walking or even just going to work, is that people who see you can't remember *when* they saw you. Everyone says they often do see Meeks and the enormous Buster, but not always, and they can't remember which days they did see him. Darren Meeks was out delivering his papers, so he doesn't know. Scott was in bed. The primary schools didn't break up for the summer till that afternoon, but young Scott's not a candidate for a perfect-attendance prize, always supposing they have them anymore. Linda Meeks says he always takes the dog out without fail, no exceptions."

"Reg," said Burden, "do you honestly believe Carl Meeks killed Devenish? It's more than two years since Devenish threw him down those stairs—or whatever he actually did to him. If he was going to get revenge on Devenish, why did he wait so long?"

"And if he did wait so long, what triggered off his doing it last Tuesday? I suppose it's possible Meeks encountered Devenish somewhere, even went to one of Seaward's offices, had another go, and was again manhandled."

"No, it isn't," Burden said triumphantly. "I've had it checked out. No one among the staff at the Kingsmarkham, Brighton, and Gatwick offices of Seaward has had sight or sound of Meeks since the stairs-throwing incident. It's just possible Devenish met him in the street and insulted him or some such thing..."

"But we've no reason to think he did."

"Now I'll tell you something," said Burden. "I wonder if you've noticed."

"Noticed what?"

"Gillian Ferry."

"What about her?"

"Mrs. Ferry is a teacher at the school Edward and Robert Devenish go to. She teaches English at the Francis Roscommon School in Sewingbury."

Wexford thought about it. "So she does. Is it significant?"

"I don't know. But it makes, so to speak, a double connection between the Ferrys and the Devenishes. Don't you think it's a bit odd?"

It was a little after ten o'clock when Sylvia put down the phone. She had been talking for twenty minutes to the woman who called but refused to give her name. Thank God no one else had phoned in the meantime. She got up, went to the window, and looked down into the gardens. The bright windows of houses in Kingsbrook Avenue punctured the darkness. Lawns looked like strips of gray velvet and cypress trees like hooded figures. Sylvia thought there was nothing like hours of solitude working on the helpline for sharpening the imagination. She would so much have liked to tell someone what the anonymous woman had said. Griselda could be told, of course, or Lucy—Sylvia wasn't a priest and it wasn't the confessional—but Griselda was on holiday and overworked Lucy was probably asleep.

It was her father Sylvia really wanted to tell, but she would only do that with Griselda's or Lucy's permission. Standing there, looking at the backs of houses where the lights were beginning to go out, she thought about her father, and how attentively he would listen and how wisely he would respond. If she didn't feel much better about her husband, Sylvia thought, she did about her father. Another good thing The Hide had done for her.

Reflected in the black glass, the door behind her opened and Tracy Miller came in, wearing a pink tracksuit and with her long hair pinned to the top of her head.

Sylvia turned around and smiled, glad of some company. Tracy often came in for half an hour on her way to bed. Her children would have her up at six in the morning. "I've had such a frightening phone call, Trace."

"One of them bastards wanting to chop your tits off?"

Sylvia laughed. She actually laughed, which only proved how hardened you could get or how the passage of time *softened* the worst horrors. "Not a man. A woman. I want to tell you but I can't. You know the rules. It's absolutely in confidence."

"I know. It's only on account of they know that, they trust you, that the poor cows give you a phone at all."

"Did you call a helpline before you came here?"

"Me? I phoned all of ten times before I screwed up my courage and made the break. By that time he'd nailed up the doors on the cupboard so I couldn't get at my clothes and cut up my shoes. I went barefoot for a week. Well, you know what he's like. He scared you when he got over the wall, didn't he?"

Sylvia nodded. "She asked my advice and I gave it. For what it's worth. I'm not a lawyer. I just remembered something I'd read and I said to be careful. If you've got to lie, lie. Was that wrong, Trace?"

"Don't ask me, love. What do I know? You've got to do what you've got to do, that's what I say."

The crematorium chapel was no more than five years old, its walls paneled in fine hardwoods, its windows owing a good deal to Chagall's designs for stained glass. The curtains, of dark green linen, had been embroidered by a local craftswoman with heavenly bodies, galaxies, and long-tailed comets, and the pulpit was a cylinder of polished steel with star-shaped cutouts through which light faintly gleamed. But for all that, it was a dismal place, cold, stark, and designed to hold more mourners than were likely ever to occupy its inlaid maple pews. Often the number was limited to ten, as was the case today, when his family and a few acquaintances came to cremate Stephen Devenish.

A representative from Seaward Air, Wexford thought the man in a raincoat very like his own lost Burberry must be. The representative sat, looking uncomfortable, with a pale gray felt hat on his lap. Devenish's PA Wexford recognized, a smartly dressed young woman in a black suit and very high-heeled, black patent shoes, sitting two rows behind him. It was extraordinary how ostentatiously the English avoided sitting *next* to anyone they didn't know. Four seats from her was Trevor Ferry.

Anyone may go to a funeral, it isn't obligatory to be asked. But still Wexford was surprised to see him there. Had he come to rejoice and gloat or simply quietly to celebrate? Ferry didn't look in his direction but sat staring at the abstract up on the wall that might have represented an angel or a tree of life, it was impossible to tell.

Fay came in with her father and mother, Jane Andrews walking behind with Edward. That was the extent of the congregation. Devenish had had no parents living, but though he had a sister, she had stayed away. There were no flowers, and if any request had been made by Fay that, instead of flowers, donations should be made to a charity, no mention was made of such a suggestion. At one point the Seaward representative got up and seemed to be about to deliver some kind of eulogy of the dead man, but Fay touched his arm, whispered something to him, and he sat down again.

No hymns were sung. Handel's *Water Music* was quietly piped, some words from the Alternative Service Book were muttered, and the coffin was slowly drawn away to disappear behind the beige velvet curtains and to send Devenish's body to the fire. Without waiting for any valediction, any closing of the ceremony, Fay got up and walked out, the small congregation gradually following her. The officiating cleric looked embarrassed. The music stopped.

Outside, the Seaward man got into the black Mercedes that was waiting for him and was driven away. Wexford found himself walking down the long gravel drive in the company of Trevor Ferry.

"That was a funny old carry-on," Ferry said conversationally. "Talk about a good-riddance gathering."

"Is that what you'd call it?" Wexford said, amused.

"Well, wouldn't you? I suppose you want to know what took me there."

"If you want to tell me."

"I don't mind, I'm not proud. The fact is, I'm a poor man—well, you know that. I'm unemployed and likely to remain so, I'm bored. I can't afford cinemas and I certainly can't afford to join clubs. I've got square eyes—that's what they used to call it when I was a kid—from watching TV. So I like to get out sometimes to whatever I can that's free."

"Like funerals?"

"Why not? You can't get in to weddings. Not if they're any good. Besides, believe it or not after what's happened, I felt sorry for the poor devil. He wasn't so bad. It's an outing, isn't it? Sometimes I go down to the station and watch the Intercities go through."

Wexford said nothing. It was raining again, a drop fell on his nose, and he could see the coin-size spots on the paving.

"Anyway, I got to talk to you. It all makes a change. For instance, another thing I do, I've joined the Kingsmarkham Neighbourhood Clean Streets Campaign."

They had almost reached the car park, where Donaldson awaited

Wexford. He turned back and cast a look at the sugar-loaf-shaped crematorium, with its steel doors and glass cross on the top. "The what?"

"Haven't you heard of it? Groups of us are organized to go to specific areas picking up litter. Oh, you don't get paid, it's on a voluntary basis. But you get people to talk to, I've met some very decent people, and they give you midmorning coffee and biscuits. Tuesday's my day. The only drawback is you have to start so damned early, before eight A.M. on the green outside the Town Hall."

Wexford was so astonished and at the same time so aghast that anyone would be in such desperate straits of boredom and idleness as to welcome this kind of diversion that it was some moments before he realized what Ferry had said. And when he did, and Ferry was saying he must be off before it started pouring, he had to catch the bus, Wexford said nothing at all beyond good-bye.

That evening Patrick Flay and Monty Smith were caught burgling a house in Orchard Drive. Kaylee was not with them. The neighbors recognized Flay, or they recognized the intruder they saw cutting a pane of glass out of a next-door window, as the man they had once seen in a drunken brawl outside the York Arms public house. Whoever he might be, they were sure he had no business gaining entry to their neighbors' home and they dialed 999.

It was eleven forty-five. The police came quietly, entered the house by the same means as Flay and Smith had entered it, and found both men in the master bedroom, putting jewelry and ornaments into a canvas holdall. Monty Smith said he was a law-abiding man who had been led astray by Patrick Flay. Flay's wife had been putting Smith up since his girlfriend turned him out. Even so, he would never have done it if he hadn't been thrown out of his home and left destitute on the streets. Flay said nothing at all but jumped out of the window.

The result was that he broke one of his legs and, while Smith was driven to the police station, had to be taken away in an ambulance. Next morning, at the Princess Diana Memorial Clinic where he was in traction, he told Burden that apart from the one he had given Colin Crowne, he had sold two of his petrol bombs to John Keenan and two to Peter McGregor.

"Who's Peter McGregor?"

"Chap who lives with Sue Ridley, next door to the Crownes."

Burden had no comment to make.

"Don't matter telling you lot now," Flay said, "seeing as I'll be going down for Christ knows how long. I never said nothing before on account of I was scared they'd get me."

It all sounded highly unlikely to Burden. "How about that business with Kaylee and the cat flap?"

"Before I'm sentenced," said Flay rather grandly, "I shall be asking for a number of offenses to be taken into consideration."

"I bet you will."

"I can't talk any more now, I'm in pain. My leg feels like it's on fire. D'you know, you've been in here an hour and you haven't once asked me how I'm feeling?"

Burden met Wexford for lunch in the Europlate. Wexford said three-quarters of an hour was all the time he could spare and he hoped Henri would get a move on. The big Glaswegian appeared as if on cue to tell them that today's specials were *soufflé pomodoro secco* and *osso buco à l'orange*. Wexford said to forget it. He'd have the pike and boiled potatoes and his friend the roast lamb.

"Good choice," said Burden, and refrained from adding that he hadn't been consulted. "Do you know, Jenny's sister's got an Italian friend who's lived in Tuscany all her life and she'd never heard of dried tomatoes till she had some in a restaurant in Soho."

Wexford laughed. "I met Trevor Ferry at the funeral." He told Burden about their conversation. "When I got back, I phoned the Town Hall—well, not the Town Hall at all, really, these days—the building that used to be the Midland Bank, which now houses Kingsmarkham Neighbourhood Clean Streets Campaign. What do you think they told me?"

"That Ferry turned up at the rendezvous covered in blood," said Burden sourly.

"Not quite that. They told me that the area covered on Tuesday mornings was Winchester Drive, Harrow Avenue, Eton Gardens, and adjacent roads."

"So? Winchester Drive's the nearest to Ploughman's Lane and it's still a good half mile away."

"Right. I asked for a lot of details about the campaign. Apparently, people may work in groups or individually—that is, one man or woman could work a street on their own. And last Tuesday very few people turned up—the usual fate of this kind of enterprise, I fear."

Burden considered. "You're saying Ferry could have been left on his own and while he was alone slipped away up to Woodland Lodge?"

"At any rate I mean to find out. Here comes our delicious Euro-grub."

A bottle of sparkling water came too. Burden poured them a glass each.

"Karen's gone to Brighton to have another word with Mrs. Probyn. Or another ten thousand words. Barry and Lynn are at Muriel Campden, still hoping to find some evidence for Meeks's assertion that he went out with that dog as usual on Tuesday. Or if he didn't, they haven't given up hope of finding someone who saw him out *without* the dog around half-seven."

Wexford tasted his pike, nodded with grudging approval. "Not bad. The thing is, Mike, Ferry lied. He lied when he said he was in bed at eight o'clock on Tuesday morning, then, caught off guard, he forgot what lie he'd told last time and told the truth."

"You mean he was definitely out with the Clean Streets people?"

"The organizer remembered him. So few turned up, you see, that she remembered those who did. One of the others who did, by the way, was Shirley Mitchell."

"What, the Shirley Mitchell who lives next door but one to the Orbe house?"

"The very same."

"Have you talked to her?"

"Not yet," Wexford said. "But if she tells me Ferry disappeared once they got up to Winchester Drive, I'm going to have that house of his turned upside down."

Arriving at the police station as requested, dead on time, Shirley Mitchell told him just that. She began with a preamble on the need to be a good citizen and the importance of what she called "community values." Litter was the scourge of the age and the principal destroyer of the environment. Wexford listened patiently. Then she said most people who volunteered to take part in the campaign "fell by the wayside." Trevor Ferry was one of them. It was her belief he only took it on for the sake of getting a lift up to the top of the hill to enjoy the otherwise unattainable view across the countryside and the Kingsbrook valley.

He was always skiving off. They didn't necessarily work singly, the idea was to work in groups, but when she'd worked in a group with Ferry, as often as not he disappeared. It was her belief he went off for a quiet cigarette, which he couldn't do on the job, Kingsmarkham having a ban on council workers, paid or otherwise, smoking in public places.

"Smokers are some of the worst litter offenders," she said. "A lot of people don't know that. They say to themselves, what's one fag end? Well, fag ends mount up. And they're not bio-whatsit, they're not destroyable."

Wexford saw he had a fanatic to deal with. "But does Mr. Ferry smoke?"

"Don't ask me," Shirley Mitchell said sharply. "I don't want to know about his filthy habits. You asked me if he was there when I was there and I'm telling you he wasn't. We got up there in the minibus, just the four of us. He got Winchester Drive, I got Harrow Avenue, and the other two got the rest of it. Well, I had my tools ready and my bag—"

"What tools were those?"

"We have a pole kind of thing with a spike on the end, and you can have a smaller thing like a kind of—well, not a dagger, you wouldn't call it that, more like a metal rod kind of thing with an end that's been sharpened. You can picture it, can't you, sharp so that you can stab something with it and pick it up."

Silent for a moment, Wexford thought about Devenish and his wounds. Only a knife could have made them, not a spike with a sharpened end. But it was a strange business, far stranger than he had expected. Instead of saying any more, he asked her to excuse him for a moment and went outside. There he picked up the nearest phone and got on to Barry Vine.

"See if the council got all their tools back last Tuesday, Barry, after the morning cleanup session. And if they didn't, what was missing?"

Shirley Mitchell was sitting in his office, staring fixedly at an object that had once, many years previously, been used as an ashtray. When he came back and took his seat opposite her, she pushed the ashtray a little farther away from her as if it still presented a threat.

"So at what time would you say you last saw Mr. Ferry that morning? You met at seven-thirty, probably got going in the minibus at twenty-five to eight, got to the set-down point at—what? A quarter to?"

"Bit before a quarter to. The set-down point's in Harrow Avenue.

That's my patch. The others just went off with their tools. Oh, and Ferry had a bag he was carrying."

Wexford felt his muscles tense. "What sort of a bag? A briefcase?"

"I wouldn't call it that. He always brings that bag. Like a canvas thing with sort of leather binding—correction, more like plastic binding. Brings his fags in it, I shouldn't wonder, and maybe a bottle. I've seen him drinking on the job. I've seen him eating sandwiches."

She could even make this last sound like a crime. Wexford frowned a little. "So you didn't see him for a while after seven forty-five. When did you see him again?"

"When I got to the end of Harrow Avenue where it joins onto Winchester Drive. I'd got to the end and I was starting down the other side. He waved to me. You want to know what time it was? All of nine, if not a bit past."

After she had gone, Barry Vine told Wexford that one of the campaign's short spiked tools had gone missing on the previous Tuesday morning. The loss hadn't been noticed until after the volunteers had been dropped on the green outside the Town Hall. Wexford sat down and reread the medical report on Stephen Devenish. He had read it at least three times before. It told him once again that Devenish's wounds had been made with a flat-bladed knife with a blade eight to ten inches long. He had taken it for granted the campaign's tool was cylindrical, with a sharpened point like a pencil. He would have to see one.

But first he set about applying for a warrant to search Ferry's house.

"He could have got there in time," Burden said. "He could have done it on foot, walked to Ploughman's Lane, up the path to Woodland Lodge, rung the doorbell, gone in, and done the deed by eight."

"The time's tight, though, isn't it?" It was Wexford's idea but he was dubious just the same. "It must have been exactly eight when he arrived, because Edward and Robert got to Mrs. Daley's by five past. I wouldn't call him a very fit man and it's uphill all the way."

"A gentle slope," said Burden. "Even a very unfit man can walk half a mile in fifteen minutes. Once he got there, he had all the time in the world. Stephen Devenish may have been killed at any time between seven forty-five and eight-thirty. He could have stood there arguing with him for ten minutes before he did the deed."

"Wouldn't Devenish have thrown him out the way he did Meeks?"

"It's not important," Burden said airily. "Besides, the conversation might have been amicable at first. Then they quarreled. Surely the point is Ferry could easily have done it in the time. He had the means, the opportunity, and the motive."

"Revenge?"

"Look, Reg, we've known all along that whoever did this did it for revenge. That's the only possible motive."

"I'm off to look at spikes," said Wexford.

The old Midland Bank building in Brook Road was opposite the Job Centre and the Nationwide Building Society. Brutal refurbishment had removed the pillared portico and the Parthenon frieze and replaced the front entrance with swing doors in a white metal-mesh arrangement rather like a freezer basket. This was the headquarters of Kingsmarkham Domestic Environment and Landscape Department, and the man-with-flowers, woman-with-spade logo was over the door.

Entering the foyer, Wexford encountered Rochelle Keenan coming out of the lift. This made little impact on him beyond reminding him that she was some relation to his informant of the morning, Shirley Mitchell, sister or sister-in-law or something. He went upstairs to the room that housed the Clean Streets Campaign and was shown the tools supplied to the volunteers. Shirley Mitchell had described them accurately, and nothing he saw much surprised him.

Undoubtedly either of these spiked implements could have been used to kill a man. The smaller one reminded Wexford of something he had never actually seen but had often read and heard about: the ice pick, once beloved of the writers of American murder mysteries. But perhaps it didn't in fact look much like this at all.

"The missing one hasn't been returned to you?"

It had not. The woman who had shown him the tools took a philosophical view. So much went missing from the council's property, issued for various reasons to the public—went missing or was destroyed—that really she was surprised more of these hadn't disappeared. Had he heard, for instance, of the fatal damage to Jodi the virtual baby?

"Fatal?" Wexford said. "It wasn't real."

"Maybe not." She sounded huffy. "But it was very valuable."

By this time the search of Ferry's house in Oval Road would have begun. Wexford said to Burden, "There is no way the wounds in Stephen Devenish's chest are going to match up with one of those spikes. They are very precisely described in the medical report. It was a knife, not a spike."

"What if you find the thing inadequately washed and wrapped up in a towel in Ferry's bedroom?"

"I doubt very much that we will. Even if we do, the fact remains that a knife of precise measurements was used and not a spike of any kind."

"With Devenish cremated…"

"'Two handfuls of white dust, shut in an urn of brass,' only she won't have wasted a good brass urn on him. Makes no difference, anyway. The medical report is a marvel of precision."

Burden looked dubiously at him. "Then what are you going to find?"

Possibly nothing. Possibly something unconnected with Devenish's death. You remember what you pointed out to me and I'd missed? About Gillian Ferry being a teacher at the school the Devenish boys go to?"

"Sure I do. She teaches English at the Francis Roscommon."

"Sit down a minute, Mike." Wexford took his seat on one side of the desk, motioned Burden to the other. Wexford pushed away the ashtray Shirley Mitchell had moved toward his side. "Gillian Ferry is also Robert Devenish's—well, we used to call them form mistresses, I expect there's another term now. I'm no expert in these things but I think Robert is a badly disturbed child, a child who was perhaps more affected by his father's treatment of his mother than either his brother or his sister was. Did he have anyone to confide in? Anyone to tell about the horrors that went on at home?"

"I think I see what you're getting at."

"Yes, he had his teacher, his class teacher. Suppose he confided in her? She already had cause to hate Devenish, he was responsible for her husband losing his job and, incidentally, for forcing her back to work. Almost any woman—any man, come to that—would be moved by a child telling them his father constantly assaulted his mother. Many would be outraged and angry…"

"Are you saying Gillian Ferry killed Devenish?"

"No, Mike. I'm saying she wrote the letters."

CHAPTER

25

IT WAS TOO SMALL A HOUSE AND TOO SPARSELY FURNISHED TO give the searchers much difficulty. Less than half an hour after they began, they found the spiked tool that was the property of the local authority. Trevor Ferry had made no attempt to hide it but put it into a kitchen drawer along with a hammer and a couple of screwdrivers. Technically, he had stolen it, but more realistically, he had simply taken it home by mistake. In any case, even a cursory examination of the tool made it clear that though it was capable of being used as a lethal weapon, it hadn't been so used.

The bag Ferry had carried with him the Tuesday before and yesterday could never have been described as a briefcase, even by a twelve-year-old. It was a soft, unstructured holdall, shabby and almost dilapidated, made of dark green canvas with tan-colored plastic binding. Wexford wasn't going to waste time showing it to Edward Devenish. Would he ever have mentioned a briefcase if his younger brother hadn't?

Ferry's indignation at the searching of his house was extreme, and he accused Wexford of "disloyalty" and even of "betrayal" solely, it seemed, on the grounds that they had left a crematorium together and carried on a reasonably amicable conversation. "I call it dirty and underhand. Worming details out of me under the guise of friendship."

Wexford ignored the last bit. It was too ridiculous to be taken seriously and reminded him of Brian St. George. "You volunteered the information, Mr. Ferry," Wexford said mildly. "I didn't ask you."

"I should have known better than to open my mouth to you people."

"Why did you tell me you were still in bed at eight in the morning when in fact you were out with the cleanup campaign?"

"Because that time I had the sense not to open my mouth. I knew what you'd think if I said I'd been in Winchester Drive at a quarter to eight. You already knew there was no love lost between me and Steve Devenish. I may as well say it now."

"You told me, I quote, 'He wasn't so bad.'"

The blood came into Ferry's face and swelled the tissues. It even seemed to get into his eyes. "I hated him."

"Did your wife also hate him, Mr. Ferry?"

Many men would have seen the question as a hint that there might have been sexual relations or a desire for sexual relations between Devenish and Gillian Ferry. In that Ferry did not, in that he hesitated and slightly narrowed his eyes, Wexford understood her husband had half guessed she had written the threatening letters.

She had been out while the search was done and knew nothing about it. The anger she had suppressed burst out when she saw police in her home, and she turned on Ferry, calling him a fool, a spiritless fool with no gumption. "You're as weak as a baby! You *are* a baby, you've never begun to grow up."

Wexford had found no evidence of the letters but he hadn't expected to do so. She would hardly have made copies and kept them in a reference file. A Word for Windows program had been used to produce them, but the searchers hadn't found a computer. He would have been surprised if they had in this household where money was tight. She would have used one of the computers at the Francis Roscommon School. He showed her the letter, the last line of which threatened to make Devenish's wife a widow and his children orphans, and asked if she was its author.

She held it in her hand and took a long time reading it. He could see in her face that she admired her achievement. When she had finished, she was smiling. Defiantly, she admitted authorship. "Yes. I wrote it. I wrote a lot of letters to that man. More than a hundred. A hundred and sixteen in all, if you want to know."

She lifted her eyes, opened them very wide so that they looked spherical. In the dark, Wexford was sure, sparks would fly from that white-blond hair. Her face was contorted as she spoke. "I wrote them. I enjoyed writing them. I kept them courteous, even quite formal. They all started, 'Dear Mr. Devenish.' They were in very good prose, though I doubt if he appreciated that." Her tone made it clear she believed she had been clever and amusing. "It was for my own pleasure, my own revenge. It made me feel better about a whole lot of things."

Her husband stared at her, then put his head in his hands. Gillian Ferry looked at him contemptuously. "I didn't do it out of love of *you*, so don't think it. I should have left you when you drank yourself out of that job, when you got sozzled every day—God knows why I didn't."

To Wexford she said more calmly, "It wasn't for him. At least, it was only a bit for him. Mainly it was because Devenish was such a bastard, punching his wife in the face and cutting her, and letting his kids see, wanting them to see. Robert told me, I teach Robert at school, or I tried to, but you can't teach much to a child who's living a nightmare at home. Kids like that aren't exactly receptive."

"He told you about his father beating his mother."

"*Beating* is a word for it, I suppose. It's not the one I'd choose. He told me how the torture started. The poor woman put a horn-handled knife in the dishwasher by mistake once, and when it came out, the powder or the hot water or whatever had bleached the handle. Devenish cut her for that, he cut her with the same knife." Her eyes flashed. "I'd like to meet the guy who killed Devenish, I'd shake him by the hand."

Wexford cautioned her. She took no notice of his words.

"Will I go to prison?"

"Probably not."

"Pity. I'd quite like to go to prison. It'd be a change from here and *him*, and that bloody school."

When he got back to Kingsmarkham, Lynn Fancourt was waiting for him with the news that Carl Meeks could be eliminated from the inquiry. Two people had been found who remembered seeing him in the Kingsbrook Meadows with Buster at 8 A.M. on the day of the Devenish murder. Her report was on his desk but she'd like just to tell him that the witnesses weren't Carl's neighbors or among the more dubious of Kingsmarkham's citizens. Both were dog owners dog-walking, the woman the proprietor of a boutique in York Street, whose premises Patrick Flay had robbed, the man a college lecturer who taught computer studies at Myringham University.

But it was really Buster who was responsible for getting Carl Meeks out of trouble. Once seen, never forgotten, as Burden had said, Buster was a dog to remember. The First Gear owner (with her spaniel) had seen him for the first time that Tuesday. She recalled it because Tuesday was her birthday and she'd wished she could ask her boyfriend for a Great Dane for a birthday present, only she already had the spaniel.

Buster got into a fight with the lecturer's Jack Russell. While gentle enough with human beings, Danes were apparently in the habit of seizing upon smaller dogs, hurling them in the air, and shaking them to death. Or so the lecturer said. He had had to take Jake to the vet, which was a nuisance because that Tuesday was the day he was due to begin teaching a course at a summer school in Sewingbury.

Carl Meeks was off the hook, as Burden put it.

Wexford said, "But Ferry isn't, is he? Not really."

"What d'you mean?"

"Just because he didn't do it with the litter spike doesn't mean he didn't do it all. And equally, because it was his wife who wrote the letters, that doesn't exonerate him. He still has no alibi. He was within walking distance of Devenish's home at the relevant time. He admits he hated the man. And there's another thing—he seems to me not to find life worth living. What has he to look forward to? His retirement pension in twenty years' time. He has no children. His wife dislikes him. His home is a tip. Maybe he did it because, like his wife, he doesn't care what happens to him, anything for a change, even prison."

"Bit extreme, isn't it? People don't really behave like that."

"'People don't do such things,' as Ibsen says? Maybe. Anyway, we have a far more likely suspect."

"We do?"

Wexford nodded. Then he said that he'd had it for today and how about a drink in the Olive and Dove? "I want to tell you a story."

They walked there, the length of the High Street. It was a mild evening of hazy sunshine, humid and still. A bereavement charity was holding a wine and cheese party in St. Peter's Church Hall, but by the look of the trickle of visitors it was sparsely attended. Conversely, on its closure at six, crowds poured out of the Heaven Spent mall, laden with carrier bags, flushed from the triumph and deep inner fulfillment shopping brings. Wexford spotted Maria Michaels and Miroslav Zlatic among them. He thought about his lost raincoat and the dismal prospect of buying a new one, then about a previous visit to the Olive and Dove when a newspaper had taken a photograph of him with a beer tankard in his hand and printed it above a ribald legend. He had never forgotten it; he dreaded its happening again. But that had been outdoors, in the hotel garden, and this evening they would be in the quiet and seclusion of the landlord's snug.

"You're very silent," said Burden.

"I'm thinking. Anyway, I don't think one can be 'very' silent. You're either silent or you're not. It's like saying someone is very dead."

"Like Devenish. I don't think I've ever come across a dead man so many people were glad to be dead. Not a dissenting voice."

"I doubt if his children are glad, Mike. Children have a rare faculty of loving parents who are unworthy of their love. You might say children love their parents as a matter of course. It's sad."

The garden of the Olive and Dove and its bar were crowded this evening, mostly with people under thirty, many probably under eighteen.

"In the United States they make you produce identification to show your age," Burden said.

"That's fine if you've got any. If you don't have a passport or a driving license or a rail pass, what then? Don't tell me they do in America, I know that. The point is they don't here."

No one was in the snug. It was too small and, with its only window overlooking a yard full of beer-can crates, too dimly lit to attract Kingsmarkham's youth. The three tables had marble tops and the chairs were upholstered in worn, dark red leather. Another feature of the place, discouraging to many, was a notice on the wall that read DON'T EVEN THINK OF SMOKING HERE. You either went to the bar and queued up or rang a brass bell for service. No one came in here otherwise.

They both asked for Adnams. It arrived in glasses, which pleased Wexford, though he had once preferred tankards. He hadn't drunk out of a tankard—they called them mugs in here—since that never-to-be-forgotten day. He said an unaccustomed "Cheers" to Burden and took a long draft of his beer.

"Cheers," said Burden. "I've been thinking about that boy Edward, Edward Devenish. He could have killed his father. After he'd seen his mother come into the kitchen with her hand bleeding. He could have gone into the study, picked up the knife, and stabbed his father, taken him by surprise. He's a big, strong boy, though not as tall as Devenish, and it's someone shorter than Devenish we're looking for."

"How about the blood, Mike? Did he cover up his clothes before he went in there? Or wash his clothes before he left for school? And what about Robert? Was he in it too? You're forgetting what I said about children loving their parents."

"Maybe, but children do kill their parents, it's not unknown, patricide. Yes, by the way, why do we call the act patricide and the perpetrator a parricide?"

Wexford said rather impatiently, "I don't know," and uncharacteristically, "Does it matter?" He didn't wait for an answer. "In France when they had capital punishment, parricides were sent to the guillotine barefoot and with their faces veiled. I read that somewhere. But Edward and Robert Devenish aren't parricides." He hesitated. "I know who did this murder. And it wasn't any of our suspects. I think," he added reflectively and rather sadly, "I've always known it."

Burden simply looked at him, saying nothing.

"I said I was going to tell you a story." Someone carried a crate of empty bottles out into the yard, dropping it with a crash. Wexford winced. "Silent," still less "very silent," were no longer descriptions that had much relevance. The countryside was as noisy as the town. He took another drink. Beer was still pretty good. "Fay Devenish and her son Edward and, more or less, her son Robert, have told us a man, unknown to Edward, came to the front door of Woodland Lodge that Tuesday morning at eight A.M. Give or take a little, I suppose. It may have been two or three minutes to eight, or two or three minutes past. We also know that Stephen Devenish was stabbed to death, receiving three stab wounds to the chest, at some time between seven forty-five and eight-thirty.

"The scenario goes like this: At seven thirty-five or seven-forty, again give or take a little, Stephen Devenish, seriously displeased with his wife's failure to provide fresh orange juice, gets up from the breakfast table, leaves the room, and goes into his study. Perhaps he shuts the door, perhaps he doesn't. Fay, her sons, and her daughter, Sanchia, remain in the kitchen.

"Within five minutes Devenish calls out to his wife from the study—

presumably from the study doorway. He calls out, 'Come in here, Fay,' or even, knowing him, 'Come in here, darling.' She knows what is going to happen and the boys probably know, but she goes. She hasn't much choice, has she? If she doesn't go, he'll fetch her, drag her out of there, an act of violence which Sanchia will witness.

"She goes into the study. Devenish tells her she has to be punished, she's a hopeless housewife and mother, she's mad, she has to learn, and a load more of that stuff, no doubt. He tells her to hold out her hand and he cuts her across the palm. Probably she cries out. She may even scream out, loudly enough for the children in the kitchen to hear. Devenish wipes the knife clean on something—maybe his own handkerchief, which she will have to wash—and tells her to go. Her hand is bleeding heavily, so she goes across the hallway into the cloakroom where she holds it under the cold tap, then wraps it in the towel that hangs there."

"Okay," said Burden a little impatiently. "We know all that."

"Wait. The study door is left a little ajar. Fay goes back to the kitchen, her hand wrapped in the towel. Neither boy asks what has happened. They know. Fay tells them to get ready for school, it's their last day of term, and they know they have to be at Mrs. Daley's by five past eight.

"Within the next five minutes or so the boys go out into the hallway, use the lavatory, wash their hands, and prepare to leave the house. The doorbell rings. Edward opens the door and there on the doorstep is a man he has never seen before. This man is about the same age as his father—that is, middle to late thirties—is wearing jeans and a jacket, and carrying a briefcase. He says he has come to see Stephen Devenish.

"Edward calls out something like, 'Dad, there's someone to see you,' and says to the man, 'He's in there,' indicating the slightly open study door. Fay, in the kitchen, also hears the man's voice but not Edward's. Possibly this is because a boy of twelve's voice is naturally higher and lighter than a mature man's. Moreover, though Edward can't remember the man's precise words, Fay can. She remembers he said, 'I'm here to see Mr. Devenish.'

"Now, whether Devenish had come to the door by then or was still inside, unseen, we don't know. Edward can't remember and Robert is too young to be a reliable witness. But the man goes into the study, shutting the door behind him. Now, this is quite remarkable. If a stranger calls on you in your house and is shown into the room where you are, he only closes the door if asked to do so by you, doesn't he? Unless he's not a stranger but well known to you and is in fact someone accorded the privileges of a friend, at least of a familiar acquaintance."

Burden nodded. "I'd put it more strongly than that. The person coming in would either be a friend of some duration or a person in authority. I mean, I close the door behind me when I come into your office, but Lynn wouldn't. On the other hand, Southby would and the chief constable would."

"That's true. However, it's not relevant here. I think there's a third category. And in that category comes someone who is an acquaintance, not a friend. Indeed, it's an acquaintance who *has become an enemy* and, as an enemy, need no longer observe customary social usage or even politeness. He or she wants seclusion and silence, so he closes the door without asking permission of the man inside.

"The door shuts. The boys leave the house, closing the front door behind them. In the kitchen Fay is giving Sanchia her breakfast and trying to staunch the blood still coming from her hand. She has the breakfast dishes to put into the dishwasher and the day's washing to do, not to mention housecleaning, bed-making, shopping, and the daylong care of a three-year-old.

"She doesn't hear Devenish's visitor leave the house, and of course, she doesn't hear Devenish leave. Devenish is dead, his body lying on the study floor, with three stab wounds in his chest, including the fatal one to the heart. Fay thinks he's left for work. She tidies and cleans the kitchen, puts the breakfast things in the dishwasher and starts it, takes Sanchia out of her high chair, and gives her things to play with. At some point in the next hour or so she takes her into the playroom and puts on children's television for her or a video. Then she goes upstairs, makes the beds, gathers up the dirty washing and, along with the towel in which she wrapped her hand, takes it into the utility room and puts it in the washing machine."

"I suppose all these household management hints are necessary?" Burden grumbled.

"I think they are." Wexford swallowed the last of his beer, set down the glass, wondering why a glass always leaves a damp ring on a surface even when it's not wet. One of life's little mysteries, only he had the big ones to solve. "At nine or thereabouts," he went on, "Fay checks on Sanchia in the playroom, perhaps puts on a new video. Then she goes into the study to clean it, carrying no doubt a duster and pushing a vacuum cleaner. She finds Devenish dead on the floor and calls us."

"Yes, but look here," Burden objected, "are you saying there were two knives? The one Devenish had used to cut his wife's hand and the one the man at the door brought with him? Because, if you're not, you must be saying the man at the door brought no weapon with him, either because he didn't intend to kill Devenish or because he knew the knife would be there waiting for him, which is absurd."

"I might be saying that he only thought of killing Devenish when he saw his opportunity in the form of the knife. Perhaps because Devenish said something insupportable to him, he picked up the knife and stabbed him."

"Well, okay, perhaps. But who was he, this mysterious man no one recognized but who had the authority or the familiarity to close Devenish's study door behind him?"

"First of all," said Wexford, "I'd like to talk about the knife—or, rather, the knives. But let's have another drink, shall we? Ring the bell."

Feeling like someone in a Victorian mystery story, literature his wife sometimes encouraged him to read, Burden picked up the brass bell and gave it three vigorous shakes. There should have been a candle on the table in one of those metal candlesticks with a snail-shaped handle, or at least an oil lamp. The snug looked as if it hadn't seen a coat of paint on its grimy ocher walls and dark brown woodwork since such a story was first published. The barman came. He was a man who could only have lived at the end of the twentieth century, with the ring in his pierced lip, matted dreadlocks, and endangered-species tiger-face logo on the back of his hand.

But he had a pleasant manner and an old-fashioned politeness, and he took their order cheerfully, returning in only a few moments with the two glasses and a free packet of cashews, compliments of the management.

"I don't suppose taking these smells of corruption, do you?" Wexford said after the man had gone. "It won't make us look more favorably on him at the next Brewster Sessions." He laughed. "Now, the knives. We both know that the knife block is made to hold eight knives but it contained only seven. However, the remaining slot is too small and short to have contained a knife wide enough or long enough in the blade to have made Devenish's wounds. There was no eighth knife, and when Fay told us there never had been an eighth knife because to insert one made the block too crowded and inhibited the removal of any of the others, she was speaking the truth."

"We've been through that before."

"All right. We have. Of those seven knives, all have horn handles, but five of the handles are dark brown and two a much lighter brown, almost a fawn color. Now this is the effect of putting horn handles into a dishwasher and through a very hot wash. I know. I've tried it and Dora wasn't too pleased with me when she saw what I'd done."

"Shame," Burden mocked, "and when it was all in the cause of justice and truth."

Ignoring him, Wexford went on, "Edward Devenish has told me that he knew this happened *to one of the knives* in the block and Gillian Ferry has told me that for this—that is, putting a horn-handled knife through a hot wash—Devenish cut Fay's hand. In fact, it seems this was the first time he cut Fay and the damage to the knife put the idea into his head."

"But only one knife, not two?"

"Edward spoke of just one. But there were two. So when was the second knife put through the hot wash? Not, surely, *before* Devenish's death. Fay was often enough punished for nothing, she wasn't going to stick her neck out committing an offense for which she was deliberately cut across the hand the first time."

"Right. And why was it put through the dishwasher?" Burden answered his own question: "Presumably, because such a wash, extending over—what? Forty minutes?—would effectively have removed any blood and any prints that might be on it."

"Certainly its blade matches Stephen Devenish's wounds," Wexford said. "Don't you want to know who the man at the door was?"

"I know you well enough to be quite aware that you'll only tell me when you're ready."

Wexford grinned. He drank from the new Adnams, nodded. "Remember, according to Edward, it was a man of about thirty-six or seven, tall but not so tall as his father, wearing jeans and a jacket, and carrying a briefcase. Now there is a woman involved in all this whom, when I first saw her, because of her hair and her lack of makeup and her height, and her thinness and her clothes, I took for a man. Very briefly, a matter of seconds rather than minutes, but I took her for a man."

"Jane Andrews," said Burden.

"Without being in the least unattractive or what used to be called 'mannish,' she can make herself look like a man. She's flat-chested, she's tall, she has the right haircut. These days women's jackets and men's are scarcely different from one another. Jeans are the same for men and women. Let us suppose that Jane Andrews dressed herself in her jeans and jacket, and perhaps added some other masculine touches, men's shoes in a size seven—her size, anyway, I'd guess—a white shirt? A tie? Edward says the man wore a tie. And the briefcase. Most people still associate briefcases with men, though the concept is slowly changing. That would be enough.

"She leaves the house in Brighton at seven or seven-fifteen. Her mother is still in bed asleep and likely to remain so for a couple of hours. There is no one else to see her go or care whether she goes or not. She arrives in Ploughman's Lane, a place she knows very well, though she hasn't been there for years.

"She parks somewhere. Maybe in Ploughman's Close or even down the hill to where it meets Winchester Drive. She walks to Woodland Lodge, carrying her briefcase, in which she has a thin, lightweight raincoat and a weapon, for she intends to kill Stephen Devenish. That is the purpose of her visit."

"Then what happened...?"

"To the other knife? The one used to cut Fay and which she afterwards put through the hot wash? Wait. Presumably Jane brought a knife with her or even a gun. Why she chose that time of day I don't know. Perhaps she had already tried to set up a meeting alone with him outside the house but he had refused even to speak to her."

"Her motive, of course, is her affection for and sympathy with Fay Devenish?"

"That and the rage she felt, and has felt for years, against Devenish. Perhaps too, her empathy with her sister, Louise Sharpe..."

"It would be a very illogical empathy," Burden said hotly. "Devenish may have been a villain and a miscreant, but no one could say he was to blame for Louise Sharpe's problems."

Wexford sighed. "We're talking about emotion, Mike, not logic." He paused, looked down at the table, then said, "Jane Andrews rang the doorbell and the door was opened almost immediately by Edward. She recognized him, of course, but he didn't recognize her. Why would he? He hadn't seen her for years, and when he last saw her, *she had long hair.* Mrs. Probyn told us that her daughter used to have 'lovely long hair.' No doubt Jane deepened her voice for the few words she had to speak to Edward, not a very difficult undertaking. She already has a deep voice for a woman.

"She goes into the study and for a moment he doesn't know who this stranger is. He says hello or something and what can he do for her—well, him, as he thinks. She speaks in her normal voice and then he does recognize her..."

"Why doesn't he throw her out?"

"I don't know, Mike. There are a few loose ends to tie up. The point is that he doesn't. Maybe he welcomes a confrontation. He may suspect she and Fay were still in touch, he may know that they were and he wants to tell her what he'll do if she doesn't stop communicating with his wife. And we know what that might be, don't we? More and severer punishment for Fay. Or he may prefer to deny what Jane says or tell her she's mad, a favorite retort with him. One thing you can be sure of, he doesn't think she's come to kill him.

"What he says drives her over the edge. A knife is lying on the desk. She has a weapon with her, but why use that when one is here to hand? She picks it up, catches Devenish unawares, and stabs him.

"She wipes the knife—on what? Her own clothes perhaps, which in any case will already be splashed with blood—puts it back on the table, having guessed why it was there and what it was used for *and knowing that in due course Fay will take it away and wash it.* She knows her Fay.

"She puts on the raincoat she has brought with her and leaves the house, picks up the car, drives home, where her mother is still in bed. How's that? It covers everything, I think."

"Yes, it does. It's the only solution that does." Burden lifted his glass. "Well, congratulations, if that's appropriate."

Wexford nodded. He didn't drink. "The only drawback is that it isn't true."

CHAPTER 26

THE NEW RAINCOAT LOOKED UNCOMFORTABLY NEW. YET IT wasn't uncomfortable but an excellent fit, the right breadth on the shoulders, the right length. Burden would have enjoyed wearing it. Mystifyingly, Burden loved new clothes, the pleasure of putting them on for the first time, of seeing himself look elegant. Wexford could never understand it. Part of the trouble for him was the newness, the *looking* new. He wasn't a self-conscious man, nor shy, nor desirous of making an impression, but in new clothes he felt everyone was looking at him. With a kind of nostalgia, he thought of his old raincoat, so comfortable, so pleasantly worn, so mildly battered. He even loved the ineradicable small stain, the heart-shaped blotch of something unanalyzable that defied the efforts of dry cleaners.

But once again it was raining. The warm, dryish weather had lasted no more than a day. He would have to wear it, make a start, break it in. The faint sheen on its fabric, the stiffness of its lapels, discomfited him.

On the phone to Burden he said, "If we have even a week's dry spell after all this rain, the water moguls will say we're in drought and put on a hose-pipe ban. You see if I'm not right."

"What are you really ringing me about, Reg?"

"How well you know me."

"Perhaps. So what's new?"

Wexford told him, in a somber voice and with a heavy heart. But Burden knew already. He'd see him later, and never mind, what must be, must be. Justice must be done.

The rain was so heavy that Donaldson had to stop the car in Winchester Drive, pull under the trees, and wait for it to abate a little. Wexford, in the back, not even bothering to clear a space with his hand in the steamy window, sat thinking whether there was anything he could say, any hint he could give, any adumbration of the terrible risks involved, without jeopardizing his career and his very job. Through his head ran such phrases as "mandatory life sentence" and "provocation beyond bearing." The rain crashed on the car roof. Condensation trickled down the glass. "Give it another go, will you?" he said with unaccustomed roughness. "We can't sit here all day."

As he spoke, the rain diminished a little. The roar lessened. The wipers could just cope with the flow down the windscreen. Donaldson started the car and drove slowly up the hill, sending fountains of water onto the pavements as the wheels rolled through puddles. In the driveway, an overhanging branch brushed against the car and sent down a cascade of water.

The rendering on the walls of Woodland Lodge was stained dark gray with water. A puddle lay at the foot of the front doorstep, and Wexford was faced either with an undignified jump or the prospect of inundated shoes. He jumped. Lynn Fancourt's small leap was more elegant. The bell rang hollowly through the house. He must have rung this bell a dozen times, but he had never noted its loudness before, nor the echo that seemed to follow it. At any rate, he reflected while he waited, that cuckoo was gone.

Jane Andrews came to the door with Sanchia close behind her. In a long skirt and silk jumper, she looked very unlike a man today. Her hair seemed longer, and a hairdresser had put blond highlights in it. "She's expecting you," she said, then, "She knows why you've come."

"Thanks," he said because he didn't know what else to say.

"I'm going to take the children out. In the car somewhere. I'll think of somewhere we can go in the rain."

The house looked like a place people lived in, women and children lived in, no longer like a country-house-interiors museum. Someone's cardigan hung over the banisters. The flowers in the big Chinese vase were dying. In the big living room where Fay Devenish sat alone, books were scattered on the coffee table among two or three days' newspapers. She jumped up when he and Lynn came in.

"Please sit down, Mrs. Devenish."

In a slow, sad voice, not at all hysterical, she said calmly, "You know, don't you? I knew you would. I just want you to know I wouldn't have let anyone else take the blame for this. I mean, if you'd arrested someone else, I'd have stopped it."

"I'm sure you would."

"I killed Stephen, of course I did. Didn't you always know?"

He wouldn't admit to her that in his heart he had indeed always known. At any rate, had always feared. It was really that he hadn't wanted to face up to it. Had he, of all people, been wasting police time these past few days?

He said quietly, "There was no man, no stranger who came to the door. It was just the story that any frightened person would invent, it's the first thing that comes into one's head. It came into your head and into your son Edward's—perhaps *because* you're mother and son—only he went further than you did. He gave the mystery man an appearance: height and clothes and an age. You only gave him a voice." He cleared his throat. "Edward loves you, you see. He didn't think twice about lying for you. That morning, when he was at school and the head teacher came and told him, I think he knew then that you'd killed his father. It was so obvious to him. He'd have done it himself—one day."

Lynn made a small sound behind him, a little indrawing of the breath. Fay had been looking at him impassively, but when he spoke of her son, her lip trembled. He knew he was talking to postpone the incriminating confession she would soon make.

"No one came to the door," he said. "Edward invented that, not knowing that you'd also invented it. He and Robert left for school, but by then, for ten minutes before that, your husband was dead. Your husband took the knife from the knife block after breakfast and took it into the study. That's how you knew what he would do when he called you in. You killed him after he cut you with the knife."

"Yes."

"Did he cry out? Scream?" She wasn't going to answer him. "It would have made no difference if he had. If Edward and Robert and Sanchia had all heard him. It would simply have been a change to hear a cry from him instead of from you."

He saw her wince. A conviction for murder, he thought, carries a mandatory life sentence. Self-defense doesn't always work, often doesn't work. If a woman gives evidence of repeated abuse and it is known that on the final occasion she reacted by killing, a jury is going to want to know what was so special about the last time. Why kill then when in the past she had borne the abuse passively? Pick up a knife and kill an unarmed man? That's murder. It's just as much murder as if a stranger came up to him in the street and stabbed him. And murder carries a mandatory life sentence, there's no choice about it, no second- and third-degree murder such as they have in the United States. Here murder is murder and the punishment is life.

"I am going to take you back with me now, Mrs. Devenish, and you will of course want a solicitor to be present."

"Are you arresting me?"

"Of course."

"This is what I'm going to say. Stephen always said I was—was mentally unstable and he was right. That morning he cut me and I went mad, I lost control, I don't know what I did or why I did it. I must have just grabbed the knife and stabbed him in a frenzy. I don't remember it, it's all a blur, it was then. They say you see red. I did, I just saw red in front of my eyes. I lost my mind. I didn't even see him when I struck out." She stared at Wexford as if she saw red now and her whole body shook. "I went mad."

He felt an inward sigh relax him. She might be lying, but he didn't care. If she stuck to that story—and her solicitor, her counsel, would love it—she would be saved.

"Jane will look after my children," she said in the most tranquil tone he had ever heard her use. "I know I may not see them for a long time. They will be fine with Jane."

CHAPTER 27

IN THE MONTHS THAT FOLLOWED, THE HUNT WENT ON FOR Ted Hennessy's killer, but inquiries had reached a stalemate. It was thought that the petrol bomb had been thrown by John Keenan or Joe Hebden, but neither of them would give evidence against the other—and no one admitted possessing or handling any bombs.

In the middle of October, Brenda Bosworth took her three children out of school for a week and up to Clacton for a holiday in her mother's caravan. As soon as she was out of the way, Miroslav Zlatic and Maria Michaels were married in the new Bridal Bower at the Cheriton Forest Hotel with the maximum of celebration and the minimum of secrecy. Heavily pregnant Lizzie Cromwell, along with her mother, attended the wedding and the buffet lunch afterward, not at all upset. For, as Lizzie told everyone over the Spanish champagne, Miroslav had only got married for the sake of British citizenship and Maria was years and years older than him.

Two weeks later Lizzie gave birth to a daughter in the maternity wing of the Princess Diana Memorial Clinic and named her Millennia. During the single day and night Lizzie was in there, Colin Crowne, who had been consoling Brenda for Miroslav's defection, moved in with her. Debbie said there was no way she was going to live three doors away from that pair, but instead of 16 Oberon Road (now tenanted by cousins of the Meekses) Kingsmarkham Housing Department, delighted to repossess 45 Puck Road, allotted Debbie and Lizzie and Millennia a two-bedroom flat in Glebe Close.

Further reshuffling took place in the tower when John Keenan finally accumulated enough money to buy DNA-testing equipment, used it, and proved he was not the biological father of the redheaded Winona.

He rented a room in the Mitchells' house—which was strictly against Kingsmarkham housing rules—while determining his future. Shirley Mitchell, though his wife's sister, was entirely on his side. Shirley's husband was seriously worried about her since she had taken to grabbing and shaking any child she came upon dropping a chocolate bar wrapper or crisp packet in the street. Sooner or later she would hit one of them and get taken to the European Court of Human Rights.

Doing well at the University of Myringham and showing a particular aptitude for social sciences, Tasneem Fowler had also been rehoused. Kingsmarkham Housing eventually gave her a "studio" flat quite near where Debbie and Lizzie Cromwell lived. At their divorce hearing she and Terry were awarded joint custody of Kim and Lee, but Terry got care. The two boys, asked with whom they would prefer to live, opted for their father.

Tracy Miller made so much money working from morning till night that she set up her own house-cleaning business with ten employees, called it Tracy's Treasures, and put down a deposit on a house for herself and her daughters in Eton Road.

One morning, leaving a house in Titania Road that the occupants had been using as the headquarters of a cocaine-dealing syndicate, Wexford saw a man come out of the tower wearing a Burberry. It was a fawn-colored raincoat with a heart-shaped stain at the hem on the left-hand side. It took him a few seconds to identify the man as Peter McGregor, partner of Sue Ridley, once the Crownes' neighbor in Puck Road. What he had been doing in the tower Wexford didn't know, and seeing the general goings-on, perhaps it was just as well he didn't. McGregor gave him a calm, innocent stare before looking away. Wexford knew he couldn't prove anything. Besides, he had the new one now, no longer new, really, but becoming comfortably battered and even slightly stained.

He had another call to make, this time in Harrow Avenue. Donaldson drove him there but Wexford was early, so he walked up the hill and saw, with some undefined satisfaction, that the estate agent had put a SOLD sign up at the gate of Woodland Lodge. Good. It was hers, in her name. If it had been in Stephen Devenish's, God knew if she would ever have got the money, seeing that no one may benefit from his or her crime.

Now, nine months after Stephen Devenish's death, she was living in Brighton, she and her children, in a house she had bought next door but one to Jane Andrews. She would still live with and carry through her life the stigma of a conviction for manslaughter. Her plea of diminished responsibility, that she had gone mad and scarcely knew what she was doing, had saved her, and she had received no more than probation.

Sentencing her, the judge said, "We are taught that we should not speak ill of the dead. *De mortuis nil nisi bonum.* 'Of the dead nothing but good.' There must be exceptions to that axiom. Stephen Devenish was a hard worker, a good provider, and, I believe, an honest man. He was also, in other respects, a monster. This woman lived a life of unimaginable suffering, abuse, and torture at the hands of a miscreant who used her as a punching bag for his sadistic impulses."

Louise Sharpe had remarried. Her husband was the man who had rescued her when she attempted suicide by walking into the sea. Six months pregnant, she expected the birth of her baby at the end of July.

Revengeful as ever, Rochelle Keenan went to the police with the film she had made of the Kingsmarkham riot, claiming that it showed beyond a doubt that it was her husband, John, who had thrown the petrol bomb that killed Detective Sergeant Hennessy. Burden, who confronted her, was a little taken aback. He thought he had seen everything, become hardened to everything, and that nothing remained to astonish him. But a wife endeavoring to secure for her husband life imprisonment merely because he resented a cuckoo in his nest, that shook him. He put the film on his video transmitter—what else could he do? He was almost glad when the picture that appeared wasn't much of an improvement on a store's closed-circuit television, grainy, gray images of barely recognizable people. He certainly saw someone throw a bottle with a rag stuffed into its neck—he saw three men throwing bottles and a woman throwing a brick—but whose hands these missiles came from he had no idea at all.

Still, he would keep trying to find Hennessy's killer. He would never give up, he said.

"When you're dead," said Wexford, "and they open you up, they'll find *Get Hennessy's Killer* written on your heart."

"I hope they'll find *He Did* written underneath."

"We all hope that, Mike."

These days Wexford often found himself in somber mood. Sylvia and Neil had at last decided to divorce. Strangely, they got on better since they had come to this decision than they had for years, and sometimes Wexford hoped that this new accord might lead to reunion. They were still living in the same house, if on different floors of it, the old rectory being quite large enough to accommodate this arrangement. The children knew but showed no signs of minding while both parents were under the same roof. It would be a different story, Wexford thought, when Neil moved out.

Or when there was someone else for Neil or for Sylvia? "An intervener," as Stephen Devenish had called it, in another context. Dora took the attitude that while they were still together, nothing was decided, nothing was definite. But he, when he considered it quietly to himself, asked how he would feel about this pair if they were not his own daughter and son-in-law, the parents of his grandsons. If they were strangers, wouldn't he perhaps think the best course for everyone's ultimate happiness was an absolute separation?

Sylvia was in the house when he got home that evening. He never mentioned the imminent divorce unless she did. She usually did, particularly when she could take advantage of the children's being out with their father to list Neil's manifold faults and sometimes, to do her justice, her own. But this evening she gave him an especially loving kiss when he came in and said she had something to tell him, she had a confession to make.

Wexford's heart sank a little. If her mother had been in the room, this couldn't have happened. Neither daughter cared to shock their mother, knowing her tongue could be rough and her opinions strong. But they told their father anything. He was unshockable, or so they believed, and now he was afraid she was going to tell him she had a lover. Or had met someone who would soon be her lover. Or Neil had a girlfriend. Things of that sort—what else could a confession be?

Something quite different.

"Dad," she said, "do you remember once saying to me that you couldn't imagine me breaking the law?"

"I think so," he said guardedly.

"Well, I don't know if I have broken the law, but I may have covered up a crime." She looked at him warily. "I can't remember if I ever told you how, when I was first working for The Hide helpline, a woman calling herself Anne phoned. Her husband was out in the garden with the baby, she said, and then she saw him coming in and she was afraid of being found talking to me."

"Maybe you did. Very discreetly, I'm sure."

"Yes, well, that must have been last April. She was terrified of her husband, but like so many of them she wouldn't leave. Her name wasn't Anne at all, of course it wasn't, they do give false names. Well, she phoned again but what she had to say was quite different. He wasn't abusing her anymore, all that had stopped, she didn't say why. She said she wanted to ask me about the law relating to—well, to abused women who kill their husbands."

"Go on."

"First of all I said I wasn't a lawyer, I couldn't help her. I said The Hide had the services of a solicitor—we have, she does it for free—who would advise her if she'd like to ring this number. And I was going to give her the number when she said she wouldn't do that, she didn't want that, all she wanted was to know what was the best *excuse* a woman could use if she killed her husband. Could she plead self-defense?"

A gentle chill, not unpleasurable, ran through Wexford's body. "So what's this confession?"

Sylvia looked at him speculatively. "I told her—what I knew. What I'd learnt, that is, when I had my couple of days' training for working there. I said that if a woman used a knife or a gun to kill an unarmed man or a sleeping man, she couldn't use self-defense. And that was because no matter what he'd threatened to do to her in the future or what had happened in the past, the 'criterion of immediacy' for manslaughter—I remembered that phrase—wouldn't be there. A jury might be understanding, but they couldn't acquit her and she'd get life imprisonment because that's the sentence that's mandatory for murder."

"And?"

"She said, but what about being provoked to it beyond bearing. I said to forget all that. The only thing was to plead guilty to manslaughter on the grounds of diminished responsibility. In other words, a woman goes mad, picks up the gun or whatever, and loses control. You'll always be stamped a criminal, I said, but you probably won't go to prison.

"And then, a few months later, that woman I recognized as abused in the photo came up in court and pleaded guilty to manslaughter on the grounds of diminished responsibility, and it all came back to me what I'd said. I knew then, I just *knew* Fay Devenish was Anne and I'd told her how to avoid a life sentence for murder. And my own father was the investigating officer in the case.

"I've wanted to tell you for ages, but I've only just plucked up the courage."

Wexford drew a deep breath. So much depended on when this phone call had been made. Stephen Devenish had died on the morning of July 29. "When was this, Sylvia?"

"*When* was it? Let's see. It was ten at night, I do remember that. The end of July, I think. The children's school had broken up."

"When did they break up?"

"I don't remember. 'Anne' probably phoned on a Wednesday or a Friday, because those are the nights I usually work. I mean, there are exceptions, but there weren't that week. I've checked. Dad, tell me, have I done something dreadful?"

Seriously perturbed now, Wexford went to find last year's calendar. He always kept calendars for a year or two. If "Anne" had made that phone call before July 29, it meant Fay Devenish's attack on her husband had not been a reaction to his cutting her—perhaps he hadn't cut her, perhaps she had cut herself—but premeditated murder, planned possibly for a long time. Wexford closed his eyes, opened them, found the calendar in his desk pigeonhole, and took it with him, reading it on the way, nearly falling down the bottom four stairs.

"Tell me, Dad," Sylvia said. "Don't keep me in suspense."

"The twenty-ninth, when Stephen Devenish died, was a Tuesday. That was the day school broke up. Your punctilious mother has written it on the calendar. It must have been a Wednesday or a Friday when Fay Devenish phoned you, so it was either Wednesday the thirtieth or Friday, August the first." He gave her a half smile. "You're off the hook."

"Thank God," she said, "but I did tell her how to get herself off the hook."

"I know. But by then he was already dead. Sylvia..." He went over to her and took her hand. "There's no harm done."